"Kisses." Fire shot into her cheeks. "I will give you a kiss for each chore you complete. You sweep the kitchen, you get a kiss. Haul in supplies from the cellar—kiss. Build a new shed. Kiss." Sliding her gaze sideways, she regarded Reno's bemused grin and wondered what he must be thinking.

"Kisses," he repeated finally.

"Yes. You want to kiss me, don't you?"

His chuckle was downright lusty. "Oh yes, I sure do, honeybee. But the way I see it, there's a big difference between sweeping the floor and building a shed. I'm going to have to ask for more to do that."

"More kisses?"

"More *than* kisses. I figure a shed's worth a whole"—he took one step closer to her—"night of lovin'. What do you say, Dellie? That would be a mighty sweet reward—for both of us."

Other **AVON ROMANCES**

Coming Soon

And Don't Miss These
ROMANTIC TREASURES
from Avon Books

TOUGH TALK AND TENDER KISSES

DEBORAH CAMP

AVON BOOKS  NEW YORK

AVON BOOKS
A division of
The Hearst Corporation
1350 Avenue of the Americas
New York, New York 10019

Copyright © 1997 by Deborah E. Camp
Published by arrangement with the author
Visit our website at **http://AvonBooks.com**
Library of Congress Catalog Card Number: 96-95180
ISBN: 0-380-78250-2

First Avon Books Printing: May 1997

AVON TRADEMARK REG. U.S. PAT. OFF. AND IN OTHER COUNTRIES, MARCA REGISTRADA, HECHO EN U.S.A.

Printed in the U.S.A.

RAI 10 9 8 7 6 5 4 3 2 1

A mail-order marriage is trickier'n braidin' a mule's tail.

—Cowboy saying

Chapter 1

The 10:10 chugged down the tracks toward Whistle Stop, Indian Territory, right on time, much to Adele Bishop's regret.

"Reno Gold," she whispered, and just the sound of his name sent her temperature up a degree. She'd been barely out of pigtails the last time she'd seen him and today she was supposed to marry him!

Of course, she wouldn't. And she was certain he didn't expect it of her. Why he had answered her advertisement for a husband was a mystery to her, but she was sure his acceptance had been as lighthearted and frivolous as her offer. They would catch up on each other's life since their shared days in Lawrence, Kansas, six years ago, and Reno would be on his way again.

She placed a confident smile on her lips, reminding herself that she meant to teach this backward-thinking town an important lesson about humanity. After today the men of Whistle Stop would reconsider their practice of ordering brides as they would a new saddle or stove.

1

Her mother—a notorious, right-thinking suffragette, may God rest her soul—would have been proud.

"Here comes the bridegroom," Yancy Stummer said, displaying the four yellowed teeth he still had in the front of his mouth. "Ain't this excitin'? I 'member when my bride come on the train. *Wooweee*, that was one happy day, I'm here to tell ya."

Adele tipped up her chin. "I wonder if your bride shared your enthusiasm."

"She was damn lucky to get me." Yancy stuck out his scrawny chest. "Why, she was a widder-woman with two crybaby kids when I agreed to take her in. She'd been livin' with her pappy, and he treated her like a plow mule."

"Ah, yes, and you ordered her up like you would a fried-chicken dinner at the restaurant." Adele looked back at the eating establishment she managed. The two-story building sat to the south of the depot and was the center of activity for the small town of Whistle Stop. She faced Yancy's gap-toothed jeer again. "I'm sure Stella felt awfully special," she added in a droll voice that diminished Yancy's grin a fraction.

Past Yancy's stoop-shouldered form Adele caught sight of Taylor Terrapin, the pitted-faced owner of the Black Knight Saloon. He never missed a chance to flirt with her, not even on this day, the day she would supposedly collect her bridegroom. His smile made her skin crawl. She not only disapproved of his dubious character, but she strongly disapproved of his business, which used women of easy virtue to attract customers to his gaming tables.

She yanked her attention away from Terrapin's oily visage and tried to shut out the snickers and snide comments directed at her by the observers. The train squealed to a stop, and the engineer gave a jaunty salute to the brakeman. Adele's nerves quivered while the conductor placed the steps at the train door and made ready for the passengers arriving at Whistle Stop. The hour stopover enticed riders to stretch their legs and order something from the restaurant, but few ever chose to remain in Whistle Stop.

However, one passenger would not get back on the train this morning.

Reno Gold.

Oh, that name sent delicious shivers skittering across Adele's skin. How had the years changed him? Why had he answered her advertisement for a husband? Was Sally Baldridge right in her assumption that he was down on his luck and looking for room and board until he could get back on his feet? Would he make a bigger fool of her than she already felt, with the town yokels gawking at her as if she were the main attraction in a carnival sideshow?

She smoothed her hands down the front of her restaurant attire of white dress and black apron. Sally had wanted her to remove the apron, but Adele had resisted, thinking the dress would seem too bridal without it, and she didn't want to give Reno any wrong ideas. She had advertised for a husband, but she had no intention of actually claiming one. Sally, a friend since her days in Kansas, had tried to talk her out of this scheme—especially after Reno had responded. She'd never approved of Reno.

Adele watched as bodies stirred behind the train

windows and the porters pushed open the narrow doors. Someone near her whistled the wedding march. A woman laughed raucously.

"It's shameful! Downright shameful!" the woman said loudly. "You've got no right advertising for a man."

Adele bristled and glared at the scolder, who turned out to be one of the saloon tarts in Terrapin's den of ill repute. "I have as much right as any man to advertise for a mate."

"Men are easy to find out west, but women aren't. Men got to do what they got to do to get women to come out here," the other woman charged, her painted face contorting in disgust.

"If a man wanted a woman so desperately, he could find one at Mr. Terrapin's saloon and ask her properly to be his wife," Adele retorted. A woman standing back from the others caught her eye. She had a plain face that was somehow off-kilter, but when she smiled at Adele, she was transformed into something almost pretty. Adele gave a sigh of relief. At least one woman here today was in her corner!

"It's a man's place to pick his mate, not the other way around," Yancy declared. "Besides, nobody wants no whore for a wife."

The plain woman's smile slipped. "Us whores don't want none of y'all neither," she declared, then shrank back when Terrapin turned to glare at her. "I mean, uh, that is . . . not as h-husbands." Her smile trembled on her thin lips and her eyes were wide with anxiety. Adele realized what accounted for her unbalanced appearance; one eye was blue and the other was dark brown.

Terrapin nodded and gently knuckled her pointed chin. "That's right, Doris. Glad you remembered who butters your bread."

God's nightgown! Strengthening the moral fiber of this town could very well be beyond her capabilities, Adele fretted. Terrapin turned his smile in her direction, and she looked quickly away from him, feeling the same revulsion as she felt for snakes.

"You want a man? There are able-bodied men right here in town willing to wed ya," Yancy piped up. "I betcha Willie Halderon there would make an honest woman of ya."

Halderon, all six feet and one hundred fifty pounds of him, shuffled forward. He blushed, and to Adele's astonishment, lowered himself to one bony knee before her. The onlookers applauded and whistled.

"Willie, get up," Adele whispered, stepping away from him as her face heated like a stove lid.

"Won't you marry me, Miss Adele? I think you're real nice to look at." His Adam's apple slipped up and down in his long throat.

"No, Willie, I will not marry you. Now please get to your feet."

"Is that him?" Yancy asked, as a crippled, elderly gentleman accepted a porter's help to leave the train.

Adele made a face at Yancy's quip, but the crowd laughed. With a sigh Willie stood and shuffled back among the others.

Adele almost hoped that Reno Gold had decided not to board the train after all. Suffering rejection wouldn't be so bad. Yet she knew she'd be disappointed if he didn't show up. In all truth, she wanted to see Reno again to discover for herself if he had fulfilled the potential for greatness she'd seen in him back in Kansas. With his agile mind and a fair chance, he could have made a mark on the world. But she worried this wasn't the case. He'd written that he'd tried his luck in the goldfields; an idle, foolish quest to her way of thinking. Men chasing after luck usually ended up luckless.

"Hey, here's another stranger. Is he the fortunate feller?" Yancy called out, clearly enjoying his role of ringleader for the group of gawkers.

A blond man with a patch over his left eye departed the train, and Terrapin came forward, one hand extended.

"Glad you could make it, Buck," he greeted the one-eyed stranger. "Collect your baggage and I'll take you to the saloon."

"I've only got this," the man said, indicating the carpetbag he held. "Good to see you again, Taylor."

"What happened to your eye?"

"Lost it back when I was in Montana. A Blackfeet son of a bitch cut me. But don't you worry. I'm still a dead-on shot."

"I don't doubt that, and I don't doubt that you'll earn the big fee I've agreed to pay you."

The snatch of conversation sent uneasiness through Adele. Was this man a hired gun? If so, who was his target?

She watched the other passengers leave the train one by one, all the while conscious of Terrapin and his tarts escorting the blond stranger away from the depot and to the saloon owner's waiting buggy. A chill of foreboding seeped into her bones. A hired gun. In Whistle Stop. Who or what threatened Taylor

Terrapin so much that he felt compelled to hire an assassin?

"Looks like your sweetheart got hold of his good sense before it was too late," Yancy said, giving a hoot of glee. "Yup, he musta seen that this mail-order husband plan is 'bout as natural as a hog trying to mount a goat."

"Watch your filthy mouth, Yancy Stummer," Adele admonished him. "I have every right to buy myself a husband and lay down the law to him." She hardened her heart against the sting of rejection. Reno wasn't on the train. He'd stood her up. "My question is, does any of us really have that right? We fought a war to end slavery and yet we practice—"

"Is this Wet Your Whistle, Indian Territory?"

That voice, slurred but achingly familiar, sliced through Adele's sermon, and all eyes swung back to the train. A man stood on the top step, swayed slightly, and pulled his hat more firmly down on his forehead. He reached out a hand, settled it on the porter's shoulder, and descended the two steps with slow deliberation. Another porter was behind him, one hand under his elbow to steady him. He was obviously inebriated and could barely place one foot in front of the other.

Gaining the platform, he squared his shoulders and tipped up his chin so that the shadow cast by the brim of his hat inched back to reveal a square jaw, lopsided smile, and chiseled nose. His eyes glinted from the murky depths beneath his hat, and he shrugged off the helping hands of the porters.

"Thank you, gentlemen. You're so very kind." Southern charm dripped like honey off the words. "I do believe I spy a sweet flower from the Kansas plains. Dellie? Is that you?''

Adele's heart climbed into her throat and lodged there, beating furiously. The nickname sent her back to her girlhood.

He strode forward, his path not quite straight, but in her general direction. Doffing his hat to reveal a head of jet-black hair, he manufactured a sweeping bow.

"My dear Dellie, I have answered your call," he announced, the words bumping into one another. "Your intended has arrived on sched—schedule." He straightened and his smoky blue eyes crossed. "Rrreno Gold, at your ssservice."

That said, he pitched forward, face first, at her feet.

From her bedroom window Adele watched the 10:10 power its way down the track away from Whistle Stop. Though the noise of the train gradually diminished, the noise in the room did not.

Adele turned and examined the sprawl of drunken maleness snoring in her bed. The spare bed-pillow enticed her, and she had to summon every ounce of will not to place that pillow over Reno's open mouth and smother him and his obnoxious snoring sounds.

His dark hair tumbled across his forehead and tomorrow's beard shadowed his jaw. A dimple snuggled into his chin. He made smacking noises, shifted his rangy body on her bed, kicked at her quilts, then settled deeper into his liquor-induced unconsciousness.

She had tried to rouse him, but he had barely batted an eyelash. Three men had hauled him from the depot to the restaurant. Because there were no guest rooms available in the sleeping quarters upstairs, he had been dumped in Adele's bedroom. His hat lay on the floor along with his fancy-stitched boots, satchel, and saddlebag.

His dusky hair contrasted starkly with the white bed linens. Adele leaned closer and sniffed the aromas of leather and cigar smoke underlining the smell of whiskey. She snagged the chain attached to his watch and slipped the timepiece from his vest pocket. It was expensive. His initials were etched in the hinged gold lid. She popped it open, and sweet chimes greeted her. Humming the snatch of song, she recognized it. A Chopin Nocturne.

Ah, a glimpse of the Reno Gold she had once known! A Reno Gold who recited poetry and played Chopin and Liszt on the piano. Smiling, she leaned even closer to his sleeping form. He had stopped snoring for a few moments, giving her a chance to admire the fan of his stubby lashes, the straight bridge of his nose, the allure of his masculine lips, full and firm and . . .

A tentative knock on her bedroom door spun her around to confront Sally Baldridge.

"Sorry to bother you—" Sally tipped her head to one side. "What were you doing just now?"

"I . . . uh . . . I was just . . ." Adele stared at the watch she'd dropped onto Reno's chest. "I was admiring this timepiece. It's beautiful." She tucked it back into the watch pocket of his black satin vest. "In fact, his clothes must have cost a tidy sum. Perhaps he isn't a gold digger."

"And perhaps he spent what little money he possessed on this finery to impress you." Sally came forward and peered down her nose at him. "He hasn't changed a bit. He's just taller and bigger."

Adele glanced around, feeling helpless. "How will I get him off this bed? He weighs a ton. It took three men to carry him in here."

"Yes, dear, I know. *Everyone* knows."

Adele winced at the truth of that. Yes, everyone knew by now that Adele Bishop had ordered herself a husband who had arrived on the 10:10 so drunk that he'd passed out at her feet. Oh, the humiliation!

"What am I going to do, Sally?" she whispered.

"About him?" Sally cast the snoring man another glare of disgust, then flicked her hand at him as if he were nothing but a bothersome fly. "When he rouses up, tell him to remove his sorry self from your sight. You have more important issues to tackle right now. Our cook is causing trouble again."

Adele groaned. "What is she refusing to do this time?"

"She won't make grits and she's serving stew for the fifth day in a row. Our regular customers complained about that yesterday, Adele. Why must the woman be such a sore tooth?"

"I'll speak with her." Adele ran her hands down her black apron and mentally prepared for battle. She marched past Sally and through her private parlor and office to the door that opened onto the restaurant.

Only a few men loitered at the counter, sipping coffee and eating toast and jam. The next train due in was the 12:48. There was enough time for the cook to whip up something besides beef stew. Fixing a determined expression on her face, Adele entered the domain of the irascible and impossibly testy Minnie Ball.

"Good morning, Minnie."

The rotund, sour-faced woman aimed her beady eyes at Adele and gave a sniff of contempt. "That your weddin' dress?"

Adele examined the pots simmering on the stove. "I see you're warming up the stew. That's good. However, we'll need another main dish today. How about potato soup? The customers love that." She peered into the big ovens at the pies baking in them. "Apple and pumpkin? They smell delicious. Now about breakfast—"

"*I'm* the cook," Minnie said, almost growling. She reminded Adele of a bulldog, with her pushed-in nose and the folds of skin around her mouth and chin.

"Yes, of course, but I'm the manager and I must be sure everything is in order. We've served stew too often lately, and we don't want our customers to complain and go elsewhere, do we?"

Minnie folded her big arms against her big breasts. "What's yer point?"

"Point?" Adele swallowed the knot of nerves forming in her throat and wished she didn't find this woman so intimidating. "My point is simple, Minnie. Add potato soup to the lunch menu today, and tomorrow morning I expect you to serve grits."

"No grits. I ain't got time to mess with grits."

"Minnie, we've discussed this already. Our customers want grits for breakfast, and we will provide—"

"I ain't no Reb. I'm a Yankee. I don't eat grits and I don't cook what I don't eat."

"It's 1884, Minnie, and the war ended some twenty years ago. We're serving grits."

"Then you fix 'em."

"*You're* the cook."

"You're right there, missy."

Adele stood toe to toe with the woman and felt her resolve begin to shrivel. "What about the potato soup? Have you an equally illogical reason why you won't prepare it?"

Minnie glared at her for nearly a full minute, then she narrowed her eyes and turned away. "I guess I could stir up some 'tater soup."

Adele released her breath. She decided to accept the small victory and not insist on a larger one by forcing the grits issue. The swinging door popped open and Sally peeked in, much to her relief.

"Very good, Minnie. Carry on," Adele said brightly, then escaped from the kitchen with Sally right behind her. "She's agreed to fix potato soup."

"And the grits?"

Adele shrugged. "That remains to be seen."

"You're frightened of her," Sally charged.

Adele released a harsh laugh. "And you aren't? I should fire her and I will once I locate a suitable replacement."

Sally shook her head. "A hedgehog would be more friendly than that woman. Maybe we can hook her up with Reno."

"Don't be cruel, Sally. We couldn't do that to our old friend."

"Friend? Pray tell, when was Reno Gold ever our friend? As I remember it, we tried to shake him off like a saddle burr."

"You always misunderstood him, Sally. He wasn't

the ruffian you made him out to be. He often quoted poetry to me when we were alone."

"Alone?" Sally widened her eyes. "When were you alone with Reno Gold?"

"Oh, from time to time he did odd jobs for my aunt." Adele moved to the sun-struck window and looked out on the depot. Autumn leaves skittered across the gray wood platform, swept clean by the prairie wind.

The sight of the gold and yellow leaves whisked her back to her four years in Lawrence, when she and Reno had woven a frayed, fragile friendship on the windy Kansas plains. He had been unlike any other boy she'd ever met. One moment he'd seemed as dangerous as a mountain cat and in the next he was reading Shakespeare's sonnets to her in his husky voice, the sound of which always made her heart triphammer.

Back then Adele had imagined that he could be anything he wanted to be because of his quick mind and intense curiosity about the world around him. No machinery had escaped his attention, no book had gone unread. And yet he had also possessed a wild streak that had made Adele wary of him even as she was drawn to him.

True, the others she'd socialized with had shunned him, calling him Winston Baldridge's poor relation. In his hand-me-down clothes and wearing his hair too long, he had seemed a vagabond to the others, who had been put off by his mixture of blood—Cherokee, Cheyenne, French, and Gypsy. But to Adele his patchwork of ancestry only added to his appeal.

Winston had never been mean to Reno, but he'd

never actually included his cousin in their activities. Like a stray dog, Reno had hung *around* Win, but not *with* him.

Adele had let Reno kiss her twice—once on the cheek and once on the mouth. Both times proved unforgettable and were responsible for her turning down Winston's marriage proposal. Having experienced the heart-hammering delight of Reno Gold's kisses, Adele found she simply couldn't bind herself to Winston for life, for Win's kisses were sweet and brotherly.

Sally had married him instead and had confided to Adele that she and Winston had never been blissfully happy. When Winston had died a year ago of a weak heart, Sally had told Adele at his funeral that her grief was softened by relief.

Adele had felt sorry for Winston and had excused Sally. She knew she gave Sally too much credit, was too soft-hearted where her friend was concerned. And she knew why. Moving so often as a child, Adele had not made close friends until those precious years in Kansas, when she and Sally had shared secrets, giggled over boys, and attended dances together. Sally had been Adele's first girlfriend—actually, her only girlfriend. It was a relationship Adele clung to tenaciously, blissfully blind to Sally's faults. She valued the friendship too much to look too closely at Sally's tendency to snobbery.

Now Sally rested a hand on Adele's shoulder, bringing her back to the present. "You've proved your point. As soon as he's awake, show him the door."

"Sally, just because we live in Indian Territory

doesn't mean we must all behave like savages."

"You sound like your mama."

"Good." Adele beamed.

Sally sighed. "He's the savage, not us. Why, he was so drunk he could barely walk under his own power! He's lucky you even allowed him to darken your doorstep. You should have known this would happen when you read that letter of his. How did he put it? Something about how he'd been knocking around the Dakotas, sniffing for riches and trying his luck? That means he's penniless, like all the other fools who went searching for gold and silver, and now he's hoping he can marry you and let you make a living for him. Why else would he have answered that crazy advertisement you placed in the *Territorial News* for a mail-order husband?"

"Don't be so dramatic, Sally. I have no intention of marrying anyone who stepped off that train. You're right. I've proven that what is good for the rooster is good for the hen."

Pushing through the swinging door, Minnie Ball heard Adele's last statement. She made a sound of contempt as she placed two hot pies on the counter. "What point will you make when you back out on marryin' the husband you ordered?" she taunted.

A knot of anxiety tightened in Adele's chest. Minnie released a burst of hateful laughter and went back into the kitchen.

"Pay her no mind," Sally said. "Who cares what people in this town think of you?"

Adele closed her eyes, hearing her mother's voice ringing in her ears. *All you have is your reputation, daughter. Once that is compromised or sullied, you have defeated yourself.*

Chapter 2

Someone had pasted Reno's tongue to the roof of his mouth. With a supreme effort he peeled it away and grimaced at the awful taste. Good God, his teeth felt furry!

Opening his eyes, he got the fright of his life when he saw a woman who looked very much like a bulldog glaring down at him. She grinned, and he was sure *her* teeth were furry, too. He shut his eyes again.

"She ain't gonna marry your sorry ass," the hag said, her voice, coarse and offensive, a perfect match for her face. "She only used you. Don't matter none that you knowed her once. She still ain't gonna marry your sorry ass."

He vaguely comprehended what she said. Mainly he was trying not to breathe, because her breath was as foul-smelling as a midsummer slop jar.

"Mrs. Ball? Where are you, Mrs. Ball?" A melodic voice drifted into the room, and the dog-faced woman whispered a word that would have made a barkeep blush. She finally left his field of vision. He coughed, his lungs rattling, and pushed himself up on his elbows. The woman was gone. He blinked several times, forcing his eyes to focus so that he could examine his whereabouts.

The bed he was in belonged to a lady. No man would choose to sleep amid lace-edged linen and ruffled pillows. A patchwork quilt hung half off the bed and another was draped across the foot rail. White eyelet curtains filtered early morning sunlight, and rag rugs dotted the highly polished plank floor. Spying a pitcher of water and a glass on the bedside table, he helped himself and found that his hands shook and his muscles were rubbery. His stomach clenched against the cold water and he almost heaved. Pain exploded in his head, and he fell back onto the feather pillows with a groan.

When he had been younger and more foolish, he'd swiped a bottle of moonshine from his uncle's stash and had tried to mend his broken heart by pickling it. The next morning, when he'd been sure he was about to die, he'd sworn that he would never indulge in too much liquor again. Here he was, six years later, having broken that vow over the same female who had broken his heart.

Dellie.

Surveying the room again, he smiled and relaxed. He was in Dellie's room. A picture of her mother sat in a silver frame on her dressing table. Another framed photograph, this one of his late cousin Winston and Win's widow, Sally, decked out in their wedding finery, perched on a tallboy. The room overflowed with femininity. Tiny yellow flowers filled a green glass vase on the bedside table, where it shared space with the water pitcher, two leather-bound books, and a crystal-shaded oil lamp.

He gathered in a breath and let the scents of lavender and roses seduce him.

"Dellie," he whispered, his voice emerging from some deep and hollow place. Clearing his throat, he reached for the water pitcher again and drank another glass of the cold, bracing liquid. His head pounded, but his stomach's rebellion was milder this time.

Shouldn't have started on that second bottle of whiskey, he thought, finding his wisdom too late to ease his splitting head. But he had been forced to get stinking drunk to go through with this crazy notion. The further that train had chugged toward Whistle Stop, the tighter his nerves had stretched. Answering Dellie's advertisement had been a moment's surrender to temptation, but answering her summons to join him in holy matrimony—well, that was a good enough excuse for any man to get bow-legged drunk.

It had all started off as a laugh, his answering Dellie's ridiculous request and receiving her reply. Remembering his innocent, youthful times with her, he'd longed to see her again. She'd been his first brush with love and impossible to forget. He groaned, thinking of his drunken arrival on the train. Right about now he figured she wanted to forget she ever knew him.

When she'd sent him the money for a train ticket, he hadn't wanted to hurt her feelings by refusing. Besides, he wanted to strut. Maybe once she saw that he wasn't a failure, she'd have a change of heart. They could renew their friendship and share a laugh or two.

He scowled at his wavy reflection in the full-length

mirror across the room. His hair stood on end, spiky and sleep-tousled, and whiskers darkened the lower half of his face. His clothes were wrinkled, and he smelled as if he'd slept in a whiskey keg. Nope, she wouldn't want him on a bet. Not the way he looked—and the way he'd acted. He couldn't quite recall, but he must have passed out right after he'd left the train.

Running a hand through his hair, he scolded himself for being such a fool. *Shouldn't have started thinking so hard on the train*, he decided. That's when things had started falling apart, when he'd realized he couldn't face Dellie and tell her he was joshing her about being her husband.

Damn, damn, and double damn! He had to find her and explain himself, redeem himself, and then buy a ticket on the next train out of here.

He swung his legs over the side of the bed, and the world slipped out from under him. Somehow he ended up on his rump in the middle of the floor. Looking down, he saw one of the throw rugs wadded up underneath him. Slippery little devils. After a couple of awkward tries, he found his feet and stood swaying in the center of the room while demons applied hammers to the back of his eyes. Clapping a hand to his forehead, he struggled to defeat the morning after, but gave up.

With a groan, a twist, and a letting go of every muscle, he fell back onto the bed and passed out again.

When he next awoke, the sun had set, draping the room in purple and indigo. Reno patted down his hair, drank two more glasses of water, located the outhouse in back of the restaurant, then he went to find Dellie.

With the eating establishment closed for the evening, the place was quiet and peaceful. Reno examined the outside of the structure. Lights were shining upstairs, but only one lamp glowed downstairs. He figured the lower level was where he'd find Dellie. Following the light, he located her in a room off the parlor. She sat at a desk, her back straight as a board, her mouth set in an unrelenting line of disapproval. Her ebony hair lay in soft curls across her shoulders, framing her oval face and complementing her ivory complexion.

The years had been good to her, filling her out, giving her skin a healthy glow, adding touches of character to her face. As he'd known she would, she had become a beautiful woman, so beautiful that he felt like a sack of manure in her presence, and he was not a man void of conceit. When he looked into a mirror, he didn't wince—except when he'd sucked down a bottle of whiskey and managed to live through it to the next morning.

Staring at the scuffed toes of his boots (had someone *dragged* him into this house?), he felt the awkward weight of shyness that he thought he'd shed years ago. He cleared his throat and hoped to God he wouldn't stammer like a lovesick schoolboy.

"It's g-good to see you, Dellie." *Damn it to hell!* "I'm sorry about my conduct earlier. I seem to have indulged in a glass too many of whiskey. I was nervous seeing you again and . . . Dellie? Are you going to look at me or keep pretending you've been struck deaf?"

She turned to him, her gaze icy green, freezing his heart. "You seem to have completely forgotten the manners you were reared on, Reno Gold. A gentleman dresses appropriately before he seeks a lady's company." She gave a disdainful sniff and returned her attention to the open ledgers on the desk.

Reno glanced at his wrinkled pants, half-buttoned shirt, and unbuttoned vest. Anger built in him like a summer squall, and something else—disappointment. Disappointment that she would treat him so callously, so coldly, after all the years he'd spent wondering about her, daydreaming about her, wishing for this moment when he would be reunited with the girl who had branded his heart and made him believe in himself. He buttoned his shirt and vest, needing something to do until he could speak civilly to her.

She scratched something in a notebook and then closed it with a snap. Laying the pen beside its matching inkwell, she gave a little sigh. "I won't marry a drunkard."

He stiffened, her words cutting like a knife.

"I only meant to make a point to the townspeople anyway," she went on. "The men here have a disgusting habit of ordering their wives and then treating them as chattel. I placed an order for a husband to make them see how wrong it is to purchase another human being."

She ain't gonna marry your sorry ass. The words came back to him, jolting his hazy memory. Had the woman, the hag, who had said this to him been real or imagined? He could recall her stench, so he figured she must have been real. Apparitions rarely had foul breath. So where was the woman who had sneered at him? Was she someone Dellie knew, someone who worked for her?

This sent another jolt through him. Dellie had not only brought him here to reject him, she'd also told other people of her intentions. Otherwise that hag wouldn't have been jeering at his circumstances and so damned sure that Dellie had no intention of tying the knot with him.

What had happened to harden Dellie's heart? Back when he'd known her, she'd been full of forgiveness and charity. That's why he'd fallen in love with her. What had life dealt her to make her look at him as if he were dirt under her feet?

He had sought her out to apologize and to be truthful and explain to her that he wasn't penniless, that he had made more money than he could spend in his lifetime, but her snippy attitude toward him choked off the confession. Damn her for believing the worst of him instead of hoping for the best! The Dellie he had known in Kansas would never have been so churlish, so unrelenting in her disapproval.

Chafing under his scathing regard, Adele chanced a glimpse of Reno through the cover of her thick lashes. His face was ruddy with suppressed anger, and his long-fingered hands were clenched at his sides. Was he still in the grip of demon rum? Had she been foolish to scold him, this tall, powerfully built man who could snap her bones like matchsticks if that were his will?

Eyeing him, she could see that he had not an ounce of spare fat on him. His body was whipcord lean and sculpted of muscle and sinew. Dusky hair fell upon his furrowed brow and a blaze of anger flickered in his smoky blue eyes. But it was his expressive mouth that demanded her fullest attention. While his lips were pale with tautly controlled fury, she noted the downward tilt at the corners and the vulnerability there. Had she hurt his feelings? Did he still possess a sense of honor, a remnant of pride?

Suddenly remorse riddled her and she had to ball her hands in her lap to keep from reaching out to him, gathering him against her, and whispering to him that she understood him, just as she had when they were youngsters in Lawrence.

He was so handsome, even with his clothes wrinkled, his cheeks whiskered, and his hair disheveled. Why hadn't he put down roots and made something of himself? With the right woman to love him, he could have achieved so much! He still could. She had an instinct about such things, inherited from her mother. Her instincts were telling her that a diamond in the rough stood before her and all he needed were skillful hands to give him polish, a loving heart to shine him up, make him gleam with self-esteem. She could offer him her resources.

Besides, those old feelings were stirring inside her, and she couldn't very well blame them on her youth anymore. Warmth bloomed in her belly and sent tendrils of passion down between her legs. She shifted, unfamiliar with the burst of sensations, but knowing what they meant. Reno Gold was a wizard and he could still cast a spell over her. She could certainly care for this man, she thought, regarding him with tenderness.

Reno saw the tenderness glow briefly in her eyes even as the evening light spilled through the open window beside the desk to bathe her in violet. Her beauty wrapped itself around Reno like a soft cloak, and he stepped closer, drawn by the kindness glinting in her eyes and tipping up the corners of her lush mouth. He yearned to touch her, to draw a lazy fingertip down the smoothness of her flushed cheek and along the firmness of her jawline. He smiled at her, and he saw a glimmer of pleasure in her eyes, but she refused to allow it to blossom on her lips. Why? What had happened to that sweet girl in Kansas? Why was she so determined to teach lessons, forgetting that the best lessons are ones the heart already knows?

She blinked rapidly and turned away from him, shifting so that her shoulder created a wall and her profile presented indifference. "I don't suffer fools or drunks gladly, Reno Gold. I must say that I am disappointed in you. You were a very bright and ambitious boy. I had hoped that you would have made something of yourself as a man."

Her words wounded him far more than they should have, and he realized that the boy in him was still trying to win her over, to secure a place in her heart. The man he'd become, however, rebelled and demanded a pound of flesh from this stern woman.

She ain't gonna marry your sorry ass.

The words smoked in his brain and burnished his heart. No, he couldn't let her sit there and condemn him, treat him like a no-'count vagabond. She had summoned him, sent him a train ticket, and by God, she was going to honor her word!

"When did you reckon we'd marry, Dellie? Tomorrow morning? Or maybe you were planning evening nuptials." He found victory in the leaping fear in her eyes and in her soft gasp of dismay.

"M-marry? I . . . There will be no marriage, sir." She tipped up her chin, all haughty and superior.

Reno ached to destroy her high-falutin' air. "Now, listen here, *ma'am*." He leaned forward from the waist to peer into her forest-green eyes. "You brought me here to marry you, so what's the problem? Isn't there a preacher in these parts?"

She pushed aside her ledgers with a flourish of agitation. "You arrive drunk as a honey-dipped bear and expect me to wed you?" Her laugh was brittle and grating. "I think not!"

"My part of the bargain was to get here on the 10:10 and I fulfilled it. I expect you to be as good as your word and make an honest man of me by marrying me."

The words sent a sobering chill through him. Christ Almighty! He was actually asking Adele Bishop to marry him. No, not asking, demanding. Even in his dreams he'd never gone this far. Staring into her startled green eyes, he willed her to obey him. *Damn her!* Every time he'd seen a beautiful woman, he'd thought of Dellie, wished for Dellie, hated Dellie for haunting him. He had wondered if she ever thought of him, had even wondered what would have happened if she had allowed him to make love to her as he'd wanted to do back in Lawrence, when she'd been promised to his cousin Winston.

Hard to believe no man had claimed her for his wife. Maybe it was fate, her waiting for him and not even knowing she was waiting, and him seeing that advertisement in a newspaper he had never read before that day, that fateful day on which she had placed a request for a husband.

Yes, strong forces were at work here, he decided, as his heart boomed in his chest and his blood thickened in his veins, coursing to his extremities, rushing to fire his loins with wanting. Yes, yes. He wanted her.

"There is no need of a marriage, don't you see?" she implored. "I have made my point."

"Good for you, but what about me? I dropped my life and boarded the train to begin a new life with you. I didn't know anything about any 'point'. You didn't tell me I was part of a lesson in the letters you wrote me."

Her eyes sparked with anger. "And you didn't tell me that you lived out of a whiskey bottle in your letters."

"I don't."

"You deny that you were stinking drunk and are standing before me this minute with whiskey on your breath?"

He arched a brow and straightened away from her. "No, I admit those things, but it's not every day that I travel to Indian Territory to marry a woman I haven't clapped eyes on for six years. I was nervous and I drank more than I intended. But I arrived, and now it's up to you to honor your part of our deal." He propped his hands at his waist and stared at her, unblinking, unflinching. "Have you become a liar and a cheat, Dellie?" Suddenly he remembered her Achilles' heel. "Your sweet mama taught you better than that. She'd be ashamed of you for using another human being to paddle the evil-doers."

"I'm not!"

He jutted his chin at her. "Prove it."

She narrowed her eyes and crossed her arms. "You don't want to marry me. You don't even know me anymore."

"Dellie, put your cards on the table or fold. What's it going to be?"

She frowned. "I don't know what those gambling terms mean, but I know a challenge when I hear it."

"I'm not challenging you. I'm just waiting to see what you're made of, whether your word is as good as gold or as worthless as Confederate currency."

Adele pushed back her shoulders and faced him. "I assure you, my word is solid gold."

A smirk worked its way up through him to find his mouth. "So how does tomorrow morning strike you? Think you can lasso a preacher to marry us?"

"Yes." She sized him up, her green eyes flashing. "I expect I can fashion you into a decent human being. You've lost your way, obviously, but I believe I'm just the woman to herd you back onto the right path."

"Is that so?" Reno asked, resentment rising in him like a fist. He ached to tell her that he could buy and sell her ten times over, but held his tongue because he suspected she had decided to wed him only to change him. She was, after all, her mother's daughter. Victoria Bishop had been one hell of a woman; she never saw an injustice she didn't try to put right or a lost cause she didn't join. "Aren't I the lucky bastard."

She gasped at the ugly word. "Watch your tongue, Reno Gold. You are in the company of a lady!"

He grinned, glad to have ruffled her feathers. "Pardon me all to hell and back, Dellie." Chuckling, he removed his pocket watch and checked the time. "Guess I'll stay in a hotel tonight and be back here bright and early to collect my bride." He winked and she blushed. "Say eight o'clock?"

"Make it nine. We can marry between the breakfast and dinner rush."

"You expect to work tomorrow?"

She gave a definite nod. "And I expect the same of you. I won't allow any freeloaders around me."

He gritted his teeth to keep from speaking his mind and pivoted sharply away from her.

Locating his belongings piled by the restaurant door, he gathered them up and stepped outside into the velvety night. He realized he was sweating and felt sick. And why not? he mocked himself. He'd just demanded that a woman make an honest man of him!

With a soft groan he struck out for the inconstant lights of town and tried not to think too hard about tomorrow or listen to the voice in his pounding head that was calling him one vile name after another.

Inside, Adele slumped in the chair and stared blindly at the flicking flame in the oil lamp.

"Well, I've gone and lost my mind," she said to the room at large. "And very possibly ruined my life."

She didn't blink for a long spell, and when she did, a fat tear rolled down her cheek. The first of many.

Chapter 3

"**Y**ou may kiss the bride."

Everything went very still inside Adele when the preacher intoned those words, then her nerves fluttered through her like a flock of startled birds. Beside her Reno turned and placed a hand on her shoulder. She trembled and looked up into his face.

His face. She had dreamed of this face and had imagined how it would have changed over the years. Actually the changes were subtle yet telling. His eyes, dark blue and glinting with deep-seated mischief, had acquired crow's feet at the corners. His jaw had squared with maturity, his dimples had deepened; his whiskers had darkened and become more plentiful, the evidence of them faintly shading the lower half of his face.

As a boy he'd been tall and gangly. As a man he was tall and lean, graceful and powerfully built. His mouth was quite beautiful, the most beautiful mouth she'd ever seen on a man, with its full lower lip and wavy upper one.

He'd changed his hair. It used to be too long and sometimes shaggy; now it was shorter and straight, sometimes falling in a sweep across his forehead until he pushed it brusquely back into place.

And the way he looked at her was altogether different. Back in Lawrence he had hardly made eye contact with her, his gaze darting away any time she tried to engage it. Now he looked boldly into her eyes and held her hands in his. She noticed that his lashes were thick and sooty and that one brow arched sardonically.

"Mrs. Reno Gold, so glad to make your acquaintance," he said, and his voice was the same as old, husky and soft, so that it always seemed he was whispering.

His lips touched hers, cool and light, like a snowflake. She knew a moment's madness when she wanted to fling her arms around him, open to him, and press her beating heart against his. Shocked, she moved backward with a jerk and touched her fingertips to her stinging lips. He smiled at her reaction, as if he had read her thoughts, had tracked the restlessness of her soul.

"This is a sham," Adele stated, then turned quickly away when she noticed that Pastor Simons had heard her and was looking at her with concern. "I mean . . . Oh, never mind. Thank you, Pastor. I do appreciate you marrying us on such short notice."

"Why, I'm pleased to do it, Sister Adele, but you sure have stirred up a hornet's nest with this marriage of yours." Pastor Simons craned his neck to see out onto the sunlit porch steps of the small chapel. Disgruntled voices floated in from outside. "Some of the men don't think too kindly of you sending off for a husband when any number of them would have been all too willing to wed you."

"Yes, I know." She clutched the bouquet of wild-flowers Reno had presented to her when he'd collected her at the depot restaurant. "And they could marry the available women in this town as well."

"Not many of those," the pastor noted.

"Oh?" Adele arched a brow. "From what I understand, the saloons are full of them."

"Well, yes, but those women are sinners, Sister Adele!" The pastor's eyes grew large behind the thick lenses of his glasses.

"So are the men who pay for their pleasures, Pastor Simons. You should know that."

Reno gripped Adele firmly by the elbow and ushered her toward the door. "I'm sure the preacher doesn't have time for a sermon this morning, Dellie." He pressed a shiny coin into the man's hand. "Much obliged."

Pastor Simons glanced at the coin and smiled. "Bless you, Mr. Gold. I trust you will be a member of our congregation, beginning this Sunday."

Reno gave a wink. "I'll be honeymooning this Sunday, I reckon."

Adele felt her face flame. She twisted out of Reno's grasp and headed swiftly for the arched doorway, her shoes tapping smartly on the plank floor.

The first face she saw outside belonged to Yancy Stummer. He jeered at her, then flapped a hand in sheer disgust. Beside him Willie Halderon skulked, his lower lip pushed out and his eyes small and moist.

"I woulda married ya," Willie muttered. "Didn't

hafta join up with that there drunken coyote."

Adele tried to ignore them as she positioned her bonnet over her black hair and tied a big bow under her chin. What was done was done, she told herself, and it was too late to wallow in regrets.

Of course, deep down she knew she had married Reno not to prove anything so much as to appease the call of her own womanhood. Reno Gold had meant something to her back when she was a girl, and now that she was a woman, she had a better understanding of those feelings. When she was in his presence she felt sublimely feminine and supremely attractive. If Reno could make her feel such wondrous things, then she owed it to him to make him realize his true magnificence. He needed someone to love him, and she felt certain she could do that—quite easily, if he proved to be an enthusiastic student.

Her mother would have been proud of her for having the fortitude to carry through with the wedding and help Reno reach his potential. Besides, her mother had always liked Reno.

"That young Reno is like a sunrise," her mother had once said of him. "Colorful and chock-full of possibilities."

Smiling to herself, Adele slipped on her gloves and turned a deaf ear to the angry voices both inside and out that were telling her that her marriage was wrong.

Reno savored the shape of Adele's body against the sunlight pouring through the doorway. God, she was a beauty in her dress of pale yellow, fitted close to her small waist and flaring at her hips. He loved the set of her shoulders, so proud, so dignified.

And she was his wife.

A bolt of alarm shot through him. Any man would be pleased to stand beside Adele Bishop and marry her, but he felt rotten for not telling her the whole truth concerning his prospects in life. Of course, if he had told her, she wouldn't have married him. She was on some kind of crazy mission to save him from himself, and he didn't want to ruin her picnic by raining on it.

Oh, no. He'd let her think he was a ne'er-do-well. Once they were reacquainted, he'd pick his time and reveal that she had not married a pauper, down on his luck and in need of a savior. He fervently hoped she would be justly chagrined when she realized she had misjudged him. If any lesson was to be learned here, she was the one who needed to learn it. He stood slightly to the left and behind her for a few moments, watching her smooth her gray gloves over her hands. He could see a mysterious smile teasing the corners of her mouth. Running the tip of his tongue lightly over his lips, he hoped he could still taste her, but he couldn't. The kiss had been too brief. Ah, well, there would be plenty of time to remedy that . . .

A series of cracks split the air. Adele let out a startled cry. Acting on pure instinct, Reno grabbed her arm and pulled her behind him, shielding her from what he knew to be gunfire.

"You rotten devil!" a man screamed, clutching his chest as he stumbled backward out of a saloon directly across the street from the white church.

Another man, gun in hand, strode out of the saloon and aimed his firearm carefully, deliberately. "I told you I don't like coffee drinkers in a saloon. It ain't natural." The gun shot fire again, discharging a bullet that plowed through the wounded man's heart and killed him before he hit the dust.

Reno shook his head, baffled by the killer's lack of humanity. The gunman holstered his Colt .45, turned slowly, and sauntered back into the saloon. Reno looked up at the gold lettering: BLACK KNIGHT SALOON. Feeling Adele trembling behind him, he pivoted to face her.

"Are you all right?"

She drew in a quick breath. "I suppose. Is that man . . . should I run for the doctor?"

"He's dead," Reno assured her. "The man who shot him, was that the saloon owner?"

"No. Taylor Terrapin owns that despicable place."

"Terrapin." Reno glanced up thoughtfully. "That name sounds familiar. I might have met him somewhere before."

"I wouldn't be surprised, seeing as how you seem to love what he sells—rotgut whiskey and the road to ruin."

He studied her and bit back a denial. If she was so damned determined to make him a rotter, maybe he should oblige her. Might be fun. Tearing his gaze from her stern countenance—she sure didn't look like a happy bride!—he noticed that the dead man had been left in the street.

"Shouldn't someone collect the body?"

"Someone will," she assured him. "Terrapin will send for the undertaker."

"Sounds like you're used to this kind of gunplay."

"Happens all the time in Whistle Stop," she told him, her tone heavy with resignation.

"Where's the sheriff?"

She wrinkled her nose and bobbed her chin at the saloon. "In there, upstairs probably. Most nights he sleeps with one of Terrapin's two-drink whores."

"Two drink ... ?" He shook his head. "Haven't heard that one before."

"Two drinks and you own them for the evening," she translated, one slim brow lifting in cool disdain. "Since our sheriff is in bed, so to speak, with the criminals, we decent folks don't expect much from him."

"Charming town you've picked to live in, Dellie." He grinned, trying to engage her good humor. She moved down the church steps without cracking a smile. "Dellie, my dear, you'd better look more pleasant. This is your wedding day and you have a lesson to teach these folks, remember?" He nodded at a scrawny, snaggle-toothed man. "Say there, partner. Can I do something for you?"

"You ain't got no pride," the man said. "What's wrong with you, marrying some uppity gal who sent you a train ticket? You don't look like a man who has to go beggin'."

"Shut up, Yancy," Adele snapped, hooking her hands around Reno's bicep. "This is none of your business. Come along, Reno. We mustn't tarry. Dinner customers will be arriving on the next train soon."

"Yeah, hop to there, boy," Yancy said with a juicy chuckle. "She done bought and paid for ya and she's ready to get some work outta ya."

Reno wanted very much to yank the rest of the crooked, yellow teeth from Yancy's white gums, but he allowed Adele to pull him away. There had been enough violence on their wedding day, and he figured he would have another chance to set this grinning jackal to rights.

Making his way along the street with his bride at his side, Reno had a chance to get a good look at his new home. He could have used a stiff drink.

Whistle Stop reminded him of Deadwood in the Dakotas, lawless and in need of a fair, firm hand. The boxy buildings were unpainted, except for two: the grand saloon, painted black with gold lettering, and beside it, a bright-red building with gold lettering—the RED QUEEN GAMING HALL. They looked like two painted-up whores in a roomful of Quakers. Traffic choked the wide street, which was deeply rutted and muddy in places. Few women lingered on the boardwalks. Men dominated this town, and women had little or no say in how things were run.

A whipcord-thin man dressed in black strode from the saloon with authority, stepped over the dead man in the street, and moved briskly toward Adele and Reno. The silver ends of his string tie bounced in the breeze, and he squinted beneath the brim of his hat as he raised a hand. Reno noticed that people scurried out of his way and tried not to snag his attention.

This is a dangerous animal, Reno thought, figuring him to be Taylor Terrapin.

"Miss Adele, might I have a moment?" The man's long legs swallowed the distance between them, and he stood in front of Adele and Reno, effectively blocking their path. He laid one hand on his black vest in the region of his heart and fashioned an expression of regret. "I am so terribly sorry for this unfortunate altercation on the morning of your wedding."

His voice was high and slightly nasal, at odds with

his appearance. Indian blood ran in this man's veins, Reno noted, Cheyenne and possibly some other tribe. He would have been handsome if not for his pitted complexion. His cheeks looked as if they'd been hit by buckshot. As he directed his attention to Reno, his hand moved to the butt of the Peacemaker in his holster. "This must be the lucky man." He held out his other hand. "I'm Taylor Terrapin, owner of the Black Knight and the Red Queen and a great admirer of your bride."

Reno shook his hand. Terrapin squeezed harder than was necessary, but Reno refused to engage in such childish comeuppance. Besides, he was busy trying to place Terrapin. He'd seen him before somewhere. Deadwood, maybe? Lewis would remember. Lewis Fields, his business partner, had a mind like a steel trap. All Reno had to go on was a feeling that Terrapin was like a plague. Wherever he went, people died.

"Reno Gold. Glad to meet you, or have we met before? I seem to recall—"

"Doubtful, doubtful," Terrapin interrupted, switching his focus back to Adele. "Don't you look ravishing this morning. I must say, the bachelors in this town are in mourning, Miss Adele, what with you taking yourself out of circulation. We had all harbored secret dreams that you would choose one of us. Now we have only Miss Sally to set our hopes on."

Adele seemed unaffected by his compliments. "Are you going to remove that dead man from the street any time soon, Mr. Terrapin?"

"Of course, of course!" He pursed his lips and leaned closer. Reno suspected Terrapin was inhaling the bouquet of Adele's perfumed skin, and he didn't like that one little bit. "As I said, I'm sorry for the ruckus. When I looked outside and saw you leaving the church, well, my heart went out to you. Such an unpleasant business on your wedding day." He made a *tsk-tsk* sound.

"Your heart should go out to the man who was murdered for nothing but sport," Adele said, her words falling like chipped ice. "Excuse us." She arched a brow, and her frosty stare forced Terrapin to step aside.

Smiling, Reno shook his head as he allowed himself to be led away. "Is there anyone in this town you like, Dellie?"

She looked startled by his question. "Of course. There are many people here who are dear to me."

"Name one."

"Sally."

"Miss Sally," he said, remembering Terrapin mentioning the woman. "Who is she? Does she work for you?" He had no sooner asked the question than he spotted a small woman standing at the window of the depot dining room. He knew her. "Not Sally Baldridge!"

"Yes. Didn't I mention in my letter that Sally had moved here to work with me?"

"No, you didn't." He sent her a swift glance, wondering if that omission had been by design. He and Sally had never gotten along.

"After Win died, Sally was so unhappy. I invited her to join me and she accepted."

"How does she feel about you marrying me?"

Adele shrugged. "Why should that matter?"

Reno set his jaw and opened the restaurant's front door. Adele moved quickly to her living quarters. She tugged off her gloves and swept off her hat, then glanced his way.

"I'm going to change into my work dress. You might want to wear something more practical yourself."

He ran a hand down his silvery satin vest and gray suit coat. "Why don't we take a few minutes to talk about our life together, Dellie?"

She turned her back on him, nervous as a cat. "I can't right now. I . . ." Her gaze flew to the doorway, where Sally stood. "Oh, Sally, come in. Say hello to Reno. I was telling him that we must change into our work clothes. We have a full day ahead of us. Are the trains running on time?"

"Yes," Sally said, stealing a glance at Reno. "Hello, Reno. It's been a long time."

"It has," he agreed, just as careful as Sally not to engage in falsehood or insincerity. She was still pretty and small, like a life-sized doll. But her face was fuller, as were her hips, and her dark hair was not as thick and glossy as it had been when she was a girl. Her brown eyes, always melancholy, were now even more lackluster. Life had been hard on Sally Baldridge, doling out too much disappointment and unhappiness to a girl who had delighted in Southern charms and full dance cards.

"I heard gunfire," Sally said, twisting a handkerchief between her small hands.

"Yes, another saloon brawl," Adele told her. "Terrapin apologized for it happening right after our wedding."

"That was nice of him."

"Nice?" Adele stared at Sally. "Nice and Terrapin are strangers. He makes my skin crawl, that one. I was telling Reno how Terrapin rules this town with an iron fist, a keg of whiskey, and a stable of prostitutes."

"You can't fault him for being a shrewd businessman. He's merely providing the town with what it wants."

Reno studied Sally and saw an opportunist. That hadn't changed about her. Sally had always been drawn instinctively to the people she thought could help her social status or put coins in her pocket.

Adele propped her fists at her waist. "Sally, how can you compliment that skunk? He preys on weaknesses, and you admire that?"

Sally waved her handkerchief like a flag of surrender. "I'm not going to fuss and fume. I only came to warn you that Mrs. Ball is being impertinent again. We had a few slices of pie left from yesterday, so she didn't bake any today."

"God's nightgown," Adele muttered, reaching back to unbutton her dress while she headed for her bedroom. "That woman! Why must she be so vexing?"

With Adele out of the room, and finding herself alone with Reno, Sally twisted the handkerchief again and edged toward the door.

"I have to get back to the restaurant," she said, almost in a whisper.

"Who is Mrs. Ball?"

"The cook. She's a trial."

"Why doesn't someone fire her?"

"I-I don't know."

"I'm surprised to find you here, Sally Ann. I

thought you'd stay in Kansas with your folks."

"And I thought I'd seen the last of you back in Kansas. Why did you do this to Dellie?"

"I didn't do anything to Dellie she didn't want done."

"You're a scavenger," Sally hissed. "A gold digger."

"And you're an uppity little hypocrite."

Sally gasped and hurried from his sight.

When Reno entered the restaurant after changing into black trousers and a boiled shirt, he was confronted by Adele, who came flying out of the kitchen, her face flushed and tears standing in her eyes.

Sally stepped around the counter toward her. "What happened? What did she say?"

Adele released a quick breath. "She won't bake any pies today."

"But we only have three slices of apple left and one of pumpkin. Why is she doing this?"

"Why does she do anything?"

Reno leaned against the counter, enjoying the small drama. "Who are you talking about?"

"Minnie Ball, the cook." Adele sat wearily in the closest chair. "She is quite obstinate, and I have a difficult time handling her."

Reno strode into the kitchen, curious to meet someone Dellie couldn't intimidate or cajole. The dog-faced woman was standing before a cooking stove, stirring a kettle of soup. She turned and glared at him. Reno resisted the impulse to growl at her. So this was his apparition, his bad dream.

"I don't allow no men in my kitchen. Git!" She tasted the soup and added salt.

Reno moved closer. "You were wrong," he told her, keeping his voice low and his tone modulated. "She *did* marry my sorry ass."

Minnie Ball set the soup ladle aside and turned to face him. She planted her big fists on the long wooden table between them and leaned on them. "What do you want?"

"I want you to obey your boss lady and bake some pies."

She gave a *hurrumph* and shook her head, making the folds of skin on her face and neck jiggle. "I done told her I ain't baking nothin' today. They can eat them leftovers from yesterday. There ain't nothin' wrong with them."

"No, but there are only two or three slices, and you know there will be more customers than that wanting dessert."

"Wanting and getting ain't the same, I reckon." She chuckled. That sound alone raised Reno's hackles.

This unpleasant bully had frustrated Dellie for the last time, and Reno meant to have the last laugh on her.

"Bake the pies or clear out."

She widened her piggish eyes. "Who says? Says you? You ain't nobody to me."

"I'm the husband, and that makes me your boss. Now bake the pies or hit the street."

"You firing me?" she challenged.

"That's right. I'm firing your sorry ass."

She removed her apron and slapped it down on the

table. "She ain't gonna like this. She'll be begging for me to come back afore sundown."

He nodded toward the back door. "You leaving, or do I have to toss you out?"

She made a face that would have scared the Devil, picked up her purse, and waddled out the back door. Reno went to the stove and tasted the soup. It was vegetable soup with too many onions and not enough carrots and potatoes.

Adele pushed open the swinging door and glanced around. "Where's Mrs. Ball?"

"Gone." Reno faced her. "I did what you should have done. I fired her."

Adele's lips moved, but no sound emerged.

"That's right. I fired her," he repeated. "She's an insolent, foul-mouthed hag and not even a very good cook, if this soup is any indication."

"And who do you think will cook for our customers?" Adele demanded.

"You can find someone to replace her. This is a sizable town. I'm sure you can locate a woman who needs the work."

"Oh, you're sure of that?"

"Yes."

She folded her arms and tapped one foot. "Then by all means, go get one."

"You mean . . . you want me to—?"

"Yes, and have her here before the dinner trade starts."

"Be serious. I can't hire someone that soon."

"Then put on an apron and start cooking." She turned and started to leave, but stopped and faced him again, her expression stern, but her eyes revealing a glint of mischief. "For your sake I hope your efforts are satisfactory. You've seen how the men in this town handle differences of opinion." She snatched up the apron Minnie Ball had taken off and tossed it to him. "Better strap a gun on along with that. I'd hate to be made a widow over an unsavory bowl of stew."

Chapter 4

The Black Knight Saloon beckoned like a Siren. Reno let his long legs carry him from the foreign soil of the depot restaurant to the familiar oasis of the saloon. Inside all was quiet, save for the tinkling of glass as the barkeep shined and stacked jiggers. The bartender nodded, and mote-filled sunlight reflected off the top of his bald head.

The main room was huge. It was not unlike most of the saloons Reno had frequented, with its staircase crawling up the back wall and its bar stretching in front of a mirror that reflected the entire room. A bad oil painting of a naked lady adorned one wall. Tables and chairs took up the rest of the area, along with a piano and strategically placed spittoons.

The place smelled of linseed oil, tobacco, and beer. Reno inhaled the mixture of aromas and felt right at home. He strode to the bar and slapped a coin onto its surface.

"Whiskey, please."

"Yes, sir." The bartender poured him a measure. "You're new in town."

45

"Yes, I'm Reno Gold. I married Adele Bishop this morning."

The man raised his thick, black brows and shook Reno's hand. "That so? You're the one, huh?"

"I'm him. Fill me up one more time."

The barkeep obliged with a smile. "My name's Hector. You're not gonna get drunk, are you? You should be tangled in the sheets with your bride right now."

"Couldn't agree with you more, but my bride is busy running that damned restaurant."

That restaurant was quickly becoming the bane of his existence. Dellie was married to the place and expected him to devote his life to it as well.

She could expect all she wanted, he thought crossly. He wasn't going to step into Minnie Ball's place and labor over a hot stove, no matter what Dellie said. If she thought she could order him around as she did the women who worked for her, she was in for a surprise. She had it all planned. She would change him, whip him into shape. But he had a scheme of his own. Reno meant to change her back into the sweet, inspiring girl she'd been in Kansas.

His immediate task, however, was to make himself scarce until the meals were served and the restaurant was closed for the day, because he wasn't about to become the cook and bottle washer.

Movement caught his eye. He turned to see two women standing in the shadows near the piano. "Hello, ladies. You aren't hiding from me, are you?"

"No. We ain't hiding." The older, broader one stepped forward. "We're just waiting for an invitation."

Reno motioned them forward. "Come on, then.

You're invited to share a drink with me. Line them up, Hector." Reno laid a bill on the counter. "That ought to keep the whiskey flowing."

"Yes, sir." The bartender seized the money and set two more jiggers on the counter. "This here is Dead-eye Doris and Little Nugget."

"Gold." Reno grinned at the women. "Reno Gold."

The younger female stepped into the sunlight. Reno was struck by her youth. She couldn't have been more than sixteen or seventeen, he figured, and she had a pretty, almost angelic face. Her pale blond hair was fine and shimmered like gold dust. Her eyes, light brown and widely spaced, sparkled with curiosity and zest. Her companion, older and wiser, smiled with jaded affability.

"I'm Little Nugget," the blonde said.

"Then you're Dead-eye Doris," Reno said to the other woman, noticing as she approached that one of her eyes was blue and one dark brown. Her smile, he also noticed, wasn't just jaded; it was slightly sad. But then, who wouldn't be sad, working in a saloon, past her prime. She probably had trouble competing with the young ones like Little Nugget.

Reno reared back, a flash of brilliance striking his mind.

"Thanks for the drink," Doris said, downing it neatly. "And congratulations on your marriage."

"Yeah, congratulations," Little Nugget chimed in, sipping her whiskey slowly and swallowing it as if it were medicine.

"Can either of you ladies cook?" Reno asked.

Little Nugget slapped her thigh and laughed. "Mister, do we look like we belong in a kitchen?"

"I can cook," Doris spoke up, narrowing her eyes at him. "Why? You hungry?"

"No, I'm looking to hire a cook for the depot restaurant. You interested?"

The blonde nudged Doris. "Want to strap on an apron?"

Dead-eye Doris studied Reno intently, and he realized she thought he might be joking. He reached into his pocket and withdrew his money clip. From it he selected a bill and laid it on the bar. Doris's eyes widened.

"First week's salary. I imagine Dellie will want you to sign a contract of some kind. I hear that the women at these depot restaurants are required to remain employed for a designated period of time. Six months to a year, I think. Dellie might offer you less per week, but I'll make up the difference as long as you keep that just between us." He winked. "A man has to have a few secrets, even from his wife. What do you say? Are you worth that salary? If there are complaints, I'll take it from your pay."

"I work here," Doris said softly, reluctantly.

"He doesn't own you, does he?" Reno asked. He could tell by her pinched expression that they were both talking about Taylor Terrapin. "You want out of this trade, don't you?" He gave her arm a light squeeze. "What do you say? Do you think you could satisfy some hungry travelers?"

Doris's mouth quirked. "I've been doing that for a good many years, mister." She cleared her throat and covered the currency with her hand. "I used to cook for my brothers and sisters and they never complained. I even had a husband once and he got fat living with me. I reckon I could manage."

Little Nugget gripped Doris's shoulder. "You better think about what you're doing. Better ask Taylor first or he'll be rootin' tootin' mad."

Doris shook her head. "You're the only one he cares about anymore. He won't miss me." She snatched her hand off the bar, and the currency was no longer there. "I gotta pack a few things. I get room and board, don't I?"

Reno nodded. "Sure do. I didn't catch your last name, ma'am."

She looked startled, but answered, "McDonald."

"Can you start cooking today, Mrs. McDonald?"

A shy smile of pleasure curved her lips. "I guess."

"Good." Reno tossed back the shot of whiskey. "I'll wait and escort you to the restaurant."

Dead-eye Doris hitched up her skirts and almost flew upstairs. Little Nugget watched her, worry etched on her elfin face. The barkeep was frowning, too.

"Hope you know what you're doing, mister." Little Nugget said. "What do you think, Hector?" she asked the bartender.

"He won't like her leaving without asking first."

"He'll get over it," Reno assured them. "Where is Terrapin? I'll tell him Mrs. McDonald is working for Dellie now."

"He's asleep and he don't like being disturbed," Little Nugget said. "I'll tell him later when he's awake. I'll handle it."

Reno observed the stubborn set of her mouth, the courage evident in her straight posture. "So you're his favorite. How old are you? And don't lie to me. I figure you can't be more than eighteen or nineteen."

"I don't lie," she told him, her eyes taking on a hard sheen. "I'm seventeen. Something wrong with that?"

"No, but it's a shame that a fine-looking lady like you had to start such a life so early. Where's your mama?"

"Dead, and you don't have to worry about me. I'm sitting in the catbird seat."

Reno grinned. "I thought you didn't lie."

She looked startled, then averted her face from him, and Reno realized he'd struck a nerve.

Doris McDonald came charging down the stairs, suitcase in hand. Her cheeks were flushed and excitement sparkled in her eyes.

"I see you're ready, ma'am."

"Yep." She backhanded a stray lock of her brown hair from her eyes. "I used to dream about leaving this life, but I never managed it. If I pass up this chance to get out, I'll never forgive myself."

Little Nugget hugged her. "Take care. I'll do what I can to smooth things over when he finds out."

Doris rested one hand alongside Little Nugget's face. "You should get out, too. You're young and pretty and can find a husband if you try. You ought to leave here, so you can catch yourself a good man."

Little Nugget gave her a playful push toward the door. "I've had all the good men I can stand. Go on. I'll stop by and see how you're doing in a few days."

"Honey, you can't fool me. I know you've got dreams just like the rest of us," Mrs. McDonald said, looking over her shoulder as she moved with Reno toward the bat-wing door. "Don't be a stranger, you hear? And don't let him hurt you."

Reno glanced back at the small blonde, struck by her friend's parting advice. He saw the glimmer of tears in Little Nugget's almond-shaped eyes before she turned away. She wasn't as tough as she pretended to be.

"Is Terrapin mean to you gals?" Reno asked the new cook, slowing his stride to match her shorter steps. "Does he hit you, beat you?"

"Sometimes." She shrugged. "I hope he won't be too disturbed about me leaving. I'm the oldest he's got and not many of the regulars ask for me. Little Nugget is different. He's real possessive of her."

"He won't hurt her?"

"I wouldn't go that far. She thinks she can handle him." She gave a sniff of derision. "Thinks that if she acts like a lady, she'll be treated like one. She's young and doesn't know that some men are evil to the core and will strike out when they feel threatened. Kill, even. Terrapin's like that. No woman is safe around him."

Reno frowned and stuffed that into a corner of his mind. Placing a smile on his face, he winked at his companion. "I think you'll like it at the restaurant."

She laughed humorlessly. "Mister, I think I'd like it just about anyplace where I don't have to lie down and spread my legs." She gave him a sharp-eyed look. "You sure your new missus will want me around? I never heard of her hiring any saloon girls before."

"Why, she'll be as proud as a hen with her first chicks to hire you, Mrs. McDonald," he assured her, wondering if she could tell he was lying like a rug.

*   *   *

Adele closed the door to her private quarters slowly and turned to face Reno. She wanted very much to yell and scream and call him every vile name she could conjure, but she refused to allow him to reduce her to a red-faced shrew.

"You had no right to hire that woman as my cook," she said, proud of her level tone and her logical words.

"You told me to hire someone," Reno reminded her with an insolent grin.

"I run a respectable establishment and I can't have that kind of woman here. You'll have to tell her you made a mistake and she must leave."

"I didn't make a mistake. Did you hear any complaints from your customers? No, because they were too busy shoveling her food down their gullets. She beats that other cook of yours all to hell, so why would you want to fire her?"

"You know why. She is a . . . a soiled dove."

Reno rolled his eyes. "Will you listen to yourself?" He stepped closer, and she flattened herself against the door. "I should think you'd be the first one in town to offer your help to the downtrodden." He pointed behind her. "That woman out there was desperate to leave her life as a *soiled dove*. I offered her a way out and she took it. I thought you'd be happy to lend her a hand. If you don't approve of the work they do, then you should be eager to do what you can to get them out of that business."

He was making sense. She hated that. "Naturally I want to help if I can, but what if it gets around that she was once a . . . a lady of the evening? What will the customers think about that?"

Reno made an off-hand gesture. "Most of your customers are passing through town and couldn't care less about who is cooking up the vittles in the back room. Come on, Dellie, give Mrs. McDonald a chance." He grinned and gave her a sly wink. "She's a big improvement over that dog-faced crone."

Adele ducked her head to hide her smile. She didn't want him to think all was forgiven. "That's true, but from now on I won't allow you to hire and fire anyone at this restaurant. I am the manager of this place, not you."

"I was only doing what you told me to do."

"Yes, I know." She edged away from the door and walked past him, pausing on the threshold of her bedroom. "Why have you placed your belongings in my room?"

He rubbed his jaw, baffled. "Where else would I have placed them?"

"Not in my room, I assure you." She gave a flick of her wrist. "You'll have to remove them. I have secured quarters for you out back in that shed. It used to be for . . . well, for servants who—"

"For the slaves," he finished, folding his arms against his broad chest and pinning her with a dark scowl.

"Yes, that's right. A good sweeping out and it will be fine. I'll put a cot in there and—"

"No, thanks. I'll sleep in there." He nodded at the room behind her.

Adele glanced over her shoulder, then whipped back around to face him. "In my bedroom? No, you'll sleep out back."

He shook his head. "I'll sleep with you. That bed

is plenty big enough for two if we cuddle real close."

An image of the two of them wrapped in each other's arms in her narrow bed flashed in her mind and sent a quiver of awareness through her. Adele closed her eyes tightly for a moment to ward off the vision.

"Reno, you know quite well that I have no intention of being intimate with you. I think now is a good time to establish some rules." She moved from the threshold and paced in front of the sofa. "The quarters out back will be yours. I won't have you sporting with other women and embarrassing me further. I have a reputation to uphold in this town. I won't have you tarnishing it with your behavior."

"Stop right there." He lifted one hand, palm out. "Just how am I supposed to scratch my manly itches if we keep separate bedrooms and you don't want me hanging around other women?"

She felt her face flame, but she strove to keep a passive countenance. "Ignore those itches. Women do it all the time. I'm certain you can abstain if you set your mind to it."

To her surprise he laughed and seemed genuinely amused. She sat primly on the sofa, folded her hands in her lap, and waited for him to get serious again.

"Dellie, you are a blue ribbon, you are. What if I don't want to ignore my itches?" He shook his head, warding off her answer. "No, save your breath. Sugar, I know you don't like this, but I'm not sleeping in any slaves' shed, so get that out of your mind. If you won't let me sleep with you, then I'll use that cot you mentioned." He looked around the parlor and indicated a space near the window. "I'll set it up there.

You can rant about it all you want, but it won't change anything. I'm not about to sleep outside in that drafty, old shed. Why, even the cats won't go in there."

She could tell by the hard edge to his voice that he meant what he said. *Blast him!* Why couldn't he simply follow the rules? She decided to concede the point and press on to the next one. "You will work at the restaurant, and I expect you to pull your load and not be a layabout. I don't know what you're used to or what you thought life would be here, but everyone here works hard. You will be no exception. Honest work will do you good. My mother always said that kicking a man when he's down is sometimes the only way to make him get back up."

Reno's expression changed from pleasant to poisoned. The muscles in his jaw twitched and his mouth thinned to a straight line. Adele drew in a cautious breath, realizing too late that she'd overstepped.

"You know, Dellie, if I didn't think so much of you, I'd saddle a horse and leave you to the gutless, heartless life you've carved out for yourself here. I keep remembering the girl you were in Lawrence and I cling to that."

"Heartless? Gutless?" Angry tears stung her eyes. "My life is exemplary compared to yours." She stood and walked briskly to the door, his words hurting her more than she cared to admit. "There are potatoes to be peeled and a kitchen to clean. You're going to be the new cook's assistant and your duties begin right now."

Reno watched her flounce out and imagined applying the toe of his boot to her swaying backside. He whirled, wanting to send a lamp crashing to the floor or to plow his fist through a wall, but he fought back the demons and took a few deep breaths.

It galled him that she had him pegged for a penniless drifter, a lazy no-'count. She was used to everyone jumping when she gave an order, but he refused to allow her to treat him like a servant. Every once in a while he saw a glimmer of the girl he knew in her eyes, in the tilt of her head, in her gestures. He had loved that girl, loved her so much he had never been able to forget her.

What she needed was someone to stand up to her, to loosen her corset and unpin her hair. She didn't know it yet, but she needed him.

He'd sleep on a cot in the parlor for now, but he meant to win his way into her bed and into her heart. For now, he'd live up to her low opinion of him and do as little as possible to please her. The potatoes could rot and the kitchen could stay dirty. Grabbing his coat and hat from the hall tree, he ducked out the back door and headed for town and a poker game at the Red Queen Gaming Hall.

Chapter 5

Toward the end of the evening, when the moon had slipped below the horizon, a heavy hand landed on Reno's shoulder. He shifted in his chair, pressed his cards closer to his chest, and looked up into a stranger's smile. The man wore an eye patch. Reno had a faint memory of seeing him on the train to Whistle Stop.

"Mr. Terrapin would like a word with you."

"I'm in the middle of a card game, pal," Reno said, glancing around at the other players. They all looked decidedly nervous.

"After this game, then?" The man's smile stiffened and his fingers dug into Reno's shoulder.

"Sure thing." Reno faced the other players and shrugged off the man's hand. The bets had been made. He laid his cards on the table and won the money piled in the center. "Much obliged, gentlemen," he said to the three ragtag, bleary-eyed drunks, who all seemed glad for the game to end now that Taylor Terrapin had summoned Reno for a little chat. "The owner has need of my attention, so I must call

57

it a night." He stuffed his winnings into his pockets, bowed to the losers, and joined Terrapin at a table near the door.

"What are you drinking?" Terrapin asked.

"Whiskey, neat."

Terrapin signaled to one of the daringly dressed barmaids. "I wanted to speak to you about your way of doing business, Mr. Gold."

"What business is that?"

The barmaid placed the drinks before them. Reno recognized her from that morning in the saloon. Little Nugget. Terrapin's favorite. She smiled at Reno before moving back to the bar, obeying Terrapin's casual gesture of dismissal. Reno sampled the whiskey. It had more bite and flavor than what he'd been served all night. Only the best when the boss was buying the drinks, he thought, glancing at Little Nugget again and tossing her a wink and a grin.

"Nugget, you get on upstairs, undress, and wait for me," Terrapin ordered.

The petite blonde stared at him, her lips trembling, but her chin tipped up in rebellion.

"Did you hear me?" Terrapin asked, his voice raspy soft and full of danger.

"I'm not hurting nothing by standing here."

Terrapin's eyes glittered with malice. "You get upstairs now or there will be hell to pay. Don't sass me if you want to keep your teeth."

"Hey now," Reno said, unable to sit quietly when threats were made against women. "There's no call for—"

"This is none of your business," Terrapin snapped. "This is between me and my woman."

"I'm going," Little Nugget said, and dashed up the stairs and into a room, slamming the door behind her.

Reno settled back in his chair, his temper simmering. In that moment he sized Terrapin up as a coward and a bully. A deadly combination.

"You hired someone away from me today." Terrapin unbuttoned his suit coat, revealing a silver vest and a tooled leather gun belt. "Dead-eye Doris. She's been on my payroll for three or four years."

Reno glanced around, making sure no one was taking an interest in their conversation other than the one-eyed man, who stood behind Reno and slightly to the right of him. Reno repositioned his chair and sat sideways so as to keep both Terrapin and his hired gun in view.

"I didn't catch your name," Reno said. "We came in here on the same train, didn't we?"

The one-eyed man nodded, but said nothing. He wore a fancy gun belt with a silver-handled Colt .45 decorating it. The handle was rubbed shiny in places, a clear indication of it being well used.

"Allow me," Terrapin said. "Mr. Gold, this is Buck Wilhite, an old friend of mine. He works for me now."

"Oh yeah?" Reno eyed him. "Doing what?"

"Whatever needs to be done to keep things running smoothly around here." Terrapin nodded at the three drunks Reno had engaged in a poker game. They shuffled out the door, casting edgy glances at Buck and Terrapin.

The piano player snoozed in a far corner. Two men, both elderly, played checkers and drank beer. The waitresses sat on the bar, swinging their legs and talking in whispers.

"You did know that Doris worked for me," Terrapin said. "I believe you met her at my saloon this morning."

"That's right." Reno finished the whiskey and let his right hand dangle at his side. "I met Little Nugget this morning, too. I offered them both a job as cook at the restaurant, and Mrs. McDonald accepted. Something wrong with that?"

Terrapin made circles on the tabletop with his index finger, his expression faintly friendly, but his eyes starkly sinister. Light flickered over his face, casting deep shadows on his pock-marked skin. "What's wrong, friend, is that you didn't ask me first."

Reno arched a brow. "Hell, that never crossed my mind. You cook, do you?"

Terrapin's face flushed a ruddy hue and his eyes snapped with anger, but his voice was pure silk. "No, I don't cook, and that's not what I meant, as you well know. Let's not jerk each other's reins, Mr. Gold. This hiring of someone on my payroll vexes me." His dark brows met. "It truly vexes me. Do you know why?"

Reno stared at him, refusing to fetch up the answers Terrapin wanted. After a few moments, Terrapin's mouth thinned to the width of a knife blade.

"It's vexing because you show disrespect by not conferring with me first, Mr. Gold."

Reno glanced around, keeping Buck and Terrapin in sight, and sighed, feigning boredom. "Uh-huh. Well, respect is earned, not given." He grinned broadly, playing the country fool, an act that had often served him well when dealing with undesirables. "My mama taught me that."

"I fear I'm not getting through to you." Terrapin

moved quick as a snake and clamped a hand on Reno's left wrist. His fingers felt like a band of steel. "I am willing to overlook your bad manners, Mr. Gold, if you apologize and give me your word that you won't tread on me again."

Every muscle in Reno's body tensed, but he strove for icy composure. Deadwood had taught him to stay calm even when his back was against the wall and the Devil was breathing in his face.

"Take your hand off me, pal," Reno told Terrapin, his voice soft and deadly. "I appreciate the drink, but I've got to be going. It's my wedding night, you know."

"Yes, I know, but the night has nearly expired. I wonder if your bride is disappointed or relieved by your absence. How much do you know about her?"

"Enough to know I'm a lucky man."

"Yes, but I don't think she approves of the way I do business. I was hoping you would have a calming influence on her. I thought you might rein her in. She tends to be flighty, too high-spirited for her own good."

"She's a woman, not a horse." Reno stared at the hand clamped to his wrist and gritted his teeth against his rising aggravation.

"I'm waiting for that apology, friend."

"And I'm waiting for you to let go of me, *pal*," Reno said, lacing the last word with insolence.

Terrapin flexed his fingers and inched his hand back across the table, but his eyes continued to hold Reno in their inky grip. "What's your tribe, Mr. Gold?"

"Tribes," Reno corrected. "Cheyenne and Chero-kee."

"Ah, I've got Cheyenne blood myself. That and Pawnee. We should be able to reach an understanding, don't you think? I'm an important man in this community, Mr. Gold, and I have earned respect here. Ask anyone." He essayed an expansive gesture with one hand.

Reno wasn't much concerned with that hand, but he did have an interest in the one hidden under the table. He suspected it rested on the butt of a revolver.

"You can understand how distressed I'd be with someone like you coming into town and hiring away one of my most valued girls. A simple apology will appease me for now, friend, seeing as how you're a stranger and acted impulsively. I'll allow one mistake."

Reno let his right hand drop lower until his finger-tips brushed the hem of his pants. He said nothing, letting silence speak for him. He felt the tension in the room tighten like a screw. He wanted to stand and make his way out of the gaming hall, but caution held him in the chair.

"Are you going to apologize, Mr. Gold?" Terrapin asked, his eyes going blacker, starker.

Reno shook his head. "No."

The tension cracked and split the two men apart. Terrapin leaned back to clear his gun from its holster. Reno slipped his fingers around the small butt of the .41 Colt strapped to his right ankle, his actions smooth and lightning-quick from countless hours of practice. With his other hand he gripped the back of the chair as he vacated it and swung it sideways, catching Buck in the chest and face. Wood splintered, and Buck stumbled backward, tripped, and fell. Terrapin froze, staring with surprise at the gun barrel inches from his nose. His brown lips stretched into an unpleasant grin.

"You carry a little ladies' gun?"

"It shoots big manly bullets," Reno assured him, backing toward the door as he divided his attention between Terrapin and Buck, who had surged to his feet, his one eye bulging from its socket. "Like I said, my bride is waiting for me, so I'd better mosey on home." Feeling the swinging door at his back, Reno shouldered it open and nodded to Terrapin, who had both his hands on the table now. "Good evening."

"You've made an enemy tonight, I fear," Terrapin said, drumming his long fingers on the tabletop, his eyes without any sheen of humanity, like a doll's.

"And I fear that the next time you start to draw on me I'll have to shoot you," Reno countered, before slipping between the swinging doors and into the gray night.

"Let him go," he heard Terrapin tell Buck.

Nevertheless, Reno stepped lightly, his eyes searching for any movement, his senses reaching out, feeling for danger. His footfalls sounded like gunshots, so he stopped off the boardwalk and onto the softly packed dirt of the street. His heart flung itself against his chest wall and he was sweating as he neared the fog-shrouded lights of the train depot. A lamp burned in the shed out back, testing his patience.

Reno opened the shed door and stared at the cot, table, and trunk. He gnashed his teeth, doused the lamp, and grabbed the rickety bed. Carrying it easily and dragging the bedclothes with him, he went to the front door of the restaurant. Locked. He carried the bed around to the rear entrance. Locked.

Setting the cot down, Reno backed up a step, aimed, and kicked. The heel of his boot connected smartly with the thin wood, splitting it and allowing the door to swing open. Reno picked up the cot and went inside. He headed for Adele's quarters, feeling damn near invincible.

"Well, where is he?" Sally demanded, tapping one foot and fixing that chastising expression on her face that never failed to fire Adele's anger.

"Who?" Adele asked. She was polishing the front counter until it gleamed. She looked toward the front door, hoping for another group of customers, but the tracks were empty and the depot deserted. In the hours between dinner and supper, the trade slackened off, giving Adele and her staff precious time to get ready for the evening rush. Usually there were stragglers wanting coffee and pie, but no one was approaching the depot, leaving Adele to deal with Sally's persistent questioning and unrelenting disapproval.

"You know who," Sally retorted. "Your lazy husband. I know he didn't sleep out back, because I checked early this morning and the cot's not even in there. So where is he?"

Adele lifted a shoulder in a half-hearted attempt at indifference. She knew exactly where he was, because she had discovered him passed out on the cot he had placed in her parlor. She'd heard him break down the door early this morning, but had remained shivering in her bed, afraid he meant to force himself on her. Only when she'd heard his noisy breathing had she realized she was safe. She'd crept out of her bedroom to stare at him, his face painted by moonlight, his powerfully built body too large for the narrow cot.

Feeling Sally's keen regard, Adele pushed aside her musings. "I'm too busy to keep track of a grown man's whereabouts."

"Adele," Sally said, making her name a lament. "Why don't you admit you made a big mistake marrying him? You can get an annulment. You don't have to keep up this charade. I can see you're upset."

"I'm upset because I don't want to discuss this endlessly with you, Sally."

Doris McDonald came in from the kitchen, and Adele seized the opportunity to change the subject.

"The customers seem to have fallen in love with your chicken and egg noodles," Adele said, stepping around Sally to address the new cook.

"That's nice to know." She wore a bright-green dress of fine quality and had tied on an apron. "I checked the staples today, ma'am, and we're getting pretty low on lard and potatoes."

"The first train in tomorrow is supposed to be bringing us some supplies, including potatoes," Adele assured her. "We buy our lard at the butcher shop. I'll send someone around for it later."

Mrs. McDonald nodded and turned to go back into the kitchen.

"Mrs. McDonald." Adele waited for the woman to face her again. "Do you sew?"

"Used to. I haven't for a long time though. Why?"

"I have some material and patterns you can use to

make yourself some work dresses like ours, if you'd like." Adele reached out to touch one of her sleeves. The satin slipped across her fingertips. "This is too fine for the kitchen."

Mrs. McDonald's face flushed bright pink. "Yeah, well, this was what I used to wear to work. I'd appreciate the material and patterns, ma'am."

"Fine, and you can call me Miss Adele." She noticed the woman's startled reaction. "If you have a problem with that, you can call me Miss Bishop."

"But you're married now, aren't you?"

It was Adele's turn to be startled. For a few moments her tongue refused to move as her mind whirled. Married. Yes, she was married. She had taken the vows and had signed her name to the certificate of marriage, but should she take Reno's name? Should she carry the farce that far? "I meant . . . Well, yes, I'm married now, but you can still call me—"

"Mrs. Adele," Reno spoke up, as he entered the restaurant. "Or Mrs. Gold," he tacked on with an insolent grin. "Just don't call her Dellie, Mrs. McDonald. That's reserved for those closest to her." He essayed a wink, which garnered a big smile from the cook. "How about a cup of coffee and a bacon sandwich? My belly's so empty it's rubbing up against my backbone."

Sally released a sharp, bitter laugh. "Will you listen to that? He comes staggering in here and barks orders like he's lord of the manor." She glared a challenge at Adele. "Are you going to obey or rebel?"

"Good day to you, too, Sally Ann." Reno swung a leg and landed on one of the counter stools. A band of sunlight streamed through the windows and fell on him. He squinted his blood-shot eyes and turned his back on the light.

His clothes were rumpled, having been slept in, and his hair had received a rough finger-combing. Unshaven and smelling faintly of whiskey, he was every bride's nightmare.

"No gentleman would show his face in public looking like that," Sally said, pointing at Reno. "He stinks like a still."

Reno grinned at Sally, opened his mouth, and released an horrendous, eardrum-rattling belch. Sally fell backward as if she'd been shot, her eyes growing huge and all color draining from her face. While Adele knew she should be shocked to the soles of her feet by such behavior, she had to bite her lips to keep from laughing.

"You are a heathen!" Sally declared. "Just like your ancestors."

"Oh, that's right. You never approved of my bloodlines, did you?" Reno said, running a hand along his whiskered jaw. "Never had much use for Indians or Gypsies."

"I appreciate *civilized* Indians," Sally corrected, wrinkling her nose at him as if he were a cow pattie. "You seem to enjoy being the black sheep, the poor relation. Win used to say you made a vocation of it."

"Did he now?" He smirked at that, then pounded the counter with his fist. "Where's my coffee?"

Adele stepped forward and Reno swung his attention to her. Immediately she saw the frost in his eyes melt and his grin lose its bitterness. For all his blustering and surliness, she could still reach his heart, and that softened hers toward him. Once again she yearned to fashion him into the man she knew he could be.

"If you'll clean up, comb your hair, and change into fresh clothing, I will see that you are fed."

The corners of his wide mouth dipped in displeasure. "I have to meet with your approval before I get fed, huh?" He shook his head. "I don't think so." With that he stood and strode into the kitchen. The door flapped behind him.

Sally placed her hands at her waist in defiance. "Are you going to let him run this place and you?"

"Oh, hush up, Sally," Adele said, then went after her obstinate bridegroom. She found him rummaging through a basket of biscuits. Four slices of bacon already sizzled in a frying pan on the stove, where the cook tended to it.

"Mrs. McDonald, would you mind going to the butcher's for that lard?"

The cook glanced anxiously from Adele to Reno as she untied her apron and laid it on the long table. "Yes, ma'am."

"Thank you." She motioned for the cook to leave the frying bacon, taking her place before the stove. When Mrs. McDonald had departed, Adele set the skillet off the fire and turned to confront Reno. "If we are going to continue with this odd relationship, there are a few things we must get straight between us."

One side of Reno's mouth tipped up in a rakish grin. "I can think of one thing in particular," he said, jeering at her and making her blush when she realized he was making a ribald joke. "But we can remedy that tonight."

"Such talk does not impress me," she asserted. "I'm

appalled by your lack of ambition, Reno Gold, but I'm here to tell you that you will turn over a new leaf, because I have no use for lazybones around here. You will earn your keep."

"You're going to make a new man of me, is that it?"

"Exactly." Adele lifted her chin to meet his eyes. He stood before her, blocking her view of everything with the width of his body and the power of his presence. "And I'm not pleased that you broke my door and planted the cot in my parlor. After you have cleaned up and made yourself presentable, your first chore today is to fix that door. You may have a bacon sandwich, and once you have completed your chores for the day, I will instruct Mrs. McDonald to prepare you a delicious supper."

He said nothing, just gripped her shoulders and eased her off to one side so that he could finish frying the bacon. Adele decided to leave it at that. She had made herself clear, so there was no use in laboring her points. Giving him a tight smile, she whirled and went back into the restaurant, where Sally was sitting at a table by the window while Colleen and Helen, the two other waitresses, mopped the floor.

"Congratulations on your marriage," Helen said, her blue eyes bright with mischief. "I hear he's quite a catch."

Colleen, a tall brunette with deep dimples in her round cheeks, stifled a giggle.

"Yes, ma'am, you've got the whole town buzzing over this mail-order husband of yours," Helen continued. "That's all I heard this morning at breakfast and again during the dinner hour. Everybody was asking me if it was true you actually married that fella who fell off the train at your feet."

"Adele, I hope you're enjoying being the laughing-stock of this town," Sally said, giving Colleen and Helen a silencing glare. "Did you have a word with him? Did he listen or burp in your face?"

Adele went toward the door that led to her private quarters and motioned for Sally. "May I speak with you, please?"

Sally joined her in the parlor, and Adele shut the door to give them privacy. She sat on the camel-backed sofa and patted the cushion next to her. Sally took a seat.

"I know you want the best for me," Adele began, selecting her words carefully, "and I do appreciate that, but you must let me deal with Reno. By fussing with him, you are simply making things more difficult for me."

Sally threw up her hands. "Heaven knows, he's your problem. But Adele, you can't go on like this, with the town snickering behind your back. You were so well respected, and now this." She glanced at the cot where Reno had spent the night. "Enough is enough, don't you think?"

"I believe he has potential. With my help, he could become a respected member of this community."

Sally stared at her, aghast. "He's not a stray cat, Adele. Please don't make him one of your causes. Reno Gold will never amount to anything but disgrace. As a boy he was worthless and as a man he has not increased his value."

Adele flinched at Sally's scathing opinion. "I don't think he was worthless and I don't think he's worthless now. He was a good friend to me back in Lawrence, and I savor my memories of my time with him. Regardless of your thoughts about his future, Sally, he is my husband now and I am his wife. Please remember that and don't criticize us in front of others. Believe it or not, I'm not the only one with feelings. Reno has his pride, as well."

Sally shrugged. "It's your problem. I was only trying to make you see how degrading this could be for you."

Adele placed a hand on Sally's. "Believe me, I can handle Reno."

"Humpf." Sally stood up and smoothed the wrinkles from her apron. "Oh, well. If anyone can mold him into a decent human being, it's you." She pulled a finger across her lips, sealing them. "No more public displays from me, I promise."

"Thank you." Adele stood up from the sofa.

"But if you need someone to talk to or a shoulder to cry on, if things get too tough for you, Dellie . . ."

Adele nodded, placing an arm around her friend's waist. "I know I have you, Sally, and for that I am grateful. But I assure you, I can handle him."

"Humpf," Sally repeated, and Adele swore to herself that she would prove to Sally and the whole darned town that a good woman could bring out the best in any man—even the stubborn, ill-mannered Reno Gold.

Chapter 6

"This isn't working out at all," Adele murmured to herself as she stood up from her desk, where she'd been working on payroll ledgers. Late-morning sun spilled into the room and warmed the crumpled covers on Reno's cot. Adele turned her back on it, preferring not to dwell on the odd, irritating sleeping arrangements. "Why he won't sleep out back is beyond me," she grumbled.

A train whistle split the air. Adele sighed. The 10:10, she thought. The very same train that brought Reno Gold back into her structured life and set it spinning crazily like a child's top. He'd been living with her for nine days, and she'd made no headway with him. In fact, he seemed to become more lazy and aimless with each passing hour. She took his poor behavior as a personal failure and she was certain everyone looked at her with diminished respect. After all, a good woman brought out the best in her man.

All Adele had been able to bring out in Reno was his penchant for bedeviling her and spooking Sally. He chanted in Cherokee under his breath and sharpened his hunting knife at the supper table and had taken to wearing a medicine bag tied to his belt, all for Sally's benefit. Sally thought of him as a savage, and he was bound and determined to live up to it.

Then there were the long, tension-filled evenings, when Adele lay in her bed and listened for Reno to come to his. She had no earthly idea where he spent his evenings and she would rather have cut out her tongue than ask him, but her mind was alive with scenarios.

Each evening she imagined him flashing his infamous smile at the painted women in town while he told tall tales and spoke disparagingly of his new wife. Her imagination tortured her with images of him kissing rouge-painted lips and palming rounded backsides, of him dancing close and buying drinks. She hated to even ponder where he was getting his money. She certainly hadn't given him any, so she surmised he was gambling at the Red Queen and winning enough to impress the ladies.

During the evening she listened for the sweet notes of Chopin's Nocturne, for Reno usually checked the time on his pocket watch when he arrived home. The haunting notes would signal the beginning of those excruciating minutes when Adele would lie stiffly in her bed, barely breathing, and wait to see if Reno would go peacefully to his cot or try to exercise his husbandly rights.

So far he had opted for the cot. Adele told herself each evening that she was glad, relieved, thankful. But deep in her heart she was resentful. What was wrong with her? What was wrong with him? Why did he prefer the attentions of bought women to hers? The least he could do was *try* to seduce her! Not that she'd let him get very far. After all, she had her pride.

Yes, her pride. Adele sat heavily in the straight-backed desk chair and stared glumly at the cot. Pride was a heavy weight for a woman to carry around for nine whole days and nights. Things just weren't working out well at all.

Things sure were looking up, Reno thought while he composed a telegram to his partner, Lewis Fields, telling him just that and thanking him for sending money, which Reno had deposited in the Whistle Stop Bank.

His lucky streak was holding, giving him winning hands during the games of poker he and a handful of other gents enjoyed in the back room of the bank. Reno had taken a liking to Paul Green, the bank president, and had confided in him about his situation in life, both financially and matrimonially. On the nights he hadn't played poker at the bank, Reno had gone to Paul's house for dinner.

The only problem with this pattern was that Adele didn't seem to care where he was spending his evenings or with whom. Or maybe she did care, but she didn't want him to know it.

At least he had Sally on the run. Hell, that gal headed in the opposite direction every time she saw him, which suited him fine. He never could stomach Sally's uppity ways. She'd always acted as though she was better than most people and that the world owed her a good life. No wonder Win had been so melancholy. To want Adele and end up with Sally would plummet any man into the doldrums.

Having conversed with the town gents around the poker table, he'd learned that Adele had garnered a heap of respect for herself in Whistle Stop but not any beaux. Oh, sure, there were men who had their eyes on her, but nobody other than Taylor Terrapin had tried to court her. Nobody dared. She was a formidable presence and intimidated men with her intelligence and sharp tongue. Her progressive thinking turned some townspeople against her.

Funny that all the characteristics that put off most were the very ones that drew Reno to her like a pin to a magnet. She was the most challenging, most infuriating, most independent, most exasperating, most beautiful woman he'd ever known. Simple as that.

Which is why it raised his hackles that she hadn't asked him where he'd been spending his evenings. Hell, he wasn't even sure she knew he was sleeping on the cot at night.

But things were looking up. This morning Doris McDonald had told him that Adele had been inquiring about the women who worked at the Red Queen and the Black Knight and why she thought men enjoyed the company of such women. Reno figured there was only one reason why Adele would be interested in those gals and that was because she thought he was spending his time with them.

"She's jealous, bless her stubborn heart."

"Say what?" the telegrapher asked, peering at Reno through the thick lenses of his glasses.

"Oh, nothing. I was talking to myself. Did you send that message?"

"Sure did. You waiting for a reply?"

"No." Reno paid the man, adding a bit extra.

"Much obliged. If there is a reply, I'm staying at—"

"The depot restaurant," the man finished for him. "I know who you are. Everybody knows."

Reno grinned. "Guess I'm famous."

The bespectacled man laughed sarcastically. "Kings and fools always make for good gossip."

Wishing he could take back the extra money he'd given the smirking telegrapher, Reno swept his hat off the counter, wedged it onto his head, and left the small office.

This town was hard to figure. Some of the people were gems, like Mrs. McDonald and Paul Green, and some were mean as snakes, like Terrapin and Yancy Stummer and Buck, the hired gun Terrapin had brought to town. Green, the banker, was right about Whistle Stop being at a crossroads. It could become either a nice town to live and raise a family in or the next Deadwood or Dodge City. Everything depended on what class of people took hold of it. If Terrapin continued to rule, Whistle Stop would be good for nothing but losing money and dying young.

"*Psst! Psst!* Mister!"

Reno stopped in his tracks and looked around. At first he saw nothing, but then movement in an alley caught his eye, and he stepped cautiously between the two buildings flanking it. A petite blond woman emerged from the shadows. Reno smiled, recognizing her.

"Little Nugget, isn't it?" He glanced around. "Who are you hiding from?"

"Nobody," she said, but she seemed nervous. "I was wondering about Dead-eye Doris. How is she doing?"

The young woman's concern for her friend touched Reno. Something about Little Nugget tugged at his heart. Her youth, probably, he thought, and her lost innocence. She should still be with her mama and papa, not working for trash like Terrapin in a whorehouse saloon.

"Mrs. McDonald is fine. You should come on by the restaurant and visit her. I'm sure she'd be plumb tickled to see you again. You two are good friends, aren't you?"

"We used to watch out for each other." She bobbed her narrow shoulders. "I miss having her around. She was always good for a laugh, you know."

"Then come by sometime. Any time."

Little Nugget released a soft, sad laugh. "Hell's bells, I could never do that. Your missus would bust outta her corset if I showed up in her restaurant, bold as brass."

"What makes you think that? Has she said something to you to give you that idea?"

"No, nothing like that. I've never said a word to her or her to me. It's just that . . ." She glanced down at her gloved hands, twisting, twisting, and she swallowed hard enough for Reno to hear. "She's a lady and I'm—not." Her gaze swept up to his, defiant and shining with inner fire.

"But you're Mrs. McDonald's friend, and your money spends the same as anyone's. I'd wager that Dellie wouldn't care if you came by to share a cup of coffee and a piece of pie with your old pal."

"Dellie? Is that what you call her?"

He nodded. "I've known Adele Bishop since she was in pigtails."

"I didn't know that." She sized him up, her gaze quick and cunning. "You reckon she wouldn't mind if I showed up?"

"Shoot, no." He tapped a knuckle gently under her chin and made her smile. "She's not as straitlaced as you think. In fact, I bet she'd hire you if you needed a job."

Her eyes narrowed and she stepped back. "I don't need a job. I got one."

"I just thought you might want a different job. It would be great working with Mrs. McDonald again, wouldn't it?"

"I gotta go." She started past him, but he snagged her arm and stopped her. "Let go."

"What's your hurry? You scared?"

"No. I got things to do."

"Does he own you?"

Her chin trembled and a muscle ticked in the corner of her mouth. "Nobody owns me."

"Then you must love him."

"Him? Who we talking about here? God?"

"Maybe you think that highly of him, but I don't." Reno leaned down to whisper in her ear. "Terrapin. You love him, do you?"

She wrenched her arm from his grasp. "No. Why'd you think that anyway?"

"Because I can't see a pretty, smart girl like you staying with a skunk like him unless you owed him money or you were crazy in love with him."

"You think you got me pegged, do you?" The muscle near her mouth ticked faster. "I can make more in one night than Doris makes in a whole week, beating that bread dough, so I don't think I'll be tying on an apron any time soon. I'm doing just fine, cowboy. Just fine."

"You're not as smart as I thought," Reno said, letting his gaze slip contemptuously over her face. "If life is so fine for you, how come you're slinking around in alleyways and wishing you were respected enough to drink a cup of coffee with an old friend at the depot restaurant?"

His words stung. He could tell that by the way her eyes narrowed and then watered before she moved backward into the shadows. He knew their chat was over and she wouldn't hear anything else he had to say to her, so he dipped his head in a silent farewell and returned to the boardwalk that fronted the buildings. He looked back once and saw her crossing the street, one gloved hand holding her skirt above the mud, the brim of her stylish hat hiding her profile from him.

The image of a lady, he thought, watching her. He'd met his fair share of whores and he'd known only a handful who actually liked the night life. Little Nugget wasn't one of them. Any gal who wore spotless gloves and a fashionable hat in a town where everyone knew her for a whore wasn't cut out for a life of hard knocks and shame. She had too much pride and she still had dreams. To Reno's mind there was hope for her.

Withdrawing his watch from his vest pocket, he checked the time and grinned. Dellie and her crew would be in between meal servings. Time to stir up the pot again, he decided with a wicked chuckle. He'd turn up the flame a little bit while he was at it. Dellie needed a sample of what she was missing at night, then she'd be more interested in where he was keeping himself every evening.

Yes. Things were looking up.

Adele walked over to the man who sat alone at one of the tables and wondered what had brought him to the restaurant. Sure wasn't the coffee or the atmosphere. Taylor Terrapin never came calling unless he wanted something. She hoped this wasn't about Doris McDonald. But if it was, she was prepared to cut him off.

"You want to speak with me, Mr. Terrapin?" she asked, her tone frosty.

He had risen from his chair at her approach and now he offered up a polite smile. "Miss Adele, it's so very good to see you today." His high-pitched voice grated on her. He motioned to the other chair. "Won't you join me?"

"I suppose I can spare a few minutes." She sat down, straight-backed, and with an edge of impatience. She'd rather be scrubbing greasy pots in the kitchen than sharing a table with Taylor Terrapin, but she told herself to be civil. "Is there a problem you wish to discuss?"

He shook his head. "Now why would you leap to that conclusion?"

"Because you never dine here."

"True, but I have a business to run, same as you. Surely you can understand how difficult it is to get away."

She nodded and folded her hands on top of the table, waiting for him to get to the point.

"How do you like being married? Do you believe you've chosen the right man?"

She stiffened. Was this about Reno? "Has my husband run up a gambling debt?"

His brows arched and a calculating expression crouched in his eyes. "Sounds as if you don't know much about your husband's comings and goings. Actually, your husband has only been in my gaming hall once."

"Once?" She shook her head, having trouble digesting this latest revelation. If Reno wasn't gambling every night, then where was he keeping himself? She noticed that she no longer had Terrapin's full attention. He was smiling across the room at Sally. "What about your saloon? Has he been there? Is this about a bar bill he's run up?"

Terrapin jerked his attention back to Adele. "No, no. I haven't come here to dun you for money, although your husband is at the root of my visit, I must admit."

"What have you come to say, Mr. Terrapin?"

"Is Dead-eye Doris working today?" He glanced around the nearly empty restaurant. "She was certainly a popular item at the Black Knight."

"Mrs. McDonald is my cook and works in the kitchen. I'm very happy to have her here."

"I'm glad you're happy, but I spoke to your husband about how unhappy I am over the way she was hired. He failed to understand my position, but I trust you have more intelligence. You see, Miss Adele, I have a reputation in this town I have worked hard for and I won't have anyone diminishing it. If you wanted to hire Doris, you should have spoken to me first."

"Is that so?" Adele arched a brow and her temper simmered. The audacity of the man, acting as if he had a right to speak for Mrs. McDonald! She leaned back, distancing herself from him.

"Your husband hired one of my most valuable girls right out from under me without so much as a please and thank you. I'm not used to such shoddy business practices, and, I trust, neither are you."

"What I'm not used to and what I shall never be used to is a woman being treated as chattel."

Sally chose that moment to join them, coffeepot in hand. "May I offer you more, sir?"

Terrapin eyed Sally with relish. "How have you been, Mrs. Baldridge? I just don't see enough of you."

"I am as well as can be expected, Mr. Terrapin. Thank you for asking."

Was it Adele's imagination or was that a rosy blush on Sally's cheeks? And her voice was so soft and demure. Horror of horrors! Could Sally actually be flirting with Taylor Terrapin? Adele shivered with revulsion and hoped her friend had better sense. Sally moved the coffeepot closer, but Adele placed her hand over the cup in front of Terrapin.

"Let's save that for our paying customers, Sally."

Terrapin and Sally gave her twin arch looks.

"I assure you, Miss Adele, that I intend to pay for this cup of coffee," he told her, his tone dangerous, like the rattle of a snake's tail.

"I can't accept your ill-gotten gains, Mr. Terrapin," Adele said.

Sally gasped, on the verge of apologizing for

Adele's rudeness, so Adele spoke up first.

"Mr. Terrapin has come to scold me for hiring our new cook, Sally."

"That's not what I meant to do," Terrapin corrected her. "I simply wanted to talk to you about acceptable business practices. You, being a woman, aren't familiar with how things are done in the course of commerce."

"And what would you know about an acceptable business?" Adele charged, tipping her head to one side in an inquiring manner. Inside, she thrilled, giddy with her courage in the face of such serpentine menace. "You run a whorehouse dressed up as a saloon. That's not acceptable to any right-thinking, God-fearing person."

Sally made a sound of displeasure behind her, but Adele didn't care if she offended Terrapin. He offended her by having the temerity to question her methods when he was nothing but a black plague let loose on Whistle Stop.

"Is that what Doris told you?"

"I haven't discussed you with Mrs. McDonald. Besides, no one has to tell me what you do at that place of yours. It's common knowledge."

Terrapin drummed his fingers on the tabletop. "Your husband has had a bad influence on you, I fear."

"He has nothing to do with this. I have never approved of your business, and you well know it."

"I don't interfere with your operation here and I expect—no, I *demand* that you extend me the same courtesy." He leaned forward; she thought of a striking snake. "There are plenty of women in this town for you to hire. Don't come stealing any more of mine, and keep your husband away from my gaming hall and saloon. Next time he pulls a gun on me, I'll have him drawn and quartered and dumped on your door-step." He stood, jerking at his vest and snatching his hat off the rack by the door. "Good day, Miss Adele."

"That's Mrs. Gold to you, sir," Adele sassed him, almost automatically, because her mind was wobbling with what he'd said. Reno had pulled a gun on him? When? Why? And where in heaven's name was Reno spending every evening if not at the saloon or gaming hall? Had he already found himself a mistress?

"How could you speak to him like that?" Sally demanded, breaking into Adele's troubled thoughts. "If you want this place to succeed, you can't insult the town's most prominent citizen."

Adele blinked and realized that Terrapin was gone and that Sally sat across from her. Balling her hands into tight fists, Sally pounded the table in frustration.

"Taylor Terrapin could help us, Dellie. He has money and power and everyone respects him. What if he does hire loose women?" She shrugged, as if the practice were insignificant. "They come to him of their own free will. He doesn't force them to work. If you're going to disapprove of someone, what about that cook? Why, she's slept with nearly every man in town and yet you treat her as if she were as pure as the Virgin Mary!"

Sally's back was to the kitchen, but Adele saw the swinging door edge out and back. She figured that Doris McDonald was listening in and had probably been eavesdropping ever since Terrapin had entered the restaurant.

"For the life of me, I can't understand how you can defend that piece of cow dung," Adele said. "Terrapin might not force those women to work for him, but he exploits them, nonetheless. The spider does not force a fly into its web, but it devours that fly all the same. Our society leaves few choices for unmarried women, and men like Terrapin certainly take advantage of that."

"Oh, you sound like your mama."

"Good!" Adele said. She stood. The kitchen door eased shut again. "I think Terrapin is cheeky to stride in here and try to intimidate me."

"I heard what he said to you, Dellie. He was trying to advise you about your lout of a husband. Obviously the man has made a nuisance of himself around Mr. Terrapin. I heard something about a gun."

The front door opened and Reno strode in, effectively ending Sally and Adele's spirited disagreement. He grinned at them, cocky as a rooster in a hen house.

"Hello, ladies. What's cookin'?"

"Trouble, that's what, and it has your footprints all over it." Adele motioned him to follow her. "I'd like to speak to you alone for a minute." She went into her quarters, but he followed more slowly. He closed the door softly behind him and grinned at her.

"Now what?" he drawled with deliberate insolence. "Have I been naughty again? Do you have another list of chores for me that I have no intention of doing? When are you going to get it through that hard head of yours that I'm not your new mule?"

"I have been extremely tolerant of your behavior," Adele said, trying hard to keep a cool head. Her hands were shaking and she picked up a throw pillow to hide the tremors. "But I would like a straight and honest answer to one question, if you can manage that."

Reno shrugged and threw out his hands in an open challenge. "Hit me, darlin'."

Adele chewed on the inside of her cheek, tempted to haul off and wallop him. His smirk was back. It symbolized what she thought was happening all over town behind her back.

Something snapped within her, and before she could check herself she cocked her arm and hammered Reno's head with the pillow.

"Hey, hey!" He grappled with her for the harmless weapon and wrestled it from her. "What's wrong with you?" His hat, knocked askew by her attack, slipped the rest of the way off his head and fell to his feet. "Have you gone loco, Dellie?"

Fury surged through her. "Answer me, Reno. Do I know her?" she asked, voicing the question burning in her mind and poisoning her heart. "Who is she? Who have you taken as your mistress?"

Chapter 7

⟨～⟩⟨⟩⟨⟩

"Am I being accused of something?" Reno asked, picking up his hat and sailing it across the room, where it landed neatly on his cot.

"I am asking for the simple truth. Can you manage it?" Adele trembled inside, her nerves getting the better of her. She told herself she wasn't jealous, and yet this writhing, gnawing feeling certainly felt like that vile beast.

"I believe I can. You want to know about my mistress." He removed his coat and unfastened his shirt cuffs. "She's fickle, I'll give her that. I'm certainly not the first or the only man she has smiled upon and offered her favors to."

"Ah-ha!" Adele raised a shaking finger. Anger heated her face. "She's one of Terrapin's tarts, I suppose. Which one? Little Nugget?" Just the thought of him dallying with that painted-up child made her want to retch. She couldn't continue having him in her home if he had such low morals. Not even her mother would have faulted her on that. A man who would have relations with a girl nary a year or two

87

out of her pinafores, a girl who had fallen into a nest of snakes and could see no way out—well, that was a man she could never respect, never join with heart and soul. "How disgusting! How despicable of you! But I shouldn't expect anything more, should I? Sally is right about you. You're common and lazy and heartless."

He came across the room so suddenly that she had no time to defend herself or move away. His hands clamped on her upper arms, and she found herself pulled solidly against his chest, her head flung back to stare with shock into smoky eyes narrowed to dangerous slits.

"I've had about enough of you telling me I'm this and I'm that, when you don't even know me. Nor have you even tried to get to know me again. For your information I have not been spending my evenings with Little Nugget."

"Who, then?" she asked, her voice emerging choked.

"Lady Luck, my dear. I've been playing poker in a private game, not in a saloon, with some of this town's most respected gentlemen and coming out a winner."

Adele swallowed her heart from where it had lodged in her throat. "I wish you would find something you're good at besides gambling."

"I'm good at making love," he responded, drawing a fingertip down her cheek. "Would you like a demonstration?"

"No." She wriggled, but he wrapped an arm around her to keep her captive. Her traitorous heart hummed and a lethargic sensation floated through her. He was going to kiss her, and she was fairly certain she was going to like it.

"I'm feeling magnanimous," he said, his gaze fastened on her lips. "I'm going to give you a sample of what you're missing. Night after night I come back to this dark room and climb into that hard bed to dream of you. I think it's about time I renewed my memories of what it's like to kiss you, Dellie."

His mouth was a welcomed visitor and her lips parted, bidding his tongue entrance. At the barest touch of his flesh, her body temperature spiked and her arms found their way around him. The tip of his tongue outlined her lips, sending shivers down her spine, and then surged fully into her mouth in an intrepid, carnal passion only a fully grown man could orchestrate.

Her own passion stampeded through her, almost violent in its rending of her willpower. She sagged against Reno and raked her fingers through his silky, black hair. Breathing him in, she experienced his scent mixed with rawhide and Whistle Stop's dust. His mouth left hers and he peppered the side of her neck with fire-tipped kisses as he feverishly whispered her name. His hands stole down her back to her hips.

"Come to bed with me," he said. He scooped her up in his arms. "Let me show you how much I want you."

He carried her into her bedroom and lowered her onto the quilt. Joining her there, he plucked out her hairpins and kissed her eyelids and cheeks and throbbing lips.

"You've been waiting for this, same as I have," he told her, one hand moving down between their bodies to unbuckle his belt. "I knew you were burning for me."

His conceit acted like a hard slap to her self-esteem, and she turned her face away from his and shoved at his shoulders. Adele scrambled off the bed and straightened her clothes, then pushed her hair back from her forehead and flaming cheeks.

"I have *not* been on fire for you, Reno Gold," she informed him. "This may come as a crushing blow, but every female who claps eyes on you does not pine for your attentions."

He stretched out on his side and cradled his head in one hand, his gaze roving over her as if she were standing nude before him. "I have been for yours."

"Then speak for yourself and not for me." She spied her hairpins and scooped them up from the floor.

"Okay, I'll do that. I'm a stallion, not a gelding, and if you don't start warming up to me, I'll be forced to go looking for a willing woman. Is that what you want?"

"I ask for your discretion." She piled her hair back on top of her head and secured it haphazardly with the pins. "And I hope you won't make any more trouble for me with Mr. Terrapin. I don't like him coming around here with his veiled threats."

He came up off the bed with the agility of a cat. "What do you mean? When was he here bothering you?"

"Just minutes before you showed up. He is very upset by the hiring of Mrs. McDonald."

"I don't care and I don't like him coming around

here. If he's got business to talk about, he should talk to me." He jabbed a thumb at his chest.

"Excuse me, Mr. High And Mighty, but *I* am the business person in this room. Not you. Certainly not you with your layabout ways, your late nights and later mornings, your total disregard of this restaurant and the disbursement of funds. Mr. Terrapin was correct in coming to me to talk business. Whatever would *you* know about it?" She spun away from him and went to the dresser, where she finished rearranging her hair.

Behind her Reno tried to bank his anger. Damn her for belittling him! Yes, she had him dead to rights, but how did she think a man could pick himself up if she kept kicking his legs out from under him?

"Mr. Terrapin said you pulled a gun on him."

"That's right. I was defending your honor," he joshed, but he saw the sparkle of interest in the eyes that were reflected in the dresser mirror. He placed a serious expression on his face and played the rest of his hand. "He spoke disrespectfully of you, and I couldn't abide that."

Adele lowered her gaze, a thrill racing through her. No man had ever defended her honor. It was like something out of a novel. Still, she couldn't endorse gunplay.

"Violence is never an answer among the civilized," she said, repeating something she'd heard her mother say many times. "What if someone had been injured or worse?"

"Would you have cared if that someone had been me?"

"Of course." She traced the back of the silver-handled brush with her fingertip, unable to meet his gaze. "But please use more tact, Reno. Waving a gun at someone like Taylor Terrapin is most unwise."

So often she reminded him of her fiery, too-smart-for-her-own-good mother. Except that Dellie was beautiful, while Victoria Bishop had been handsome in a robust, apple-cheeked way. Dellie was more fair-skinned, more fragile, yet just as spirited and as sharp-witted as Victoria.

"Do you miss your mother, Dellie?" he asked. Her lashes lifted to reveal her green eyes in the dresser mirror. "How did she die?"

"Pneumonia," she answered, unable to manage more than a whisper. "It was pneumonia. The winter had been harsh and she'd spent it in Maine, setting up another library. She'd had some meetings with an influential man named Carnegie. He wanted to do what she'd been doing, but on a much larger scale. She was terribly excited, but then the sickness went into her lungs and she could barely draw a breath. It was quite sudden." She released a shaky sigh. "And yes, I miss her very much. Just knowing she is no longer in this world casts a shadow over me." Her eyes found his in the mirror. "How is your family?"

"Alive and well. Thanks for asking—finally."

His words poured over her, drenching her with guilt. She turned slowly toward him, seeing him fully for the first time, this broad-shouldered, handsome man she had married.

His dark hair, sleek as a crow's wing, fell across his forehead and brushed the tops of his well-shaped ears. She could see where his beard would grow in if he allowed it, but she was glad he didn't, for whiskers would hide the dimple in his square chin. He had rolled his shirtsleeves up to his elbows and unbuttoned his shirt almost to his waist. He wore black suspenders and trousers and shiny black boots. Suddenly her bedroom seemed small and overly fussy with this man standing in it. He extended one hand, palm up, and she responded without thinking by placing her hand in his.

"I should have asked after your family sooner," she allowed, averting her gaze while feeling his keenly on her hair, her face, her breasts. "They were always kind to me."

"Why did you take up this work, Dellie? I thought you would walk in your mother's footsteps."

"I wanted something of my own. Besides, opening libraries means moving often, and I'm tired of that. Mother loved to travel, but I wanted roots."

"You could have found a better town than this one to put down your roots."

"Oh, Whistle Stop isn't so bad." She hitched in a breath when his thumb moved sensuously across her knuckles. "If Terrapin would pack up and leave, this place would be almost heaven."

"I wouldn't bet on him doing that, Dellie."

Dellie. Nobody said her name quite like he did, she thought. His gentle Southern accent drew out the sound of it, caressed it.

"Terrapin's not going anywhere. He likes it here," Reno said. "Being a big man in a small town is a profession to someone like him."

"Reno, while I appreciate you standing up for me, I must ask that you not threaten or challenge Mr. Terrapin. You'll get yourself killed. He is a ruthless man."

"Again you demonstrate your appalling lack of faith in me." He released her hand abruptly. "You assume that I can't handle Terrapin, that I'll end up the loser."

"It's just that I know him and—"

"And you know me?" he finished. "Well, you don't, Dellie. You *don't* know me." He pointed a finger at her, and she was surprised to see the slight tremor of his hand. "What's more, you haven't even tried to get to know me. You labeled me common and lazy and what was it?" He snapped his fingers, remembering. "Heartless, that's it. Heartless." He shook his head and a mirthless laugh tumbled from him. "You thought you could put a yoke on me and lead me around like a dumb ox and you're aggravated because I won't mind you." He stepped closer, one step, and his body bumped hers. "I'm not a dumb ox. I'm a man. Treat me like one, treat me with common decency, and you might find out a little more about me. I guarantee you'll like what you find."

He cupped the back of her head in one hand and slanted his mouth over hers. Adele's fingers curled against his chest, fastening on his shirt, while her breath caught in her throat. Oh, kissing him was a celestial experience! He kissed with his lips and tongue and even his teeth, taking tiny soft bites while his tongue tussled gently with hers. He had learned a few things about kissing since his boyhood and he was teaching her. Adele was lost in her lessons.

So lost that she didn't hear Sally until she had nearly invaded the bedroom to stand on the threshold, her jaw dropping like an egg from a tall chicken.

"Adele! What are you doing?" Sally asked, staring at Adele as if she'd caught her in an illicit act.

"I . . . that is . . . I didn't hear you—"

"We're spooning, Sally," Reno said, wrapping an arm tightly about Adele's waist. "I'm stealing a little sugar from my wife here. Surely you and Cousin Win locked lips every now and then."

"What my husband and I did is none of your concern!"

"Exactly." Reno stared at Sally, letting his message settle, smiling patiently while she grasped his meaning.

Sally looked at Adele. "You can do better than this. You know you can."

"Sally, please, you promised." Adele slipped out of Reno's embrace. "What can I do for you?"

"Do?" Sally blinked, then remembered her mission. "Oh, yes. One of those whores from the Black Knight is here, asking to see Doris McDonald. I told her that Mrs. McDonald was working. I thought she'd have enough sense to leave or at least call on the cook at the back door, but that little tart sat down and ordered coffee and pie!" Sally gave a sniff of contempt. "You should have a word with her and explain why we can't serve her."

"What?" Reno's voice sounded like the boom of thunder and his eyes flashed with inner lightning. "Why won't you serve her? It must be Little Nugget."

Sally glared at him. "I wouldn't know her name, but we won't serve her because of what she is, of course."

"You served Terrapin today, didn't you?" Reno asked.

"He is a businessman," Sally rejoined. "And I'm not speaking with you. I'm trying to have a conversation with Dellie."

"*I'm* speaking to *you*," Reno bellowed, "you hypocritical, tight-lipped little—"

"God's nightgown! Hush up, the both of you!" Adele stepped between them. "I'm tired of this bickering. Reno, will you tell the cook she has a visitor and ask Helen to oversee the kitchen while Mrs. McDonald takes a break? Sally, you know that we don't turn away any paying customer."

"But you can't approve of how she made that money," Sally objected. "You wouldn't take Mr. Terrapin's."

"That was different. Terrapin is older and should be wiser and he is a man. He has far more opportunities to make a decent living. He isn't trapped. He is the trap." Adele shouldered past Sally, but not before she caught a glimpse of Reno's proud grin. She ducked her head to hide her own smile and was surprised that his pride in her created a warm glow around her heart.

Entering the restaurant, she saw that Mrs. McDonald's visitor was indeed Little Nugget. Sally swished past and filled the girl's order, placing it before her without so much as a smile. Reno strode into the kitchen, then came back.

"Mrs. McDonald says she'll be with you in a few minutes," he told Little Nugget. "She's got her hands full of bread dough right now."

Little Nugget nodded and flapped a hand. "Tell her I'm in no hurry."

Reno winked at her. "We'll do," he said, before returning to the kitchen.

Adele hung back, observing the young woman and thinking how lovely she looked bathed in sunlight, her hair shining like pale gold, her pert features seeming angelic. Adele's heart went out to her, and she found herself approaching the table slowly but with purpose. Little Nugget looked up, startled to find her there.

"Something wrong? I got money to pay for this."

"Oh, I'm sure you do," Adele said, smiling. "I don't think we've ever been formally introduced." She held out her hand. "I'm Adele Bishop."

The girl hesitated a moment before placing her gloved hand in Adele's and giving it a squeeze. "I'm Little Nugget. Pleased to meetcha."

"Must I call you by that made-up name?" Adele asked. "You have a last name, don't you, Miss—?"

She frowned slightly, then shrugged. "Little."

"Miss Little?" Adele smiled. "Very well." She eyed the chair opposite Little Nugget. "May I join you?" When the girl looked as if she might object, Adele added, "Just until Mrs. McDonald comes out."

The girl shrugged again. "I guess."

"Thank you." Adele sat down and saw Reno come halfway out of the kitchen. Seeing her sitting with Little Nugget, he retreated out of sight again. Evidently he wanted her to talk to the saloon girl. "This is your first time in here, isn't it?"

"Yeah."

"Your boss was in here for the first time today, too."

"He was?" Little Nugget's brown eyes widened.

"Yes, he dropped by to talk about Mrs. McDonald. He wasn't pleased that I'd hired her without consulting him first."

Little Nugget fashioned a quick smile. "Yeah, he's like that. He was blowing smoke out his ears when he heard about her leaving and coming here to work."

"I'm happy to provide honest work for women in this town." Adele traced a circle on the wood grain of the table. "I might be able to find work for you here, should you ever be interested."

Little Nugget sat back in the chair, wariness in her posture. "What makes you think I'd be looking for other work? I got a job. A good job."

"Is it good? Is it good for you, Miss Little? A young lady as lovely as you could be bettering herself instead of lowering herself to pander to the base needs of menfolk."

Little Nugget wrung her gloved hands. "I don't like lectures, especially from someone I just met. You want to preach a sermon, go find a congregation, but don't be wasting my time. Besides, I'm not the one who ordered herself up a husband. Not that I blame you. I mean, I've sampled the men in this town and I wouldn't want to be hitched to any of them either."

"I was trying to make a point," Adele defended herself, but she could tell by the sparkle of laughter in the girl's eyes that she would never be taken seriously by her. "Never mind. I'm sorry if I've offended you. I'm glad you've stopped by to visit your friend."

"Your husband told me to."

"He did?" Adele glanced toward the kitchen door, wondering if this was further evidence that Reno was sporting with Little Nugget.

"Yeah. He said you'd let me come in here, but I wasn't so sure. I wanted to see Doris, but I figured you'd hustle me right out the door if I showed up."

"Don't be silly. Mrs. McDonald will be so pleased you've dropped by to see how she's doing."

"Your waitress isn't pleased," Little Nugget noted, jutting her chin at Sally. "She wasn't going to serve me."

"She was confused."

The girl's smile became brittle. "I don't think so. But it's mighty Christian of you to serve up your vittles to the likes of me. Why, I'm so touched I might puddle up and cry." Her eyes were anything but liquid with tears.

Adele refused to rise to the bait. She found it disconcerting to have such a grown-up conversation with such a young person. Most girls of Little Nugget's age talked of parties and socials and the latest dance step. They giggled and blushed and spent a good amount of time in front of mirrors. Little Nugget didn't giggle or blush. She stared at Adele with eyes that were beautiful but cold, like marble. "I'm trying to place your accent, Miss Little. Where are you from?"

"Lots of places. My pa moved around a lot."

"And your mother?"

"She died when I was a kid. We used to live in Montana and Wyoming, but we headed for California 'cause my pa thought he could strike gold and get rich."

"But he didn't."

"Shoot, no. He struck rock bottom is what he struck. My ma died on the way to the coast. She lost a baby and just never could recover from it. We kids had to look out for ourselves 'cause Pa was busy drinking and whoring and talking about how he was going to find a pot of gold."

"When did you strike out on your own?"

She considered the question for a few moments before she answered. "The day before my fifteenth birthday."

Adele gasped. She'd expected the girl had left home at a young age, but not that young. "Oh, my dear. What were you thinking? How did you expect to make a living at that tender age?"

Little Nugget rounded her shoulders, as if the memories suddenly weighed on her. "I was tired of changing diapers, doing the washing, cooking up the food and taking care of my brothers and sisters. I was sick of it and I didn't want to spend another birthday growing old. So I left with a young drifter."

"Terrapin?"

Little Nugget laughed. "No, he didn't come along for years. The drifter and I parted pretty quick. He tried to get under my skirts, and I got hold of his gun and shot him in the foot. He didn't like me much after that, so he lit out in the middle of the night, leaving me with a horse, a saddle, and a bedroll. That's it. No water or food and no earthly idea where I was or where I was going."

"Whatever did you do?"

She sipped the coffee, her lashes sweeping down over the windows of her tattered soul. "I thought about running for president or maybe opening a bank, but I finally decided on whoring. Seemed like a thriving business just about everywhere I went." Dimples sprang into her cheeks, accompanying her small, snide smile.

"Miss Little, my questions are not meant to demean you. Like every unattached woman, I am keenly aware of the limited opportunities available to us. I must humbly point out, though, that there *are* choices, however few, and it's never too late to change one's mind, to choose something else to do with one's life."

The kitchen door eased open to admit Mrs. McDonald into the dining area. Impulsively Adele slid her hand across the table and captured one of Little Nugget's. Her gloves were made of silk and finely stitched.

"You are welcome here, Miss Little, and if you ever want to make a change, I will be here for you. I'll do whatever I can to help you."

Little Nugget tugged her hand from Adele's, and her expression was stony, even belligerent. "Why? You don't even know me. You don't even like me."

Adele smiled. "That's not true. I like your courage and your honesty. They are traits I admire." She glanced at Mrs. McDonald and gestured her forward. "I've kept your guest entertained, Mrs. McDonald. Here, take my seat." Adele stood and pulled out the chair for the cook.

"I'll only be a minute, ma'am."

"Nonsense," Adele admonished her. "You've been working hard today. Take a break and enjoy your company. I insist." Adele held out her hand. "Good day, Miss Little. It was so nice to finally meet you."

The girl took Adele's hand awkwardly. A faint blush stained her rouged cheeks. "Same here."

Adele moved away, giving the women their privacy, and joined Sally behind the counter.

"Next thing you know we'll be serving whiskey in here," Sally grumbled.

Adele sighed and tapped Sally on the shoulder, making her look up from the pie she was slicing into equal pieces. "If you keep up this griping and grousing, I'll *need* a good, stiff drink." She smiled, taking the edge off her declaration, and was relieved when Sally laughed softly under her breath.

"I can't help it, Dellie. I worry about you. These crusades are getting completely out of hand."

"But they make life interesting, don't they?" Adele quipped.

"Maybe for you." Sally covered the pie with a clean dishcloth. "Are you ready for the next interesting slice of life?"

The cold finger of anxiety slipped down Adele's spine. "I guess so."

"Then you'd better hustle on out back. Mrs. McDonald told your husband that we needed more kindling, and he picked up an ax and announced he was going to reduce the shed to firewood."

"He *what?*" Adele was already making for the kitchen. "He was joshing, surely." But as she neared the back door she heard the crack of an ax and the moan of old lumber splitting.

Throwing open the door, she watched the old slave quarters crumble to the ground.

Chapter 8

❦❧

❝What have you done?❞ Adele said with a moan as she strode toward the ax-wielding Reno. ❝Who gave you permission to tear down this shed?❞

❝Nobody. I don't need permission to turn this eyesore into kindling. This shack wasn't fit for humans or even rats, but you expected me to stay in it. It was a reminder of an enslaved South, a scar left by human suffering.❞ He turned toward her, his eyes blazing with a strange intensity. ❝I'll build you another one. A proper, upright, shiny new one.❞

❝Oh, really? Just as you sweep the floor and carry in the supplies and fix the broken wagon wheel? You don't mind if I don't hold my breath while waiting for this new shed to be built, do you?❞

He made a disdainful gesture and hoisted the ax, swinging it savagely to splinter a beam in two.

Watching him, Adele suddenly realized the error of her ways. The old saying about catching more flies with honey than with vinegar took on a new significance for her. Reno was a man, after all, and men

103

valued their pride above nearly everything. Carping at him had not produced any change in his lazy habits, therefore it was time to try a different tack. What could she offer him as a reward for any work he performed? The most obvious answer sent a wave of red-tinged embarrassment through her, but any other answer seemed frivolous. She had only herself to offer and she knew Reno wouldn't refuse her.

He continued to swing the ax, his muscles working under his shirt, his face set in lines of concentration.

"Reno, I have a proposition," Adele said, then cleared her throat nervously when he stopped and looked at her.

"That sounds interesting. What have you got in mind?"

"I was thinking that . . . Well, my browbeating you hasn't been successful."

"You just noticed that, did you?"

She chose to ignore his sarcasm. "Therefore I'm prepared to give you some—well—sweet rewards for any work you accomplish around here."

He leaned on the ax, bestowing upon her his full attention. "Sweet rewards? Exactly what are those?"

This was the hard part, she thought. Explaining to him and waiting for his reaction was torture. But she was beginning to think she was onto something important.

"Kisses," she blurted out, and fire shot into her cheeks, but she trudged on. "I will give you a kiss for each chore you complete. You sweep the kitchen, you get a kiss. Haul in supplies from the smokehouse and cellar. Kiss. Fix the broken wheel and put it back on the wagon. Kiss. Build a new shed to replace the one you are currently destroying. Kiss." She blew out a breath, glad to be done with her explanation. Sliding her eyes sideways, she regarded his bemused grin and wondered what he must be thinking.

"Kisses," he repeated finally. "Those will be my sweet rewards."

"Yes. You want to kiss me, don't you?"

His chuckle was downright lusty. "Oh yes, I sure do, honeybee. I surely do."

"Then this is a good plan, isn't it?"

"Almost perfect."

"Almost?" She studied him from the corners of her eyes. He seemed to be trying hard not to laugh.

"The way I see it, there is a big difference between sweeping the floor and building a shed, but you're offering the same reward for each task. That's not fair, is it? I'll accept a kiss for sweeping the floor, but I'm going to have to ask for more than that if I build a shed."

"More kisses?"

"More *than* kisses," he explained.

"Oh, I see." She looked away from him, while her mind scurried about for a solution. "I'll tell you what, I will openly and publicly take your name, Mrs. Reno Gold, if you fix the wagon wheel. That's a fine reward, isn't it?"

"You took my name when you married me," he pointed out.

"Yes, but people still call me Miss Adele, and I haven't corrected them. I shall correct them once that wagon wheel is fixed and the wagon is operational again."

He grinned, that lop-sided, devil-may-care grin that

made her heart do double time. "Done. What about the shed? What will you give me for building you a shed? I figure that little chore should be worth a whole"—he took one step closer to her—"night of"—another step closer to her—"lovin'." He stood next to her, his breath playing over her face, his body heat searing her. "What do you say there, Dellie? That would be a mighty sweet reward—for both of us."

Adele could hardly breathe. Suddenly perspiration slicked her body and every breath she took burned her lungs. Knowing the source of that incredible heat, she inched away from Reno and forced words from her parched throat.

"I might not like the shed you build. I have certain specifications that must be met."

"You draw up a list of specifications and I guarantee they'll be met. Is it a deal, Dellie? A shed for a long, hot night of lovin'?"

Adele hitched in a breath and expelled the word that she knew would seal her fate. "Deal." She glanced at him and saw that he had extended his hand and expected her to shake on it. She'd have to touch him, and if she touched him, she would surely melt.

She offered her hand slowly and he grasped it, held on, squeezed gently. But when he should have released her, he wove his fingers between hers and brought their clasped hands up for his examination.

"You know, Dellie, I like this idea of yours."

"Do you?" She could hardly speak, barely breathe. The simple joining of their hands was somehow erotic, sensual, fantastic. His skin was darker than hers, his fingers longer, the palm of his hand rougher.

"I do believe it's a mighty fine idea," he murmured,

drawing her gaze to his just by the provocative purr of his voice. "The best idea you've had in years and years."

She smiled, enjoying his teasing, his touch. "I wouldn't go that far, but I'm glad you find it acceptable."

"I was thinking, Dellie . . ." He glanced at the ruined shed and the firewood that was piling up from his ax. "Providing kindling is a chore, right?"

She nodded, already seeing where he was headed. "That's right."

"So I should get one of your sweet rewards for it, shouldn't I?"

"Yes, I suppose so. However, you aren't finished yet. This is only half done. I can't give a half-kiss, now, can I?"

He pursed his lips. "Yes, you can."

She shook her head. "No. There is no such thing as half a kiss or half a chore, for that matter."

"No, you're wrong, Dellie. I've got enough kindling there to fire up the cook stove for the rest of the day and I'll have the rest chopped and stacked by tomorrow. As for half a kiss, you just stand there and leave it all to me. You don't have to kiss me back. That'll make it half a kiss."

She laughed to relieve the tightening in her chest, the thrumming of her pulse. "Don't be silly."

His fingers, still linked with hers, tightened as he pulled her hand forward and around to his back, bringing her breasts against his chest, her lips in line with the swoop of his mouth. His kiss acted on her like a lightning bolt, stunning her into submission, charging her blood while rendering her senseless. He groaned, the sound filling her head, and she answered with a soft moan. His tongue slipped inside her mouth and she thrust her own tongue into his. Instantly his ardor increased. His free hand cupped her breast, his fingers locating the bud there with ease.

As quickly as he'd struck, he subsided. His mouth lifted from hers and he moved away, letting go of her breast, her hand, her heart and soul.

Adele blinked, clearing her eyesight and her foggy brain. She tasted him on her tongue, felt the sting of his passion on her lips, the blushing tingle of her nipple.

"Did you decide I deserved a whole kiss, after all?" he asked, teasing her.

For a moment she tried to think of something scathing to say, but she decided not to reward him with ire or irritation. She shrugged and released a nonchalant sigh.

"It's a small price to pay to have that shed torn down. You're right. It was an eyesore."

"I do believe I'm going to like being on your payroll."

She touched a fingertip to the corners of her mouth, trying to tame the smile there. "I hope you prove to be a tireless worker, Reno. I so admire that in a man."

Her uncharacteristic attempt at ribald humor caused his jaw to drop, giving Adele a sweet reward of her own.

Hours later, when the supper trade was at its peak and every one of Adele's employees was working frantically to keep up with the orders and impatient customers who were afraid they'd miss their train,

Reno marched in and made a beeline for Adele.

Glancing up from dishes she'd set before a tableful of anxious passengers, Adele was allowed only a few moments to read his expression before he stopped beside her and wrapped an arm around her waist.

"Wh-what . . . ?" Adele sputtered, rendered speechless by mortified shock.

"I swept the floor," he announced, then stamped her mouth with a hard, soul-shaking kiss. "And I finished carrying in all the supplies Mrs. McDonald needs for tomorrow's trade." His mouth claimed hers again, this time passion-tinged and lingering.

Hearing the titters around her, Adele pushed him off, huffing and puffing in the face of his smugness. "How dare you! This is a place of business."

"Well, I've finished my work for today and collected my pay, so I'll be moseying along." Reno winked and then gave a jaunty wave to the room at large. "Y'all enjoy your meals and don't worry about this young lady's welfare. She's my wife, and this is how she pays me for the work I do around the place."

More laughter. More whispers. Adele felt as if her face would burst into flame.

"Get out of here," she whispered.

Reno bowed from the waist and strode past her and out the door. Adele's knees wobbled and she gripped the edge of the table to keep herself upright. Somehow she managed to move across the room and around to the other side of the counter, where she busied herself, her back to the patrons. She sliced pie and cake with a vengeance.

"You should have slapped him," Sally whispered, standing next to her.

"Slapped him? If I'd had a gun, I would have shot him."

"What was he talking about? You're paying him for working?"

"After a fashion," Adele allowed. "I don't want to go into it now, Sally. Suffice it to say that I think my cleverness has landed me in a sticky situation."

Sally removed her apron and folded it. "I had the early shift, so I'm off now. It's six o'clock."

Adele glanced at the white-faced clock on the wall. "So it is. Go on up to your room and relax. I'll join you later and fill in the details."

"Yes, do. But I might go out for a stroll."

"Be careful," Adele warned her. "This town isn't fit for a lady after dark."

"I'll be fine." Sally slid behind her, patted her shoulder, and offered a commiserating smile. "I hope his abominable behavior tonight has opened your eyes to the utter impossibility of this marriage."

Outside the home of Whistle Stop's bank president, Reno lit a cheroot and inhaled the biting smoke. He tipped back his head to examine the stars that had come out since he'd arrived at the house two hours ago for a friendly game of poker. It was a revolving game, meeting in the banker's home one evening and in the back room of the bank later in the week. The game had broken up unusually early, each man full of excuses for the shortened evening of cards and whiskey and inflated stories of heroics and conquests.

Even Ellie Green, the banker's wife, had been noticeably aloof. Usually she was good-natured and brimming with hospitality. Tonight she had said no more than ten words to him and had kept her distance.

Reno turned back to the house and saw Paul Green silhouetted in the doorway. "Good night, Paul. See you Friday at the bank. Same time as usual?"

"I can't make it Friday night, Reno." Paul came out onto the porch. He was shaped like a barrel, with a round face and bald head. His beard was black and curly and trimmed close. "Sorry, but I promised the wife I'd cut back on the games. She's become cranky about my spending so much time at the poker table."

"Has she? But you told me that we meet one night a week in your home at her request. You said she enjoyed the company and our doting on her."

"Ah yes, so I did." He scratched at his beard. "Who knows the workings of a woman's mind?"

Reno smiled and examined the stars again. "Don't try to play me for a fool, my friend. Tell me the real reason why you've decided to shut me out of the game. I deserve the truth."

For a moment, Reno thought Paul would offer up another lie, but then he dropped his gaze and gave a sigh of defeat.

"You're right. I'm sorry, but it would be better for everyone if you didn't come around anymore. Of course, I appreciate your bank business, but anything social, well, it could be uncomfortable."

"Uncomfortable? Why?"

Paul pulled at his beard, clearly in anguish. "It's Terrapin," he said, lowering his voice and glancing around his own front yard, as if he expected to be overheard. "He had a talk with me today and asked me not to continue my friendship with you."

Reno angled his head back, surprised by Paul's explanation. "And you'll end our friendship just because Terrapin asked you to? What's he got on you, Paul? Why are you afraid of him?"

"Reno, Taylor Terrapin is one man you don't want to cross. You've done both, or so I hear. You've made yourself an enemy, which was a damn stupid thing to do. Terrapin's hired gun—I think his name is Wilhite?"

Reno nodded. "Buck Wilhite. I've met him."

"He told me that Terrapin thinks you're bad for the town and that anyone who befriends you is bad for the town. He told the others that were here tonight the same thing. It's a message we can't ignore, Reno. Terrapin already isn't pleased about our poker games. He sees it as taking money out of his pocket. I hope there are no hard feelings, but I have a family and a business to protect."

Reno inhaled on the cheroot and let the smoke escape in a thin stream. "How could he destroy your business or your family?"

"He has his ways, and no one will go against him to stop him. He's burned people out, and accidents have happened to others who didn't listen when he gave them advice. He's the law in Whistle Stop."

"Not the sheriff?"

Paul gave a harsh laugh. "He owns the sheriff. I tell you, Reno, you've stepped in a nest of rattlers. You might ought to apologize to him for whatever you did. He says you tried to shoot him."

Reno grinned. "If I had tried, he'd be dead. I just wanted his attention and I got it." Reno rolled the cheroot between his thumb and finger, watching the end glow in the dark. "He could close your bank?"

"All he'd have to do is open his own, and everyone who had any sense would take their money out of mine and put it in his."

"He'd do that?"

"He's threatened before, and I believe him. Look, it's not so bad. We keep Terrapin happy and he leaves us alone."

"What if he asked you to kill me? Would you do that to keep him happy?"

Paul made a choking sound. "God, no! I'm not a barbarian, Gold. I'm simply a cautious man. I don't believe in asking for or buying trouble."

"I didn't mean to insult you, Paul," Reno assured him, reaching out to clasp his shoulder. "I was curious as to where you'd draw the line. You'll end our friendship by Terrapin's request but not my life. I suppose I should take some comfort in that."

"I like you, Reno. I hope you understand the situation I find myself in."

"I understand. You're not completely happy with the situation as it stands, are you?"

Paul stuffed his hands in his trouser pockets. A frown creased the skin between his eyes, and his mustache drooped. "Can't say that I am, but there is little anyone can do about it."

"I wonder." Reno threw aside the cheroot and clapped a hand on Paul's shoulder. "I'll be seeing you, Paul. Thanks for the hospitality."

Paul grabbed Reno by the arm before he could stride away. "You're not going to do anything crazy, are you? Don't try to go up against Terrapin. He's a dangerous individual, Reno. Several men who opposed him are dead or have mysteriously disappeared."

Reno grinned. "Paul, I survived Deadwood, North Dakota, when I was still wet behind the ears, so I reckon I can deal with Terrapin and his one-eyed assassin."

Paul nodded. "You've proved yourself to be a lucky son of a gun, that's for sure."

With a low chuckle Reno left Paul and swung up on the wheat-colored mare he'd borrowed from Adele. He clucked his mount into a sedate walk and headed for the depot. Night creatures sang to him with squeaky chirps and deep-throated calls. The stars seemed to press down, and he felt as if his hat was skimming them.

Beautiful, he thought, and Dellie's face appeared before his mind's eye. Yes, she was beautiful to him, with her darkly lustrous hair and glittering green eyes. Even when she was fussing at him, he found himself admiring the bright spots of color in her cheeks and the grit in her voice. Oddly enough, he was having the best and worst time of his life.

Best because he was getting to know Dellie again and delighting in teasing her and stealing kisses from her. Worst because she kept herself from him while he ached to take her to bed and lose himself in the smell of her, the feel of her, the very core of her.

Nights were unbearable unless he drank enough whiskey to numb his mind. Knowing she was in the next room was a sore temptation. His patience was nearly expended. He couldn't be sure anymore that he could continue with his campaign to win her affections. Each time he held her now he felt his resolve crack. He had never wanted a woman more keenly, and she had made him realize that he didn't have an iron grip on his self-control. One night, he knew, he would not be able to remain in his bed. One night even whiskey would not keep him from her.

Ahead, in the hazy light of the moon, Reno saw a woman rushing toward a man who stood under the shelter of the depot platform. Reno reined his horse into the black shadows of a hickory and watched, trying to see which of Adele's waitresses was meeting a secret paramour. The man embraced the woman and held her for a few moments before moving back to smooth his hands over her hair. The woman was petite. The man was slim and neatly dressed.

Reno narrowed his eyes, his senses sharpening. Terrapin? Yes, it was Taylor Terrapin, cavorting with one of Dellie's waitresses. Not Doris McDonald. This woman was too small. Good God! Reno held his breath for a moment, his pulse booming in his ears. Of course, he should have known.

Sally Baldridge.

Stifling the chuckle that tickled his throat, Reno shook his head slowly in sardonic amusement. Sally the hypocrite. He should have guessed immediately.

So she had taken up with the town bully. More important to Sally, she'd caught the eye of the richest man in Whistle Stop. That is, the richest man before Reno had taken up residence there. Reno had no doubt that if Sally knew how much he was worth, she'd do an about-face and become his new best friend. She'd been a gold digger as a girl, and age and misfortune had only deepened her desire to be the most admired and respected belle of the ball. Like her new beau, she related admiration and respect to money, not to character.

Sally and Terrapin moved stealthily to a horse and buggy. Terrapin helped Sally into the seat, then sprang up beside her. Cuddling close, with Sally's head on his shoulder, Terrapin reined the buggy away from the depot—toward some hideaway, Reno presumed.

His luck was holding, Reno thought. Dellie's allegiance to Sally was obviously misplaced. He'd bet Dellie did not know that Sally had a suitor.

Nudging his horse from the shelter of the hickory, he made for the restaurant, debating with himself how he would use his newfound information to his best advantage. He'd have to be careful. Dellie was fond of Sally, and this revelation could blow up in his face. Women, like dynamite, were often unpredictable. And damned dangerous.

Chapter 9

Having purchased a spool of thread with which to finish Mrs. McDonald's work dresses and a bag of lemon drops for her own sweet tooth, Adele emerged from the General Store and hurried home. Smiling to herself, she placed one of the candies in her mouth and thought about how Reno called her *sugar*. She liked it. Loved the way he said it, so slow and Southern. *Shugah.*

Afternoon shadows striped the muddy street. The horses and vehicles made sucking sounds in the muck. It had rained early that morning, but the clouds had been chased away by noon.

When Adele had left the restaurant, she'd expected to see Reno out back working on that confounded shed, since he wasn't in the kitchen with Mrs. Mc-Donald. No sound of hammer or saw rent the air, making her wonder where he was hiding. He'd come home at a decent hour last night, although she had already gone to bed. She'd listened to him moving about in the front parlor and had pictured him stepping gingerly so as not to disturb her. When the cot had groaned under his weight, she had envisioned him lying flat on his back, staring at the ceiling, just like her. Did he think of her, or was his mind occupied by other things, other women?

"Such nonsense," she muttered to herself, jerking her thoughts from their preoccupation with Reno Gold. "What do you care?" Then she caught sight of him and stumbled over her own feet.

Getting her balance again before she could pitch forward onto the boardwalk, she stared at Reno and Little Nugget sitting side by side on the balcony of the Black Knight Saloon, Whistle Stop's whorehouse. Pretty as you please, they sat in big wicker chairs and laughed at something Little Nugget had said.

Adele glanced around and was relieved to find no one else staring at them. What was he thinking, sporting with that woman right on the main street of town? It was one thing to hire a soiled dove. After all, Mrs. McDonald had become quite an asset, Adele admitted. And she could turn a blind eye when Little Nugget visited Mrs. McDonald at the restaurant. But for Reno, a married man, to sport with one of Terrapin's trollops right under the town's nose! Well, it was unpardonable.

"He's been up there with her most of the afternoon."

Adele whirled to confront the man who had spoken to her. He leaned against a post, his thumbs tucked into his gun belt, a faint smile quirking his lips. The one eye revealed to her was blue and cold.

"You're Mr. Terrapin's hired gun, aren't you?" Adele asked, making her tone convey her displeasure.

He nodded. "Buck Wilhite's the name. I'm Mr. Terrapin's assistant."

"Assistant, hmmm?" Adele poked into her small sack of purchases and popped another lemon drop into her mouth. "I wonder what kind of assistance Mr. Terrapin requires."

"Mr. Terrapin has asked your husband to stay away from Little Nugget, but there he sits." Wilhite returned his attention to Reno and the pretty blonde. "Guess your man don't have much respect for his life—or for you."

Adele almost choked on the hard candy. "He told Reno to stay away from that woman? Why? Anyone with enough money can buy her time."

"She's the boss man's favorite and he don't much like your husband." His blue eye slid sideways to find her. "If I was your mister, I wouldn't be wasting my time with whores."

"If you were any kind of decent man, you wouldn't be working for a whoremonger and taking money to threaten and bully people." She smiled, not caring that she had roundly insulted him. "Good day, sir." Turning on her heel, she marched smartly toward the restaurant. She glanced back once to find that Wilhite wasn't the only man interested in her departure. Reno had taken notice, too.

Cranking the pump handle for all she was worth, Adele filled the wooden bucket to the brim with water, her thoughts churning. She tried to lift the bucket and groaned when her shoulder socket burned.

"Let me." A shadow fell across her at the same time

as a warm hand brushed against hers on the rope handle.

Adele snatched her hand away and stared up into Reno's face. The brooding quality in his eyes belied the smile on his lips.

"I saw you in town," she said, her tone accusing.

"And I saw you."

"I was merely on a shopping trip." She gave him her back, wishing he didn't look quite so handsome in his work pants and shirt of dark blue that matched his eyes.

"So was I."

Adele gasped and swung around to him. "I thought we had an understanding about this."

"About what?"

"About you embarrassing me in public!"

"And how did I embarrass you?" He placed his hands on his hips and waited for her explanation.

Adele ground her teeth, resenting his act of innocence. "You know perfectly well how. You were doing your shopping in public where everyone and God could see you." She gave a sniff of contempt. "And you're asking for trouble by cavorting with Little Nugget. She is supposedly Terrapin's favorite, and I believe you've been told to stay away from her."

"Who told you that?"

"Terrapin's *assistant*. Buck Wilhite."

"Yes, I saw you talking to him. You should be careful who you associate with, Dellie."

"Me?" She almost sputtered with affront. "How dare you suggest that I—" She snapped off the rest of her tirade, her words drowned out by Reno's laughter. She felt her face heat and her hands tremble.

Spinning away from him, she wished she wasn't a lady, so that she could slap him quiet. A pillow! Oh, for a pillow! But violence was never the answer, she counseled herself, her hands curling into impotent fists.

"Ah, Dellie, you are a constant amusement." Reno struggled to control himself and rested his hands lightly on her shoulders.

Adele jerked away and put distance between them.

"Hey now, don't be that way. I'm only having a little fun with you. Remember how we used to tease each other back in Lawrence when we were just a couple of green sprouts? Hell, we had some good times back then."

"We were children then and we are grown up now," Adele pointed out, however needlessly. "I see nothing amusing about you cavorting with whores in town, thus sullying my good name."

"I wasn't cavorting. I was shopping for some information. Information, I might add, for you."

She issued a harsh laugh. "For me? Little Nugget has nothing to say that could possibly be of interest to me. Unless, of course, she has decided to leave her life of sin. I will be glad to help her, if that's the case." She glanced at him and read his expression. "But that's not the case, is it? She enjoys her servitude to Taylor Terrapin."

"Dellie, people can't change overnight." He sighed and shook his head. "You should know that by now. But that's not what I want to talk to you about. First, I want you to stay away from Buck Wilhite."

She arched a brow. "I assure you I have no intention of striking up any kind of relationship with that man. However, if I was so inclined, your orders would not deter me."

He grinned and reached out to tap the end of her nose with his fingertip, then laughed when she back-pedaled. "He's right. You're a spirited filly."

"What are you talking about? Who said that?"

"Never mind. I'm glad you have enough sense to stay away from Terrapin's henchman. What was he saying to you on the street?"

"That you had been with Little Nugget most of the day and that Mr. Terrapin had asked you not to consort with her."

"I think he's tailing me."

"Wilhite? Why would he do that?"

"Because Terrapin would like for me to be dead or gone."

Adele took an involuntary step toward him, non-plussed by his assertion. "If that's true, Reno, then you must be careful. Don't sell Taylor Terrapin short. He's a vicious man, with no moral conscience."

"Then you won't like what I have to tell you."

His ominous tone stiffened her with dread. She set her jaw and waited for him to drop the other shoe.

"Terrapin is courting Sally."

She felt her eyes go wide and her jaw slacken. "That cad! Oh, poor Sally. She hasn't said a thing to me about this, so he must not be pestering her too much. Who told you? Little Nugget? She's probably jealous, so we shouldn't take what she says too seriously."

He held up a hand, palm out, to stop her flow of words. "Sally hasn't discouraged him, Dellie." Bending down and leaning in close until his gaze arrested hers, he fashioned a determined scowl. "Sally likes his attentions. She sneaks out two or three times a week after dark to meet with him."

Fury clamped down on Adele's good sense. She retreated from Reno as if he'd grown horns and a tail. "You liar! How dare you spread such vicious gossip about a woman who is like a sister to me! You should be ashamed, Reno Gold. Just because you and Sally don't get along is no reason for you to consort with a soiled dove and make up horrid stories about—"

Reno hooked an arm around her waist and pulled her against him, crushing the breath from her and abruptly ending her tirade.

"I'm not a liar. I saw them with my own eyes last night when I came home. While I admire your steadfast loyalty, Dellie, you should open your ears before you let your mouth run free."

Adele glared with belligerence at him, since there was little else she could do with him holding her captive so that she could hardly breathe.

"When I came home last night, I saw Sally run and throw herself into his arms. Then they hopped into a buggy and headed out of town."

"Where to?"

"I didn't follow them, but I figure they have a secret place where they can do their spooning."

Adele made a face, finding the whole scenario distasteful and impossible to believe.

"I wanted to be sure that I saw what I saw, so I went to the saloon and had a talk with Little Nugget. She said that Terrapin has been sneaking around with Sally for a few weeks. She's glad, because that means he spends less time with her. In fact, Little Nugget is hoping Terrapin will marry Sally. Not that he'd stop sleeping with Nugget, should that happen, but he won't bother her nearly as much."

"Are you finished?" Adele asked, getting a nod from him. "Then please let go of me. I can barely draw breath."

His arm loosened, but he did not release her. "I like holding you. You're about the softest, sweetest-smelling female I've ever encountered, Dellie Bishop Gold." He grinned. "By damn, I sure do like the sound of that."

"You are mistaken."

"About you being soft and sweet-smelling? I don't think so." He sniffed her hair, then nuzzled her temple where her hair curled damply against her skin. "Ummm, you smell like spring, Dellie. Like the best spring ever."

She closed her eyes, the touch of his lips upon her skin intoxicating, his gentleness and flowery words disarming. She no longer wanted to be released.

"Remember when I gave you your first kiss?"

She smiled. "Who said it was my first kiss?"

"You did."

"I did?" She knitted her brows, trying to recall that confession.

"Sure did. You weren't lying to me, were you?"

"No. It was my first real kiss. I'd been bussed on the cheek, and Winston had brushed his lips over mine once or twice, but you were the first to truly kiss me."

"The first," he whispered, his lips moving across her cheek toward her mouth. "And I pray the last. When I draw my final breath, Dellie, I want you beside me. I want you to give me a sweet good-bye kiss."

While the image was not one she wished to contemplate, Adele savored the sentiment behind it. Dusk draped them, and she let the world slip away. When Reno's lips touched hers, she sighed and melted against him. She felt his momentary surprise at her unconditional surrender, then his tongue slipped between her lips and sparked a passion so divine, so unexpected, that Adele's knees nearly gave way. She flung an arm around his neck to keep herself upright.

His lips stroked hers and his hands roamed her back and hips. Adele's fingers touched the curls at his nape and moved up into his inky hair. The kiss continued far longer than was prudent and increased in its ardor to the point at which her breath was depleted and she had to tear her mouth from his or die.

Sucking in air, Adele stared into Reno's eyes and saw the bright fire of desire there. A flame within her leapt in response.

"Adele? Oh, Dellie!" Sally's voice floated to them before Sally rounded the side of the depot. She stopped in her tracks when she spotted them. "What's going on here?"

Adele disengaged herself from Reno's embrace and smoothed wisps of her hair back from her face. She knew she should be embarrassed to be caught kissing passionately in the backyard, but Reno's tenderly teasing smile bewitched her. She turned toward Sally without a trace of self-consciousness.

"What do you need, Sally?"

"Nothing. I was just . . ." Sally looked from Adele

to Reno and then back to Adele, clearly puzzled. "You should come inside now, Dellie."

"Why?" Adele asked, not liking Sally's maternal tone.

"Because it is the proper thing to do." Sally's face was visible, lit by the light shining through the kitchen window. "The dinner trade is beginning."

"I'll be in shortly." Adele stood her ground, refusing to obey. Reno's earlier announcement wove through her mind like an evil potion, and she wanted to question him thoroughly about his accusation against Sally. She wanted to dismiss it as unfounded.

Sally lingered another few moments before making a sound of frustration and leaving them.

"She has her nerve," Reno said, "making scolding noises at us when she's carrying on with a skunk."

"I can't believe she'd take such a man seriously."

"Dellie, don't be so pig-headed."

"I'm giving her the benefit of the doubt."

"Why her and not me?"

"What do you mean?" She studied him, puzzled by the strain in his voice.

"I mean, you are quick to condemn me at every opportunity, but you refuse to believe that Sally might be fluttering her lashes at Terrapin. Why is that? We used to be friends, Dellie. Why would you assume I'm a rotten scoundrel and insist that Sally's motives are as pure as snow?"

"I know Sally better." Something inside her squirmed. Her conscience, perhaps?

"I'm your husband."

She frowned and heaved a sigh. "In name, yes, but Sally has been part of my life for a long time. I know her and I can't for the life of me see her sneaking off with any man, much less a man like Taylor Terrapin."

"She defended him the other day. Remember? I don't think she shares your low opinion of Terrapin, Dellie. I think you are once again making a mighty big assumption."

"Once again?" She arched a brow, wondering just what he meant by that.

"You have a habit of assuming a lot about people, Dellie. You're going to regret that one day." He smiled and tapped her nose lightly with his fingertip. "Mark my words."

She curbed her natural instinct to defend herself and her friend, forcing herself to think through what he'd said. "You saw her last night. What time?"

"Must have been close to midnight."

"She retired shortly after nine and was up with the chickens."

"I saw her, Dellie. I saw *them*."

The certainty in his demeanor made Adele restless with anxiety. She paced, head down, searching frantically for an explanation. But all she could grasp was the memory of Sally going up to her room for a nap after the dinner trade had tapered off. She'd looked tired, like a woman who hadn't gotten much sleep last night.

"I think you should have a talk with her, Dellie, and try to make her see that Terrapin isn't the kind of man she wants to entice. He might be worth some money, but his heart is as black as the ace of spades."

"If this is true, if she is carrying on with that man behind my back . . ." Adele shook her head, the idea turning sour in her mind. "Sally must be mad."

"You going to talk to her?"

"I'll ask if it's true. I trust you are willing for me to tell her how I came on this news?"

He shrugged. "Sure. I'll be interested to hear what she says. Little Nugget thinks it's only a matter of days before Terrapin and Sally make it known around town that they're a couple. Little Nugget says Terrapin is pleased to have a town lady interested in him. One he doesn't have to pay or threaten, that is."

"It's appalling," Adele said, and would have left him there in the darkness if he hadn't grabbed her hand to stop her. "Something else?"

"Just this."

His mouth found hers and touched off sparks, even though the kiss was light and airy. "You go ahead and have a private chat with her, and I'll see you later tonight in the parlor."

Adele eased her hand from his. "I suppose you're going to another poker game. Or will you find your pleasure at the saloon tonight?"

"There you go making assumptions again, Dellie."

"I am guessing based on your usual behavior."

"What do you know about my usual behavior?" He waved aside any answer she would have made. "Never mind. I'm going to feed the horses, Dellie dear. Sorry to disappoint you."

She knew she should offer an apology, but the words stuck in her throat, lodged there by her own monumental pride. Reno strode away from her. She turned and moved slowly toward the back door of the restaurant, her heart heavy and a crack in her certainty that she knew what was true and what was false.

Sally sat at the kitchen table, a lamp spilling light across her face and a book open in front of her. Mrs. McDonald dried a big pot and set it on the stove, then reached behind her to untie her apron.

"I was cleaning up so that Colleen can take over in here for the evening trade," Mrs. McDonald said. "You need anything else before I go upstairs?"

"No. By the way, I put the finishing touches to that work dress of yours. I laid it out on your bed."

"Really? Oh, thanks ever so much." Mrs. McDonald smiled and clapped her hands in anticipation. "I'll look like part of the place now instead of somebody just passing through. I'll wear it tomorrow. Good night, ma'am. See you in the morning, Mrs. Baldridge."

"Mmm?" Sally looked up from the book. "Oh, yes. Good night, Mrs. McDonald." She watched the woman leave the kitchen and shook her head. "She's a strange one. I told her she could call me Sally and I'd call her Doris, but she said she preferred last names. She said she liked being called Mrs. McDonald."

"I believe it's been a long time since anyone called her that," Adele noted, sitting across the table from Sally. "What are you reading?"

"A love story." Sally placed a strip of leather in the slim volume to mark her place and closed the book. "I'm sorry if I interrupted out there earlier. When I saw you with *him*, I thought you would welcome the interference."

"Reno told me something that has me quite in a stir."

"Is that why you were letting him take advantage of you?"

"He wasn't," Adele said softly. She looked away from Sally's scolding expression, then swung her gaze back to her friend's face to catch her reaction. "He said you have a new beau in town."

Sally's face tensed and her eyes narrowed a fraction. For the first time Adele noticed the small lines fanning from the corners of her wide-spaced eyes and the shallow creases bracketing her mouth. The years had put them there. Long, bad years of turbulence and heartache.

"He was gossiping about me? Spreading tales?"

"No, he was telling me what he witnessed last night and what some people in town are saying about you. Reno says he saw you meeting a man last night and riding away with him. Reno says the man was Taylor Terrapin and that the talk in town is that you and Terrapin are courting."

"He has no right snooping around and peering at me from the bushes!" Sally stood up, her skirts rustling. "I hope you told him to mind his own business."

"I told him I didn't believe you would take up with a man like Terrapin but I would ask you about it. I'm asking, Sally." Folding her hands on the tabletop, Adele waited, but she knew the answer in her heart. Good Lord, it was true! Was Sally so unhappy as a widow that she would accept the advances of a bloodless man like Terrapin?

Sally faced her, her expression haughty and her brown eyes snapping. "He is not what you think, Adele. Taylor is kind and has been nothing but a gentleman to me. He's misunderstood by so many. Those women at the saloon, he gives them a roof over their heads and—"

"Oh, stop." Adele covered her ears with her hands, blocking out the paltry excuses. "Please, stop. You're breaking my heart, Sally, and Win is rolling over in his grave."

"Don't bring Win into this. You'll never know what I went through for that man. Winston was no saint, Adele. He never loved me. I was second choice after you."

"That's not altogether true. He always had his eye on you. But that doesn't excuse this. What can you be thinking, accepting the attentions of such a man?"

"He happens to run this town, Adele. Unlike your husband, who is little more than the town drunk."

Adele flinched, and anger burst in her like a storm. "Don't even try to compare Reno with Terrapin. Reno makes no pitiful excuses for his actions. What balderdash has Terrapin been feeding you? He said he was providing a roof over those women's heads at the saloon, did he?"

"They would be doing what they do in the streets, in the alleyways, in the barns and stables, if he didn't provide them a clean, safe place," Sally informed her. "Taylor says they like the life. He gives them a place to ply their trade away from the eyes of respectable people like us."

"I hope he doesn't include himself in that lot." Adele sprang up from the chair. "God's nightgown, Sally! Will you listen to yourself? You are attempting to make a silk purse out of a sow's ear, and it can't be done. Before it's too late, end this. Tell Terrapin you will not see him again, that you no longer want his company. Most people in town don't know about you two yet, so your reputation can be saved."

"Save your own, Adele," Sally said, almost hissing. "Yours is worse than mine. Why, you're the town laughingstock, wedding that no-'count Reno Gold after you fetched him from the dustbins of some saloon up north. However, nobody has anything but respect for Taylor. When he walks down the street, people smile and greet him. He has carved a niche for himself in Whistle Stop."

Adele clutched the edge of the table, rocked off balance by Sally's tongue-lashing. "He has not carved a niche, Sally. Your new beau has cut through this town with the finesse of a dull ax, chopping and hacking away, scaring everybody and chasing off anyone who doesn't like the way he runs things. How many men do you think he's murdered in cold blood, Sally? How many women has he ruined?"

"Hush! You don't know these things. You don't understand him as I do." Sally's face contorted with her anger, and spots of pink flecked her cheeks and throat. "I'm going to marry him, Adele."

Adele sat heavily in the chair again. "No. Don't say that, Sally. Please."

"You didn't listen to me when I begged you not to marry Reno, so I will return the favor. Don't try to talk me out of it. I believe Mr. Terrapin means to ask me to marry him soon, and I will accept his proposal. We have discussed things. He wants to build a big, fine house out on that property he bought by Bobcat Creek. We'll build it on the crest of a hill and have a view of the cattle ranch we mean to start out there."

Adele shook her head and wondered if she'd ever really known Sally Baldridge. Until this moment she hadn't seen her clearly. Friendship had lightened the darker colors of Sally's character. Now Adele identified the stark streak of greed in Sally's soul. Sally had always wanted to be the richest woman around and she'd stop at nothing to achieve that. Everyone had said that she'd married Winston for his money and that when he lost his fortune he also lost Sally's affection, but Adele had refused to believe it. She'd been a fool. Acquiring money was Sally's chief ambition and money was the only commodity that could entice her to wed.

"You can't marry him."

Sally laughed. "You aren't my mother, Adele. I don't need your permission or your blessing."

"I am your employer and you signed a contract," Adele reminded her, grasping at her last straw. "That contract prohibits you from marrying for three more months. If you marry him before that time expires, I'll take you to court."

Chapter 10

❦

‘ ‘**Y**ou *told her you'd take her to court?''* Reno sat
on the cot in the parlor and stared at Adele,
not knowing whether to groan or laugh or do a little
of both.

"That's right. I have a contract that states clearly
she cannot marry or leave my employ for another
three months. By that time, I'm sure she will have
come to her senses."

"Yes, but will you have come to yours?" Reno held
up his hands to stop her sharp retaliation. "Sally is
your best friend. You can't treat her as though she's
your wayward daughter or your disloyal worker."

"I am trying to save her from herself." Adele
roamed the room, skirts rustling and flags of color
rising into her cheeks. "She might hate me now, but
later—"

"She'll despise you," Reno finished for her, earning
a dark scowl. "She's a grown woman and she has
decided to take up with a grown man. There's not a
damn thing you can do about it. If you try to force
her to stay here, you'll be buying trouble and ending

your friendship with her forever. Even if she comes to believe that you know what you're talking about when it comes to Terrapin, she'll never be your friend again, because she'll resent the hell out of you for being right."

"Then what do you suggest I do? Let her marry that blackguard?"

Reno rested his hands on his bent knees. "I was hoping you could talk her out of it, but failing that, then, yes, stand back and let her get on with it. That's my best advice."

She stopped and shoved her fists onto her hips. "Well, your best advice stinks to high heaven."

He grinned, thinking she was the prettiest, orneriest, most stubborn woman on God's green earth.

She narrowed her eyes. "You weren't really surprised to see Sally with Taylor Terrapin, were you?"

"No." He bent over and pulled off his boots. "Makes sense once you figure out what's important to Sally. Money makes a man a prince in her eyes."

Adele winced. "Oh, I hate to believe such a thing of her, but why else would she even give that man the time of day? What can I do, Reno? Other than enforce that contract, what else can I do?"

Reno unbuttoned his shirt. "I've told you. Nothing. It's not up to you to pick her husband for her." He twisted around to pull the curtains across the window behind him and caught sight of Sally moving quickly across the side yard. "There she goes."

"Who? What?" Adele rested a knee on the cot and peered out the window. "God's nightgown! She's sneaking off to see that cold-blooded snake this very minute! I must stop her."

Reno grasped her arm. "No, Dellie. It makes no nevermind to me whether you keep Sally as a friend, but I know it means a lot to you, so I'm telling you to leave her be."

She looked as if she meant to ignore his advice, but then she seemed to melt. Sitting on the cot beside him, she placed her hands over her face and released a tortured groan.

"Tear up the contract, Dellie."

"How can I? Everyone else is expected to abide by those contracts. I hire nice women, and they are rare in these parts. They're all looking to marry. If I don't hold them to the contracts, I'll be searching for waitresses so much that I won't have time to manage the restaurant. It's what the owner wants."

"He gives you no leeway?"

"Yes, Mr. Harvey leaves the business pretty much to me. He trusts me."

"Okay. Sally is your friend, not just a waitress. You talk to her. You tell her that you're releasing her from her contract, but that you don't want her telling the other women about it. Let the others think that you signed Sally to a shorter contract, seeing as how you two are girlhood friends. They'll understand. You keep a civil tongue in your head. Then, when Sally needs someone to talk to, she can still come to you."

She bowed her head, defeated. "You're right. I know you're right. If she marries that man, she'll need my friendship more than ever."

"There you go." He patted her hands resting in her lap. "And there's an outside chance she might change her mind and not marry him. Of course, he could decide not to marry her, but I don't look for that to happen. I figure they both see this marriage as a good thing, a fine trade-off. Sally will be the belle of the ball again and Terrapin will gain more respectability in town through the marriage." He chuckled. "She sure isn't going to listen to your advice on who to marry. Sally doesn't think much of your choice of husband."

"She knows I never really meant to marry you."

"Oh?" He cocked a brow. "And what did you mean to do with me once I arrived?"

"Well, I hadn't thought that far at the time. I didn't expect you to agree to come, and when you did, I suppose I thought I would make you see that this was an experiment, a lesson to the bull-headed men of Whistle Stop. I didn't think you'd want to marry me."

"That *was* the deal, wasn't it?"

"Yes, yes." She sighed, clearly agitated. "Placing that advertisement was impulsive of me. I didn't expect to find a husband and I surely didn't expect to hear from anyone I knew! I was dumbstruck when I got that letter from you."

"But you answered it and sent me train fare."

She wound a lock of her ebony hair around her finger. "I thought . . . that is, I wanted to see you." Her eyes found his; stars seemed to have gathered in them. "I was curious as to why you wrote me, why you had reached out to me. I wondered what had become of you."

"And I got off the train and fell in a drunken heap at your feet." He stood and peeled away his shirt, needing some means to expend some of the frustration coiled in his muscles.

"Are you overly fond of alcohol?"

He smiled crookedly at her. "Maybe I'm overly fond of you, Dellie. Maybe I was so damned nervous over seeing you again that I drank too much and made a fool of myself."

Her color heightened. "Is that true? Is that what happened?"

Sorely tempted to confess, he turned away from her instead, unwilling to give her more leverage when she already had so much. Besides, she was sitting on his bed, and that brought to mind enticements that made his loins burn. She'd come to him this evening for advice, a good sign that the ice was thawing from around her heart. He didn't want to take advantage of her lowered defenses. Facing her again, he settled his hands on his belt buckle, figuring she'd bolt and run when she realized he was getting ready to strip for bed. She stared at his hands and didn't move.

"Guess I'll turn in," he said.

"It's early," she noted. "Won't you be going out to play poker or flirt with Little Nugget?"

He grinned. "The poker games have been closed to me and Little Nugget isn't my type of woman."

"She isn't?"

"She's too young. I like my women in their prime."

"And what is prime to you?" She folded her arms at her waist. Moonlight bathed half her face.

"Dellie, do I need to tell you that I think you're prime womanhood? Of course, you could use a little seasoning, but that's nothing I can't handle."

She turned her face away from him, hiding it in shadow. "Seasoning? I dare not ask you to explain that." Whipping her gaze back to his, she squinted cannily. "Why are the poker games closed to you?"

"Terrapin decreed it."

"Are you in debt to him?"

"Hell, no." He unbuckled his belt. Still she didn't move. "For some reason he just doesn't like me. Breaks my heart."

She smiled and then laughed, her starry eyes gleaming, her teeth flashing. Reno's manhood stiffened. God, she was pretty! And she was in his bed.

Suddenly she sprang from the cot and was across the room before he could blink.

"Good night, Reno," she said, and closed the door to her bedroom behind her.

Reno stared at the door and wanted to kick it in, but he walked off his burst of frustration and drove his fingers through his hair in silent agony.

He was plumb crazy for her, and she was immune to his condition and his charms. Here he was pacing like a penned-up bull in sniffing distance of a heifer, and she was blithely preparing for bed with no thought of him.

She'd responded to his kisses, but he had misjudged her response. She didn't want him.

She wanted him.

On the other side of the bedroom door Adele stood before a full-length mirror and examined her flushed face and crimson throat. A deep trembling seized her.

Who was she? Did she really know herself? What had happened just now between her and Reno?

Her heartbeats boomed in her ears and a warm ache pulsed between her thighs. Smoothing a palm down her midsection, she felt her face heat up again as she glanced almost fearfully at the bedroom door. She wanted him.

More precisely, she had wanted to see him disrobe.

Adele covered her hot face with her hands, mortified by her admission. When he'd taken off his shirt, she should have left the room, but she had pretended not to notice that he stood before her in his red knit undershirt, black chest-hair curling over the top of it. Sitting on his bed, she had watched his lean fingers unbuckle his belt and she had wanted to stay right where she was and wait for his trousers to drop.

She groaned into her hands. Maybe she was more lonely for a man's touch than she cared to admit. After all, she hadn't exactly fought him off when he'd kissed her. Oh, she'd fumed and scolded him, but she had wanted every kiss he'd given her.

After her mother's death Adele had thrown herself into finding meaningful work. That hadn't stopped men from approaching her, of course, but she had rarely encouraged them. She'd wanted to be a businesswoman, to make her own way in a man's world, just as her mother had done.

But her mother's life had not always been like that, Adele reminded herself. When her mother had been Adele's age, she was already married to Lowell Bishop and a few months away from giving birth to her only child. Victoria had been madly in love with Lowell Bishop, as she had often told Adele.

"When he died, part of me went with him," her mother had stated. "If I hadn't already had you, I think I would have curled up and faded away like a shadow, for that's how I felt, like a shadow of the woman I had been with Lowell at my side. But I wanted a good life for you and I couldn't give that to you by hiding and crying and feeling sorry for myself."

Adele could barely remember her father and she could recall nothing of her mother's relationship with him. But she had only to remember the expression of devotion on her mother's face when she'd talked about Lowell to know how rich, how passionate that love had been for Victoria.

Reno could never love her like that.

She could never love him.

Reno threw himself on the cot and stared morosely out the window at the stars, stars that had been in her eyes. Starry-eyed, but not for him.

Sally was out there somewhere with Terrapin, and he'd bet a saddlebag full of gold that they weren't admiring the heavens. They were doing what he would dearly love to be doing with his wife.

His wife. He chuckled silently, his chest heaving, almost hurting. She'd never be his wife. She thought of him as a brother.

No, that wasn't true. She had kissed him back. He had that to cling to, at least. She had raked her fingers through his hair and had opened her lips to him more than once. She had responded, but that didn't mean she wanted him.

He'd bet another saddlebag full of gold that she was in bed now, fretting about Sally and not wasting one thought on him. Out of sight, out of mind. He was squandering his time with her. He should get out of the marriage, set her free and be on his way.

Dreams were for dunces. He couldn't live on

dreams. And he certainly couldn't make the ache in his groin go away by dreaming of Adele. No. Dreams of her only made it worse.

She'd probably dream of him again tonight.

Adele whirled from the mirror and flung herself on her bed. Night after night her dreams were full of Reno Gold, each more agonizingly wonderful than the last. Sometimes he was a knight in armor on a powerful steed. Sometimes he was a riverboat gambler. Always he was handsome and dashing and seeking her favor.

If only he possessed more ambition, she'd feel better about these dreams and these feelings she wrestled with during every waking hour. How could she be so attracted to a man who had so little self-esteem? A man of pride would have already found himself a job, instead of doing what his wife made him do. A man of self-worth would have already made something of himself, instead of coming to her penniless and aimless.

Surely he had an abundance of charm and certainly he knew how to make a woman's head swim, but none of that would sustain a real marriage or support a strong relationship. She could not commit herself to a man of so little means and so few scruples.

But she could lust for him, and lust for him she did.

Ah, the lust, the lust, the goddamned lust!

Reno sat up in bed, his skin slick with sweat, his breathing shallow, his mind roiling with carnal images of Dellie.

Her midnight hair streaming over his chest, tickling

his loins. Those hands, those beautiful hands of hers, skimming over his ribs, gripping his hips. Lips pulling at his. Tongue laving him. Legs tangling with his. Pelvis grinding against his. Breasts rubbing him. Nipples firming under the massage of his tongue.

He sprang up from the cot and stared at the bedroom door. He couldn't stand it, could not tolerate one more second of this agony!

This agony! Adele wailed silently, staring at the shadows writhing on the ceiling.

What was that? She sat up, thinking she'd heard something at her door. Reno? Was he moving about in the parlor? Had something disturbed his sleep?

Straining to hear any other noises, she was disappointed by the quiet inside and the chirping of crickets outside. Must have been her imagination. Or wishful thinking?

She lay back in the bed. It felt like a prison of solitude. Cold. Lonely. Barren.

Barren? How odd that she should think that.

Another sound, faint but close by, made her sit up again, eyes straining to see the door handle. Was it turning? Should she call out to Reno? She placed her fingertips to her lips to keep herself from doing just that, from inviting him into her room, into her bed. Why, she'd be no better than a trollop!

No, that's not true, she argued with herself. He was her husband. She had every right . . .

Every right . . .

Switching off her thoughts, she rose from the bed and moved like a sleepwalker to the door. The handle was cool on her palm. She shoved it down and opened the door slowly, fully expecting to find Reno right on the other side.

The parlor was dark, but moonlight illuminated his narrow bed. His *empty* narrow bed.

"Reno?" She searched the room, frantic, wide-eyed. Her heart sank, its wings clipped.

He was gone.

Chapter 11

The next morning Sally was making coffee when Adele came into the restaurant. The place smelled of the freshly made brew and the mouth-watering aroma of yeast rolls that drifted in from the kitchen. Sally afforded Adele a rapid glance and then turned her back on her.

"I wasn't sure you'd work today," Adele said, checking the wall clock. In ten minutes she'd have to open the door and let in the first of the breakfast crowd. People were already milling outside, coming early for a meal before they boarded the train or went to their businesses in town.

"According to you, I have no choice. I must work, no matter how much I loathe it."

"Loathe it?" Adele laughed lightly. "Really, Sally, don't be so melodramatic."

"I'm not. I hate to work." She pushed aside the coffee urn and dried her hands on her apron. "This is not what I was meant to do. I always wanted a husband and children, not tables to wait on and strangers to please. I detest this life I've had forced on me."

145

Adele flinched, taking Sally's denouncement personally. "No one forced you to come here, Sally. I wrote and asked if you'd like to work here and you jumped at the chance."

"To leave Kansas, yes, but I did not jump at the chance to plunge my hands into hot water day after day until they became rough and red. Nor did I jump at the chance to carry heavy trays of food to table after table and sweep floors until my back aches. I suppose you must gain something from this, Dellie, but not me. I don't want to work here one minute longer than I must."

"I make a decent living here, Sally, the same thing I offered you."

"I am marrying him, Dellie, and there is nothing you can do about it. I'll work here, if I must, until my time is up and then I'm leaving to become his wife."

Adele slumped against the front counter. "I wish you'd reconsider, Sally. Marriage is not always the answer for a woman, you know. You and Winston—"

"Win is dead and I'm not." Sally faced Adele, her eyes as hard as diamonds. "Don't preach to me about marriage. Not when you married that mongrel."

Adele's anger flamed and every charitable thought disintegrated to ash. "Mongrel? Terrapin is a mongrel."

"He happens to be a rich and powerful man, who loves me very much and wants the best of everything for me."

"Forgive me, Sally, but it seems to me that you are selling your soul to the Devil."

"And you'll forgive me if I tell you to stay out of my personal business. If you are determined to keep me here with that employment contract, then we are just a boss and her worker."

"Sally, we can't end our friendship over this," Adele said, reaching out a hand to appeal to Sally's better sense.

"It seems you have chosen to do just that." Sally rounded the counter and went to unlock the front door and let in the people waiting outside.

". . . two more sacks of flour and a jar of molasses," Mrs. McDonald recited, moving around the kitchen and checking the supplies. "Your mister says several of the older hens aren't laying like they used to, so we'll either have to raise some young ones or buy extra eggs from someone else. I ran out of eggs yesterday morning and I only have six left today."

Adele nodded and added the items to her list. "We should have some chicks hatching soon, but I'll speak to a few farmers and see if we can't buy some young hens. That will be cheaper in the long run, I think." She rubbed her temple and glanced at the kitchen door, wondering if Sally had gone upstairs to her room or into town after her shift was over.

The day had been fraught with tension, almost as if Adele was working with a cold stranger instead of her best friend. Sally had avoided any contact with her and had been almost surly to the customers.

"Is she going or staying?" Mrs. McDonald asked, then smiled when Adele shook her head in confusion. "Mrs. Baldridge," she clarified. "That's who you're thinking about, isn't it?"

"Yes." Adele sighed and fell back in the kitchen chair, letting the pencil drop from her hand. "She's staying, but only because she is honoring the contract she signed. Do you understand what she sees in him?"

Mrs. McDonald sat down at the table across from Adele. "This will be hard for you to swallow, but Taylor can be quite the gentleman when he puts his mind to it."

"That is hard for me to believe," Adele agreed.

"He's got a way about him. Quiet and steady and sort of like the king of all he surveys. It's easy to get caught up in that, into thinking that you're his queen and you'll be sitting pretty on a throne. He's real generous at first, too. He gave me all kinds of baubles and bolts of cloth so fine I almost cried when I touched the fabric."

"But he sells women," Adele said with a shiver of revulsion. "How can anyone forget that?"

"Women are fools for love, Mrs. Gold. I guess every one of his saloon girls had the same notion I did when I first started up with him." Her mismatched eyes misted. "We all thought we'd be his only one, that he'd give up the rest. I convinced myself he'd marry me, that he loved me better than anybody. But then things turned ugly."

"How?"

"He started hitting me, kicking me, making me do things I didn't want to do."

"Why didn't you leave the first time he put his hand on you that way?"

"Because by that time I was into a life that sucked me dry of any pride I ever had."

"I can't stand by and let him do that to Sally."

"Oh, I don't think he will," Mrs. McDonald said,

wiping her eyes on her apron. "No, I do believe he'll marry her."

"Why?"

"Because she's a lady, and Taylor's always had a hankering for a lady. That's why he puts such stock in Little Nugget. She looks the part. But he knows underneath all that finery and pretty gloves and hats, she's just like the rest of us. Soiled and with nobody to care about us, nobody but him to look out for us."

"So you believe he will treat Sally differently?"

"Yes. She's respected in this town. He wouldn't think of putting her up in one of them rooms at the saloon. No, ma'am. He means to marry Mrs. Baldridge and start a family with her. The one I'm worried about is Little Nugget. He's been treating her real bad lately. I'm afraid for her."

"Have you told her?"

"Yeah, but she tells me I should watch out for myself. She says Taylor is hopping mad about me leaving him and working here. He keeps telling Little Nugget that he won't put up with it much longer."

"What can he do about it?"

Her smile was full of fear and worry. "Plenty. He's got no conscience. Nobody would raise a hand to stop him if he decided to line up me and Nugget in the middle of Main Street and—"

The back door opened and Reno stepped in. He swept his wide-brimmed hat off his head and stamped his feet, dislodging bits of dirt onto the mat.

"Where have you been all night and day?" Adele asked, taking her frustration out on him. "You certainly know how to make yourself scarce."

Reno looked from her to Mrs. McDonald, and

Adele could tell from his expression that he didn't like being scolded in front of the cook. "I've been fixing the wagon," he stated tersely.

"I went out early looking for you," Adele said. "You weren't in the barn."

"I had to take the wheel and axle to the blacksmith's to get it repaired." He frowned and hung his hat on a wall peg. "Good afternoon, Mrs. McDonald."

"Afternoon, Mr. Gold." The cook turned to the deep sinks and began filling them with hot water from kettles steaming on the stove.

Reno looked at Adele and gestured toward the swinging door. "I'm going to wash up. Mrs. McDonald, could I trouble you for a bowl of beans and a hunk of cornbread?"

"No trouble at all," she said. "Want to eat in here?"

"Yes, thanks. Be back in a few minutes."

Adele followed Reno from the kitchen, through the restaurant, and into her quarters.

"The wagon is fixed and ready for you to use." He turned suddenly. His eyes were turbulent with emotion. Reaching out, he clasped her shoulders and pulled her to him. His mouth branded hers, hard and hot, taking her breath away. "And next time you want to snap and sass at me, do it in private."

"Let go. You can't grab me on your every whim and force your will on me." She pushed at his upper arms and felt his muscles tighten to hold her fast.

"You owe me."

"Owe you?" She looked up into his eyes and was momentarily adrift in the blue-gray pools.

"I fixed the wagon." His mouth slanted into a grin. "You remember our deal, don't you? Tit for tat." He loosened his hold, but only so that he could skim his lips down her neck to the open collar of her dress. "Speaking of tit . . ."

"Stop!" Adele bolted from his arms, getting a robust chuckle from him. He went to the sideboard, where he poured water from a pitcher into a shallow bowl. "Fixing that wagon caused me to work up an appetite, but once my belly's full, I'll be ready to satisfy another hunger." He chuckled again and looked over his shoulder at her. Catching her fretful expression, he sighed and picked up a ball of soap. "What's got you in such a snit? Sally? I thought you two would have ironed all this out by now."

"It will take longer than a day for that."

He soaped his arms up to his elbows. "You told her you tore up her contract."

"I haven't."

"Not yet, but you mean to." He glanced at her again. "You told her that?"

"Not exactly." Adele sat on the parlor sofa and watched him rinse suds from his forearms. His trousers and the shirt pulled taut across his wide shoulders were smudged with dirt and flecked with bits of hay and grass. He'd been working hard outside, and she had greeted him with sharp words and spears of doubt. He wasn't the one she was mad at. She was mad at herself and at Sally and most definitely at Taylor Terrapin.

"What exactly did you say to her?" He faced her and dried his arms and hands on a soft cotton towel.

"I told her that . . . I left things as they were."

"Dellie," he said, drawing out her name in a gentle scolding tone, "I thought you were going to square this with her. Why didn't you tear up the contract and save your friendship?"

"I don't know." Adele bounded up from the sofa and walked to the windows. How could she explain to him that all her good intentions had gone up in smoke when Sally had called him names? She couldn't even explain her reaction to herself, much less to Reno. "She was in such a horrible mood today and I decided to . . . that is, I simply postponed my decision. I'm hoping she'll have second thoughts."

Reno shook his head. "Leave Sally to her romantic tussles and concentrate on your own."

That brought her up short, and she gave him her undivided attention. The glints of mischief in his eyes didn't console her.

"What do you mean?"

"I mean I'm a hard-working man, sugar, and I'll be expecting my payment in full come tonight. After I have something to eat, I'll work on the shed. With any luck I might just finish it by nightfall."

Adele whirled away from him and stared out the window, her nerves jangling. Gray clouds met her view. "Looks like rain," she said brightly.

Reno laughed behind her. "Maybe. We'll see. Anyway, the wagon's fixed."

"And you were paid for that."

"What? That little kiss I stole? Dellie, be fair. Working all day on that wagon deserves more than a kiss."

"I thought you said the blacksmith fixed the wagon."

"He did some ironwork, but I supplied the muscle." He moved closer to her. "No, I'll be 'round to collect tonight after the restaurant is closed."

Adele released her breath in a soft hiss. What was he planning? If he wanted her, why did he leave last night? And just where had he gone?

"By the way, you never told me where you slept—" She abandoned the rest when she turned and found that she was talking to an empty room. "Reno?" She glanced around. Alone again. Blast that man! He was as hard to pin down as a feather in the wind.

She started after him, but made a detour outside when she spotted Taylor Terrapin's buggy pulling up alongside the restaurant. Terrapin lowered himself from the vehicle and tipped his hat when he saw her. Now what? Adele wondered, sensing his visit would add to her burgeoning headache.

Rail-thin in his all-black clothing, Terrapin's physique was as duplicitous as his demeanor. Adele knew he was much stronger than he appeared and much meaner than his courteous behavior implied.

"Looking for Mrs. Baldridge?"

"No, I was hoping to have a word with you, Miss Adele. You have upset Mrs. Baldridge and I have come to negotiate a peace treaty." He smiled and hung his thumbs in his gun belt. "She's meeting with my builder and discussing the house I'm having constructed on some property I purchased outside of town. It's going to be a grand place and I hope you will visit us often."

"Will it be another whorehouse?" Adele asked, folding her arms and giving him a cold appraisal.

He lowered his brows menacingly and his fingers twitched. Itchy trigger finger? Adele wondered.

"It will be our home, Miss Adele."

"Her name is Mrs. Gold," Reno spoke up from behind her, having come from around the side of the building. "I believe in fairness, Terrapin. I figure it's only fair that you stay away from here, seeing as how you told me to stay away from your businesses."

Terrapin extended Reno a disparaging glance. "This restaurant is not your business, Gold. I'm speaking to the lady. You'll excuse us."

Reno walked to Adele's side and placed an arm around her shoulders. "Dellie, darlin', you don't mind if I give a listen to what Terrapin has come to say, do you?"

She shook her head, glad for his company. "I don't mind at all." Slipping an arm around his middle, she smiled at him with her eyes before facing Terrapin again. "You want peace, Mr. Terrapin? Please stay away from my friend. Don't ruin her life. If you care anything for her, then you must admit that she deserves a better man than you."

Beside her, Reno found himself startled by her bold, brash honesty. He admired her profile, the tilt of her chin, the way her nose poked at rarefied air. Her arm felt good around his waist, and the curves of her body fitted perfectly with his, as a wheel fitted an axle.

But she was also foolhardy and a mite too stubborn, he surmised, sensing the explosive heat behind Terrapin's cold anger.

"I care deeply for Mrs. Baldridge," Terrapin said, "which is why I intend to marry her and do everything in my power to keep her safe and happy." He squared his shoulders. "I have come in hopes of reasoning with you. Sal—that is, Mrs. Baldridge has informed me that you are holding an employment contract over her head."

Adele arched a brow, wondering just what he intended to accomplish with this visit. He wasn't stupid, so he surely knew that her doing him a favor was highly unlikely. "Sally signed an employment contract and she has three months left before its provisions are met."

"But given the circumstances, you could void that contract."

"What circumstances?" Adele asked, being purposefully thick-headed. Let him spell it out. Let him ask.

"Her impending marriage to me. She wants time to plan the wedding and oversee the design of our house. And I don't think it would be seemly for my intended bride to work. Her job here can be given to some other young lady."

"Maybe Little Nugget," Reno spoke up, gaining a quick, cutting glare from Terrapin.

"Nugget is happy where she is, and you'd better leave her alone. I haven't forgotten that you hired Doris out from under me. That situation is intolerable and will be corrected." His smile was chilly. "Excuse me, Miss Adele, for the rude interruption."

"I told you, her name is Mrs. Gold."

Terrapin kept his gaze pinned on Adele, as if Reno hadn't spoken.

"The point of having the ladies sign a contract is so they can't marry and leave before the year is up," Adele told him. "You see, decent ladies are hard to come by out west and are snatched up so quickly that keeping waitresses is hard. Thus, the contracts."

"Of course, of course, but Mrs. Baldridge is your friend and exceptions can be made. Must be made."

Adele bristled at his authoritative tone. "If I make an exception, then others will expect the same. I might as well not have any employment contracts."

"Ah, well, that's probably best. If you can't keep them working here without making them sign their lives over to you, then your ability to conduct a business successfully certainly should be scrutinized."

"Are you saying that you think I'm inept?" Adele asked, narrowing her eyes with contempt.

"I'm simply saying that I'm a successful businessman and I've never required anyone to sign a contract to work for me."

"No, you just threaten them with their lives," Reno said. "I don't think Dellie would like doing business that way."

Terrapin paid Reno no heed outwardly. However, Reno knew he was getting under the man's skin. He'd seen the flexing of Terrapin's long fingers and the subtle bracing of the man's legs in a wide stance. Reno recognized the signs of readiness. Giving Adele's shoulder a gentle squeeze, he released her and set himself a few inches apart from her, clearing his body for action. He didn't think Terrapin would try anything with Dellie present, but men like Terrapin were hard to read. A fella just had to stay ready and expect the worst.

"I run my business as I see fit," Adele informed him. "And I don't believe I'll be taking your advice. Sally is employed by *me* and I won't discuss this with *you*, Mr. Terrapin."

"She sent me here to persuade you," Terrapin said. "She is distressed by your lack of faith in her. I don't like seeing her unhappy, so I offered to intervene. You must release her from the contract. It will go better for you if you do."

Adele tipped her nose even higher into the air. "You'll have to excuse me, sir. I have a business to run." She made to turn and leave him.

"Very well, I will buy out Mrs. Baldridge's contract." Terrapin reached into his coat's inner pocket and withdrew a slim leather wallet. He flipped it open. "How much?"

Adele stared at him, never thinking he would offer her a bribe. She couldn't conjure up anything scathing enough to say to him and he took that as acceptance.

"Let's see, three months' salary plus another twenty-five to sweeten it." He waited for Adele to speak, and when she didn't, he fumbled in the wallet again. "Make it an extra fifty dollars to show you how much I appreciate your willingness to be reasonable." He held out the folded bills.

Reno examined Adele's shocked expression and waited for her to explode. Blood crept from her neck to flood her cheeks, and her eyes narrowed to green slits.

"Keep your filthy money," she said, her voice husky with emotion. "You will not pay me off or threaten me, as you do everyone else in this town. I'm not one of your saloon girls you can buy and sell and neither is Sally Baldridge. If there is one scrap of decency in you, you will end this courtship." She held her arms stiffly at her sides. Her eyes smoldered in their deep sockets. "I'd sooner see her marry the town drunk than you."

"How could she? You already did." Terrapin's gaze flickered over Reno. "If you keep making these tragic

mistakes, Miss Adele, they will be your ultimate un-
doing."

"You bastard," Reno said, stepping forward, his
hand moving so quickly that Adele failed to see the
knife at first. "I told you, her name is Mrs. Gold."

The knife ripped through the front of Terrapin's
white shirt, slicing the fabric to ribbons. Reno backed
up to appreciate his handiwork and the mottled rage
on Terrapin's face. When the man would have
pounced on him, Reno displayed the knife blade, tilt-
ing it so that the orange rays of the setting sun caught
and were reflected by the shiny surface.

"Think twice," Reno cautioned. "And don't go for
your gun. I'll bury this knife in your black heart before you can clear that pistol from its holster."

Terrapin pointed a shaking finger in Reno's face.
"You have gotten in my way for the last time, Gold.
You're a walking dead man, you hear? A walking
dead man!"

"Get gone before I carve up your chest." Reno
gripped the knife handle more tightly. "And don't
come around here anymore bothering my wife or
me."

"Or Sally," Adele added. She couldn't keep from
staring at the ruined front of Terrapin's shirt, stunned
by Reno's quickness and audacity. The knife seemed
to have materialized from thin air. And the way he'd
used it! Deftly, almost gracefully, like an artist with a
brush.

Not a bad man to have around, she thought, examining him in a whole new light. Yes, it was nice
having a strong man on her side, especially against a
lowlife like Taylor Terrapin. Pride crowded into her

chest, and her heart swelled with it. Reno might be a tad lazy, but he made up for that in courage. In fact, he had to be the most courageous man in Whistle Stop.

And he was her husband.

"This isn't finished," Terrapin said, his voice and intent as low as a snake's belly. "You can't treat me with disrespect and get away with it. I've tried to reason with you, but you've rejected my offer and have ended up buying trouble, my friends."

Reno carved a Z in the air with the knife inches from Terrapin's nose. "You're wearing out your welcome, pal."

Terrapin retreated to his buggy and climbed nimbly to the seat. He snatched up the reins, threw Adele and Reno one last black glare, then rode away with a jingle of harness and a tapping of hooves.

Adele watched him go and let out a long sigh of relief. "He is insufferable." She slanted Reno a worried glance. "But maybe we should have handled him differently."

"Too late for that. The gauntlet has been thrown down, Dellie. All that's left is to deal with whatever comes from it."

"I suppose he'll drive Sally even further away from me."

"Dellie, Sally didn't take up with Terrapin just to rile you. I'm telling you to forget that contract and save yourself more trouble and your friendship with her."

"I can't, Reno. I just can't. I find it impossible to turn my back on those I love." She moved to go back inside, but he caught her hand and detained her.

When she looked over her shoulder at him, the soft light in his eyes made her catch her breath. "What is it?" she whispered, mystified.

"Don't turn your back on me, Dellie," he said, his tone as soft as the light in his eyes.

"I wasn't . . . I have to get back to work, that's all."

His smile was sadly sweet. He linked his fingers with hers. "Meet me for supper tonight."

"Supper? Where?"

He laughed. "Here. After the restaurant closes, meet me for supper. Just the two of us. Say eight o'clock? I'll have everything ready for us."

Adele looked down at their clasped hands and pleasure swirled through her. "All right." It was all she could say, what with sweet emotion blocking her throat.

He straightened his fingers and let hers slip free. Adele glanced up at him through the veil of her lashes, saw that he, too, was pleased, then went into the restaurant, which was filling up with hungry patrons.

She was wrapped up immediately in her work, helping to take orders and carry trays of steaming food to the tables. More than an hour later, she caught a glimpse of Reno as he moved away from the restaurant and toward the shed he was building. It was only then that she realized he'd been sitting on a bench outside, watching her through the restaurant windows. For how long she couldn't guess, but the realization sent another swirl of pleasure through her.

The enticement of a supper just for two kept her on edge the rest of the evening and made each minute pass like an hour. She let Colleen and Helen close the restaurant while she dashed into her quarters to change her clothes, splash on some rose water, and brush her hair to a glossy sheen.

From seven o'clock until eight, she sat on the parlor sofa and tried to remember the last time she'd been so excited about sharing a meal with a friend.

Except that Reno wasn't just her friend.

Chapter 12

❦

Entering the restaurant, Adele smiled shyly when she spotted the table by the window, draped with a white linen cloth and set for two. Candles glowed in its center, casting a romantic light over the shiny china and glinting silver. A delicious aroma lured her closer. She lifted the lid off a serving dish to reveal creamed peas and new potatoes. A platter of thinly sliced roast beef made her mouth water. Freshly baked rolls filled a basket, and creamy balls of butter slowly melted in a shallow bowl. Another bowl contained fluffy rice. Beside that sat a boat of brown gravy.

"You are a vision."

Adele spun around to find Reno standing in the kitchen doorway. He carried a bottle of wine and two glasses to the table, his gaze never wavering from her.

"I decided to dress up, since you were going to the trouble of fixing me supper," she said, glancing down at her dress of dark-cherry satin with black lace edging. She ran a hand up her nape, checking for curls that might have fallen from their pins.

"You're beautiful, Dellie," he said, dropping a light kiss on her cheek, "as always."

"Aren't you the smooth-talker," she teased, admiring the fit of his dark-gray suit, his boiled white shirt, and black satin vest. His clothes looked expensive, and she wondered where he'd found the money for them. Fingering a lapel, she tipped her head at a questioning angle. "This is a tailored fit. Must have cost you something."

"In the great Southern style, I sold a few pieces of my mother's jewelry to buy these duds. I wanted to look so good that you couldn't resist me."

She smiled at his joshing. "Speaking of something irresistible, the smell of this food is making me weak-kneed. I was so busy today that I skipped dinner."

"Then have a seat," he said, setting the wine and glasses on the table and holding out a chair for her. "I must confess that Mrs. McDonald helped me with some of this. The meat and gravy I could handle, but the rest—well, she took pity on me."

"She's a good woman."

Reno took the chair opposite her. "Yes, she is. You won't have to worry about her wanting to leave before her contract is up. She's found a home here."

Adele shook out her napkin and draped it over her lap. When Reno started to pour wine into her glass, she shook a hand at him. "I never—that is, I don't drink."

"Have a few sips tonight," he said, filling the glass halfway. "The taste will enhance the food. Trust me."

"I doubt this food will need enhancing." She shrugged and took a sip while he selected a slice of beef, cut it in half, and placed it on her plate. "You're rather handy with a knife," she noted. "Where did you learn to use one so deftly?"

"I suppose you're talking about what I did to Terrapin's shirt earlier." He grinned and placed two large slices of beef on his plate. "That's a little trick I learned from a Cheyenne cousin."

"Very impressive." She nodded when he offered her a serving of the peas and potatoes. "This is nice, having supper together."

"It's what married people do, I'm told."

"I usually just eat with the others after the restaurant closes. I expected you to show up, but you never have."

He smiled. "I was never invited."

Adele blinked, taken aback. "But I assumed—"

"There you go assuming again, Dellie. You assumed I knew this rooster would be welcome at your hen parties?"

Contrite, she pursed her lips and forced herself to apologize. "I'm sorry, Reno. From now on you must join us for supper."

"Must I?"

She sighed, irritated by her poor choice of words. "That is, you may if you wish."

He lifted his wine glass. "To a better understanding of each other."

She hesitated a moment before honoring the toast with a clink of her glass against the side of his. The wine was fruity and sweet. She was glad he'd selected a mild one, since she wasn't used to the effects of liquor or the taste of it.

"If you'd given Terrapin the time of day, he would have asked *you* to marry him."

"Me?" Adele laughed. "Don't be ridiculous."

"I'm not. The day we married I noticed how he looked at you. And why should he be any different from any other bachelor in this town? You were the most coveted woman in Whistle Stop, and then I had to come along and ruin every other fellow's chances."

"I believe you're trying to turn my head."

"No, I'm trying to make it clear to you that I know what I have and I'm grateful. I took a shine to you years ago, Dellie. Did you think I hung around because I was overly fond of my cousin?"

"You and Win were close," Adele insisted.

"Not that close. We had little in common, other than blood and our infatuation with you."

She felt herself blush, but covered it by tucking in her chin and concentrating on buttering a roll. "You were the only one who didn't say I was crazy for not accepting Win's proposal of marriage."

"You and Win weren't a good match."

"Oh?" She arched a brow. "How did you come to that conclusion?"

"He couldn't handle you. You're a strong woman and you need a strong man. One should fight fire with fire."

"Personally I don't think of a love match as a fight. When looking for a mate, I seek someone who does not want to dominate me or subjugate me."

"That's right. You want your equal, and Winston wasn't that. He was too weak. You led him around as if you had a halter on him."

"I did not!" she protested hotly, but Reno only smiled indulgently at her. "My mother said that Winston was a dear, but he didn't understand my ambition. She was right. Winston wanted a wife who would be content to stay at home and never leave the confines of those walls."

"That's why he and Sally were a good fit. If Win had possessed a knack for keeping his money, he and Sally would have been as happy as cream-fed cats."

"Sally isn't a gold digger. She is simply terrified of being poor, which is a common ailment among certain Southerners." She waved her fork to dismiss any more argument from him. "But I'm tired of talking about Sally. This meal is delicious. Let's enjoy it."

"Very well. Let's talk about us."

Adele had trouble swallowing. Glancing at him, she admired his casual air. Of course, he was directing this grand seduction, so he could afford to be cavalier. Although she felt like a deer being lured into a clearing, she had to admit she liked this side of Reno.

His mannered air, his handsome clothes, his attempts to impress her, all served to weaken her defenses. She could have done much worse in choosing a husband, she thought. Then she realized that she must have influenced him. Yes, that was it. Her plan had worked! She had uncovered his pride, his desire to achieve something, and his self-respect. Savoring her triumph, she was too late in refusing the wine he poured into her nearly empty glass. Ah, well, another glass wouldn't compromise her.

"Your mother liked me, didn't she?"

Adele nodded. "Yes. She found you quite exotic."

"Exotic?" He laughed, a low, purring sound. "I've never been called *that* before."

"Your mixed bloodlines intrigued Mama. She was especially taken by the Gypsy in you. She met a band of Gypsies once and found them intoxicating." Adele partook of more wine. "You're right. This does enhance the taste of the food. And it's not much stronger than fruit juice."

His smile lured the timid deer inside her further into the clearing. "Did you find me the least bit exotic back then?"

"Yes, of course. You were the wild spirit among us. We never knew what to make of you or what you would do or say next. Winston said your family were the black sheep of the Baldridge flock. Your father married your mother amid furious protests, Win said."

"Yes, but my father and his brothers were all renegades. They were raised to be independent thinkers. My grandfather married a dusky-skinned Gypsy, and they raised their children to follow divergent paths."

"Then why did they protest when your father wanted to marry an Indian?"

"They didn't like her because she had already had two husbands. My grandmother was superstitious and she was afraid my mother was cursed and that every man she married would suffer an early death. But my father is still alive, so the curse must be broken." He buttered another roll for himself. "Winston's branch of the family wouldn't have had anything to do with us if we hadn't owned so much land and had success at farming."

"Your family still has the farm?"

"Yes, and my cousins on my mother's side have a large spread out by Guthrie. I was visiting them when I saw your advertisement in the Territorial newspaper."

"And you thought I'd gone mad."

"No, but I couldn't imagine why you would need to advertise for a husband, so I decided to find out what kind of trouble you'd landed in."

"You wrote that you'd been trying your luck at prospecting. When I read that, I wondered what kind of trouble *you'd* landed in."

His smile was veiled, secretive. Standing, he went to the restaurant counter and lifted the lid from a box there, producing the sweet notes of a waltz. Turning toward her, he held out his hand as he approached.

"Would you dance with me, Dellie?"

"Dance?" She rested a hand on her throat, where a pulse fluttered like a bird's wing. "I never expected this!"

"I recall that you were the most graceful dancer I'd ever seen. You moved as light as a feather. I always wanted to dance with you."

"But you never asked."

"I was afraid you'd refuse or I'd make a fool of myself by stepping on your toes. Will you accept my invitation, Dellie, now that I've found the courage to ask?"

She placed her hand in his. "I'd be delighted, Mr. Gold."

They moved to the center of the floor. He had pushed the tables and chairs to one end, creating a space for them, Adele noticed, touched by his forethought. Moonlight spilled through the windows, its white light mingling with the golden glow of the candles and transforming the restaurant into a romantic sanctum. She recognized the music as the same tune that his pocket watch played.

"I take it you are fond of this Nocturne."

"Yes. It touches something inside me. As you do." His free hand curved at her waist.

Looking up into his eyes, the timid creature inside her advanced fully into the clearing and trembled at its own courage. She moved closer to him and followed his lead, her feet moving of their own volition while the rest of her body thrilled at the intimate press of his.

He had underestimated himself, for he had no peer on the dance floor. As straight-backed and lithe as a cat, he guided her in flowing steps and sweeping turns, his gaze never wavering from hers. Excitement built within Adele as she watched his eyes change from blue-gray to dark blue, and she sensed the quickening of his pulse to match hers. Something was in the air. Something that quivered and sparked like a lightning charge. Her breath shortened and warmth flooded her breasts, her neck, her face. She wanted to fling herself into his arms and bury her hands in his thick mane of hair. She wanted to feel his hands on her body, his mouth on her skin.

So this is lust, Adele thought disjointedly. Oh, it was incredible!

"Dellie," he whispered, his voice rough and magical, "you have no idea how long I've wanted you. The only reason I tolerated Win and his other friends was so that I could be near you."

She thrilled at the confession, but couldn't form any words of her own. Her heart pounded in her throat.

"And I never got you out of my mind. Did you ever think of me, Dellie? Did my name ever cross your mind?"

Her lips moved, but she could make no sound. She swallowed and forced her tongue to work, but before she could answer him, she was distracted by movement outside the windows. So was Reno. They both turned toward the disturbance at the same moment.

Men on horseback—Adele counted two—sped by the windows. She thought she knew one of them, perhaps both. "Is that Yancy and—"

Noise erupted all around them. Choking off the rest, Adele stared dumbly at the wine bottle, which had exploded in a shower of glass, spilling its contents onto the white tablecloth. Before she could comprehend what had happened, the rest of the world erupted in a volley of gunfire, shattering glass and splintering wood. Adele screamed. Reno clutched her shoulders and slung her to the floor. Bullets whizzed over her head, and the acrid smell of spent gunpowder burned her nose.

Fear coated her mouth with a coppery taste, and her head ached with the reverberating sound of the gunshots. Then it was quiet, save for the drip, drip, drip of the wine and the tinkle of falling glass. Reno lay on top of her so heavily that he squeezed the breath from her.

"I'm okay," she whispered. "Get off me, please." When Reno didn't move, she did, shrugging and twisting out from under him. His body slid off hers, unnaturally limp.

"Reno?" On her hands and knees, she looked at him. He lay sprawled on his stomach, his face turned away from her. "Reno?" Grabbing him by the shoulder, she pulled him onto his back. He was pale, his dark lashes creating crescents against his skin. "Reno, this isn't funny." She patted his cheek and he didn't even flinch. "Reno!"

Colleen and Helen burst into the restaurant. The glow of the lanterns they carried revealed their frightened expressions. From beneath their nightgowns and robes their bare feet flashed.

"Be careful!" Adele shouted. "There's glass everywhere."

Both women slid to a halt and stared at the glittering floor.

"Are you hurt?" Helen asked.

"What happened?" Colleen demanded.

Doris McDonald came puffing in behind them. She'd thought to stick her feet into leather slippers. "God Almighty, did somebody get drunk and mistake our windows for empty whiskey bottles?"

"No mistake," Adele said, patting Reno's cheeks again and getting no response. She ran her hands over his clothes, searching for wounds. "Reno's hurt."

"Did he get shot?" Helen asked.

"I don't know." Panic skittered through Adele as she bent over him. "Reno, please. Open your eyes." She pressed her ear to his chest, and for a few moments heard only her own heartbeat. Was he dead?

"No, no, Reno." A sob tore at her throat and a black, ominous cloud moved across her vision. For an instant she thought she might faint from the sheer terror of losing him. "Reno, please don't leave me," she whispered in his ear, tears streaming down her cheeks. Her heart seemed to cave in on itself.

Then he moaned.

"He's alive!" she shouted, sitting up to beam at the women. "Thank God, he's alive."

"Why, sure he is," Mrs. McDonald said, squatting beside her. "Looks like he's getting a bump on his head." She indicated a swelling above his ear. "Probably hit his noggin when he dove for cover."

"Of course. I was afraid he'd—" Adele realized how she must look to the others, cradling Reno's head in her lap, her face streaked with tears and her voice shivering with fear. She strove for composure and grappled with the numbing realization that her feelings for Reno Gold surpassed infatuation and ran deeper than lust.

Mrs. McDonald reached toward the table for a glass of water. With no warning she tossed the liquid into Reno's face. He gasped and sputtered.

"Mrs. McDonald!" Adele flung out her hands and stared at her wet lap. "Was that really called for?"

"I thought you wanted him awake." The nononsense woman peered into Reno's bleary eyes. "Hey there, you know your name, partner?"

"Gold," Reno said, his voice sounding like a bullfrog's croak.

"How about me. Do you know me?"

Reno squinted at her. "Mrs. McDonald."

"He seems to have his wits about him."

"Dellie?" Reno's voice rose to near panic.

"I'm here," Adele assured him. He relaxed when he saw her face above him. "I'm all right. Everyone is safe."

"My head," he said, groaning.

"You hit it against something. Can you stand?" Adele looked toward Helen and Colleen. "Open the door to my quarters. Mrs. McDonald, will you help me get him to the bed, please?"

"Sure. That's the best place for him. You two go put on some shoes," Mrs. McDonald told the other two women. "After we get him settled, we'll clean up the glass. Good thing tomorrow's Sunday. We can use the day off to board up the windows until glass can be ordered and put in. Did you see who did this?"

"I'm not sure. Everything happened so fast. I thought I recognized them, but..." Adele shook her head, unwilling to share her impressions with anyone yet, in case she might be wrong. "Reno, can you help us get your legs under you?"

With Mrs. McDonald assisting her, Adele managed to steer Reno into her parlor. When she would have stopped there and let him fall onto his cot, Mrs. McDonald veered toward Adele's bedroom. Adele started to protest, then thought better of it. After all, Reno had received a hard bump on the head and needed a soft bed, at least for tonight.

They backed him up to her bed, and Mrs. Mc-Donald held him steady while Adele turned down the spread and sheet. Then she let him go, and he fell like fresh-cut timber. Mrs. McDonald swept her palms against each other in satisfaction.

"Let's get his boots off him, then I'll leave the rest to you."

"The rest?"

The older woman looked at Adele with a cagey squint. "The rest of his clothes."

"Ah, well, he can sleep in those."

"In a suit?" Mrs. McDonald frowned. "You want him to sleep in his Sunday best?"

Adele smiled sheepishly. "Well, tomorrow *is* Sunday." She felt her color heighten under the woman's scrutiny. "You want me to undress him?" Mrs. McDonald offered. "Won't bother me. He's got nothing I haven't seen before on lots of other men."

"I believe that would be best," Adele said, already retreating from the room. "I'll be out here in the parlor."

"He's got a cut on his head and it's bleeding."

"I'll fetch a basin of water and bandages," Adele said, seizing the opportunity to leave Mrs. McDonald to her task.

Helen and Colleen were sweeping up glass when she entered the restaurant. Adele waved off their anxious expressions.

"He'll be fine. He's woozy from hitting his head. I'm going to clean the cut."

"Should we fetch the sheriff?" Colleen asked.

"Why?" Adele asked. "Oh, you think he'd catch the men who shot out our windows? Not likely. Don't you think someone heard the shots and the shouting? Do you see any of them here to help us?" She didn't wait for answers she already knew, but went into the kitchen for a shallow bowl of hot water, clean strips of cloth, and a tube of ointment she used for cuts, scrapes, and burns. When she joined the others again, Helen was peeking out the front door.

"What's going on?" Adele asked.

"Here comes somebody. It's a buggy, letting somebody off." Helen gasped. "Why, it's Mrs. Sally!"

Adele had stopped at the table that she and Reno had shared. She turned toward the door just as Sally crossed the threshold. Sally's color was high, but Adele couldn't determine if she was elated or afraid.

"Was anyone hurt?" Sally asked, glancing around

at the destruction but not seeming very surprised.

"Reno received a bump on the head," Adele related. "He threw me to the floor and then dove for cover. It's a wonder we weren't killed. We were standing right here when those men started shooting."

"I'm sure they weren't aiming at you. They didn't mean to kill anyone."

"How do you know that?" Adele challenged her.

"I don't know it. I only presume it," Sally said. "They were probably drunk."

"How did you hear about it?"

"I . . . Someone in town told me. You know how news travels. People heard the shots, saw the riders." Sally shrugged. "As long as no one was hurt—"

"I told you, Reno was hurt."

"But I'm sure he's fine. Maybe the incident knocked some sense into him." Sally's smile was tight and false.

Adele approached her, carefully studying her and finding her more a stranger than a friend. "Sally, what do you know about this? Where were you tonight?"

Sally flinched as if Adele had struck her. "Just what are you implying? I was in town, as I told you."

"I want to believe you. I want very much to believe you." Aware of the other two women, who had fallen still and quiet and were carefully watching her and Sally, Adele curbed her tongue. If she had been alone with Sally, she could have been brutally blunt, but she had to remember that she was the manager of the restaurant and that called for some decorum. "Who brought you home tonight?"

"You know who," Sally said, her voice tight.

"I suppose he had nothing to do with what happened here tonight either."

"If you had been the least bit civil to him, he would be rounding up those men right now and taking them to the sheriff. He could be a valuable friend, Dellie. But you won't give one inch, so why should he go out of his way to help you?"

"I'm not asking for his help," Adele shot back. "I came close to being shot tonight, Sally. Do you understand that?"

Sally's mouth dipped at the corners and her shoulders slumped. "I couldn't stand to see you harmed. You must know that." She reached out and grasped Adele's hand. "But think about what happened tonight. Think about the consequences of foolish actions."

"We should both do some powerful thinking," Adele agreed, "before something happens that can't be rectified with an apology or a regret."

Mrs. McDonald joined them, her nightgown wrinkled and her hair frizzing around her sweating face. "Mrs. Gold, your husband is as naked as the day he was born and in there waiting for you." Planting her hands on her hips, she puffed out a breath that made the curls on her forehead dance. She took in her audience of four slack-jawed women and her lips curved into a bawdy grin. "I can attest to the fact that he's all man—and he's all yours. Better hurry on in there. Like my seafaring papa used to say, 'When you get yourself a good, stiff one, you best hoist your sails and thank the Lord for the ride.' "

Adele closed her eyes slowly in embarrassment.

"Dellie, whatever is this woman talking about?

What has she been doing with your husband in your quarters?" Sally asked, almost sputtering.

Adele opened her eyes, caught the mighty struggles of Helen and Colleen not to laugh aloud, and issued Sally a long, cool glare. "Sally, if you don't want to miss our shenanigans, then you'll have to quit sneaking off to be with the town plague. Now excuse me." She swept past them and escaped to her quarters.

Chapter 13

A lone in her parlor Adele leaned against the door and closed her eyes. The voices of the other women floated to her. She heard her name spoken, then Reno's. Laughter followed, then angry words from Sally. Adele heard Sally's heels tapping against the floor and up the stairs.

"... none of your business anyway," Sally called hotly to the others. "You're all just jealous!"

"Not likely," Colleen called out. "You can have him."

"I *have* had him," Mrs. McDonald said, her low voice carrying easily to Adele. "He's nothing to crow about."

Adele bit her lips to smother a spate of laughter. Opening her eyes, she stared at the bowl of water she held. Maybe she'd let Reno sleep and tend to his wound by the light of day. She'd curl up on his cot and not bother him.

Who are you fooling? she asked herself with a self-mocking smirk. *You don't want to see him because your heart has revealed itself.*

She was falling in love with him. What other explanation could there be for her reaction when she'd thought he might have been felled by a stray bullet? Shivering at the memory of her overwhelming grief, her inconsolable pain when she'd listened for his heartbeat and couldn't hear it, she realized that she hadn't felt such powerful despair since her mother's death.

Had she loved Reno back in Kansas, and had that love lain dormant until he'd kissed her again? More important, was she falling in love with the man he was or the boy she had longed for in Lawrence?

The questions circled in her mind and found no answers. Would morning make any difference to how she felt? Would daybreak cast light into her heart and reveal the answers she sought? She could only hope that Reno, unconscious, had not been aware of her anguish.

Hearing his soft groan and the squeak of the bedstead, she heaved a sigh and pushed away from the door. Just like a man to struggle to his feet when he should be flat on his back. But she was glad to be galvanized into action, because it served no purpose to worry and question and postpone the inevitable.

She was falling in love with her husband, a development that certainly complicated her life, but she would find a way to deal with it. What was important was not to let Reno know that she'd gone soft for him, because he would surely find some way to use that to his own benefit.

Prepared to be as aloof as possible without being rude or arousing his curiosity, Adde felt her resolution crumble when saw him, disheveled and disarming. With his hair tumbling in dark waves and his eyes shadowed and heavy-lidded, he sat on the edge of the bed, the sheet wrapped around his midsection and draped over his legs, and she could tell by his expression that he didn't like being bedridden. One long, muscled leg was exposed up to the thigh. His chest, broad and lightly furred, was also revealed to her desirous gaze. Her foolish heart took wing and beat in her breast, a wild, wanton thing.

"No, Reno," she scolded, hurrying to him. She set the bowl and bandages on the bedside table, then placed her hands on his warm shoulders. "Lie back. You're not going anywhere."

"My head hurts," he said, touching the swollen flesh. "Who was it, Dellie? Did you see them?"

"It was dark," she answered, dodging the question. "Please lie back in the bed. You hit your head on something. It's still bleeding a little. Let me see to it, Reno."

He fell back with a groan, his eyes closing and his lips forming a hard line. "Damn them. He hired someone to do his dirty work."

"Hush. We don't need to talk about that now."

"Why not?" he asked crossly.

"Because you'll just get upset." She dabbed a damp cloth against the dried blood in his hair.

"I'm not upset," he said, slapping her hand aside. "I'm goddamned mad. Son of a bitch, sending those men here to shoot at us."

"I don't think they meant to shoot at anybody. I believe they were trying to shatter the windows and scare us."

"When you fire your gun, you take life and death

into your hands. Every male out of short pants knows that."

"I'm going to clean this wound, and you are going to keep your hands to yourself," she informed him.

"Is that so?" he asked, some of the anger in his eyes replaced by bemusement.

"That's so." She cleaned the dried blood and applied a dab of ointment to the cut. "This is quite a knot you have here. Do you know what you hit?"

"The edge of the counter, I think. It's a wonder it didn't split right down the middle like a ripe melon."

"What, the counter or your head?" She smiled, mischief rioting in her. "I think you'll live."

"Disappointed?"

She relaxed, realizing that he wasn't aware of her earlier display of raw emotion.

"Dellie?"

"Hmmm?" She blinked, coming back to herself. "Oh, don't be silly, I'm—"

"I seem to be naked."

"—not disappointed."

Reno's brows arched and his lips quirked. "That's a relief. I know you are a lady of high standards. Glad to hear I pass muster."

She swatted at him. "I wasn't talking about . . . Shame on you!"

"Shame on me? I didn't get naked on my own."

"Mrs. McDonald undressed you while I fetched the water and bandages." She eyed the lump on his head. "Should I dress it?"

"Now there's my problem." He nudged her chin with his knuckle. "The woman I don't care for undresses me and the one I do care for wants to dress me."

"I believe that rap on the head jostled your brains." She looked away, flustered by his gentle teasing and his lambent gaze. "You should sleep now."

"So should you, but where?" He eyed the space next to him. "There's plenty of room in here for you, and you could keep me warm all through the night."

"I'll use your cot for tonight, thank you."

"Suit yourself, but I warn you, that's a poor excuse for a bed." He sighed and gave a bounce on the bedding. "This is so comfortable I might not surrender it." He folded his hands behind his head and grinned.

The sheet slipped to his waist, and Adele found she could not look away from the spectacle of him, even though a tiny voice scolded her. She knew his body was warm, as if fire licked just beneath his skin. She knew that he was hard with muscle but gentle with compassion. It was what she didn't know about him that held her captive.

"Did you recognize the riders, Dellie?"

Only half of her mind comprehended the question. She nodded and caught off guard, answered, "Yancy Stummer was one, and I think the other was that Buck fellow. Buck . . . Buck . . . the one with the eye patch."

"Wilhite."

"Yes, that's right." She sucked in a breath and shook her head to clear her mind of sultry images. "But I'm probably wrong. It was dark."

"Are you afraid I might start trouble with them?" His voice was laced with humor, but his eyes glinted with sincerity.

"I'm afraid you'll get yourself killed," she confessed. "And nothing is worth that. Nothing."

He let his arms fall slowly to his sides. The atmosphere in the room changed. Adele looked around, sensing the change, then realizing it existed between them, *because of them.* When his fingertips caressed the side of her face, she exhaled a long breath and closed her eyes. Tipping her head into the palm of his hand, she let the sensations inside her spill like a waterfall. His thumb nestled in the corner of her mouth. She parted her lips, accepted the tip of his thumb, and ran her tongue across it.

"Ah, Dellie." His voice was rough and soft all at once. "Come here, sugar." He curved his other hand behind her neck and drew her to him.

His lips trailed over her cheek, sprinkling small kisses, his breath warming her skin. He wound strands of her hair around his fingers and framed her face in his hands. Kissing her mouth, he seduced her with lips and tongue and inexplicable technique. He tilted her head so that his mouth slanted recklessly over hers.

"So sweet," he whispered against her lips. "Kiss me back, sugar. Make me believe you love me."

Drifts of desire floated over her, through her. She inched closer, her hands moving to his hair, her lips parting to accept his thrusting tongue.

He flinched.

The night's events intruded again. Adele leaned away.

"I'm sorry," she said. "Your head. I didn't meant to—"

"It doesn't hurt."

"Yes, it does." She stood up from the bed. His

hands clutched for her, but she stepped back out of his reach.

"Dellie, come here. It's just a little bump on the head. You were making me feel fine. Real fine." He grinned around the last words.

"I don't have your constitution. I'm tired."

"Slip on into this bed and let me rock you to dreamland, darlin'."

Adele laughed at his persistence. "No, Reno. Not tonight."

Interest sparkled in his eyes. "Not tonight? Now that sounds promising. I do believe we're making progress here."

Adele went to the tallboy and selected a nightgown and robe from it. "Once you're fully recovered, you can finish that shed, and then we'll talk." She flashed him a smile and crossed the threshold into the parlor. "Sweet dreams, Reno," she said, laughing at his squinty-eyed attempt at menace before she closed the bedroom door.

She sat on the parlor sofa and relived his kisses and the beauty of his brawny chest, with its soft covering of curly black hair, his small brown paps, the line of hair that arrowed down past his navel. Crossing her arms, she hugged herself and marveled at her will of iron. If she hadn't touched that lump on his head and if he hadn't flinched, she would be in that bed with him. She knew this. But did he?

"I'm not staying in this damned bed another minute," Reno announced the next day when Adele came in carrying a dinner tray for him. He flung back the covers with a flourish.

Giving a shriek of alarm, Adele spun away so quickly that the soup sloshed out of its bowl and the glass of milk nearly tipped over.

"Have a care, Reno," she said, her voice high and uncharacteristically flighty. "A lady is present!"

"So?"

"So cover yourself."

"Dellie, I'm decent," he said, his tone grimly indulgent.

Not fully trusting him, Adele glanced over her shoulder. He was standing and pulling on a pair of trousers over his red long-handles. She turned to face him again, frowning at his determination to defy her.

"You aren't strong enough to be out of that bed."

"I know my own strength." He rested a hand momentarily on his forehead and squeezed his eyes shut. "Although there are three of you."

"Sit down before you fall down." She set the tray on the bedside table. "I swear, men are the most exasperating creatures on earth. No wonder the Lord decided He'd have to create a woman to help Adam. Didn't take Him long to figure out that man was self-destructive."

Reno fashioned a flapping mouth with his hand. "Yak, yak, yak. You aren't easing my headache any."

"Sit back against the headboard. I've brought you some delicious chicken soup, Mrs. McDonald's famous griddle cakes, and a big glass of milk. You'll feel much better after you've eaten." Shaking out a napkin, she bent close to him and tucked the edge under the frayed neckline of his long johns.

His dark scowl and brooding eyes caught her attention and she matched his forbidding countenance.

"Don't look at me as if you hate me. I'm doing this for your own good." She set the tray on his lap. "I should think you'd be glad to have a reason to lie about all day."

He sighed wearily. "Yes, I know, Dellie. Before I stepped off the train, you had decided I was a no-'count cur."

"That's not true," she admonished him. "I was looking forward to seeing you until you staggered off the train and fell like a stone at my feet."

Folding his arms across his chest, he glowered at her. "Back in Kansas you gave people the benefit of the doubt and didn't assume they were worthless and lazy. You thought well of them. Your heart was as big as the prairie sky."

"Back in Kansas I was a young girl who knew nothing of the world. I'm a woman now and I've learned that the only person you can depend on is yourself."

His mouth dipped at the corners. "Who taught you that, Dellie?"

"Life taught me that. Since Mama died, I've had my share of disappointments."

He glanced around and shrugged. "You seem to be doing well for yourself."

"Yes, well . . . I must return to my work." She stood, uneasy with the turn of conversation.

"What work? It's Sunday."

"Yes, but we're cleaning up the mess from last night and boarding up the broken windows. The railroad, which actually owns this building, is sending money for new glass, but until then we'll have to make do."

"I could help."

"No. You eat and I'll return for the tray. I want to see if Sally's back. She went to church this morning and that's the last I saw of her. I suppose she's off somewhere with Terrapin, but she could at least have let someone know."

"She'd better watch out or you'll fire her," he joked, not cracking a smile.

Adele appreciated his quip with a sour expression. "Stay in bed." With that, she left him.

Reno dissected the conversation while he tucked away the food. What she hadn't said exactly was that all she had was her work. Since the death of her mother, love had been absent from her life. That could certainly harden a heart and erect barriers. But a woman of her beauty didn't have to be alone. She had chosen the path, spurning the advances of the men in Whistle Stop and wherever else she'd lived.

His mind circled a notion, and he examined it from every angle before deciding it was sound. Dellie wanted control. She didn't like the surprises life had handed her, so she strove to be in charge of every aspect of it. That's why she had advertised for a husband.

Oh, she'd fooled herself into thinking she was making a statement, teaching the men in town a lesson, but what she was really doing was finding herself a husband she could control. Someone she could handle.

What she needed, however, was an equal, someone she could not manage, but someone she could depend on. He could be that person. He wanted to be that person. Why, he didn't know, other than that he'd had a lingering sense of destiny since the day he'd met her. And of course she was the most beautiful woman he'd ever clapped eyes on. Her green eyes haunted him night and day, and he had never seen skin as creamy and as flawless as hers. Then there was her spirit. The woman was brimming with it. And her intellect, her quest for knowledge, her insistence on achievement.

She acted on him like a potion, running through him, changing him, binding him in the spell of her. Even when she was irritating him by bossing him or frustrating him with her damning assumptions, another part of him wanted to kiss her quiet and drive her wild with desire.

Damn if he wasn't roped and tied. The woman should brand him and put him out of his misery.

Grinning crookedly at his musings, he set the tray aside and fought off dizziness to get to his feet. Locking his knees, he waited for the room to right itself, then he dressed with slow, deliberate movements. Navigating into the parlor, he strapped on his holster and he was ready to leave when he caught his reflection in the mirror.

Good God! He could scare Satan himself.

Unshaven and hollow-eyed, he was a walking specter of doom. His own mother would shriek in horror if she could see him. Yep, he'd never looked meaner or more disreputable. He felt almost as bad as he looked, which was dandy. He rocked a hat gingerly onto his tangled mop of hair, careful not to touch the knot of pain above his ear, and slipped out the side door. With what he had to do, looking scary and feeling as rotten as week-old meat would tip the odds in his favor.

* * *

In less than an hour he'd tracked down his quarry at the General Store.

Yancy Stummer sat in one of the ten rocking chairs fronting the building and concentrated on rolling himself a cigarette. A collection of other town wastrels sat with him and traded well-worn tall tales of bad tempers and bad women.

Reno approached them diagonally from across the street. On Sundays the store was closed, and most people were staying at home this afternoon. Yancy and his cohort were so involved in rolling their own and trading lies that they didn't see Reno coming until he was only a few steps away. Willie Halderon nudged Yancy in the ribs with a sharp elbow and gave a quick, nervous nod in Reno's direction. Yancy looked up, saw Reno, and gulped loud enough for Reno to hear. His eyes quivered in their sockets, and Reno wouldn't have been surprised if Yancy had watered the seat of his pants.

"You left your calling card last night, Yancy, so I thought I'd pay you a visit of my own," Reno said, keeping his voice low. He glanced left and right at the gawkers. "You men might want to make tracks. Me and Yancy have some private business to attend to, and I wouldn't want anybody getting in our way." He rested a hand on the butt of his gun. "So get."

In a blink of an eye, Yancy was left sitting alone with only wildly rocking chairs on either side of him. He jumped up and patted his sides.

"I'm not armed," he blurted out.

"That doesn't seem to matter much in this town.

You were armed last night and you nearly killed me and Dellie."

"I don't know what you're yammering about. I was home with my wife last night."

"Maybe for part of the night, but I saw you and Terrapin's hired coyote galloping by when you shot out the restaurant windows. I know you're good at lying, Yancy, but I'm better at knowing a lie when I hear it."

"Take your crazy notions some place else. I don't know what the hell you're talking about. And you'd better watch your back, mister. If you try to gun me down, the sheriff will have you swinging from a rope before sunset."

"I'm not going to gun you down, Stummer."

"You ain't?"

"No." Reno shook his head slowly and released his most evil, blood-chilling grin. Yancy blanched. "I'm going to beat the livin' hell out of you."

Yancy's pupils dilated. He lunged sideways, trying to escape, but Reno was a step ahead of him and grasped the back of his shirt, ripping it as he held Yancy in check while he introduced his fist to the man's stomach. Yancy doubled over with a groan and a whine.

"Don't hurt me," he wailed. "I never done nothing."

"Lying little bastard," Reno shouted. "You're going to confess if I have to smash every last one of your snaggled teeth out of your head." He punched Yancy in the mouth to prove he was a man of his word.

"Owww! Help me! Help me!" Yancy wailed like a stepped-on cat.

Reno had no mercy, landing blows to Yancy's jaw, his midsection, his ribs, until the man collapsed at Reno's feet. Reno shook out his hands, his knuckles stinging, his fingers cramped, and stared down at Yancy Stummer. He rolled the man over onto his back with the toe of his boot. Yancy moaned, blood leaking from a cut and swelling lower lip. A piece of tooth dangled from his upper lip.

"Listen to me, Stummer," Reno said, shoving Yancy's shoulder with his boot. "Stay away from me, stay away from the restaurant, and—listen good now, Stummer." He toed him in the ribs and Yancy howled. "Stay away from my wife, or I swear I'll kick your sorry ass from here to Texas."

Leaving him in the muddy street, Reno turned and saw a shadowy figure in the doorway of the saloon. Pausing, he waited for the man to step outside. Buck Wilhite.

"Hey there, Buck," Reno called, keeping an eye on the man's gun hand. "I've been having some fun here with your friend."

"He isn't my friend."

"Oh? He rides with you when you're out at night shooting at folks through windows."

"I heard there was trouble at the restaurant," Buck said. "Maybe you should be more careful in picking your friends and enemies."

Reno walked slowly toward the man, smiling on the outside while his temper flared inside. "Let's talk man to man." He stopped a few feet from Buck. "I know you rode out last night and emptied your gun at the restaurant windows. I figure you were doing what you get paid to do. It's a damned cowardly way to make a living, but I reckon it's all you have sense enough to do."

The one eye visible to Reno narrowed. Buck flexed the fingers of his gun hand.

"I've got no use for cowards, Wilhite. Next time I see you making trouble for me or mine, I'll let my gun do the talking."

Buck's mouth twitched in the semblance of a grin. "That right?"

"That's right. So you'd best go hunt up something you can use for a backbone. You'll be needing it." Reno walked away, each step a testimony to his courage and his belief that Wilhite wouldn't shoot him in the back. Not today, anyway.

"Shoot him!" Yancy Stummer propped himself up on one elbow and motioned for Buck to obey. "Kill him, Buck!"

"Shut your trap, Stummer," Buck drawled, "before I shoot you quiet."

Reno stifled a laugh when Yancy whimpered, scrambled to his feet, and limped away, trying to outpace Reno.

"Gold!"

Reno didn't want to stop, didn't want to face Wilhite again, but he did.

"How come you didn't try to jump me or draw on me?" Wilhite called.

Reno considered his answer a moment before he spoke. "You're not the man I've got a grievance with. It's your boss I'll call out if this trouble isn't put to rest."

"What about Stummer? You jumped him."

Reno cocked a brow and gave a shrug. "Hell, I just did that for the pure pleasure of it."

Buck dipped his head, then angled a glance toward the gaming hall as if he were scouting for his boss. Reno thought he might be laughing, but he was too far away to be sure. Issuing a short wave, Buck spun around and went back into the saloon.

Reno adjusted his gun in its holster, relieved that he didn't have to use it, but knowing he would soon. Too damn soon.

Chapter 14

The last of the glass had been swept away. The broken windows were boarded up against the dirt and debris carried by the wind. Adele sat alone in the restaurant and looked out one of the two windows that hadn't been demolished by bullets. She thought to check on Reno. He had seemed weary when she'd taken a supper tray to him, but that was to be expected, since he'd disobeyed her by getting dressed. Just dressing had obviously sapped his strength. He hadn't argued when she'd insisted that he undress and get back into bed.

She would look in on him in a few minutes, she thought, but right at that moment it felt too good to be off her feet. She wanted to sit and rest and not think about the restaurant or last night's riders or how close she had come to losing Reno.

Hearing the tap of heels on the depot platform, Adele jerked to attention, her nerves jangling and the hairs on the back of her neck lifting. She was relieved to see Doris McDonald approaching the door.

The cook let herself in with her own key and

seemed surprised to find Adele still in the restaurant.

"Everything peaceful here?" she asked.

"Why, yes, Mrs. McDonald. Did you have a nice stroll?"

Mrs. McDonald nodded. "I stopped at the boardinghouse to have a cup of tea and talked with a woman I know there. She told me about what happened earlier. I sure hope Mr. Reno knows what he's doing, yanking the Devil's tail like that."

Adele frowned and shook her head. "I don't follow you."

"Nobody's said anything to you? I thought some of the town folks would have stopped by to spread the news."

"Once the workmen were finished, I locked the restaurant. I've been taking inventory in the kitchen."

"Oh." Mrs. McDonald sighed. "I should have kept my mouth shut, I reckon."

"If this concerns me, I should know about it. You mentioned Reno?"

"Yes, ma'am. He . . . Well, he tracked down Yancy Stummer and bloodied him good. He threatened to kill Buck Wilhite if he ever came around this place or you again."

Adele fell back in the chair, her breath stuck in her throat. "When? When did he do this? He's been here—" She chopped off the rest.

Mrs. McDonald shook her head and smiled grimly. "No, ma'am, he hasn't been here all day. He snuck out while we were busy cleaning up the place."

"That rascal." Adele looked toward the door leading to her quarters. "I thought he was weak because it had taken such an effort for him to get out of bed and dress."

"He had himself a big day, Mrs. Adele. A mighty big day."

Adele knew she should be livid, but her reaction was just the opposite. She was glad, glad that Reno had given Yancy Stummer his due and had warned Buck to keep his distance. Naturally she wished he had waited until he was fully recovered from his injury, but she couldn't deny the intense pride she felt for him. His actions showed gumption, spirit, and self-confidence, all things she liked in a man.

"He didn't say a word to me," Adele said. "I suppose he knew I'd burst the ties in my corset."

"Men have trouble turning the other cheek. It ain't natural for them to let something like this"—she gestured at the boarded windows—"go without making somebody pay. He was only doing what comes natural, ma'am."

"Don't worry, Mrs. McDonald, I'm not as naive as you think when it comes to men. Granted, I never knew my father and I didn't have brothers, but I have been making my way in this man's world for a number of years and I know they are a law unto themselves."

Mrs. McDonald laughed. "Truer words were never spoken. God bless 'em. Guess I'll be turning in, ma'am. Good night."

"Good night, Mrs. McDonald."

The cook paused and seemed to struggle with something she wanted to say. Finally she sighed and met Adele's gaze. "I'll always have a soft spot for your mister. He made me respect myself again. Every time somebody calls me 'Mrs. McDonald' I hold my head up higher. Mr. Reno made me believe that I could walk away from the saloon life and he helped me. I'll be forever in his debt." She gave a short laugh. " 'Course, I never told him this, because I know it would embarrass him. But I wanted to tell you, 'cause you have a lot to be proud of in him. You just got to look real close to see it sometimes."

Adele wanted to hug the woman. "Thank you, Mrs. McDonald. I'm glad you told me." She exchanged a smile with her before Mrs. McDonald climbed the stairs to her room.

Her thoughts scurried back to the day Reno had hired the cook, and she felt ashamed of herself. She hadn't been charitable. She'd wanted Reno to take Mrs. McDonald back to the saloon. That wasn't like her, being so narrow-minded and not seizing an opportunity to help someone embark on a better life. Had her struggles in the past few years hardened her, made her think only of herself?

She pushed aside the troubling thought, confident she had a gentle heart, too gentle at times. But to be honest she also knew she had formed a bad opinion of anyone who worked in saloons and gaming halls. Too many lives were ruined in those places. However, she'd lost sight of the fact that not everyone who worked in those devil dens was there entirely by choice, but often by coercion. Adele knew from experience that a woman alone in the world was vulnerable and that her choices were few.

Smiling when she recalled Mrs. McDonald's testimony to Reno's goodness, she decided she really should cut him some slack. Oh, she would have liked to have witnessed his altercation with Yancy Stummer! But a niggling fear sent a chill through her heart when she thought of Buck Wilhite. That man was dangerous, and she worried about Reno crossing swords with that heartless killer.

She didn't want to lose him. She was falling in love with him. Shaking her head at that and still finding it stunning and sweet and totally unexpected, she wondered if he had any inkling that her feelings toward him had deepened, become more complex and almost full to bursting.

From the corner of her eye, she caught movement outside and her heart stopped, then started beating again when she recognized the petite figure of Little Nugget.

She was probably coming around to see Mrs. McDonald and make sure she had escaped harm, Adele thought, rising to unlock the restaurant door. Nearly everybody in town had been by to look at the damage for themselves and speculate on who could have done it. Of course, anyone who had half a brain knew who was behind the destruction.

"I bet you're looking for Mrs. McDonald," Adele said. "She has already retired upstairs to her room. Shall I get her for you?"

"No." Little Nugget stepped inside and examined the damage. "Is she okay? Are you okay?"

"Yes, everyone is fine. Reno had a close call, but he's in no danger now." Adele motioned to a chair. "Would you care to sit down?"

"Thanks." With a swish of her skirts, Little Nugget settled in the chair. A stylish midnight-blue hat sat atop her pale blond hair and matched the fine, perfectly fitted dress of linen and lace. She smoothed her black gloves more tightly over her small hands. "Have you heard about the fight in town today?"

"As a matter of fact, Mrs. McDonald informed me of that a few minutes ago. I suppose Reno didn't think I'd be interested." Adele sat opposite the young woman and smiled, letting her in on the joke. "Did you witness the spectacle?" A thought struck her. "Your boss didn't send you here with a message for me or Reno, did he?"

Little Nugget shook her head and wrinkled her nose, as if she found the idea ludicrous. "Do I look like a carrier pigeon to you? I'm sure Taylor isn't leaping for joy, but if he was going to send a message, I figure he'd send it with your friend Sally Baldridge."

"Hmmm, well, Sally and I are not getting along right now."

"Besides, Taylor sent you a message last night." Little Nugget raised her head to eye the planks covering most of the windows.

The light from the oil lamp on the table flowed across Little Nugget's piquant features and illuminated the dark circle under her right eye and her split and puffy lower lip. Adele sucked in a breath and shot out one hand, gripping Little Nugget's arm.

"What happened to you? Did Terrapin do that?" she asked with a wince.

"A saloon customer last night who got too rambunctious. I didn't like his manner and told him so. He didn't like my mouth, so he slugged me. Taylor didn't like me telling off his customer and he took a swing at me, too."

"Why don't you leave?"

"Why don't you cut loose your pal and let her and Taylor get on with their wedding?"

"She signed a work contract. If I let her break it, what will keep my other waitresses from doing the same thing?"

Little Nugget shrugged. "I don't reckon the others will want to leave. This is a good place. Got a roof over your head, three meals a day, fair pay, and the work ain't too tirin'."

"Because we hire respectable young ladies here, mostly from the East, they are popular with local men. We had trouble keeping our workers, so now we have them sign a contract, promising to remain one year."

"Respectable ladies," Little Nugget murmured. "Doris ain't respectable, is she?"

"Well, I made an exception there. She's the cook and stays in the kitchen."

"Hidden." Little Nugget smiled at Adele's discomfort. "That's okay. She'd rather be hidden in that kitchen than be on display at the saloon."

"What about you? Wouldn't you rather work here?"

"Maybe. But I couldn't." Little Nugget smoothed her gloves again, keeping her head bowed.

"Why not? Mrs. McDonald fits in. So would you. I bet you'd make a good waitress. I'll need another one when Sally leaves." Adele felt good making the offer. "Won't you think about it?"

"Nothing to think about. I couldn't do the work."

"Not do the work? Oh, there's nothing to it. You might have to take some joshing from the customers, but that will disappear soon enough. Before you know it, everyone will forget that you used to work at the saloon."

Little Nugget shook her head. "I can't."

"Don't say that word. You can. You need only—"

"I can't read nor write nor do numbers," Little Nugget blurted out, her gaze snapping up to collide with Adele's. Fragile pride glittered in her eyes and trembled on her lips. "I couldn't write down no orders or read no menus or add up any bills."

Adele was speechless for a few moments. Staring at the young woman across the table from her, she saw her anew. Little Nugget was seventeen and had no formal education. She worked in a saloon, being sold to men who cared nothing for her. Beaten and degraded, she had nonetheless held onto her pride, her integrity.

"You never went to school?" Adele asked.

"Nope. My pa never stayed put long. He went from gold strike to gold strike. After my mama died, nobody cared much for schooling. Even before she died, none of us were made to go to the schoolhouse, so we mostly stayed around the house and helped Mama and Papa in the fields."

"You could learn to read and write. One of the women you work with would probably teach you."

"None of them know such things either. Why do you think we do what we do?" She ran the tip of her finger along the edge of the bruise that marred her youthful beauty. "We don't like being knocked around and having babies by men we don't even know by name."

Adele sat straighter. "You have a baby?"

"Not yet, but I will."

"You're pregnant?"

Little Nugget shook her head. "No, but my luck will run out someday and I'll catch. Every other saloon gal I ever met has had babies or lost babies. But when you don't have no schooling, there ain't much you can do to get money. Once I worked doing laundry for a hotel, but the hotel owner came by my room late one night and raped me." Tears collected in her eyes and she wiped them away with swift impatience. "I packed up and hit the trail the next day. I wasn't going to stick around and let him have seconds."

Adele shivered involuntarily, her heart going out to the young woman. She couldn't imagine such a life. "I feel so sorry for you."

"Don't." Little Nugget's tone was bedrock hard, but her eyes were vulnerable. Pride tipped up her chin. "I'm not telling you this so you'll get all weepy for me. I'm telling you so you know why I can't work here. I'd be about as useful to you as a pump with no handle."

"How many women in this town can't read or write?" Adele asked. "Besides yourself, how many would you say?"

"Maybe a dozen. More, probably."

Adele tapped her fingers on the tabletop as an idea formed and sparked her enthusiasm. She felt her mother's spirit rise within her. "I could teach you."

"Huh?"

"I could teach you!" Adele laughed, tickled by the sheer pleasure the task would give her. "I could hold classes for you and any others in this town who would like to learn to read and write. I could even teach simple addition and subtraction."

"Why would you do that?" Little Nugget asked, clearly baffled. "There are plenty of others here in Whistle Stop who already know those things and would be glad to work here for you."

"Oh, I'm not worried about finding workers. All I have to do is place an advertisement in an East Coast newspaper and I'm up to my neck in replies. I think every grown woman should know how to read and write." She sandwiched one of Little Nugget's gloved hands between her own. "I could hold the classes on Sunday afternoons. You don't work then, do you?"

"No. The saloon and gaming hall are closed on Sundays. Terrapin doesn't want any trouble with the ministers and holy rollers."

"That's perfect then. The restaurant is closed on Sundays, too. We could meet right after church here at the restaurant, and I'll hold class. You'd need a few supplies, but I can get those. I'll send off for schoolbooks, writing paper and inkwells and pens."

"I don't know." Little Nugget averted her gaze, and Adele could see that she was uncomfortable. "Taylor won't like it."

"Then don't tell him. You want to learn, don't you?"

"Yeah, but why would you do this? You work hard every day. You don't want to be teaching classes on Sundays when you could be resting or visiting with your friends or being with your handsome husband."

Adele felt her cheeks heat, but she pressed on. "Spending a few hours on Sunday to help others help themselves will be good for me." She squeezed the young woman's hand. "Please, Miss Little. I *want* to do this. Will you help me spread the word?"

A shy smile curved Little Nugget's swollen mouth. "Sure. I guess."

"Splendid!" Adele let go of her hand and sat back in the chair, relieved to have struck a deal. She smiled back at Little Nugget, catching something else in the girl's expression. "What? Why are you looking at me like that?"

"You remind me of someone."

"Oh? Who?"

"Someone I met when I was a girl. Her name was Miss Tess Summar. She was full of ideas and wanted to help everybody who crossed her path, too." Tugging at her gloves, she smiled tenderly. "She gave me my first pair of these. She said a lady never goes out without wearing a suitable hat and pretty gloves on her hands."

"Was she—?"

Little Nugget seemed confused for a moment, then she caught on. "You mean a whore? No. Miss Summar was a fine lady. A doctor or nurse or something. I only knew her a few days, but I've never forgotten her kindness, her good heart." Giving a sigh, she stood. "I'll run upstairs for a minute to see Dead-eye Doris, if you don't mind, then I'll be on my way."

"Why did you want to speak to me tonight?"

"I wanted to make sure everyone was all right." She glanced at the windows. "He won't stop at this. He squashes anything that gets in his way."

"You came to warn me?" Adele asked, surprised by the gesture.

"Yes, and to warn Doris. Taylor is still making noise about making her come back to work for him. He's got me worried. He's like a stick of dynamite waiting for a match. Anyway, you probably don't need to be warned. You're a smart lady and you know you've riled Taylor." She moved toward the stairs. "When will these classes start up?"

"Next Sunday."

"I'll be here. Good night, Mrs. Adele."

"Good night." Adele sat alone in the restaurant. A knot tightened in her stomach. Was she being stubborn to the point of foolishness?

She didn't believe that Taylor Terrapin would kill her over this point of contention, but then what did she really know about the man? He could have killed women before for inconsequential things. From what Little Nugget said, he was capable of anything. It was obvious that she was worried for Mrs. McDonald's safety and for her own.

Why couldn't Sally see the evil in Terrapin? How could she love a man who hit women, who threatened to kill them?

Moving quietly into her quarters, Adele eased toward the bedroom, not wanting to disturb Reno. He needed his rest, especially after what he'd done this afternoon. Why, that rascal, sneaking off to chase down that skunk Yancy—

"Well, God's nightgown," Adele whispered, staring at the empty bed. "I'll kill him!"

Under cover of night Reno met with his banker.

Paul Green glanced around nervously as he let Reno slip in the back door of the bank.

"Did you get the money?"

"Came in this morning," Paul said, moving past Reno to his office at the back of the building. "Quite a lot of money, I might add. Who is this Lewis Fields?"

"My business partner."

"What kind of business?" Paul asked, sitting behind his desk and looking official.

"Anything illegal—slave trade, of course." Reno grinned at Paul's startled expression. "That's what you were expecting me to say, wasn't it?"

Paul cleared his throat and had the good grace to blush. "I was hoping for the truth."

"The truth." Reno sighed. "That's almost as exciting as the lie I just told. Suffice it to say, Paul, that our business is legitimate. I wanted the money sent because I've decided to purchase a building here in this cowardly little town and give the people a taste of Reno Gold's way of doing business. I figure Terrapin's had it to himself long enough." Grinning broadly, Reno hooked his thumbs into his vest pockets. "Competition can be fun."

"Competition?" Paul swallowed hard. "Just what are you scheming this time, Reno?"

"I'm not scheming. I'm dealing. I made a deal with a man named Gus Franklin today. He saw me whip Yancy Stummer and he wanted to shake my hand. Later we shook on a certain building he owns and was looking to sell."

"Gus owns several buildings." Paul started ticking them off on his fingers. "Two houses on Broad Street, the land building, the old Rusty Kettle Saloon—"

Reno made a gun out of his hand and "shot" the banker. "There you go. The saloon."

Paul blinked and stared, dumbfounded. "The saloon. What are you planning to do with that barn of a place?"

"Oh, I thought I'd open it up for business. I telegraphed for a load of whiskey and beer to be sent by rail. It should be here by the end of the week."

Paul ran a hand down his face. "I don't believe you, Gold. Have you lost your ever lovin' mind? Opening a saloon across the street from Terrapin's Black Knight? He won't stand for that."

"Then he can damn well sit for it," Reno said, giving a devilish wink, "'cause I'm going to open me a saloon." He swept a hand in front of him in a grand gesture. "The Lucky Strike. How does that sound to you?"

"Like a bad idea."

"Why?"

"Because Terrapin—"

"No more talk about Terrapin," Reno demanded, swiping aside the subject. "I'm sick of hearing about him. I'm not going to tuck tail and run every time he strides down the street."

The banker groaned. "I hope you know what you're doing."

"I do." Reno leaned forward and lowered his voice, although there was no one to overhear. "Let's keep this between you and me for awhile. I want the town to be buzzing about the saloon being sold and all, but I don't want anyone to know who bought it until the grand opening."

"You can't keep a secret like that for long."

"Let's keep it for as long as possible. The anticipation will breed gossip, and the gossip will be better than the truth. Terrapin will be running in circles trying to figure out who's aiming to be his competition."

"He's not stupid. He'll probably figure it's you."

"Then you start the first rumor, Paul. You tell Terrapin that the money for the saloon was wired in from the East from a man named Fields."

"You don't want your name mentioned. That's smart."

"No, you can tell Terrapin I'm going to run the place." Reno laughed. "Just don't tell him I'm the owner. I want to keep that to myself for awhile."

"Why?"

Reno sobered. He didn't want to tell the banker that he had been keeping a naughty little secret from Adele concerning his wealth. Adele deserved to know the truth before anyone else was told.

"Like I said, let the flames of gossip be fanned," Reno said. "Terrapin will find out soon enough that it's my money taking his."

"You've done well for yourself, haven't you?" Paul asked, leaning back in his office chair to give Reno a thorough once-over.

"Well enough."

"In the goldfields?"

"I hit it lucky," Reno allowed. "But I also worked hard to keep what I had and to add to it. I even ran into Terrapin up there in the golden hills."

"You did?"

"I heard about him before I saw him. It was in Deadwood. Terrapin killed a man—cut his throat during the night—and stole the old boy's money and other belongings. Like most cowards, he winnowed out the weak ones and went in for the kill. He never challenged anybody he wasn't sure he could whip, rape, or kill. Now he's got enough money to hire his dirty work done for him."

"I hope Buck Wilhite doesn't kill you for Terrapin."

"Don't worry about me, Paul. I'm a lucky son of a bitch."

"I'm surprised you're up and about today after what happened last night. I heard you got hit in the head."

"Yes, but my head is hard. Hadn't you noticed?"

Paul chuckled. "I reckon I have, at that."

"I'm okay. My head was spinning like a water wheel for a few hours, but that passed. Of course, I didn't let on that I was feeling fine, because I enjoyed Dellie buzzing around me." He shared a lascivious smile with the banker. "Guess I'll be getting back home for some more of her sweet medicine, if you know what I mean."

"Oh, I know," Paul assured him. "There's nothing better than a woman treating a man like a conquering hero."

"I'm her hero all right." Reno stood up and shook Paul's hand. "I appreciate you helping me out with this business deal, Paul. Remember, I'm just running the place for a rich man named Fields."

"I'll remember. And you remember to watch your back."

Reno slipped out the rear door of the bank and walked to the depot. He hummed happily to himself, caught up in his plans to refurbish the saloon and entice Terrapin's customers over to his side of the street.

Nearing the train depot, he saw lights on in Dellie's quarters. She'd be wondering where he'd gone. He'd tell her he'd been out for a walk, stretching his legs and clearing his aching head. He'd stumble and lurch a little, and she'd help him to her bed. Ah, yes. Her sweet-smelling bed.

The restaurant door opened, letting out a square of yellow light. Adele stepped outside, her slim figure casting a spire of shadow.

"Hey there," Reno called out, giving a wave so that she was sure to see him. "I'm home, darlin'."

He squinted, wondering what she held in her hands. It was long and cumbersome. She lifted it slowly and aimed it right at him.

Reno had only a moment to shout and jump before the shotgun coughed, and dust and clods of earth erupted no more than a foot in front of him.

"What the hell are you doing, Dellie!" he yelled, angry and edgy. There was nothing more dangerous than a woman with a firearm.

"We've had trouble around here, and I'm shooting any weasel that comes crawling around after dark."

"It's me, damn it all, woman! It's your husband."

"My husband?" She lowered the weapon a few inches. "My husband is in bed, where I left him. He's too weak to be out at this time of night. He knows I would be worried sick if he ventured out of his bed."

Reno heaved a weary sigh, recognizing her game. "I'm sorry, sugar. I had business in town."

"Who did you beat up this time?"

He went still, realizing she knew more than he'd thought. "You can't be mad at me for teaching Yancy Stummer to choose his friends more carefully. He deserved what he got and you know it."

"All I know is that you have a knot on your head and should be in bed."

"When you're right, you're right." He started forward, but she fired off another round, stopping him in his tracks. This time she missed the toes of his boots by inches. "Dellie, this isn't funny. I'm getting mad now. Put down that shotgun before you hurt someone."

Mrs. McDonald came rushing out, her hair and nightgown flowing behind her. "What's going on? Who's shooting?"

"I'm shooting," Adele told her calmly. "We're closed for the night, Mr. Gold," Adele called to him. "I put your cot out in that shed you've almost completed. Good night. We'll see you in the morning."

"Dellie, damn it all!" He started forward again, but stopped when she lifted the weapon and placed him in its sights.

"And don't try to break down any of these doors or I'll aim true and pick off some of your toes. My aunt taught me how to use this shotgun, and if you'll recall, she won a blue ribbon for target shooting every year at the Kansas county fair."

Reno stood his ground as Adele pivoted sharply and ushered Mrs. McDonald inside ahead of her. He didn't move toward the shed until the lights went off in the building. He did remember about her aunt being a crack shot and he was partial to his toes.

Chapter 15

Standing at the restaurant door, Adele said goodbye to each of her new students, all seventeen of them.

Seventeen! She had expected to see Little Nugget and a couple of her friends at the first class and had been surprised when women kept arriving, shy and hesitant, but eager to learn to read and write.

"You look downright bewildered," Little Nugget said, the last one to leave that Sunday afternoon.

"I didn't expect . . . that is, I thought these women knew their letters and numbers. I've seen them around town, shopping and making purchases."

"When you're ignorant, you get real clever at hiding it," Little Nugget said, looking demure and sweet in a pretty, cream-colored dress with a straw bonnet and tan gloves. Adele suspected she was something of a clothes horse.

"None of you is ignorant," Adele asserted. "You weren't provided with lives in which school was important, but you are rectifying that now. That's what is important."

"And we have you to thank." Little Nugget gave Adele's arm a quick squeeze. "Thanks. See you next week, and don't be surprised if several others show up. Word will get around about this, and women will be coming out of the walls!" Laughing, she glided out of the door and walked briskly toward the heart of town as if she had not a care in the world. But Adele knew different.

Watching her, Adele felt sad and angry and helpless. If only she could provide an escape for those women working in Terrapin's saloon. Though she'd tried to hide it, Little Nugget had been beaten again. No visible bruises or cuts this time, but Adele had noticed the stiffness in her, how she'd sat down and stood up so gingerly, one hand pressed to her ribs, her expression carefully composed so as not to show discomfort. It made Adele's blood boil.

To calm herself and work off her anger, Adele straightened up the restaurant, moving tables and chairs back to their proper places, then went outside into the afternoon sunlight. The sound of sawing drew her to the back of the property, where she knew she'd find Reno working on the shed. Since the night she'd shot at him, four days ago, he had spent his evenings in the shed and his days busy with chores and putting finishing touches to his new home. He was mad at her, punishing her for putting him out of her quarters.

She hated to admit it, even to herself, but she missed him. In fact, she was more jumpy and nervous without him nearby. Now that the windows had been shot out, she feared another retaliation, and having Reno a few steps away had been a comfort.

There was more to her missing him, she knew. She craved his attentions, his sexy teasing, his special glances and lingering looks. Her pulse began to thrum, and she tried to stem the tide of her constant yearning, frightened that she might be swept away and do something crazy.

'Fraidy cat, she called herself. *Afraid of your own thoughts, your own feelings. What's so scary? Maybe that you care deeply for him, perhaps even want him to make love to you.* She slammed the door on that possibility, finding it too powerful, like him.

Reno came into view, carrying a load of two-by-fours as if they weighed less than nothing. He didn't see her. She stood statue-still, so as not to draw his notice, affording herself a chance to admire him, shirtless and sweating, his torso gleaming and rippling, the dusting of hair on his chest slick and swirled. Her palms grew moist and her breath hitched in her throat. Good Lord, he was gorgeous!

In profile his chest and arms bulged with muscle. Work pants and work boots were his only clothing, leaving his lean, hard body exposed to her inspection. Rivulets of perspiration glimmered on his tanned skin like tiny streams struck by sunlight. His trousers fitted tightly across his backside and intimately cupped his manhood. Adele tried not to stare there, but her gaze kept coming back to that particular bulge, and her imagination flourished.

Lovemaking. What would that be like? Not just spooning, courting and deep kissing. She'd done those things. But never full, intimate, free-as-a-bird lovemaking. Never that. She hadn't even discussed it with her women friends. Her mother had talked to her about the actual act, at first making it sound strictly biological, then admitting that it was more than that.

"Oh, you feel all sorts of things if you have the right man in bed with you," Victoria Bishop had told her only child. "None of which I can aptly describe. Words aren't enough, Adele. One must feel certain things. I hope—oh, I *sincerely* hope—that you do feel those things. Those wondrous, heaven-sent emotions . . ." Her voice had faded away and her eyes had softened with dreamlike visions.

Instinct assured Adele that Reno was the right man to summon those indescribable sensations in her. As he bent to sort through the lumber, his sinewy muscles undulated beneath his skin. A knot formed in Adele's throat. Reno straightened and ran both hands through his sweat-dampened hair, exposing tufts of coal-black hair in his armpits. Then he ran a hand down his chest—his chest, with its whorls of curling hair on deeply tanned skin, the nipples small and diamond-hard. Turning his back to her, he moved with easy grace to a bucket. Lifting it high, he tipped the vessel, and a stream of water sluiced over his face and down his chest. He set the bucket down and shook his head, flinging water droplets off his wet hair.

Adele's heart beat wildly, sending blood rushing to her extremities and making her light-headed. She feared she might pass out, so she started to retreat. That's when he spotted her.

"Hey there," he called out to her. "You want something?"

Oh, yes. She wanted something. Adele forced herself to face him again. He wore a scowl, his expression of choice for her this week. When she didn't speak up, he splayed his long-fingered hands on his hips and tipped his head to one side.

"What's wrong now?" He cupped a hand to his ear. "Speak up, lady."

"I . . . nothing." Adele shook her head, hating the breathlessness in her voice.

He strode forward. "Through with your hen party? What are you doing, plotting to castrate the men in town?"

She flinched at his venom. My, my, he was on a tear! "I was not having a hen party. I was conducting a class."

"A class, huh? What are you teaching them? How to place an advertisement and get yourself a human mule?"

Adele withstood his growling tirade. "I was teaching them to read and write," she answered calmly. "I offered the instruction to Little Nugget, and we struck on the idea of seeing if any other women would like to learn. Today was our first class." She hitched up her skirts a fraction and spun about, intent on leaving him and his scowling and growling.

"Hold up there."

He moved so quickly that Adele let out a gasp of surprise when his hand closed on her arm and stopped her. His palm was calloused and hot to the touch. Her gaze flew to him and charged the air between them.

"Did you say you were teaching them how to read and write?"

"Yes." She found she could not look away from him, entranced as she was by the strong planes of his face, the streaks of sweat and water, the glisten of water drops on the tips of his hair, the musky smell of him.

"You're teaching whores how to read and write," he repeated.

"Not just ... *Any* woman who missed out on her formal education. I thought it might lead to Little Nugget breaking away from Terrapin and that life."

To her astonishment Reno smiled. "Well, well, if it isn't Victoria Bishop's feisty, crusading daughter. Where have you been hiding, Dellie?" He dipped his head until his eyes were even with hers. "Your mother would be proud, sugar. Hell, *I'm* proud of you."

She nearly preened in front of him. Sweeping her lashes down, she felt her skin grow warm with embarrassment. He took her hands in his and held them lightly.

"Oh, Dellie," he said in a singsong tone, "what do you think about the shed?"

"The shed?" She leaned sideways to see past him. The shed didn't look any different from the way it looked the last time she'd seen it. "It's nice."

"It's finished."

"That's good." Meaning dropped like a stone into her mind, and her gaze jumped to his again. "Fin ished?"

"All finished," he assured her.

"I heard you sawing."

"I'm making a wash stand for your laundry tubs, so you can stand straight to scrub the clothes and not have to bend over and give yourself backaches. I finished the shed this morning."

"Inside and out?"

"Inside and out," he assured her. "I figure that calls for something special from you."

She retreated, but could not move far, because he held onto her hands. Heat burst through her, making her knees tremble and her blood catch fire. She was afraid he'd see the hunger in her eyes.

"Can I come around tonight, say 'round about eight?" he asked, his thumbs moving lightly across her palms, making them tingle.

She nodded, unable to speak.

"See you then. Don't bring the shotgun."

His fingers stroked hers as they slipped away. Released, she turned and moved awkwardly toward the restaurant, her limbs trembling and her heartbeats booming in her ears. She prayed he wasn't watching her jerky retreat, but when she reached the door and glanced briefly over her shoulder, she discovered that her prayer had gone unanswered. He was not only watching her, he was loving it.

Grinning like a monkey, he sent her a wink and a wave before returning to his work. Mortified, Adele shut herself inside for the rest of the day, a day that seemed never-ending.

Hours dragged by and minutes stood still as Adele suffered through the rest of the afternoon and early evening. She found she couldn't eat, could barely think coherently. Reno wanted a special reward, and she had promised to give him one once that shed was finished.

Adele found herself staring at her bed, knowing she would not sleep alone in it tonight. So she changed the linens and sprinkled rose water across the pillow cases.

He found her standing before the full-length mirror in her bedroom, staring at herself. Dressed in soft, white, layered lace, she was a vision to him. Her hair, held at the crown of her head by invisible pins, was dark and lustrous, framing a face that had become more dear to him with each passing day.

His Dellie. He'd found her again. He'd rediscovered her sweetness, her gaiety, her compassion. And in return she had unearthed the boy in him, that shy, rebellious, smitten boy who had fallen in love with a great lady in the making.

God knew he should be madder than hell at her for shooting at him. But he wasn't. In fact, that night had taught him something about Dellie. She liked him. She liked him a whole hell of a lot. With a little coaxing, she might even fall in love with him.

She frowned, as if she didn't like the woman in the mirror. Reno couldn't have that.

"Don't change a thing. You're beautiful."

Spinning around, her mouth agape, she rested one hand over her heart and the other against the wide pink ribbon circling her waist.

"You startled me. I . . . I was . . ." She glanced down at her dress. "This was the last dress my mother bought for me. She said it made me look angelic."

"She was right."

"But angelic might not be how you would want me to look this evening."

Reno arched his brows and chuckled. "You think I would rather have you looking devilish? Maybe in a red dress, the bodice low-cut and saucy?" He shook his head. "Like I said, don't change a thing." He held out the box of chocolates he'd bought for her at the General Store. "Here you go."

She accepted it, her fingers gliding over the top of the red box with its gold lettering. "I thought *I* was to give *you* a sweet reward."

He noticed the tremor in her voice and the trembling in her hands. Gliding a fingertip down her cheek, he sought her gaze and held it. "Are you nervous?"

"Yes," she said, sighing the word. "Oh yes. I think I might be ill. I'm certain I'm about to faint . . ."

He caught her up in his arms just as her knees gave way. "Whoa there, darlin'." He laughed, surprised that she felt nearly weightless. "Have you eaten anything today?"

She shook her head. "Not since breakfast. I couldn't. My stomach is all aflutter."

He kissed the end of her nose. "Dellie, you are a trial. How can I ravish you when you're out cold?" He strode through her quarters and out to the restaurant.

"Where are we going now?" she asked, wrapping her arms around his neck.

"To the kitchen to rustle up some grub."

"No, I can't eat. I tell you, I won't be able to keep it down."

"Yes, you will." He set her in one of the kitchen chairs and rolled up the sleeves of his white shirt. "Something light, I think. Shaved ham and eggs? That ought to put some color back into your cheeks. And a big glass of milk to give you strength." He wagged a finger at her. "Shame on you, Dellie. You own a restaurant and you don't eat?" He made a *tsk* sound.

Reno added wood to the stove and stoked the embers into shooting flames. In the span of twenty minutes he had set a plate of eggs and ham before her and poured her a glass of fresh milk. Sitting opposite her, he watched her eat, smiling his approval of each bite.

To her surprise Adele discovered her appetite. Her stomach settled into normalcy as a strange peace spread over her. Gazing into Reno's eyes, she knew a perfect calm. He cared for her. He wanted her to be well, to be whole and strong more than he wanted her to be his lover tonight. That made her love him and want to please him all the more.

She noticed that he was freshly shaved and washed. She could smell lye soap drifting off his skin and a faint aroma of talcum powder. His shirt was clean, his black tie knotted perfectly, his black trousers knife-pleated. He'd combed his hair until it shone in the lamplight, black and glossy as a raven's wing. His blue eyes were warm tonight and glittering with a thousand twinkles.

Oh, he was a handsome man, without a doubt, and Adele could hardly believe he was hers.

"You're not mad at me?" she asked, breaking the comfortable silence that had settled between them.

He shrugged and took an apple from a bowl on the table. "I can't stay mad at you, Dellie." After grabbing a knife from a rack near him, he began peeling the red fruit. "I don't like sleeping in the shed. You miss me at night? I surely do miss you."

Smiling, she knew her cheeks were as red as the

apple he held in his big hands. "I miss you. I never realized until this week how comforting it is to have a man around, especially when other men are given to shooting up your residence."

"That won't happen again."

"At least Yancy won't do it again. I hear he was laid up for days after that run-in with you."

"That fella is as dumb as a stump." The knife sliced through the last of the peel, and a long, continuous strip of red fell to the table. Reno cut a wedge of apple and held it out to her. "Here's a change. Man offering a bite of apple to Woman. Tempted?"

Feeling devilish, she leaned forward and opened her mouth. Reno slipped the apple slice between her lips, then cut himself a bite, never taking his gaze from her. His eyes glittered with anticipation and she loved it.

He continued to dole out the fruit, a slice for her, then one for him, until it was gone. Tossing the core and peeling into the slop bucket, he wiped the juice from his hands and faced Adele across the table.

"Dellie, I mean to make love to you tonight. How does that sit with you?"

She swallowed hard. "I didn't . . . I don't . . ."

"You didn't think I was going to?" he asked, clearly surprised.

"Well, yes, I knew you were going to try." Her nerves were back again, fluttering through her like a hundred startled moths. "I just didn't think you'd come out and tell me like this."

"When it comes to important things in life, I like to lay my cards on the table. I think I've been more than patient. We've been married a spell now, and I haven't taken anything that wasn't offered. I don't want to take anything from you tonight that you aren't willing to give me. I'm assuming I'll be your first lover."

Her mouth had suddenly gone as dry as dust. She nodded and struggled to locate her voice. "I'm assuming I won't be yours."

His grin was lop-sided and self-mocking. "No, sugar, you won't be, but that doesn't make this any less special for me. Hell, I've been wanting you for most of my life, Dellie. I remember just like it was yesterday that afternoon we were in the hayloft and I kissed you. Kissed you deep with my tongue. Lord, I thought I'd bust right there, I wanted you so bad. You remember that?"

"Yes." Oh yes, she remembered. She had felt ashamed and excited and confused all at once. His tongue kissing had certainly sent her into a spin. "I didn't know what to make of it," she confessed. "I even thought I might get pregnant."

"Pregnant?" He widened his eyes and released a hoot of laughter. "From kissing? You weren't that green, were you?"

"It was the ... invasion that confused me. I knew that invasion or inserting body parts led to pregnancy. Anyway, I spoke to my mother later and she assured me I was still a virgin, but she also warned me not to allow you to kiss me that way again."

"Did she?" He winked. "You disobeyed."

"Yes, well ..." Adele shrugged and then laughed softly. "That was a minor rebellion, I suppose. But I felt that I was betraying Winston by letting you ... well, kiss me and touch me."

"Win and your mama aren't in our way anymore, Dellie," he said, his voice low and pulsating with a pagan note that warmed her blood. He slipped a hand across the table, palm up. "Come along and let me take you."

Those words, brimming with meaning, enchanted her. She placed her hand in his with certainty and confidence. His fingers closed around hers with the same.

Hand in hand they walked to her parlor, where a single lamp cast its golden glow. Reno traced the shape of her face with his fingertips, his gaze taking her in, making her feel infinitely beautiful.

In his face she could trace his ancestry. His Gypsy blood was evident in his thickly lashed eyes, which held romanticism, bravery, and passion in their mysterious depths. His mouth was Gypsy too, she fancied, because it was erotic and sensuous, naughty and generous, rakish and roguish. His Cheyenne and Cherokee bloodlines were found in his silky black hair, his teak-colored skin, his proud, slashing cheekbones. His nose was French, patrician and bold.

His face told the story of his people and of him. Brash and passionate, handsome and proud.

What did her face tell him? she wondered. Did it reveal her growing love or her fettered passion? He had to see in her eyes that she wanted him and only him but that she was afraid she wouldn't please him. She knew so much about other things, but so little about this.

"Reno," she ventured, "what should I do?"

"Nothing. I'll do everything."

"But that isn't fair."

His lips brushed hers. "All is fair in love and war, my darling Dellie. You've been teaching all day. Now let me teach you a few things."

She laughed lightly against his lips. "That sounds lovely. I shall be a most attentive pupil."

He lifted his hands to her head and removed the pins, letting her hair fall heavily to her shoulders and down her back. He combed it with his fingers and kissed her lips again before bringing a handful of her hair to his nose as if it were a bouquet of exquisite blooms.

"When I catch the scent of you, I respond," he murmured. "At night when I slept in here, I could smell you all over this room, and that alone made me miserable with longing."

Was he truly saying these things to her? she wondered. The words fell off his tongue like honey, coating her senses and calming her nerves. His voice was a benediction, his touch, a potion.

"Did you ever waste a thought on me lying out here on my cold, hard cot?"

"Every hour of every night," she assured him. "It's a wonder I got any sleep."

He smiled. "Sweet liar."

"No, it's true." She rested her hands on his broad shoulders. "I did think of you and wondered if you thought of me. When you spent your nights away from here, I knew you were in the arms of another woman."

"Yes, and her name is Lady Luck." He moved forward, making her walk backward to the bedroom. "I swear I was playing poker with the banker and his friends, Dellie. I was not with any other woman."

She sighed and closed her eyes. "I know, and I'm so very glad to hear that."

He seized the moment to drive his fingers through the side of her hair and tip her head as he slanted his mouth over hers. His lips were warm and insistent, nudging hers apart. The kiss was slick and carnal, growing more so with the flicking of his tongue. She arched against him in wanton submission and felt his arousal press into her. She imagined she could feel the pulsing of his blood, timed to her own. With a tortured moan she sent her tongue across his lips, tasting him and leaving her taste on him.

His hands slipped from her hair to outline the sides of her breasts, her waist, the flare of her hips. She learned from that and smoothed her hands across his shoulders, up his neck and in through the cool silk of his hair. He tasted of sin, dark and rich and too good to be true. Flinging her head back, she gasped for air. He dropped fiery kisses upon the column of her throat down to the lacy neckline of her gown.

The small buttons marching down her spine were no barrier to his quick, sure fingers. One by one they were dispensed with to expose her dainty under-clothes of white cotton and lace and her boned corset. But he was a man of the world, and once again he needed no guidance. He had explored such territory before and knew his way around it.

In stunned silence Adele felt her laces loosen and the rustling slide of her petticoats as they fell to the floor around her feet.

Staring at his necktie, she wondered miserably if she would be able to untie it properly, much less have success with the rest of his clothes. Suddenly feeling woefully inadequate and unsure of herself, she stepped away from him and crossed her arms over her breasts to keep her dress in place.

"What's wrong, Dellie? Are you shy?" he asked. "Want me to lower the light?"

"Douse it," she said. She watched him cross the room to lower the wick. "I do believe you can undress me quicker than I can myself, Reno Gold."

"Ah, is that it?" He sat on the edge of the bed. "Is that what made you retreat from me? Go ahead, if you would rather. Undress yourself. I'll sit here and watch."

"Oh, no, you don't." She sat on the bed next to him. "You want that kind of show, then go find a saloon girl and be ready to pay her handsomely."

Laughing, he pulled her to him. His mouth claimed hers again and his chuckles died as the fire of his desire rose high. Dellie fell back on the bed, no longer concerned with his skills and her lack of them. When he kissed her, open-mouthed and hungry as a wolf, she cared for nothing in the world but to kiss him back. His kiss transported her, transformed her.

Clothing evaporated under his warm, swift hands and she was reduced to her chemise and stockings in no time. He shrugged off his suspenders and unbuttoned his shirt. Pulling it free of his waistband, he then brought her hands to his chest. She released a luxurious sigh, her fingers exploring the springy curls, the flat nipples, the corded muscles. Ah, it was everything she'd imagined! The feel of him, so different, so tough and tender and foreign!

He rained fire-tipped kisses over her face, stamping her mouth over and over until her lips felt bee-stung.

Instinct began to rule her, urging her to stroke his sun-kissed shoulders, to knead his strong back, to caress his ribs while he untied the ribbons of her chemise and parted the fabric to reveal the soft, white globes of her breasts. She saw his eyes glow, and then he dipped his head and his lips circled one of her nipples.

She thought she had died for a moment, but then life and feeling came flooding back to her in a white-hot flash. His tongue flicked over her nipple and he sucked hard. Pleasure corkscrewed in her stomach and shot down her thighs. She clutched his head in her hands as her breath sawed in her throat.

Her mother was right. There were no words.

Reno sensed the quicksilver changes taking place in her body. Through his lashes he watched ecstasy claim her features, drawing her lovely mouth into a sweet pucker and closing her eyes in a near swoon. He wanted this to be unforgettable, but for all the right reasons. Therefore he eased off her and collected himself by gathering his iron self-control.

Folding back the bed covers and plumping the pillows, he sniffed the rose-scented air and smiled. Just like Dellie to make everything smell sweet and delicate. He spread her hair across the pillow and it looked like black fire. Starlight painted her face and shadows played across her beautiful body. After removing the final lacy scraps of her clothing, he kissed her slowly and deeply while he dispensed with his own trousers and underwear. Naked, he came to her, covering her body with his own, warming her cool skin with the heat of his.

Her smile was tremulous, and he knew she was full

of anxiety. He remembered his first time—the awkwardness, the brevity, the acute embarrassment—and he wanted something better for her.

"Aren't you glad you didn't shoot my toes off, Dellie?" he teased, trying to relax her.

She blushed and smiled. "I was mad at you."

"I noticed."

"I'd been fussing over you, afraid you might take a turn for the worse, and then I found out you'd been in town beating up on people. Then you snuck out *again* and went God knows where, leaving me to worry."

"I was visiting with Paul Green, Dellie," he reassured her. "Spending so much time with women makes a man crave man talk. Nothing wrong with that, is there?"

She conceded with a twitch of her lips. "I suppose being around here, around me, is trying."

"Maybe not so much anymore." He trailed a fingertip down her throat to the valley between her breasts. "Mainly I've been trying to keep my hands off you. After tonight that won't be a problem."

"Perhaps," she allowed, mischief dancing in her eyes.

"No perhaps about it," he promised, framing her face in his hands and kissing her soft, giving mouth.

He set about turning her bones to liquid and her qualms to dust by priming her body with moist kisses and feather-light caresses. Gathering her breasts in his hands, he kissed their pink crowns and tongued them to diamond hardness. She writhed beneath him, wrapped in emotions that he knew she could barely understand.

When her legs parted, he settled himself between them, gauging her readiness by the quickening of her breathing and the drumming of her heartbeat. He stroked her smooth stomach and touched the mass of curls. She released a sound of trepidation, so he kissed her lips before exploring further. He was glad to discover that her body had responded and prepared itself for what was to come next.

"I'm glad you waited for me," he whispered, shifting himself against her, positioning himself, sensing her wariness. "Easy, darlin'. I'll be easy."

And he was, gliding into her slick portal, pausing only a second before driving through her final defense. He sensed her moment of pain and kissed her softly and then hungrily, engaging her in the glory so that she would forget the discomfort.

She was honey and cream to him, and he lapped her up with his hands and his mouth and tongue.

With her pulse humming, she gripped his hips and fell into his rhythm. After a few strokes she felt the flames of her passion leap higher and higher still as he rotated his hips slightly and ground his body against hers. She shuddered, her senses clamoring for something just out of reach but vital.

His mouth fastened on hers, pulling at her, tugging at her, tempting her closer to the edge. Her skin became slick, sliding against his and creating an indescrible friction that added to the intensity of their coupling. Pleasure, even passion, were mild, weak words for what she was feeling.

As his pace increased, so did the wildness within her. She clamped her legs around him and lifted her hips to meet his lunges. And then, like a stampede, it was on her. She strained her head back into the pillow, mindless with desire, her body bowed and tensed, shuddering with pure ecstasy.

He bucked against her, and strange, wonderfully sexy sounds emerged from him as he released his seed deep within her.

The beauty of the moment burst in him like a sunrise. She whispered his name. Her fingers clutched at his shoulders, then her mouth moved across his jaw, skimmed his lips, nipped at his earlobe. Holding her, he shared her every tremor and took each soughing breath with her.

He was perspiring and pleasantly weak when he came to himself, back from the towering height of passion. She lay beneath him, her breasts rising and falling, her lips parted, her eyes glimmering with unshed tears. He leaned closer until she closed her eyes, and he kissed the translucent lids and gathered the salty, crystal drops with the tip of his tongue.

"Why are you crying, sugar?"

For a moment he thought she wouldn't answer, then she sighed and a smile teased the corners of her mouth.

"Because there are no words," she said.

He nodded, understanding, then rolled onto his side and pulled her up against him. Wrapping her in his embrace, he felt her body go soft and limp and trusting. His heart swelled with so many feelings that he thought he might shed a few tears himself. It had never been like this before for him. He had never cared so deeply or felt so much.

Recalling the many ribbings he'd given other men

who had been smitten with their wives or wives-to-be, Reno felt shame. Hell, he was the worst of the lot!

He snuggled closer to his Dellie, glad to be caught and happy to be claimed.

Chapter 16

Buzzing around the restaurant the next morning, Adele felt like a new woman. She wondered if any of her customers had noticed. Her fellow workers suspected what had transpired last night and delivered teasing grins and a few suggestive remarks, which Adele accepted good-naturedly. She couldn't be mad at anyone on this glorious morning, she thought, stopping by one of the remaining windows to view the arrival of another train. That was the third one since six. Monday was always a busy day.

She moved closer to the window to see the position of the red ball on its metal pole. The ball had been lowered, which signaled the train engineer to stop at the depot and let the passengers alight. This meant that the trains were running on time and business at the restaurant would be brisk. If the ball was at the top of the pole, it signaled the engineer to highball it, keep on going, because the trains were running late and schedules were skewed. Lately the railroads had worked smoothly with the telegraphers to keep the trains punctual. The ball was rarely hoisted to the top of the pole anymore.

Watching the approach of an iron horse was always exciting for Adele, but she particularly loved to witness the arrival of a night train, with its huge front headlight and twinkling red lanterns on the last car. The monstrous oil-burning headlights were made of brass and glass and emitted enough light to tear through the black fabric of night. The train's low, mournful wail would sound, and the depot flagmen would light their lanterns to signal to the engineer and brakemen. Then the evening's quiet would be shattered by the squeal of brakes, the grinding of metal on metal, the gruff shouts of men, as the massive train slid into Whistle Stop, Indian Territory.

Arms wrapped around her, jolting her from her reverie. Adele released a squeak of alarm before she recognized the voice whispering in her ear.

"Just what do you think you're doing out here, Mrs. Gold?"

"I'm working, Mr. Gold," she said, glancing back at his smiling visage. "And I have been working since five-thirty this morning. I let you sleep in because you looked so adorable. Like a little boy."

"Hmmm." Reno nuzzled her neck. "I might have *looked* that way to you, but I feel very much like a man." He rocked his midsection against her. "Doesn't that feel like a man to you?"

"Stop that," she whispered fiercely, twisting from his embrace. "We're in a public place!"

"So we are." He acknowledged the dozen or so people eating breakfast and the two waitresses serving them. "Looks like you've got things running smoothly, so let's leave this public place for our private little love nest."

"I can't. I have work to do."

"You're the boss, the queen. You can leave the work for the worker bees." His eyes smoldered, reminding her of the delights of last night. "Come along, busy bee. You deserve a day off, don't you? Consider it a"—he grinned—"honeymoon."

Adele couldn't help but laugh and be lured by his delectable offer, but she was ready to refuse until she caught Sally's narrow-eyed, stinging glare. That did it. Adele untied her apron and hung it behind the counter.

"Colleen, I'm taking off the rest of the morning to deal with some personal business. I'll check back in after the noon trade. You and Sally have this well in hand, but should you need me, I'll be in my quarters."

"Yes'm," Colleen said, smiling brightly. "We can handle things in here today." She dimpled at Reno. "You go on."

"You said I could have the afternoon off," Sally said. "I have a fitting scheduled." She hiked up her chin. "For my wedding gown."

Adele controlled the urge to sputter and lambast her. "I'll relieve you of your afternoon shift, Sally, but I'm surprised you're getting fitted this soon. Your wedding is months away."

"Is it?" Sally arched her brows, defying that presumption.

"Don't get started on this now," Reno said, grasping one of Adele's hands and leading her out of the restaurant and into her quarters.

"Did you hear that?" Adele fumed. "She as much as told me that she's planning to be married before her contract has expired."

"And you're surprised?" Reno chided. "Sugar, you are one stubborn woman—and so is Sally Ann." Taking her by both hands, he led her into the bedroom. "You broke my heart, Dellie."

"Broke?" Adele shook her head. "How?"

"By letting me wake up this morning all alone in this cold bed." He fashioned a pitiful expression. "I 'bout near wept."

"I would have loved to have seen that," she retorted with a disbelieving laugh. "You are a silver-tongued devil, Reno Gold."

Oh yes, he is a devil, she thought, examining the dancing lights in his dark eyes and the wicked grin on his attractive mouth. Sweet temptation crooked its finger, and she answered by lifting her hands to her hair and plucking out the pins. She tossed them onto her dressing table and shook out her hair, laughing lightly when Reno clutched his chest and feigned a swoon.

"Darlin', I could watch you do that all damned day."

With memories of last night's lovemaking swimming in her mind, Adele undressed slowly and allowed him to watch, though shyness painted her cheeks rosy and made her avert her own eyes from his. Her peripheral vision revealed to her that he was undressing, too. He hadn't bothered with underwear. He'd known he could tempt her back into his arms and into bed.

When she had shed her final piece of clothing, he swept her off her feet and onto the bed. Lying beside her, he rained hot kisses over her face and breasts and stomach. Adele kept her eyes open this time. Last night she had experienced his lovemaking blindly, too shy and overwhelmed to look at him or what their bodies were doing together. But now, with buttery sunlight seeping through the lacy curtains of her bedroom windows, she stretched like a cat and fastened her gaze on Reno's head of midnight-black hair. His hands slipped over her skin like a breeze. She felt the abrasion of his morning whiskers on her stomach before he surged up her body to kiss her fully on the lips.

To be kissed by him was passion itself. His lips and tongue seduced her. The tip of his tongue tickled the corners of her mouth and his teeth nipped gently at her lower lip. He slanted his mouth one way and then another, gathering her in, making her his, centering her attention on the plucking, sucking kisses so that she hardly noticed when he laced the fingers of one hand with hers and brought that hand down between their bodies.

Her fingers encountered something foreign, but they seemed instinctively to know what to do. Wrapping around the length of hot flesh and hard muscle, her fingers caressed him and moved up and down. He moaned, a sound of pain and pleasure and delirium.

"Dellie, Dellie," he chanted her name.

Adele felt him grow and pulse, and knew he was teetering on the brink of a cataclysm. She stilled her movements, giving him a few moments to recover. She kissed his shoulders and stroked his smooth, muscled back. He kissed her breasts and teased the pouting peaks with his tongue.

And then he was inside her in a swift, shuddering,

sizzling thrust. Adele bent her knees and locked her legs around his hips as he moved in and out of her like a relentless tide. She watched emotions flicker in his eyes and muscles tense in his face. The sight of his pleasure doubled hers. Clinging to him, she bit him lightly on the shoulder while the waves of her own passion climbed higher and higher until she was utterly consumed.

She cried out his name, and he answered with low animal sounds as his body jerked in rapid-fire release.

Drifting back to earth, she realized she was wrapped in his arms and his body was slick and hot and his breathing was ragged and warm against the side of her face. Adele combed his hair with her fingers and closed her eyes against her tears.

She loved him so much it hurt.

As promised, Adele returned to the restaurant in the afternoon. The day had been busy, and Mrs. McDonald was flying around the kitchen, preparing the evening menu, while Colleen and Helen mopped the floor and wiped off the counters. Sally rose regally from her perch on a stool near the cash drawer and untied her apron.

"It's about time you showed up," she said, smoothing her hands over her hair. "We've walked our legs off today. I've never seen so many people getting off those trains in all my life."

"Yeah, and just about everybody in town came in for the noon meal," Helen added, pausing to rinse out her wash rag in a shallow pan of hot water. "We ran out of beans and cornbread about one o'clock, and Mrs. McDonald had to throw together a pot of chicken and rice soup. People ate it up, didn't they, Colleen?"

"Sure did. That Mrs. McDonald is the best cook I've ever seen. She can make leather taste good."

Sally made a face. "I'm leaving now. I'm already running late." She tied her pocket purse to her narrow belt. "I suppose you'll change your tune now about Taylor and his saloon."

Adele furrowed her brow, confused. "Why would I do that?"

"Because of your husband, of course." Sally sniffed with contempt. "And he calls *me* a hypocrite." Then she sashayed out the door.

Adele couldn't make any sense of what Sally had said. Turning toward the other two women, she noticed that they were absorbed in their cleaning. Too absorbed.

"What did Sally mean by that?"

Colleen glanced up from the mop she was wringing out. "She's always talking."

"Yes, but what did she mean?"

Helen shrugged. "Most of the time I don't know what she's yammering about."

Adele rolled her eyes, knowing full well that both women were avoiding the truth. "Why would she think I had changed my mind?"

Mrs. McDonald pushed open the kitchen door. Red-faced and perspiring, she offered up a broad smile. "Whew! I can't believe this place has finally emptied out. How much longer do you reckon it'll be before the next train puffs in?"

Adele checked the clock on the wall. "The next one

is the General Star at six-forty-five, so you've got a little more than an hour."

"That's good. My bread will be ready by then. I got my liver and onions and stewed potatoes done and I just took four apple pies out of the oven." She fanned the door. "Can't you smell 'em?"

"Yes, I sure can," Adele said, breathing in the mouth-watering aroma. "We were just talking about how—"

"Let me guess. I bet you were talking about what every other person has been talking about today." Mrs. McDonald's eyes sparkled with excitement. "About your mister managing the new saloon across the street from the Black Knight." She chuckled and slapped her thigh. "Don't you know that Taylor is busting a gut?"

Adele plopped down on one of the stools at the high counter and shook her head. "Reno is managing *what*?"

Colleen stopped mopping. "You mean he didn't tell you yet?"

"Tell me what?"

"About him and the saloon."

"What's it called?" she asked Helen.

"The sign that went up today says Lucky Strike." Helen swept a hand in front of her in a grand gesture. "They say it will open up by the end of the week. There's a crew in there now hammering and sawing away. Whoever owns it is throwing some money into the place."

Sitting in stunned silence, Adele could do nothing in the next minutes except listen and inwardly deny it all.

"Yeah, and it's supposed to be even bigger than the Black Knight. It'll have gaming tables and a dance floor and a stage. I guess they're planning on bringing in some acting troupes or something," Colleen added.

"There are saloons in Arizona that do that," Mrs. McDonald said. "I worked in one that staged one-act plays and even had some singers and jugglers."

"Excuse me," Adele said, finding her voice. "But what has this got to do with Reno?"

"Like we said, he's the manager," Colleen repeated. "He's going to run the place right under Terrapin's nose!"

Adele might have fainted if Reno hadn't chosen that moment to make an appearance. Grinning cockily, his gaze met hers. In a split second he saw he was in trouble, but before he could do anything about it, Adele's temper struck like lightning. She closed her hand on a tin salt shaker and hurled it at him. He ducked and the shaker bounced off the wall behind him.

"Now what?" he asked, his own anger sparking in his eyes.

"What *else*?" Adele charged, standing to face him. "You, you lying, smooth-talking . . . saloon keeper!"

The wind seemed to leave him in a gush. He slumped and ran a hand down his face. "Aw, hell, I was just coming in to tell you about that. How did you find out?"

"It makes no difference, because you aren't going to be managing that saloon or *any* saloon."

"Says who?"

She looked down the bridge of her nose at him. "Me. Your wife and your boss."

242 DEBORAH CAMP

He glanced at the others and shook his head. "We're not having this discussion in front of an audience, Dellie." He opened the door to her quarters, kicked aside the salt shaker, and gestured for her to go inside. "You ladies will excuse us," he told Colleen and Helen.

"I am the boss here," Adele reminded him, but dropped that quibble. She had bigger fish to fry.

"I wanted to tell you about my business venture before it got around town," Reno began. "Who spilled the beans?"

"The sign is up and the gossip is rife," Adele informed him. "It's called the Lucky Strike."

"That's right." He grinned. "Catchy, huh?"

Adele suddenly felt weepy. The beauty of what they shared had shattered with the news, leaving her to grieve. Sitting on the parlor sofa, she sniffed and held back her tears. "How could you, Reno? This is so humiliating."

"I can't win for losing with you. First you're telling me that I don't have any gumption, any business sense, but when I prove you wrong by opening up a business in town, you say you're humiliated. I wish you'd make up your mind."

"Don't act stupid around me, Reno Gold. You know very well that I would never approve of any husband of mine running a saloon. If you do this, you're no better than Taylor Terrapin."

"That's where you're wrong. I'm going to run a respectable saloon."

"There is no such thing."

"Are you an expert on saloons, Dellie?"

"I know that they sell women in them."

"Not in mine," he assured her. "There will be gambling, some stage shows, liquor, of course, but no rooms for rent upstairs."

"One thing this town does *not* need is another saloon." She flattened her hands against her thighs. "No, I can't have it, Reno. You'll have to tell the owner that you won't work there." She tipped her head to one side, struck by a question. "Who *is* the owner?"

"A man named Fields from back east, and I'm not sliding out of this deal." He sat beside her on the sofa, noticing the sheen of tears in her eyes. His heart kicked painfully and his conscience told him to tell her the truth about his owning the saloon and not just managing it. "I wanted to surprise you. I thought you'd be tickled that I'd found myself some work that would bring in some money."

"You should have asked me before taking on another job," she said, her feelings still stinging. "You work here for me. I'm the boss and you—"

"No, you're not my boss, Dellie," he cut in, his anger spiking again. "You're my wife."

"Only because I put an advertisement in the newspaper and you answered it," she reminded him, even while a calm voice inside her head told her to curb her tongue. "It was clear when we went into this . . . this situation that I expected certain things of you."

"And I expect certain things of you," he rejoined. "Respect, for one."

"How can I respect someone who makes money in a saloon?" She wrinkled her nose in distaste. "And you sit there and tell me you won't hire women to work in that place?"

"I didn't say that. Of course, I'll hire some ladies."

"You see? Another lie." She sat straight, her back so stiff that she thought it might snap. "I can't trust you."

Stung by her supercilious attitude, Reno rose from the sofa. "I thought you'd changed, but you're still lording it over me, aren't you? What makes you think you have the right to boss me, Dellie?"

"I'm your employer and your wife."

"I never agreed to work for you, just to marry you." He paced, trying to outdistance his anger. "You lecture others who lord it over their spouses and treat them unfairly, but you try the same thing with me. Now you say you can't trust me. Why? Because I've shown some grit? Because I'm my own man and don't need your permission to work for a living?"

She stared at him, trying to reconcile the angry young man pacing in front of her with the tender lover she'd been in bed with less than an hour ago.

"I'm going to beat Terrapin at his own game," he said, pacing, pacing, his movements jerky. "I'll hire ladies, but they will sell drinks, not themselves. I'll have a couple of men built like bulls on hand to keep all the troublemakers out. They can trade at Terrapin's. My place will be the respectable one in this town."

Adele gave him a stern look. "I won't have you running a saloon, Reno. It's a despicable business. I won't hear of it."

Reno stopped in his tracks and glared at her. The last time he'd been spoken to in such a fashion was by his mother. Damned if he'd let Dellie get away with it.

"You won't hear of it?" he repeated, his anger flaring.

"That's correct," she said, as prim as a schoolteacher.

Reno leaned close until his nose almost touched hers. "Then cover your ears, sugar." He marched out of her quarters, her look of amazement and disappointment stamped on his mind and heart. Females! God save him from them.

Damn her. Did she have to defy him at every turn?

Adele stared after him and forbade herself to cry. He would come to his senses, she told herself. He wouldn't want to cause war between them, not when love was so close at hand. Once he thought it out, he would see that she was right and he'd tell that East Coast moneyman he could not be a party to the saloon business.

Yes, he'd come around to her way of thinking. Despair crept into her mind unbidden, and tears blurred her vision. She wished she hadn't said some of those things to him. She hadn't been entirely truthful. She did feel she could trust him. If only he weren't so stubborn, so set in his ways, so . . . so . . . male!

Damn him. Did he have to defy her at every turn?

Chapter 17

"**W**on't you even come look at the place, Dellie?" Reno asked after Adele had placed a cup of coffee and a piece of Mrs. McDonald's elderberry pie in front of him.

"I'm not interested in frequenting a saloon."

"One visit isn't frequenting. It's natural you'd want to cast an eye on your husband's business venture."

"I want nothing to do with it," she insisted, moving away to wait on customers.

The woman was a puzzle, Reno thought as he tucked into the pie. In the week that had ensued after she'd learned of the Lucky Strike Saloon, Adele hadn't budged an inch. She hated the idea and hated him for having anything to do with it. Of course, their bodies betrayed their convictions. Nightly they made heated love. Daily they exchanged cool glances.

Reno had thought Adele would thaw out and finally accept his work in the saloon. Then he'd tell her that he wasn't merely managing the place, he was the owner. But she had not fulfilled his expectations. She remained staunchly opposed to his plan to give Terrapin a run for his money.

From the corner of his eye he observed Adele interacting with her customers. She charmed them with her lovely smile and emerald eyes and she enchanted them with her grace and modulated voice. But they were seeing only the surface of her considerable assets. He had discovered the deep pockets of her soul, the well of her passion, and the magnitude of her character. And there were still volumes for him to discover in her.

Through her he had also unearthed nuggets of himself. She had swum through his blood, had shown him the complexity of his heart, and had proved to him that he had never loved, never even really lived, before she'd happened in his life.

Everyone who had come before and after her paled. Every woman he had been with faded. Each time he made her shudder in his arms with the intensity of their passion, he felt reborn.

And yet he couldn't be sure Adele shared his newfound faith in them as a couple. He sensed that she didn't trust him and therefore could not trust her feelings for him. She was too damned smart. Like her mother, she could spot a fake a mile away. He should tell her the unvarnished truth, he argued with himself, but his pesky pride blustered and persisted. Her unbending presumptions of right and wrong and her firm belief that he would fail rankled, souring his good intentions.

Sally, sullen as always these days, came around to the other side of the counter and stacked soiled dishes in a tub underneath.

"What do you think of the Lucky Strike, Sally Ann?" Reno asked, enjoying getting under her skin.

"Are you afraid I'll take away your lover man's business?"

She fashioned a bored expression on her face. "I don't worry about Taylor's businesses. He is astute and successful, two things you will never be."

Reno chuckled. "I do admire how you stand by your man. Too bad you weren't as faithful to poor Win. Once his crops started failing and he bet what money he had left on the wrong racehorses, you began to lose interest."

"That's a lie," she charged, but not too stridently.

"Is it?" He quirked a brow, and Sally turned away and hustled toward the kitchen, where Mrs. Mc-Donald held out two plates of eggs and ham.

"I'll take them," Sally said. She snatched the plates and carried them to the waiting customers.

Mrs. McDonald shook her head at Sally and wiped her big-knuckled hands on her apron. Catching Reno's eye, she smiled and came to stand by him.

"When does your saloon open?"

"Friday night, and your first drink is free. Interested?"

"No, thanks." Her smile was gentle and wise. "In my experience you don't get nothing for free."

He nodded. "I'm hoping to prove to this town, especially to one Whistle Stop citizen in particular, that saloons don't have to be evil places. I've been in some bad ones, but I've enjoyed myself in others where the music was gay and the women were sweet and weapons were checked at the door."

"Yeah, I've heard about those, but I never worked in one. I hope you can have a nice place. This town needs a place for men to gather where women don't have to worry about them being there." Her gaze strayed to Adele. "Hope it's worth disappointing your wife."

"She'll come around."

The cook looked unconvinced. "And I hope you don't get killed over a silly thing like trying to get Terrapin's goat. Sure would be a waste."

He grinned. "You think he'd shoot me just because I opened a saloon across the street from his?"

Mrs. McDonald's expression was as sobering as a splash of ice-cold water. "I think he'd kill you for a lot less."

Reno cleared his throat, suddenly uneasy. "Maybe you're right."

"You *know* I'm right. Watch yourself." She returned to her domain behind the swinging door.

Reno dropped into his own dark thoughts as he finished the coffee and pie, hardly tasting either one. He knew he was stepping on the Devil's tail by opening the Lucky Strike, but he was convinced it was the right thing to do. Terrapin had to be challenged, if not stopped. If no one in Whistle Stop stood up to him, the town would eventually be worth spit, and the trains wouldn't even stop to let off their passengers.

As for Adele, she was always trying to teach him lessons, and this would be a chance for him to turn the tables on her. Once she saw that the saloon could be an asset to the town, then he'd tell her about his real station in life and explain that he hadn't told her before because of her persistence in thinking the worst of him. She'd see things his way for once, and the rift between them would be healed. Simple as that.

But a voice inside his head cautioned him that things were never simple with her.

Easing himself from the stool, he meandered toward the door and tried to catch Adele's eye. She looked everywhere but at him. Giving up, he left the restaurant and headed for his business enterprise.

Several people on the street called out greetings. Lately he'd begun to think of Whistle Stop as his home, but he knew that had more to do with his feelings for Adele than for this speck of civilization. He could hardly believe how much he loved Adele. It was downright scary.

Of course, the love had been glowing like embers for years. It hadn't taken much to leap out of control. Just a little encouragement from her, and he'd been head over heels in love with her. Damn, if it didn't baffle him, this spell she cast so easily. Did she have any inkling how deeply he cared? In a way he hoped she didn't, because that would give her even more power, and she had enough. He'd even had some second thoughts about the saloon, all because she had so disapproved, and he wanted desperately to win her respect as well as her love.

But a man could bend just so far before he had to straighten his backbone or crack it. Dellie didn't need another man to break. She needed a man she couldn't handle, a man she couldn't tame. He would be that man.

Nearing the saloon, he headed down the alley, fumbling in his trouser pocket for the key that would let him in the back door. His attentiveness sharpened when he realized he wasn't alone. Someone was waiting there for him. He slowed his pace, then relaxed when he recognized the slight figure.

"Little Nugget, what are you doing slinking around back here like a stray cat?"

"Waiting for you," she purred, stepping into the sunlight, which added a splash of gold color to her pale blond hair. "I thought you'd be along hours ago."

"What's the hurry?" He slipped the key into the lock. "Want to come inside?"

"Yeah. I got business to discuss with you." She preceded him into a dark room filled with crates and barrels.

"Business? With me?" Reno echoed, his interest piqued. He cupped her elbow and guided her through the back room to the front, where frosted windows let in light. "Do tell."

She strode into the middle of the main room and turned in a slow circle, her light-brown eyes missing nothing. "Not bad." Moving toward the stage, she went up the four steps and fingered the blue velvet curtain. "You going to have shows?"

"A few. Not anything too fancy." He smiled, amused by her stroll across the stage and her attention to detail. She nodded after examining the suspended chandeliers, the player piano, and the shining copper spittoons.

She left the stage and ran a fingertip around the green-leather-topped gaming table, then sashayed to the long bar and surveyed the kegs and bottles. Stepping back, she admired the painting of a ravishing brunette woman clad only in carefully placed silver coins and gold dust. Reno could see her smile reflected in the mirror behind the bar.

"Somebody you know?"

He shook his head. "It's a painting I bought from a man in Denver. The title is *Striking It Lucky*."

Her laugh was girlish, reminding Reno that she *was* a girl, although she lived the life of a woman.

"The Lucky Strike," she said softly, turning toward him. "You know a lot about that, don't you?"

His boot heels sounded loud on the floor as he approached her. "Not a lot."

She made a comical face. "That's not what I hear."

"What do you hear?"

"That you're rich."

"Says who?"

"Buck."

Reno lifted a brow. "He's been checking on me?"

"I guess." She lifted one smooth, white shoulder, revealed by the daring cut of her periwinkle-blue dress. "He told Taylor that you struck it rich in the goldfields and you're the moneyman behind this place."

Reno stared at her, offering nothing. Finally she strolled the length of the room, but avoided the windows. She didn't want anyone to know she'd come here, he realized. She was running on fear, although she played the role of a nonchalant visitor. He drummed his fingers on the bar, snagging her attention again.

"Taylor says he remembers seeing you in Deadwood."

"Your boss has quite a reputation for being a mean, foul-hearted cheat. In Deadwood women cross themselves and men spit when they hear his name."

Little Nugget smiled and stood beside him at the bar. She ran one small hand across the top, admiring the wood grain. "No nicks or cuts or scratches," she noted. "I like new things. Always have. I remember the first new dress I got. It was white with pink satin ribbons."

His thoughts swam to Dellie and the white lace dress she had worn the other night when they had made love for the first time. It had a pink ribbon, too, around the waist. Dellie had such a narrow waist. A perfect span for his hands to circle . . . He yanked his attention back to Little Nugget, feeling guilty for forgetting she was even in the room. He cleared his throat and picked up the thread of conversation.

"Did you wear the dress to church?"

Her glance was a rapier thrust. "You making fun of me?"

"No." He lowered his brows. "I figured you'd wear something like that to church with your family or for a special occasion."

She rolled her eyes. "My family didn't mess with church, and the only special occasions I remember were moving days." She frowned. "We had a peck of those. I was long gone from my pa when I got that dress. Taylor bought it for me."

He looked at her from the corners of his eyes, wondering about her relationship with Terrapin and how it had started. "When was this?"

"Uh . . . last year, I guess. Yeah, last spring. I only wore it twice and a rowdy cowboy ripped the front of it. He couldn't wait for me to take it off." She puffed out a sigh of disgust. "Ruined my dress. I was so mad I dumped the contents of the chamber pot over him once he was asleep." Her grin was purely wicked. "Then I ran like hell. I'd thrown his clothes out in the hall, so I got away before he could grab me. He was a drifter, and I knew he wouldn't hang around town long, but he looked for me for three days."

"Where did you hide?"

"In Taylor's room. Taylor thought it was as funny as hell. That's when he made me his special girl."

Reno tapped his fingertips on the bar again. "And what does the special girl get, besides Terrapin's Johnson and the back of his hand, of course."

The light went out of her eyes. "Fewer customers to mess with, for one thing. He just sends me the high rollers."

"That's good?"

"Sure. It's better than having three or four men a night pawing at you."

Reno winced, the facts of her young life slicing through him. "You're afraid of him."

"I can handle him."

"Like hell." He stared her down. "Let's be straight with each other. You think I don't notice how you sneak around to see me, how you avoid those windows because you're afraid of being spotted here? You could do better for yourself. Dellie tells me you're right smart. She says you're way ahead of the others in learning your letters and numbers."

Pride glimmered over her like sunlight. "I've been studying every day. Mrs. Adele told me that I ought to be able to add numbers and read whole sentences in a month or two."

"I don't doubt it."

"I figure by then you'll be looking for somebody to help you out around here." She sent her gaze around the room. "Somebody who can read a little and take money. Until I get good at it, I could do what I already know how to do, smile and talk men into buying drinks and making bets."

He blinked again. Christ, she was taking one hell of a chance! "You're asking to work here?"

"I'm offering my services," she amended. "I'm good, you know. Men pay top dollar for me."

"Yes, but I'm not looking to open that kind of business. I won't peddle flesh in the Lucky Strike."

"That's why I'm here talking with you. I want out of the whoring part of it. I want to be a businesswoman like your wife. I want to be a lady that gentlemen help across the street and tip their hats to when they see me coming."

Reno grinned. Hell, she was still a schoolgirl at heart, dreaming of a prince of a man who would marry her and make her queen of his castle. "I do believe that Dellie has turned your head. That's good. You're too young for this life. A pretty girl like you should be rounding up her suitors and picking out one to marry."

She patted her hair, checking to make sure every curl was in place. "I'd like to settle down someday. First I want to get some respect, so I can be known as something more than Taylor's favorite whore. Then I might get a serious suitor."

He rubbed his chin thoughtfully. "I seem to recall a little gal telling me that she was in the catbird seat and wasn't interested in working anywhere else."

"That was before."

"Before what?" He tensed, immediately assuming that Terrapin had roughed her up again.

"Before your wife talked to me, made me see that I could be something more, something better. She talks and talks and before you know it, you've changed your mind so many times you don't know up from down."

Reno laughed and nodded. "That's my Dellie."

"You've done well by Dead-eye—I mean, Doris McDonald." She smiled quickly. "She don't like being called by her saloon name anymore. Anyway, like I was saying, Doris says you don't make promises you can't keep. She says you've treated her fair. That's all I'm looking for, a fair chance." Her brown eyes were bright but serious when she fastened them on him. "So you hiring?"

"Are you sure you want to work for me?"

"I'm sure."

"I suppose we can get around your boss man. He seems to have gotten over his mad about me hiring Mrs. McDonald."

She caught her lower lip between her teeth, and worry settled over her like a shroud. "I wouldn't say that. He still gets steamed up when he sees Doris. He hasn't forgiven or forgotten that. But he don't blame you as much as he blames her. He says she stabbed him in the back and that he won't let her get away with it. He swears she'll pay. I'm scared for her."

"Hey, don't worry about her." He grinned, trying to put her at ease. "I figure Terrapin's got himself a runaway mouth. After all, if he was such a dangerous man, why did he have to hire Buck Wilhite?"

"To keep folks in line. Us girls are another matter." She sighed heavily. "Anything to do with us he takes real personal. Like we're his, and we got to ask permission to do anything or go anywhere."

"You're not backing out already, are you?"

"No. He'll be mad, but he don't own me. Of course, this might buy you even more trouble with him."

Reno shrugged, although his good sense told him he was thumbing his nose at danger. He didn't want her to retreat, not after she'd found the courage to fight. He'd take her in and watch over her. Terrapin would have to come through him to get to her or Mrs. McDonald.

"He's already measured me for a coffin." Offering his hand, Reno gave her a wink. "Put 'er there. What's your real name?"

She smiled, shy, her lashes fluttering. "You're awful interested in people's real names. Ain't Little Nugget good enough for you?"

"That's not the name your mama wrote in the Bible the day you were born."

"No. She wrote 'Cassie Mae Little.' But I don't want any drinkers and gamblers calling me by my given name. I save it for people who mean something to me."

Reno nodded, finding her endearing. "Would you get mad if I called you Miss Little?"

"I guess that'll be okay."

He could tell she liked the sound of it. "Then at the Lucky Strike you'll be Miss Little. I think it's time folks around here started showing you some respect."

"Respect you got to earn." She slipped her hand into his.

"You have, Miss Little." He smiled at her, touched to see the pink blush spread across her piquant features as he squeezed her hand and sealed their deal. "You have."

"You've made an impression on Little Nugget," Reno said when Adele joined him in her quarters later that night.

"That's good." Adele moved listlessly into the bedroom, hardly comprehending what he'd said. She fumbled for the buttons at the back of her dress. Her muscles burned. "I'm tired. I never saw so many contrary people in all my born days. Everybody was in a bad mood today and nobody wanted anything we had to offer. If I told them we had beans, they wanted stew. If I said we'd just taken an apple pie out of the oven, they curled their lips and said they had their mouths set for peach."

Reno joined her in the bedroom. "Lie down there, Mrs. Gold, and let me tend to your aches and pains."

Glancing at him, she shook her head. "Not now, Reno. I'm too weary." She sat on the edge of the bed and removed her shoes. "I certainly don't feel amorous."

"I'm not talking about that. Lie back here and quit putting your thoughts into my mouth." He gripped her by the shoulders and pulled her back onto the bed.

Seeing the determination stamped on his features, she shifted and rested her head on the feather pillow.

Reno cradled one of her feet in his hands and massaged the sole gently. Adele was surprised at how good it felt and immediately surrendered to his touch.

Closing her eyes, she let herself go, sighing with relief as his hands moved up to her ankle and leg.

His hands were bathed in magic. Gentle and strong and lightly calloused, those hands could manipulate her in ways that made her blush just to think about them. Warmth infused her breasts and fluttered in her stomach. Recognizing the embryonic sensations of passion, she strove to temper them.

"You saw Little Nugget today?" she asked, seizing on something to occupy her mind besides her body and the touch of his.

"Yes. She asked me for a job."

Adele opened her eyes, surprised. "She wants to work here? That's wonderful!"

"Not here. At my place."

"Your . . ." Disappointment crashed into her. She shut her eyes again. "Oh."

"I told her I wasn't going to sell any flesh in my place, and she said that's why she wanted to work for me."

"I do wish she would show more gumption."

"Have you ever heard of compromise, Dellie?"

She gritted her teeth. "I live it every day."

"No, you don't. You're one of the most exacting, intolerant, unforgiving people I've ever met."

His words stung like an angry wasp. "If I was those things, you wouldn't be sitting on my bed, rubbing my feet. I certainly compromised when I decided to let you stay here."

"You didn't let me do anything," he said, his voice level, but his hands not so gentle anymore. "I decided to stick around and make you see the error of your ways."

"The error of my—?" She coughed and sputtered until her eyes watered. Jerking her foot from his grasp, she sat up in bed. "What did you tell Little Nugget?"

"That she could work for me, if that's what she wants."

She folded her arms against her breasts. "You should have told her to aim higher. I would have."

"She's doing what's right for *her*. The whole world isn't going to march to your tune. You better get used to that. Back in Kansas you were more loving, more tolerant. What happened to make you expect people to think and act to suit you? Hell, you're worse than the King of England!"

"If you disapprove of me, why do you stay? Why not pack up and leave?"

His gaze was steady and unnerving. "Is that what you want?"

She pressed her lips together to keep herself from telling him that what she wanted was for him to love her enough to turn his back on his life of gambling and drinking and chasing women. If he worked in that saloon, she couldn't imagine how their union could survive. And she wanted it to survive more than anything she'd ever wanted in her life.

Before he'd staggered off that train, she had resigned herself to a single existence, telling herself that it was best. She was too independent to be strapped to a man. Being alone was hard, but it was what she had known most of her life. Better that than to marry and be widowed, as her mother and Sally had been. She'd seen the acute loneliness in her mother's eyes, a loneliness that came to those who had treasured a love only to lose it.

But win her heart he had, and now she was Reno's wife in more than name. Her heart and her body were his.

And there was the matter of Taylor Terrapin. He would not allow another saloon to have any success in Whistle Stop. Reno would end up dead. A shiver raced up her spine, and she covered her face with her hands to shut out the horrible visions. She'd be a widow. Her constant nightmare.

"What's wrong?" Reno asked. "What are you hiding from? I asked a simple question: Do you want me to leave?"

"I want you to use the sense God gave you," she said, letting her hands slip away from her face and fall heavily into her lap. "You can't have anything more to do with that saloon, Reno."

He shook his head, looking bullish. "Dellie, don't talk to me like that. I'm warning you."

"And I'm warning you." She wrung her hands, wishing for words to convey her tumultuous feelings. But words were inadequate, flimsy wisps of sound, and could not bear the weight of her fears. In his eyes she had seen heaven, but just now she'd glimpsed hell and she knew she was losing him.

"You don't own me. You don't own anyone, although you'd dearly love that," he said.

"How can you say that when you know how hard I fight for every person's freedom?"

"You want them to be free only if they obey you and agree with your view of the world."

She set her jaw, refusing to cave in and reveal her

pain to him. She might lose him, but she would not allow him to take her pride as part of his spoils.

"You aren't like your mother. She let people live their lives without judging them. You're the judge and jury of everyone, Dellie. I hadn't even stepped off the train before you'd decided I was low and common and in need of your firm hand."

"Was I wrong?" she asked, recalling that day and his state of inebriation.

His smile chilled her. "Absolutely, and it is truly pathetic that you still can't see how wrong you were and are about me."

Adele felt her lips tremble and knew she was close to breaking in front of him, so she strove to shore up her defenses. "If anyone is pathetic, it's you. I'm offering you a good life, but you're throwing it aside because you can't stay away from the gaming tables."

"I don't give a damn about the gaming tables." He made a sharp, chopping motion with his hand. "I care about holding my head up high and not cowering to the likes of Terrapin. If you weren't so determined to see me as a failure, you'd understand that."

"And if you cared anything for me you would understand that I can't hold *my* head up in this town if my husband runs a saloon, when he could be making a decent living here."

"This is your restaurant to manage and you don't need me here."

"That's true."

She didn't think how that would sound until it was out and the damage was done. Reno narrowed his eyes and bunched his hands into fists. She felt him take her words all wrong. She had meant that she didn't need him, but she wanted him around. She liked having him around. The words clogged in her throat, choking her.

"Well, at least we agree on something." His eyes softened for a second, tearing at her heart, and then he turned on his heel and marched out.

She didn't see him again until the next morning, when he returned to collect his things. If he noticed that her eyes were swollen from crying all night or that her color was chalky white or that she didn't speak to him because her voice was hoarse from her wrenching sobs, he didn't let on.

After he had left, she retired to her bed and cried some more. Around midnight Sally came into her room. Without a word she held out her arms to Adele, and without hesitation Adele accepted the embrace of an old, complicated, and inexhaustible friendship.

Chapter 18

"The word around town is that he's moved into the rooms above the saloon," Mrs. McDonald said. She looked across the table, full of potatoes and peelings, at Adele. "The Lucky Strike opens tonight. You going?"

Adele shook her head and continued to slice the potatoes, concentrating fiercely on them in an attempt to control her bubbling emotions. It had been two days since Reno had moved out, and every time she heard his name it was like reopening a wound.

Mrs. McDonald shrugged. "I'll stop in. It's the least I can do. He's been nothing but good to me."

"Did he ask you to work for him?"

"No. He knows I'm happy where I am."

"I wonder how Terrapin is taking all of this. Sally says he hasn't talked to her about it."

Mrs. McDonald chewed on her lower lip and worry pinched the skin between her eyes. "Taylor don't talk to women about business and he don't share his thoughts with strangers neither. Whatever he's planning, we won't hear about it until it's too late. We should all watch our backs."

264

Adele released a shaky breath. "You're afraid, aren't you?"

"Sure. Anybody who knows Taylor is afraid. I try not to even pass him on the street if I can help it. I know he's plotting my death."

"Mrs. McDonald!" Adele stared at her, terror striking her heart when she saw that the woman was completely serious. "You think he'll try something like that?"

"I wouldn't be the first person he's killed or tried to kill."

Adele shivered. "Then don't go shopping or anywhere else unless someone is with you."

"I can take care of myself." The woman conjured up a smile with some difficulty. "Don't worry about me."

"But I do worry."

Mrs. McDonald removed her apron and laid it aside. "You should be thinking about your own troubles. Is Mr. Reno going to move back here ever?"

"I don't know."

"See? You've got enough in your own life to keep you busy. I'll see you in the morning. Sleep well."

"Yes, same to you, Mrs. McDonald."

Alone in the kitchen Adele sighed with weariness. She felt heartsick and had ever since she'd learned that Reno was opening a saloon almost directly across the street from the Black Knight. Sally found it hilarious and never missed a chance to tease her about how they would both end up being wives of saloon keepers.

Pushing herself up from the table, she grabbed a bucket and took it outside, where she dumped its contents into the slop barrel out by the chicken coop.

Leaning against a fence post, she thought of Sally and marveled at how her friend had changed. But then, they'd all changed. Even her.

She remembered Reno telling her of the girl she'd been in Lawrence. He had said she'd been open-minded, an eternal optimist, with a loving, trusting heart. Well, yes. That was normal for a young girl barely out of childhood. The world had not yet shown her its ugly face.

But that wasn't true, a stern inner voice insisted. She liked to think of her childhood as carefree, an endless string of flawless days. Actually she had been a lonely child, except for the four years she'd spent at her aunt's home in Kansas. Home. Such a lovely word, and one she hadn't been able to know person-ally until she'd arrived in Lawrence.

Her dear aunt had opened her home to them and there Adele had first had a sense of belonging to a place. When her father had died, her mother had moved from town to town, from job to job. Adele had gone to so many schools that she'd lost count. Her penchant and desire for knowledge had been her sal-vation, or she surely would have failed in her studies, being uprooted every few months and then dropped into another new classroom.

Her mind, ever nimble and valiant, had added color and glamour to her days of wandering. Others, those lucky ones who stayed in one place and were able to drive their taproots deep, envied her travels. And she let them. She never told them how she yearned for a mother who was not too busy to make a home for her and a father who was alive and well and a good provider. She let the envious think that her life was full of surprises instead of jolts, sophistication instead of insecurity.

Only her mother had sensed the dark clouds behind her sunny disposition, and so they had roosted in Kansas for a few years to give Adele a chance at lasting friendships and perhaps a betrothed. Her friendship with Sally had been forged, but although she had received a marriage proposal from Winston, she had declined it. Her mother had been greatly relieved.

"There is someone more suited to you out there, Dellie," her mother had assured her. "Winston would have tried, bless him, but he would have been incapable of making you truly happy."

Her aunt's death and then her mother's demise six months later had been cruel blows. She had been unprepared to be alone in the world and had felt as if her legs had been knocked out from under her. Acting on fear, she had scrambled to find a job, rejecting offers to continue in her mother's line of work for fear that she would never call a place home. When the restaurant had been offered, she had seized on it. Even the fact that it was in a territory and not a state had not deterred her. She was determined to stay put, no matter where, no matter what.

How could one not change when life took such sharp turns and dangerous curves? With nothing to hold onto, she had careened and wobbled. Only recently, just before Reno had showed up again, in fact, had she felt in control of her life and able to stand tall once more.

Yes, she had changed, but so had Reno and Sally and everyone else. Sally was more self-centered, Reno was more cavalier, and she was more . . . Well, she admitted she was more exacting than she'd been as a girl. But she was *not* intolerant and certainly not someone who sat in judgment on everyone else.

Shoving away from the fence, Adele kicked at grassy tufts and strolled toward the depot buildings. Her insistence rang false, and she realized she was not convinced of her own sterling character. Maybe she did judge people. Perhaps she even misjudged them. And yes, she tended to be less tolerant of certain behavior. God knew, she could be mule-headed.

Was she difficult to please, a trial to live with? Was Reno justified in leaving her? Perhaps the saloon was an excuse, a haven for him away from her. She believed in her heart that he had enjoyed their nights of lovemaking, but they weren't enough to hold him.

Stopping to stare up at the cloud-shrouded moon and dusty stars, she wondered what he was doing and if he was doing it alone or with someone. Loneliness enfolded her. She tried to shrug it off, but it clung tenaciously to her spirit. She closed her eyes for a moment to see his face, his smile, to hear his voice and his laughter.

She wanted to cry again, so she hurried inside to busy herself with sweeping the kitchen, wiping off the stove, tidying the silver and glassware. Anything but sleeping in that bed without him. Without him that bed had become her worst enemy, a feather-stuffed vessel of bittersweet memories, curdled hope, and yesterday's dreams.

Standing beside the shed he'd built, Reno waited until he was sure Adele was safely inside before he struck out for the saloon and his single bed on the second floor.

What had she been thinking about, staring up at the moon like that for so long? Him, he hoped vainly. He wanted her to miss him. He wanted her to pine for him, weep for him, fight off madness for him. Because, God knew, he was slowly going mad from wanting her.

Good thing he had the saloon to keep him busy or he would have been reduced to drinking and making a fool of himself. Working like a man possessed, he had thrown himself into getting the saloon ready for its opening night, when he would thumb his nose at Taylor Terrapin as he welcomed the good people of Whistle Stop into the Lucky Strike.

Ah, it would be a sweet, sweet victory, if only Dellie would share it with him. But she would spoil it, as she spoiled every day he spent without her. She wouldn't come to the saloon on opening night or on any night, leaving him to pretend he was proud and happy and successful, when in truth he was ashamed and miserable and a failure.

And it was all her fault.

She'd made him love her, knowing good and well that she would never allow herself to love him. He'd never be good enough for her. She'd made up her mind about that before he'd set foot in Whistle Stop, and try as he might, he had not been able to alter her opinion.

Entering through the back door of the saloon, he locked it behind him and ran up the stairs to the room that held a bed, a bureau, a chair, and a kerosene lamp. Home, sweet home.

He flung himself on the noisy bed and kicked off his boots. Hell, he'd go ahead and tell her about the money he'd made and that he owned this place. It wasn't as if he had anything to lose anymore.

Reaching out, he ran a hand over the empty expanse of mattress beside him and held back a groan of self-pity. In Deadwood folks had said that he lived up to his name. Everything he touched turned to gold. His fingers curled into an empty fist. The Midas touch was gone. Gone with Dellie and his stupid boyhood dreams.

Sitting alone at the central gaming table, Reno nursed a shot of whiskey and shuffled the deck of cards over and over again. When someone tapped at the glass in the fancy double doors that graced the front of his establishment, he didn't even glance up.

"We don't open until eight tonight," he shouted.

"Not even for an old saloon hag?" a woman shouted back.

Reno cocked an ear, then grinned. Dear Dead-eye Doris McDonald. He shoved himself up from the table and went to unlock and open the doors. Grinning, he extended a hand to the woman standing outside.

"Come on in here. How did you know I was wishing for a friendly face?"

She placed her hand in his and crossed the threshold. Dressed in the simple clothes she wore at the restaurant, she glanced around at the fancy, new-smelling surroundings. "My, my, ain't this pretty! Looks like you're all set for the big opening night."

"All set," he agreed. "I was having a drink. Want one?"

"No, thanks." She sat at the table, eyeing the whiskey and cards. "I'm not usually a betting woman, but I'd wager my face isn't the one you were wishing to see."

Sitting opposite her, he acknowledged her remark with a lift of his brows and a wincing smile. "Sure you don't want a drink?"

"I'm sure. I mostly use liquor to dull the pain of living, but I'm doing fine now and don't need it. Besides, I should keep my wits about me. How about you?"

He raised the squat glass and flung the contents to the back of his throat, then set it solidly onto the table. "I need it."

"I figured as much." Mrs. McDonald settled more comfortably into the barrel-backed chair. "She'd take you back in a second. She misses you, too. Why, she floats around that place like a ghost, pale and lifeless. Is running this saloon more important to you than being with your wife?"

He traced a wet circle on the tabletop. "The Lucky Strike is not our problem."

"Pride," the woman said, spitting out the word as if it were rancid meat. "That's your problem. Hope it keeps you warm at night."

"It doesn't, but I'm not the only one suffering from pride. She's full of it, too."

"I don't get it," Mrs. McDonald confessed. "Guess you have a yearning to die, 'cause that's what this place will do for you. Taylor has probably already given that hired gun of his orders to plug you. He won't allow this saloon to stay open. I'd understand it better if you didn't have anything to live for, but that boss lady of mine fires you up. Doesn't take a scholar to see that. So why do you want to die and break her heart?"

"I'm not going to die."

She shot out a hand and clutched his forearm. "Yes, you are. Listen to me. I know what I'm talking about. I've told you that Taylor doesn't fight fair. He's already riled about me working at the depot. Close this place and go back to your wife. Live long and happy. Don't be a fool by trying to beat the Devil at his own game."

"I suppose Dellie isn't planning on coming here tonight."

Mrs. McDonald frowned. "What do you think?"

"So she's been sad?"

Mrs. McDonald sighed and pushed at his arm, clearly exasperated, then she let go. "You deaf? I'm giving you good advice here, mister."

"And I surely do appreciate it."

"Then why ain't you going to take it?"

"Because I can't turn back now. I can't fold and expect to hold my head up in this town. I think Dellie will eventually see that I know what I'm doing, that everything I promised her has come true, and she'll forgive and forget."

"It won't get that far. You'll die before she has time to see the error of her ways."

He chuckled. "Oh, ye of little faith. I'm going to show everyone in this town that they don't have to be slaves to Master Terrapin. It's time somebody stood up to him. Otherwise Whistle Stop won't be fit to live in."

"There are plenty of other towns. You and your missus can move to one and be happy."

"But Dellie has put down roots here. She wants to make Whistle Stop her home, and by God, she deserves a town equal to her spirit and generosity and goodness." He felt himself blush, hearing his flowery words and seeing their impact on Mrs. McDonald. Her eyes rounded and she blew out a low whistle.

"Saints preserve us, I see the light. You're doing this for her, ridding her nest of the bad, old chicken snake." She slapped a hand on the table. "Well, hell. I should have seen it. Even pride don't usually scramble a man's brains. But love can do it."

In the next second an explosion rocked the room. Reno instinctively grabbed Mrs. McDonald and shoved her under the table. Glass tinkled, sparkling on the floor like diamonds, followed by the diminishing sound of horses. Reno helped Mrs. McDonald to her feet.

"Sorry about that."

"What happened?" She whirled and surveyed the shattered glass panels in the pretty double doors. "That bastard. Didn't I tell you? This is only the beginning."

"Doesn't matter," he assured her, moving to the broom closet tucked in a corner behind the bar. "Broken windows don't frighten me."

"Well, it's spoiled your opening. Folks will be here in a couple of hours and this is what they'll see." She extended her hands, indicating the ragged spikes of glass in the doors.

Reno swept up the debris and handed a dustpan to Mrs. McDonald, who helped him dispose of the broken glass. "I'll fix the doors before eight."

"And just how will you do that?" she asked.

He crooked his finger at her and carried the dustpan with him to the back room. Dumping the bits of glass into the trash barrel, he then turned to Mrs. McDonald. Winking, he nodded sideways, guiding her attention to six glass-paneled doors leaning against the wall.

Mrs. McDonald broke out in laughter. Doubling over, she cackled until tears streamed from her eyes, then she popped him playfully on the shoulder with her fist.

"You just might be a match for that old chicken snake and his friends," she said, beaming at him. "I pray you'll be able to keep one step ahead of him."

Reno rested a hand on her shoulder and leaned down until he was nose to nose with her. "Don't tell Dellie about this. It will only add to her worries. But you can tell her that you have faith in me, that you believe I'm smarter and more cunning than any old chicken snake."

The woman surprised him by placing a gentle hand alongside his face. Her eyes softened with sentiment. "She's just afraid you'll get killed, same as the rest of us who've developed a fondness for you."

"I know, but I want her trust and faith."

"Her love isn't enough?"

A sadness stole through him, and he moved away from her, evading her touch. "Mrs. McDonald, you and I both know that love is a shallow suitor if it's not accompanied by trust and faith."

She opened her mouth as if to argue with him, then shut it with a definite click of her teeth. A frown pulled at the corners of her mouth. "Damn, I hate a man who's right most of the time."

He laughed and walked with her through the main room to the damaged front doors. Several people stood outside, examining the ruins.

"Look at them," Mrs. McDonald said under her breath. "They act concerned, but they really don't care. Not enough to stand up against Taylor with you."

"Who needs them when I've got you?"

She elbowed his ribs and laughed. "I'll see you tonight, you charmer you. And don't worry. The boss lady won't hear about this from me." Glancing at the people milling outside, she chuckled. "I imagine she probably already knows about it. You can't belch without somebody running to the restaurant to tell her about it."

Reno grimaced, realizing she was right and that he couldn't keep unpleasant news from Dellie's door. "Tell her I hope to see her tonight."

Mrs. McDonald rolled her eyes. "Yeah, well, like my papa used to say, 'You hope in one hand and piss in the other and see which one gets filled first.' "

She laughed when Reno pantomimed kicking her in the rump as she made her exit.

Chapter 19

Approaching the two men on the boardwalk, Adele cocked an ear when she realized they were discussing Reno's saloon.

"Terrapin can't blame a man for accepting a free drink," Ned, the blacksmith, was saying to Chester, the feed store owner.

"That's right," Chester agreed. "This town can support two saloons. Did you hear that tonight is Ladies' Night at the Lucky Strike?"

"What's that mean?" Ned asked, scratching at his black beard.

"All drinks are free for ladies. My wife says she wants to go and sample the ginger ale. She ain't never had none before and she's always wanted to taste it."

"Free drinks, huh? Maybe I can talk Maybelle into going with me. After all, it's not like the Black Knight. The Lucky Strike is more like going to a dance or a party. No cussing or spitting or grabbing gals' asses—Oh, afternoon there, Mrs. Gold." Ned ducked his head, noticing too late that a lady was present.

"Good afternoon, gentlemen." Adele smiled stiffly

at the two men as she edged past on her way along the boardwalk. "Pardon me."

She felt their eyes on her as she walked toward the General Store. The town was abuzz about the opening of the Lucky Strike Saloon last night. She had heard little else since early this morning, when her own workers had giggled and spoken in hushed whispers about the fun they'd had dancing and singing the night away.

Adele had been surprised to find Helen, Colleen, and Mrs. McDonald already at work when she'd entered the restaurant. She knew they hadn't returned from the saloon until well after midnight, because she hadn't been able to get to sleep until a couple of hours before dawn.

Foolishly she'd entertained a hope that Reno would arrive at her door and beg her to come to the opening. She would argue but give in, and they would put aside their differences long enough for a few dances.

More foolishly she hadn't surrendered that hope until three in the morning, when exhaustion had doused the feeble flame and she'd fallen into a dreamless slumber. Feeling like a sleepwalker, she had managed to get through the morning and noon trade before leaving the restaurant to do some errands. Actually she'd taken a nap and was only now venturing out in the late afternoon to pick up a few items at the General Store.

Usually she would send Mrs. McDonald, but she was afraid for the woman. If Terrapin was plotting something evil, Adele felt honor-bound to do what she could to ensure Mrs. McDonald's safety. She wouldn't have Doris McDonald walking alone on the streets, doing her errands when she could very well do them herself.

The only bright spot in her day so far had been the sour look on Sally's face as the others had cheerfully recounted last night's excitement and how grand and bright and elegant the Lucky Strike was compared to other taverns.

"A saloon is a saloon," Sally had finally declared with a tight pursing of her lips. "Just like a pile of horse manure is a pile of horse manure."

"Takes a pile to know a pile, I suppose," Colleen had murmured.

Adele laughed under her breath at the memory. Stopping in front of the store, she couldn't help but look longingly further down the street at Whistle Stop's newest business. All was quiet, but she noticed there were more horses tied up in front of the Lucky Strike than there were in front of the Black Knight.

Wonder how Terrapin was taking that?

Trying not to worry, but failing, Adele went inside the store and nodded to the proprietor, Mr. Nolan. She went to the notions section for thread and a new needle, then went around to the stack of pumpkins in the front of the store.

"Those came in this week," Mr. Nolan said from behind the counter.

Adele glanced over her shoulder at him. "Yes, I saw them being unloaded off the train and my mouth has been watering for pumpkin pie ever since." She noticed the man who had been talking with Mr. Nolan, and the hairs on the back of her neck quivered. Buck Wilhite.

The man gave her the willies.

He smiled at her and turned back to Mr. Nolan again. The black patch stretched over the whole of his eye socket and all the way up and over his brow. Malevolence shimmered around him like a heat wave. Even without that Colt .45, he would still have been armed—armed with a lack of conscience.

He wore black from head to toe. His gun belt was decorated with silver disks and his spurs were silver and copper. Adele sniffed and caught the scent of toilet water wafting off his skin, so sickly sweet that she coughed, drawing his attention again. His one eye, pale blue, stared at her, unblinking. He smiled again, slow and oily, as his cyclops eye roved to take in her figure. Adele moved behind a barrel of brooms.

"Do you need help picking out a pumpkin?" the store keeper asked.

"No."

"Would you allow me to help carry your parcels back to the depot?" Buck asked.

"No." She realized how rude that sounded and added, "Thank you."

"You still live at the depot restaurant, don't you?" Buck inquired.

"Yes." She furrowed her brow, disturbed by the question.

"Ah, I thought you might be living with your husband above the Lucky Strike Saloon."

Adele flinched. "No . . . I . . ." She shook her head, nonplussed, and examined the pumpkins again. Bending over, she picked one up and straightened. When she turned around she saw that Wilhite was still staring at her. Revulsion crept over her skin. "I'll take this one," she said to Mr. Nolan.

"That should make a couple of good pies," Mr. Nolan said, moving aside a sack of seeds so that she could place the pumpkin on the countertop. "What else today?"

"That's all. Will you add these things to˙ my bill? I'll pay the entirety at the end of the month as usual."

"Be glad to. I'll start you a new sheet." He opened his journal to a clean page.

"But I have other items from last week and the week before," Adele said, stopping him from writing on the new page.

"That's right, but your husband paid off those things a couple of days ago." He paged backward and tapped a line where a figure had been struck out. "Paid in full."

"My husband . . ." Her mind spun crazily. Reno had paid her bill without saying anything to her? She was smiling before she knew why. Then it all caught up with her. Reno had spent some of his first pay on her. She ducked her head, embarrassed and secretly pleased. Was this his way of apologizing, of trying to prove to her that his work could be beneficial?

"Big spender," Wilhite murmured. "If you were my wife, honey lamb, I'd be buying you pretty dresses and flashy jewels instead of paying for flour and pumpkins."

Adele shot him a glare. "Luckily I am *not* your wife, Mr. Wilhite." She would have said more, but her attention was drawn to a commotion outside. Puzzled, she stepped to the open door and looked out. She saw nothing unusual, except that the horses tied to the hitching post were nervous, tossing their heads and sidestepping away from some unseen danger. Then the crack of a whip rent the air, followed by a woman's scream. Adele bolted outside.

With a gasp of alarm, she stared, aghast. Taylor Terrapin, bullwhip in hand, was driving Little Nugget ahead of him as if she were a rogue steer.

Staggering down the middle of the street, Little Nugget tried to regain her balance and escape the madness of the man behind her. Terrapin, a death-mask grin stretching his thin lips, strode confidently down the street, certain no one would dare raise a voice to curse him or a hand to stop him from whipping Little Nugget as if she were an animal. *His* animal.

"For God's sake, do something!" Adele grasped the sleeve of the nearest male, trying to galvanize someone into action before Terrapin killed Little Nugget.

The man jerked his sleeve from her fingers. "It's none of my business what he does with his whores."

"Coward," Adele charged, whirling around to find a braver man. Buck Wilhite stood before her. "Are you going to allow this to go on? Have you no decency?"

Wilhite frowned and gave a careless shrug. "She's always treated me like dirt, so I won't be coming to her rescue." He grinned. "But since you're all worried and fretting, I'll fetch the doc. She'll be needing him."

The bullwhip cracked again and laid open another piece of Little Nugget's back. Long streaks of crimson stained her yellow dress. She fell forward and crawled on her hands and knees, her sobs rattling in her chest, as she tried to escape the whip. Behind her Terrapin stalked, dressed in black, like a carrion bird.

"You think you're something special?" he jeered.

"You're nothing but an ignorant tramp. Just like Dead-eye Doris. I bought you and I own you and you're not going anywhere but the graveyard. I'll kill you before I let you work for him."

Him. Adele knew instantly what had precipitated this horrific spectacle. Little Nugget wanted to work for Reno.

"Please, Taylor . . . I w-won't w-work for him," Little Nugget said, casting fearful looks over her shoulder at him. "I was j-just seeing if you'd g-get jealous, honey. I never m-meant to leave you. You're the only m-man for me."

Sick to her stomach, Adele stepped off the boardwalk and strode with purpose to Little Nugget.

"Get away!" Little Nugget said, shoving at her. "He'll kill us both!"

"No." Adele stepped in front of Little Nugget and into Terrapin's path. Terrapin advanced, the bullwhip making lazy circles in the dirt at his feet.

"Move aside," he told her, his high-pitched voice whispery soft and sinister, "unless you want to know the kiss of this whip."

"No, no," Little Nugget said in a strangled voice. Feebly she tried to push Adele out of harm's way. "Don't let him hurt you. Get away from me!"

"No." Adele stood her ground. "Put that whip down, Mr. Terrapin, and act like a man instead of a rabid beast."

Terrapin flicked his wrist, and the whip popped inches from the hem of Adele's skirt. She flinched, then her temper flared, overriding her fear.

"You're such a big man, aren't you? Whipping girls

and threatening women. Do you slap babies and kick puppies, too?"

His face became a mask of evil intent as he coiled the whip in one hand and prepared to release it in a burst of anger. His upper lip curled to reveal small, square teeth.

"Last warning. Step aside."

Fear roared in her head and froze her heart. Little Nugget sobbed behind her. "I will not be cowed by you or obey you," Adele told him, proud that her voice didn't quiver.

Terrapin shrugged. "Suit yourself. I mean to beat that bitch until she's dead. Then I'm going after Doris. If you want to be part of it, that's perfectly fine with me."

He cocked his arm. Adele shut her eyes, trying to prepare herself for the racking pain, but the loud pop of gunfire jerked her eyes open again. Terrapin jumped sideways and glared at the man who was holding a smoking .44 Smith & Wesson.

Reno.

Never had any man looked so good to Adele or made her heart burst with such powerful, soul-shaking love. Reno strode forward, coming from behind and to the right of Terrapin, his expression one of deadly intent. He stopped a few feet from Terrapin.

Reno's coattails fluttered in the breeze. A thin stream of smoke wiggled up from the barrel of his gun. His gaze flickered to Adele, and she saw the instant softening, the quick bolt of faith and courage extended to her. She grasped at what Reno offered and knew that with him by her side anything was possible.

"It's okay," she told Little Nugget. "Reno's here." The words came from her heart. Her faith in Reno's abilities was profound and rock-solid, but it wasn't until that moment that she could acknowledge what her heart already knew. She trusted Reno with her life.

"Drop the whip," Reno said, steely determination in every word.

Terrapin let the bullwhip answer for him. It fed out and flicked Reno's gun arm, cutting open his shirt-sleeve. But Reno didn't release his weapon. Gripping the gun in one hand, he fanned the firing spur with the other, aiming at Terrapin's boots. Terrapin had no choice but to hop and skip to avoid having his toes shot off. One of the bullets glanced off one of his spurs, making it sing and whirl.

"You bastard!" Terrapin shouted, trying to recover enough to lash out at Reno again. "I'll kill you."

"Not today," Reno said, and fired again, the bullet plowing into the street an inch from the toe of Terrapin's left boot.

Leaping backward, Terrapin almost fell, but he reached behind him and grabbed onto a hitching post to keep from landing on his butt on Main Street. His face grew almost black with rage.

"Dellie, darlin', you take Miss Little on inside my saloon while me and Terrapin continue our discussion."

Torn between wanting to get Little Nugget to safety and wanting to stand side by side with Reno, Adele pulled Little Nugget to her and moved closer to Reno.

"You come inside with us," she said.

"I'll be in shortly," Reno assured her.

"Come inside *now*."

He cut his eyes at her, his jaw growing more tense. Terrapin tipped back his head and laughed.

"Better mind her, big man," Terrapin said with a leer. "She's got you by the nuts and she knows it."

Little Nugget broke loose and fled, disappearing inside the Lucky Strike.

Terrapin watched, murder written on his face. "Run, rabbit, run, but I'll get you in my sights again and shoot you dead," he yelled.

"Go on, Dellie," Reno said.

She knew he wanted her out of harm's way, but she was loath to desert him. "I won't leave you out here with this heathen!"

Terrapin turned his head and looked down the street. "Here comes Buck with the doctor." He touched the brim of his hat. "Another day, Miss Adele." His eyes glittered with black menace. "As for you"—he gathered up the whip, looping it like rope in his hand—"you're dead, Gold. You're just too stupid to know it."

Reno holstered his gun. "Get along, little doggy."

Adele held her breath, certain that Reno's parting shot would send Terrapin into another frenzy. But Terrapin merely grinned coldly, turned on his heel, and walked into his saloon, spurs jingling. Wilhite followed him.

"Where's the gal he whipped?" Doc Martin asked, bustling forward and out of breath.

"In my saloon," Reno said.

"She dead or alive? Buck didn't say which."

"She's alive," Adele assured him. "Reno stopped Terrapin before he could kill her—and me." She turned her gaze up to Reno and leaned into him, suddenly weak. His arm came around her, holding her up.

"You?" The doctor gave her an incredulous look. "Terrapin wouldn't hurt you."

Adele arched a brow, wondering if the man was really so naive. "Taylor Terrapin would shoot his own mother if she defied him." She gripped Reno's arm. "Let's see to Little Nugget. The poor girl must be suffering terribly."

"You okay?" Reno asked, squeezing her shoulder.

"Yes . . . I . . . Oh, Reno." Suddenly overcome, Adele pressed her face into his chest. His heart boomed against her cheek and she realized he wasn't as serene as he seemed. "What you did. It makes me so proud."

"I did what any self-respecting man would do." He slipped an arm around her and guided her to the saloon. A train whistle blew, and Adele's head automatically went up. Reno laughed. "Wish I could get your attention that easily."

They stood outside the saloon, arms looped around each other's waist, eyes only for the other. Adele's heart pounded furiously with unadulterated love, and she saw the promise of it in his calm, blue gaze.

"You have my attention, Mr. Gold," she assured him. "I saw in you today so many qualities that I admire. I've never been so proud to know anyone in my whole life."

He brows quirked and he grinned lop-sidedly. "That's high praise coming from you, Dellie. If you don't watch out, you'll make me fall spurs over Stetson for you."

"To tell you the truth, I wouldn't mind—"

Doc Martin came puffing from the shadows of the saloon. "I need to get Nugget to my office. Can you help me carry her, Gold?"

"Sure." Reno pecked Adele lightly on the cheek. "We'll continue this discussion later. Maybe tonight, if you'll drop by. It's Ladies' Night, you know."

She smiled. Refusing him any request would be out of the question. "Tonight."

He went inside and came back out with Little Nugget in his arms. Adele and Doc Martin flanked him as he carried the sobbing young woman to the doctor's office. When he started to go inside with her, Little Nugget reached out and snagged Adele's sleeve.

"Thanks for what you did," she said, her voice hoarse and full of pain. "I'll never forget it."

Adele patted her hand. "You'll be all right now."

The train whistle sounded again as the iron horse pulled into the station. Reno nodded toward the depot.

"Go on, Dellie, and tell Mrs. McDonald and the others. I'll stay with Little Nugget until the doc can fix her up, then I'll take her back to my place."

"I'll send Mrs. McDonald to be with her as soon as I can," Dellie promised. She rested a hand on his shoulder and rose up on tiptoe to kiss his cheek. "Thank you, Reno. You're my hero."

She thought he blushed, but she couldn't be sure, as he turned quickly and carried Little Nugget into the doctor's office. Lifting her skirts, she nearly flew down the street to the depot. Spotting her from the window, Colleen rushed outside.

"We heard gunshots. What happened?" Colleen

asked. "Holy Moses, is that blood on your dress?"

"Blood?" Adele glanced at the red drops on her sleeves. "Yes, but not mine. That animal—" Her voice shook with a flash of rage and she drew in a breath to steady herself. "Terrapin took a whip to Little Nugget right in the middle of Main Street."

"The Devil take him," Colleen said, her eyes growing wide. "Is she . . . ?"

"The doctor is with her. Reno stopped Terrapin before he could kill her."

"Mr. Reno?" Colleen sighed and looked at Helen. "Didn't I tell you he was a champion, that one? Did he slay the monster?"

"No, but he made him dance a jig in the street." Adele giggled. "Oh, he was magnificent! You should have seen him, so tall and strong and in control. Terrapin didn't have a chance against him! Where's Sally?"

"In the kitchen with Mrs. McDonald."

Adele brushed past them and walked through the restaurant to the kitchen, where she found Sally slicing pies into wedges. Mrs. McDonald toiled at the stove, her hair hanging in wet curls around her face as she lathered butter onto hot baked sweet potatoes.

Sally dropped the knife she was holding. "Good gracious, what happened to you? You're bleeding!"

"No, not me. Little Nugget is bleeding, thanks to your husband-to-be, the *pig*." Adele spat out the last word, abandoning all pretense of restraint and decorum.

"Little Nugget?" Mrs. McDonald spun around and backhanded the hair out of her eyes. "What happened to her?"

"Terrapin flayed her skin with a bullwhip while every coward in this small-minded town watched and did nothing to stop him." Adele rounded the table and pressed her face close to Sally's. "And he would have been willing and ready to apply that whip to me if Reno hadn't taken aim at him. Reno saved her. Reno, of whom you think so poorly, Sally. He stepped forward and stopped that madman."

"Did Reno hurt him? Are you telling me that my Taylor is dead?"

"No, not yet." Adele shook her head slowly, disgusted. "*Your* Taylor is like any other rat. He's hard to kill. Reno only meant to stop him from murdering Little Nugget. If Reno wanted to shoot him dead, he had a perfect opportunity today. Terrapin's hired gun had gone to fetch the doctor and wasn't around to protect him. But Reno isn't cold-blooded like *your* Taylor. Murder isn't something he can do as easily as he would clip his fingernails."

Sally fell back a step. "That . . . that . . . she must have done something terrible for him to be so angry."

"Little Nugget? Oh yes. She did something despicable, all right. She told him she wanted to work for Reno at the Lucky Strike. Terrapin took a bullwhip to her, laying her clothes and skin open as she ran, screaming." Adele narrowed her eyes. "Sally for God's sake, quit being so stubborn. How can you love such a man?"

Sally's lips trembled and her eyes filled with tears. "I can't believe that he'd . . . If Taylor did this, then he probably caught her robbing or cheating him."

"You can't justify it," Adele said. "If you do, then you're as bad as him." She grabbed Sally by the shoulders and shook her. "Please, Sally, use your head!"

Sally refused to see reason. "I'll talk to Taylor. He'll tell me why he did this."

"I give up!" Turning, Adele pushed through the kitchen door and went to her quarters, hardly aware of the restaurant customers she passed along the way.

Going straight to her desk, she removed a strongbox from the bottom drawer and unlocked it with a key she wore pinned to her garter. Inside it she located a paper folded in three and checked to make sure it was the right one before locking the box and replacing it in the desk drawer.

She tried not to think about the consequences or of the friendship she and Sally had nursed along, propped up and resuscitated again and again. Instead she thought of Terrapin and his black heart and that Sally loved him, or at least professed to love him.

Striding into the kitchen again, Adele pushed open the door in time to see Mrs. McDonald wave a spoon at Sally and Sally slap it aside.

". . . don't care what you think," Sally almost hissed at the cook.

Adele cleared her throat. "Some people are worth fighting for and some people aren't. I just figured out which kind you are." Holding out the paper, she tore it in half. "Your contract," she told Sally, then flung the pieces at her. The pages fluttered to the floor. "You can pack up and leave any time you want. You and Terrapin deserve each other."

Sally looked down at the pieces of paper. "Adele, surely you know that your contract wouldn't have held me here anyway."

"No, but I thought our friendship would. I was wrong."

With a small choking sound, Sally ran from the kitchen. The door flapped behind her, sounding like the broken wing of a huge bird. Adele turned to Mrs. McDonald.

"You go to the doctor's place and check on Little Nugget. But be careful. Terrapin is out for blood." Adele put on an apron. "I'll take over in here."

"If you're sure . . ."

"Yes, I'm sure. Little Nugget will feel better if you're with her. But I would like to go to the Lucky Strike tonight. Will you go with me?"

Mrs. McDonald's eyebrows lifted. "Why, sure thing. It's Ladies' Night, I hear."

"Yes, so I'm told. My husband invited me, and I wouldn't dare refuse him."

Mrs. McDonald chuckled and headed for the swinging door. "Now you're talking, girl!"

Chapter 20

"I'm so nervous," Adele confided to Mrs. McDonald in a whisper as they walked side by side that night down Main Street toward the Lucky Strike Saloon. Colleen and Helen were in front of them, heads together as they spoke in whispers to each other.

Mrs. McDonald smiled. "Why? Because you've never been in a saloon before? I think it's about time. It won't turn you into a harlot, you know."

"I'm not nervous about that. As a matter of fact, I have been in a saloon. My mother and I solicited money for libraries, and we always made sure we visited every saloon in each community, since that was where money was spent frivolously."

"Then what are you nervous about?"

"Seeing Reno, of course. There is so much I want to say to him, so much I need to explain."

Mrs. McDonald sent her an odd look. "You want to *talk* to him? I thought you'd want to be doing something else besides *that!*"

"Yes, but I—I only hope I can express to him how

292

much what he did meant to me. And I hope he will—
well, understand. We're estranged and I..." She
shook her head. "I just never know what he's going
to do or how he's going to act. That's one of the bad
things about him."

"Or one of the good things. Men you can read like
a book don't offer any sweet surprises."

Adele slanted her a glance, struck by the woman's
insight. Surprises had never been pleasant for Adele,
but Reno's spontaneity was refreshing. Yes, his un-
predictability could be unnerving, but he certainly
had made her life more interesting!

Colleen and Helen ducked inside the saloon ahead
of them. Adele's heartbeats accelerated. She stopped
and checked her dress, smoothing imaginary wrinkles
from the emerald-green skirt. She knew the style flat-
tered her by hugging her figure. The neckline dipped
low enough to be provocative but not so low as to be
considered scandalous. She had arranged her hair in
a loose bundle on top of her head, allowing a few
curling tendrils to frame her face and caress her nape.
She had applied the rose water Reno liked to her
pulse points and had enhanced her cheeks and lips
with a touch of rouge.

"You sparkle like a jewel," Mrs. McDonald assured
her. "It ain't like you've got to win him over. He's
already your husband." She tucked her hand in the
crook of Adele's arm. "Let's go."

Adele hung back, her gaze fastened on the saloon
across the street. The public whipping had not damaged Terrapin's business. Both the saloon and the
gaming hall were bustling. She looked up and stiffened when she saw Buck Wilhite standing on the sec-

ond-story balcony of the Black Knight. He tipped his hat to her.

"That vulture," she said, striding on with Mrs. McDonald. "He circles and waits for death, and if it doesn't come quick enough, he helps it along."

"Any man who makes his living killing for someone else ain't worth beans."

"He went for the doctor today. I asked him to stop Terrapin and he wouldn't do that, but he did go for the doctor."

"That don't earn him no admiration or gratitude from me. Any fool can run for the doctor. But there *is* something I noticed about him."

"What?"

"He don't care for the way Taylor does business. Buck ain't too pleased with what's going on around here and his part in it. I think he believed Taylor was a bigger man in a bigger town. Buck's out to make a name for himself, but it will be hard work in this town." She let loose a bark of laughter. "Whistle Stop ain't Dodge City!"

Adele sighed. "Maybe he'll move on and we can all sleep easier."

"Let's not waste another thought on him." Mrs. McDonald squared her shoulders and placed a bright smile on her face. "After I make sure Little Nugget is resting easy, I'm going to snag me a partner and dance my shoes off!"

They opened the double doors and stepped inside. The tinkling of a piano and the joyous strumming of a banjo greeted them. More than half the people inside were women. Adele was taken aback by that. Ladies' Night, she reminded herself, but she was surprised to see which town ladies were present.

Salt of the earth women. Adele spotted Clarice Nolan, the General Store owner's wife, and Lucille Miller, the proprietor of the boardinghouse. Oh, and wasn't that Opal Martin, the doctor's wife? Colleen and Helen sat at a table with Henry Staples, one of the town bachelors and a frequent restaurant customer.

Catching sight of a man's chiseled profile and blue-black hair, Adele's hungry eyes latched onto them. Reno stood beside the piano, looking sophisticated in a dark-blue suit and white shirt, black tie, and gold vest. He laughed at something the piano player said. Adele held her breath, waiting for him to notice her.

Around her the voices ceased to whisper and the bodies stilled. Reno furrowed his brow, evidently sensing the decrease in activity and the unnatural hush. He surveyed the area, and his gaze landed on her. A smile touched the corners of his mouth. Adele released her pent-up breath and realized that he wasn't the only one staring at her. She commanded all eyes in the room. The music dwindled to a few trailing notes before subsiding altogether.

Glancing around, Adele felt as conspicuous as if she were stark naked. She felt her face flame and she took an involuntary step backward; she might have fled if Mrs. McDonald hadn't kept hold of her arm.

Reno walked toward them, his gaze on Adele, his route direct, unwavering. People eased out of his way, giving him ready access to her. He dipped his head slightly.

"Good evening, ladies."

"We came to check on Little Nugget," Mrs. Mc-

Donald said when it became obvious that Adele had lost her voice.

"You've come to make a sick call in those dresses?" he asked, his eyes alight with mischief.

"If she's on the mend and doesn't need me, I hope to take a turn on the dance floor."

Reno moved to one side. "I believe she's doing well. She's upstairs. Let me show you the way. After you, ladies."

Adele followed Mrs. McDonald and Reno followed Adele. Intensely aware of his trailing presence, she tried to move with grace and quickness. She wove around tables and chairs and smiled at the people she recognized. Although it took less than a minute to reach the stairs, she felt she had traveled a mile.

On the second-floor landing, she and Mrs. McDonald waited for Reno to open a door to their left. They went inside a room lit by the low flame of a lantern, which illuminated the bed where Little Nugget was recuperating from her unspeakable ordeal. She raised her head from the pillow and smiled wanly.

"I knew you'd come," she said in a hoarse voice. Lying on her side, she lifted a hand toward them. "Come here, Doris. And Mrs. Adele. I owe you my life."

"Oh, no," Adele said, shaking her head. "Reno is the one to thank for that."

The door closed softly behind her, and Adele turned to find that Reno had left them. Her heart sank a little.

"So how are you feeling?" Mrs. McDonald asked, approaching the bed.

"Tender," Little Nugget admitted. "My back is on fire. The doctor said there wasn't much he could do. He cleaned me up and slathered the wounds with some kind of stinging, smelly medicine, then bandaged me." Her light-brown eyes filled with tears. "I'm going to be scarred."

"Oh, honey." Mrs. McDonald dropped to her knees beside the bed and stroked Little Nugget's pale blond hair. "I'm just thankful you're alive. That man almost killed you."

Adele walked around to the other side of the bed. Through the gauzy material of the girl's nightgown she could see the crisscrossing bandages, stained pink. She perched on the edge of the mattress and ran a hand down Little Nugget's arm.

She was so small and fragile, Adele thought, her stomach twisting into knots. But she was tough. That was what was so endearing about Little Nugget. That huge spirit and big heart housed in a petite package. How could anyone beat her? She'd been through so much. Her young life had been full of disappointments and loss and fear. Little Nugget turned her head and her large brown eyes located Adele. She smiled, and Adele's heart melted into a puddle.

"I'll never forget what you did," Little Nugget whispered. "I won't go back to that life. From now on I'm going to make you proud of me."

Adele swallowed a sob and pushed the damp, curling tendrils of Little Nugget's hair off her forehead. "Darling girl, you don't have to prove anything to me. I want you to leave this saloon work for your own peace of mind and your own pride. You deserve the best in life, not the worst. We all do, and that's why we must all reach for the moon and not be satisfied with less."

"I wish I'd met you sooner."

"Me, too," Doris McDonald said, her eyes brimming.

"As much as I would like to accept all the credit, I can't. Reno deserves your gratitude more than I do. He's the one who hired you, Mrs. McDonald, and he's the one who made Terrapin stop whipping you, Little Nugget."

"Did you hear about Buck Wilhite?"

"No, what about him?" Adele asked.

"The doctor said Buck told him he was leaving Whistle Stop."

Mrs. McDonald cackled and slapped herself on the thigh. "Ain't that something? We were just hoping for that."

"He's going to work on some ranch."

"A ranch?" Adele exchanged a dubious glance with Mrs. McDonald. "I can't imagine him being a cowpoke."

"He's supposed to keep squatters and cattle thieves from stealing some rancher blind. They call that being a 'Regulator.'" Little Nugget sighed and closed her eyes. "Things won't be as bad once he's gone." She moaned and tears ran from the corners of her eyes. "I'm so tired of this. I wish somebody would put a bullet into Taylor's head."

"Hush, honey," Mrs. McDonald whispered. "You rest easy."

"Let's be thankful you're safe and will be well again," Adele added. "Did you notice that Mrs.

McDonald is all dressed up tonight? She hopes to lure a nice man onto the dance floor."

"Oh yeah?" Little Nugget blinked away tears and mustered a grin. "And what's your excuse?"

Adele felt a blush bloom in her cheeks. "Me? Oh, I wanted to look nice for my husband."

"You go on and have your ... talk," Mrs. McDonald said with a grin. She pulled a chair close to the bed and sat down. "I'll stay a few more minutes with Little Nugget before I take my chances downstairs."

"Okay." Adele waved to Little Nugget. "I'll check in on you tomorrow."

Leaving the room, Adele closed the door softly behind her. Sprightly music floated up to her, marked by bursts of laughter and the tinkle of glasses. A shadow moved in the hall and she jerked, startled, before she saw that it was Reno. Adele smelled the spicy aroma of his toilet water and the flash of white teeth when he smiled.

"She's better than I thought she'd be," Adele said, glancing at the closed door. "But she'll be scarred, poor thing."

He cupped her elbow in one hand. "She's young and pretty and she'll be fine. Let's go in here and get away from the noise." He indicated another door, then reached out with his free hand and opened it. "After you. It's not fancy, but it's private."

Her nerves all aflutter, Adele entered and stood near the door while he lit a lamp and turned up the wick. The room was sparsely furnished but clean and neat. A lovely patchwork quilt draped a man-sized bed. A wash stand stood against one wall along with a large hammered-metal tub. She smelled his toilet water and saw a bottle of it sitting on top of the bureau. So this was where he'd been sleeping, she thought, noticing his clothes hanging on a line stretched across one corner.

"Wine?"

"What?" She tore her gaze away from the bed and saw that he held a decanter in his hand.

"Do you want some wine?" he repeated.

She started to agree, then shook her head. "No. I don't need it."

"God, Dellie. You're beautiful."

He set down the cut-glass decanter and gathered her into his arms. The heat of his kiss fired her desire, and she clung to him, opened her lips to him, moaned into his mouth. Tension broke in her like a storm raging through her and freeing her. She raked her fingers through his hair and breathed in his aroma, slanting her mouth under his.

"Reno, Reno," she whispered between kisses. "I'm so proud of you I could burst. When you appeared today like some knight in shining armor, oh, I wanted to throw my arms around you and kiss you until you pleaded for me to stop."

A smile twitched the corners of his mouth. His lips warmed her and his hands skimmed down her back and over her hips. He pulled her closer, his body intimate with hers.

"You're the bravest man I've ever met," she told him, closing her eyes and tipping her head to one side so that his mouth could dance along her neck.

"And you're the bravest woman I know. I brought

you in here to seduce you, not for your undying gratitude."

"Seduce me?" She ran her hands down his arms, feeling the muscles beneath his sleeves. "Did you really think you'd have to? I'm your wife, remember?"

He straightened away from her and his stormy blue eyes bored into her. "Oh yes, and I remember you asked me to pack up and leave."

"No, I didn't." She quelled the urge to argue hotly, but she wanted to get a few things straight. "I tore up Sally's contract. You were right about her. She is so determined to have money again, not to have to work for a living, that she refuses to see that Terrapin is a demon. And you're right about other things, too."

He arched a brow. "Go on."

"You're enjoying this, aren't you?"

"Immensely," he assured her, moving away to pour himself a glass of wine.

"Maybe I've lost faith since Kansas," she allowed. "But I have regained my faith in you." She waited for him to say something, but he merely sipped the wine. She stamped one foot in irritation. "Tell me you forgive me, you pig-headed fool! Don't you want to bury the hatchet?"

He laughed and finished the wine. "I forgive you, Dellie. But do you forgive me?"

"For what?"

"For this saloon, of course. What do you think of it?"

She stalled for time by cruising around the room and trailing her fingertips along the bed's counterpane. "It's not what I expected. It seems . . . respectable."

"Uh-huh. Just like me."

Smiling at his teasing tone, she sat on the bed, testing its give. "You are the most cocky man I've ever known. You take self-confidence to new heights."

"Have a drink, Dellie, and loosen up." He handed her a half-filled glass.

"You think I need this?" she asked, taking the wine from him and sniffing its heady bouquet. She tasted it, then set it aside when she noticed that her hands were trembling.

"I wanted to open this saloon mainly to help this town and you."

"Me?" Adele asked, confused. "How could the Lucky Strike help me?"

"By breaking Terrapin's reign of terror and making Whistle Stop a safe place for you to live."

"You should have talked to me about it before you agreed to run this place."

"Why?"

"Because we're married." She stared at him stubbornly. "As much as I don't want to fight anymore, I will *not* surrender on this point, Reno."

He grinned. "You don't want to fight, huh?"

"No, I don't."

"What *do* you want to do?"

She sighed, a knot of nerves shifting in her stomach. He looked so handsome in his suit of blue and his vest of gold, his eyes darkly intense, his lips full and smiling. And she felt no shame for wanting him, body and soul. She wanted his hands on her, his mouth on hers, his heart hammering in time with hers.

"Oh, Reno," she whispered, lust making her voice

husky. "There is hope for us, isn't there? Don't you want to make love to me right this moment?"

A shudder coursed down his body and the glass fell from his hand to shatter. He stared at the jagged pieces at his feet, clearly surprised, then he withdrew a handkerchief from his jacket pocket and absently wiped his hands.

Sweet, sinful pleasure gripped Adele. His actions told her what she needed to know.

"You *do* still want to be my husband," she murmured.

His eyes met hers, and passion leapt like flames in them, hot and sky high. He tossed aside the damp handkerchief. Impatience balled his hands into fists.

"Only as much as I want to breathe," he assured her, and then he was across the room, pulling her up from the bed and into his arms.

Chapter 21

Lust was in his kiss. Adele responded to it like a starving woman to a three-course meal. Sliding her hands down his chest, she latched onto his lapels and slipped the jacket off his shoulders, eager to have him.

He laughed against her mouth, his breath mingling with hers, his fingers freeing buttons, unlacing ties, dividing fabric. She caught the end of his tie in her teeth and gave a tug. It fell to ruin. Upon unbuttoning his shirt, she pressed a hot kiss against the center of his chest. He released a shuddering breath.

"Darlin', you're going to be the death of me if I don't get you naked and under me in about two seconds."

She laughed and kissed his shoulder as she peeled off his white shirt. "I'm still dizzy from this afternoon when you made Terrapin dance in the street. I've thought of nothing else but you—you and me, together again."

Catching her by the shoulders, Reno spun around and fell back onto the bed, taking her with him. He pushed the top of her dress down, exposing the creamy whiteness of her breasts to his lambent gaze. His lips sandwiched one of her nipples, and she groaned, her eyes closing, her mind shutting down for a few tumultuous moments. He rolled with her, his body pressing on top of hers.

"You're beautiful, Dellie," he murmured against the curve of her breast. "When you walked into the saloon tonight, you took my breath away."

"Let me give it back," she whispered, holding his head between her hands and pulling his mouth down to hers.

The surroundings were strange to her, but not the man. He was the epitome of her dreams, made all the more beautiful because he was flesh and blood, bone and sinew. Adele welcomed the slick stroke of his tongue on hers and the kneading of his fingers on her breasts. She needed no experience with other men to know that he was the one she lived for.

Her tongue courted his, ebbing and flowing, stroking and retreating, until he latched his mouth to hers and sent his tongue deep. Her heels climbed the back of his legs, and she realized she'd kicked off her shoes at some point. He ground his pelvis against her, and she felt him, thick and hard. That she could bring him to such readiness thrilled her, spurred her on to their ultimate completion.

He sat up and eased her dress off her body. Her underthings soon followed until she wore nothing except a passion-induced blush.

"My God, you are a vision," he muttered. He unbuckled his belt and unfastened his trousers.

Adele watched, the simple act of his undressing in

front of her unbelievably arousing. His body was long and lean, dusted with ebony hair, sculpted by muscle. When he came back to her, his skin was almost hot to the touch, and she could feel the thrum of his pulse.

"You sure you don't want to fight?" he murmured in her ear, his teeth catching her lobe, nipping gently.

"Fight? Why would you want to fight now?"

"Oh, I think a little tussle might be fun. You know, just to see who comes out on top."

"You devil," she said, laughing under her breath and knowing there would be no losers in this game. "You're on."

His mouth sealed against hers. His tongue was hot and wet. Adele's breath came in short gasps as his hands gently massaged the softness of her breasts. He rolled her nipples between his thumbs and forefingers until they became pink pearls, then he took one into his mouth and laved it with his tongue. She moaned and trailed her short nails down his back.

Giving the other rosy crest his attention, he sucked and wet her skin thoroughly. Her hands clamped onto his buttocks and pulled him to her. She parted her thighs and rocked her pelvis against him. One of her hands surrounded his straining organ and guided him into her. He gasped, flinging back his head in sweet, sweet agony.

She was everything beautiful and winsome and wild. In her, he was whole, and he grew still for a full minute to experience the intensity of his pleasure. She stared up into his eyes, hers as green as emeralds. Her dark hair fanned the white pillow, some strands still secured by pins. He leaned forward, the musky perfume of her hair enveloping him as he sought the stubborn rebels with his teeth, located each, and pulled it free. She smiled, and her inner muscles tightened around him.

"Ahhh, Dellie. Where did you learn to do that?"

"I had a splendid teacher."

"I didn't teach you that. I believe you stumbled upon that all by yourself." His voice broke on the last word as those magic muscles gloved him. He kissed her fully, his tongue dancing with hers, his body imitating that dance.

He thrust against her hard, driving her head into the soft pillow. She closed her eyes and mouthed his name, her hands still clutching his hips and her heels hooked behind his knees. Withdrawing slowly, he enjoyed the sensations bursting in his blood and firing his nerve endings. He joined with her again, and a shudder ran the length of her body. She arched against him and pushed at his shoulders. He realized she wanted him on his back.

Obliging, he hooked an arm around her waist and flipped over, bringing her with him so that she straddled him. Her long legs, bent at the knees, clamped against his sides, making him a prisoner of her desire.

Looking up at her, he felt like a favored god staring at a goddess of unequaled beauty. Her high breasts and hard, rosy nipples sent a new surge of blood to his extremities. Inside her, he bucked and hardened to near agony. She leaned forward and kissed him, laving his lips with her tongue and biting his lower lip playfully. Her fingers tweaked his flat nipples, bringing them to tingling awareness.

She caressed his chest, her hands pressing and smoothing and delving. Bending forward, she let her hair sweep over his chest and neck and face. He trembled with the exertion of holding onto the last thread of self-control. A thin veneer of perspiration covered his skin and hers.

Her eyes glinted with something carnal and her lips curved in a sensuous smile. He felt caught, pinned, branded. He loved it.

"Hard and hot," she whispered. "And mine."

To his utter astonishment and undying gratitude, she leaned back, lifting herself up and then down. Up, then down, up, down. Her pace was steady and slow, agonizingly slow. He gripped her waist, steadying himself rather than her. She needed no guidance from him. She was in control.

His heart flung itself against her ribs, and he knew he was teetering, ready to dive into bliss.

"Dellie . . . oh, Lord . . . I . . . I—" He clenched his teeth, hearing himself babble as his body trembled and his flesh caught fire.

Her tempo quickened. Reasonable thoughts melted. Primitive responses erupted.

He grasped her waist tightly and rode out his passion, his body acting on its own and exploding inside her in four sharp bursts that she answered with four long moans.

She crumpled like a rag doll, falling over him like a shower of sparks. Her skin was slickly hot and her breath burned his shoulder. He draped an arm over her and kissed her flushed cheek. He saw her smile before he closed his eyes, ready to drift away.

"Who's on top, Reno?" she whispered in his ear.

His eyes popped open and he examined the situation. "Let's go for two out of three."

Laughing, she rolled off him and sprawled at his side, her hair spread across the pillow. "You just don't know when to quit."

He trailed a fingertip over one of her pouting nipples, sending rays of pleasure searing through her.

"That's right, darlin'. Are you complaining?"

Turning onto her side, she flung one long, shapely leg over his hip. "Nope. Are you?"

"Never." Wrapping his arms around her, he pulled her close to him, belly against belly, chest against breasts. Heaven in his arms, he thought lazily. Heaven.

She realized she'd fallen asleep when she was roused by Reno's warm lips on her shoulder. Smiling, she kept her eyes closed while his mouth traveled down her arm to place a kiss on the inside of her elbow.

"Dellie?"

"Hmmm?"

"Where did you learn what to do when a woman is on top?"

Furrowing her brow, she had to think for a few moments before she understood what he meant. "I don't know. I guess I just did what came naturally. I did to you what I'd dreamed about doing."

"I like the way you dream, sugar." He chuckled and pulled her back against him.

"Why did you ask? Are you suspicious of me? Did you think I was holding out on you?"

"No. I thought you'd read about it somewhere, and if so, I wanted to borrow that book."

She laughed and snuggled closer. "I guess, like

most everything else, I'm a quick study."

"I'll say!"

"I know one thing for sure."

"What's that?"

"I like that kind of fighting."

He chuckled. "Me, too."

A snippet of music from downstairs floated into the room, reminding Adele of the rest of the world. She traced the curve of his upper lip with her fingertip and admired the bold lines of his face and the dimple in his chin. "Does this mean we're going to patch up our differences?" she asked.

"I'm willing if you are."

"I'm willing." She caught her lower lip between her teeth, seized by momentary shyness. "I've been thinking about what you said about how I've changed."

"We've all changed."

"Yes, that's true, but I can see how it's true that I've become more guarded and not as willing to give the benefit of doubt to others. Since my mother's death—well, perhaps even before that—I've been fearful. That hardens the heart and tests the faith."

"Fearful?" He caught her hand and kissed her fingers. "What are you afraid of, Dellie?"

"Of failing. Of being thrown out on the street because I can't make a decent living for myself. Of never having a real home. Of being condemned to a life of wandering—like my mother. She said she didn't mind traveling from city to city, going wherever she was needed, but I minded. I resented that life very much."

"I know, Dellie."

"You do?" she asked, surprised by his quick admission.

"Yes, you told me. Don't you remember that day we went for a swim in the pond and we told each other our most secret wish, our deepest desire?"

"Oh yes." The day came back to her in all its summer heat and wildflower beauty. The murky pond water had felt like cool silk on her skin, weighting her undergarments so that she had to stay in the shallows for fear that she might be dragged to the bottom. Reno had dared her to strip them off, but she hadn't accepted the challenge. Later, when they had stretched on the grassy bank to let their underclothes dry on their bodies, they had exposed secrets instead of skin. Far more risky, Adele thought. Far more revealing.

"You wished for wealth," she said, and he nodded. "And you desired a big family to spend your money on."

"You remember," he acknowledged. "You wished to find someone you could depend on to be around when you needed him, and you desired a home—not just a house, you said, but a home to grow old in."

She laughed softly and ran her fingers through the downy hair on his chest. "Yes, and I thought thirty was ancient back then. I figured if I reached that doddering age, all I'd want is a rocking chair by the fire."

"I didn't tell the truth that day, Dellie."

"You didn't?"

"No. My deepest desire was to be the someone you could depend on." His smile could touch any woman's heart and Adele's was no exception. "I couldn't tell you that then. You would have laughed."

"I wouldn't have laughed. I would have been surprised, because I didn't know you liked me in that way back then."

"Yes, you were blind."

"No, I was looking in a different direction."

"At Win."

"Yes. Everyone seemed to believe we belonged with each other, and I tried to make it so, but I couldn't."

"And I was damned glad."

"Yes." She smiled. "I do remember you jumping for joy and grabbing me up and spinning me around until I was dizzy."

He laughed with her and held her closer, nuzzling her hair. "It would have broken my heart if you'd married him."

His confession brought sudden tears to her eyes. She blinked them away and cleared her throat of emotion. "Probably would have broken mine, too," she admitted. She kissed his shoulder. "I'll try not to be so bossy from now on, Reno, if you'll be more careful around Terrapin. Why court trouble? Court me, instead." She breathed in his ear and tickled it with her tongue.

He hunched his shoulder. "How can I resist you, sugar?" He rolled on top of her and grinned. "You've got a deal. We bring out the best in each other, Dellie. I swear we do."

She lifted her head to seal his mouth with hers. Stroking his ribs and back, she opened her lips to the seduction of his tongue.

His pace was lazy, his kisses slow and deep, making her simmer sweetly. Stretching like a cat, she brought her hands up over her head and grasped the metal bars of the bedstead. Reno moved down her body to lavish on her breasts wet kisses that made her tingle madly. She writhed with frustration and longing, gripping the metal bars with all her might as the carnal assault continued. Her breasts grew heavy and hot, her nipples throbbing with each beat of her heart.

Gathering one in each hand, he teased the hard crests while his mouth moved ever south over her stomach, her hip bone, her thigh. He pressed warm kisses on her knees and inner thighs, making her tremble with need and abandon any notion of changing positions to get the best of him. She was already getting his best.

He kissed her most private place, and she drew in a sharp breath and released the bedstead. Her hands moved of their own accord to his head, clutching desperately as her mind fought with her body. *More, more*, her body screamed.

Then his mouth settled on that intimate place again, and his tongue touched a spot that sent fire shooting through her veins, eradicating all rational thought.

The power of her passion was almost frightening. She felt as if she'd been pulled under by an immense wave of feeling. She could hear herself gasping for breath as she clutched his head and arched her body against his sucking mouth. Her legs trembled and colors exploded behind her eyes. Moaning his name, she thought she might black out, but he lifted his mouth and moved up her body.

He entered her and she convulsed around him. The blistering pace he set left no time for tender kisses or whispered words. Theirs was a tumultuous, panting, sweating, grasping completion. Adele felt as if she'd run a race when Reno relaxed against her. Her heart boomed and her breath came in labored hiccups. She filled her lungs, and the haze of passion lifted from her mind. He was still inside her, filling her, stretching her.

She caressed his shoulders and back. He was so big and masculine! She could hardly believe he was hers to love, to build a dream on. His lips moved against the side of her neck. He pulled out of her. Her body shuddered from the long good-bye.

"Every time I make love to you, I think I've died and gone to heaven," he whispered.

"Me, too," She stroked his hair, loving this man who could speak such things to her.

"Being with you like this is so incredible. I'm afraid it's a dream and I'll wake up."

"It is a dream, but a waking one."

He shifted to his side and she nestled in his embrace. Just like home, she thought, and went to sleep on a smile.

Moving quietly around the room, Adele located her various pieces of clothing and dressed, early-morning sunlight illuminating the space. She let Reno sleep. Occasionally she glanced at him, attracted to the boyish quality of his features in repose. Her musings meandered like a stream, winding through special times she'd shared with Reno. In retrospect she realized he had secured a special place in her heart from the moment she'd met him.

Winston had introduced them. Adele had been attracted to Reno's wild side. He hadn't tried to fit in, but challenged people to take him as he was: a mis-

chievous rakehell. He didn't care about bloodlines
and ancestors, didn't try to conform or compromise
or change. He cared only for fun and trying new
things, taking a chance.

Adele had accepted him, happy to share his company because he was infinitely fascinating.

Still is, she allowed, glancing at his reflection in the
bureau mirror. His lashes were thick and inky on his
cheeks and his ebony hair was adorably tousled.
Sorely tempted to jump back into bed with him, she
focused her attention on brushing her hair and pinning it in place on top of her head. She had to attend
to business, no matter how much she would like to
stay in bed with Reno. She wanted to check on Little
Nugget before she left, too. After all, if it hadn't been
for her, Adele would have spent last night alone
again.

By coming to Little Nugget's rescue, Reno had
made Adele see that his good points far outweighed
his bad ones and that it wasn't his fault that she had
expected too much of him. She still believed he could
better himself, but she knew he would have to go
about it in his own way. If this saloon was a stepping-
stone for him, so be it. She would accept it and hope
that he moved onto something else soon.

Whenever possible she would give him a gentle
push in the direction he should go. However, she had
to remember he was a rebel and that was one of the
things she had always loved about him. Rebels could
not be tamed, but they could be guided.

When she laid the hairbrush down on the bureau,
she noticed a telegram lying open there. The saluta-
tion caught her attention and begged her perusal:
"Dear Partner."

Who would be calling Reno a partner? She glanced at the name signed at the end of the message: "Lewis Fields."

The name held a familiar ring, but she couldn't place it. Giving in to her curiosity, she picked up the sheet of paper and read the message.

DEAR PARTNER,

ASSUME YOU ARE NOW PROUD OWNER OF SA-LOON(STOP)WANT YOU TO MEET MY BRIDE(STOP) WANT TO MEET YOURS TOO(STOP)F&G PRINTING BUSINESS DOING WELL(STOP)MAKING POTS OF MONEY(STOP)PLEASE

The paper was suddenly plucked from her fingers by Reno, looking tousled and sleepy-eyed and a little annoyed.

"Morning, sugar. Looking for something in particular or are you just plain nosey?"

"I didn't think you'd mind if I read that telegram, since it was lying out in the open."

"Did you notice it was addressed to me?"

"Yes." She narrowed her eyes, thinking about what she'd read. Reno held the paper above her head, out of reach. That he was trying to keep it from her was infuriating. She jumped and snagged the telegram, then danced backward when he tried to grab it. "What are you hiding, Reno? Who is Lewis Fields? Why does he think you own this saloon?"

She regarded him, her gaze slipping down his na-ked body, her pulse quickening when she noticed that he wasn't completely . . . at ease. She grinned. He frowned and snatched the sheet off the bed, wrapping it around his waist.

"Lewis is a fella I know from back in Deadwood." He kicked at the clothes on the floor. "Where the hell are my pants?"

She pointed to the other side of the bed. "Somewhere over there, I think. Does he own this saloon?"

"No, I do."

Adele laughed, shaking her head. "Very funny. Now tell me the truth, Reno. No more games."

He sat on the side of the bed, trousers in hand, and brought his gaze up to hers. "All right. No more games." He dropped his pants back to the floor and spread a hand over his chest in the region of his heart. "As much as I hate to tell you this, as much as it pains me to burst your bubble . . ." He drew in a deep breath and shook his head in a moment of high drama.

"Just spit it out, Gold," Adele snapped.

"Okay, okay. Dellie, not only am I the bravest man you've ever met, I'm afraid I'm also the richest." He sent her a devilish wink. "My last name isn't Gold for nothing, sugar."

Chapter 22

❦

"**R**ich?" For a moment she believed him, but then the absurdity of the idea tickled her and she laughed and waved the telegram at him like a flag. "Do I look like a fool, Reno Gold? Now quit your joshing and tell me the truth."

"Sorry, sugar, that *is* the truth." He stood and turned his back to Adele while he jerked up his trousers and buttoned them. "I own this saloon and Lewis is my business partner. I met him in Deadwood after I struck it lucky. He was the only honest man in town, and I needed someone who was level-headed to show me what to do with my money and how to make more of it." He faced her again, arching a brow and waiting for her reaction.

Adele propped her hands at her waist, trying to figure out what mischief he was cooking up. "You're telling me that you struck gold in Deadwood? One in a hundred men find gold. Everyone knows that."

"You're looking at one, sugar. I struck it lucky and I doubled my money at the gaming tables. I was called the Midas Man, the man with the golden touch.

I made so much I became a target for every thief and snake-oil salesman in the territory. That's when I hooked up with Lewis. He has a nose for investments."

Dropping the telegram back onto the bureau, Adele gave him a scolding look. He was in a rare mood, but she was tired of his fun and games. "I have more important things to do than listen to your tall tales, Reno Gold. In another hour the restaurant will open for breakfast and the 8:20 Liberty Bell will be rolling into the depot. I must be on my way or—" She chopped off the rest when Reno's hand closed around her upper arm. "What is it?"

"Listen to me, damn it all!" He shook her a little, sending home his point. "I've been wanting to tell you the truth for awhile now, but you always said something snooty and I'd clam up. You have to believe me, Dellie. I'm not penniless. I own a printing business and a chain of newspapers with Lewis. I'm rich, darlin'. Filthy rich."

The seriousness etched on his face killed the vestiges of humor lingering in her. A coldness invaded her heart, and she wrenched away from him as the import of his news careened through her brain like a runaway railcar. She retreated to a safe distance from him, afraid that if she was too close she'd slap him.

"Why did you keep this from me?" She shook her head, trying to fling her thoughts into order. "When did all this happen? F&G—that is Fields and Gold?"

"Yes." Reno released a sigh and spread out his arms in appeal. "Lewis lives in Kansas City now. He married a few months ago, just before I answered your advertisement for a husband."

"Is that why you answered it? You wanted to marry because your friend had done so?"

"No, that had nothing to do with it." He ran a hand down his bare chest. His suspenders hung loosely at his sides. His bare feet slapped the floor as he went to the window and pushed back the curtains to let in more light.

Adele looked at the sun-dappled bed and its tangle of sheets. She had thought she knew the man she'd slept with last night, but when she brought her gaze around to him again, she felt as if she was looking at a stranger.

"You lied to me." The words hung like a guillotine blade between them.

"I didn't want to."

"You're saying that I forced you to lie to me?" She laughed harshly.

"I wanted to tell you the truth." He pushed a hand through his hair and groaned. "I should have, I admit it. When I saw the advertisement, I decided it would be fun to offer myself as a husband. I never thought you'd take it seriously, but you did."

"Why wouldn't I?"

One corner of his mouth twitched, but not with humor. Adele sensed irony there. "That's part of the problem," he admitted. "I never for a minute thought you'd believe me to be so indigent that I'd need to marry to pull myself up a rung."

"What was I to think? You answered the advertisement, so I assumed you looked upon it as an opportunity."

"Exactly. You assumed. It never crossed your narrow mind that I might be having fun with you."

"No." She gave him a cool look. "And my mind is no more narrow than yours. So you never wanted to marry me? You were making fun of me in answering my advertisement?"

"No, that's not right either. I wanted to see you. I thought you'd write back and invite me to visit. But you sent me a train ticket and a list of your expectations. Remember? You expected me at a certain time and on a certain day. I was to understand that you were not offering me money or property. You were only agreeing to a marriage." He frowned. "I would have sent you a telegram telling you what you could do with your expectations if it hadn't been for that last line of your letter."

She folded her arms and glared at him. "And what was that?"

"You wrote that you remembered our days together fondly and that you were anxious to see me again." The frown slipped away. "I wanted to see you, Dellie. So I stowed my pride and boarded the train."

"No doubt your pride took up one of the freight cars."

He grinned rakishly. "Two of them."

"So you came here and have lied ever since. Why did you marry me? If you have so much money, why go through with the wedding?"

"I had every intention of telling you that I'd come to renew old acquaintance and I didn't expect you to marry me, but on the train ride I started worrying that you'd be embarrassed or angry that I'd answered your summons for a husband. I started drinking . . ."

"Yes, you certainly did." She glanced at the bed

and couldn't stand seeing the aftermath of their love-making. With swift, sure movements she stripped the linens from it.

"When I came to, you were lording it over me, treating me like a vagabond instead of an old friend and—well, it singed my tail feathers."

"I knew you'd manage to make your lies my fault."

"No, I take some of the blame."

She arched a cynical brow. "How noble of you." She tossed the linens at him, hitting him squarely in the face. "You make me so mad I could spit!"

Reno's temper spiked, and he flung aside the sheets and kicked at them in aggravation. "It's exactly that kind of attitude that makes me want to teach you a lesson you won't soon forget."

He rounded on her, his face suffused with color, the cords of his neck standing out. He reminded her of a charging bull. Grabbing her by the upper arms, he pulled her to him and kissed her solidly, his lips as hard as her determination not to respond to him. Grinding his lips against hers, he continued his punishing kiss. Adele endured it, sensing that it was hurting him far more than her. Finally he pushed her away from him and cursed under his breath.

Adele folded her arms and stared calmly at him, her own irritation and fury simmering deep. She refused to shout and cry in front of him. His lying had cost her enough already.

"What was that supposed to prove?" she asked.

"Nothing!" He made a sweeping gesture, dismissing the kiss and what it was supposed to accomplish. "When you look at me like that, when you spout your rules and look down your nose at me, I can't take it,

Dellie! You sound like your snooty friends in Lawrence. All I ever wanted was for you to listen to your good as gold heart."

"How was marrying me and lying to me supposed to accomplish that?" She tapped one foot impatiently, biding her time, her throat thickening, her own anger bubbling just beneath the surface. How could he justify lying to her, letting her make a fool of herself over him?

"I don't know. Things got out of hand." He sat on the bare mattress and the bed frame squeaked under his weight. "I figured we would marry and I'd show you that you could love me without changing me. Every day I came close to confessing, and every day you'd say something that would get my dander up and I'd choke on the truth." He sighed. "I'm glad the truth is out."

He had the audacity to smile at her! Adele shook with anger. She wished she could shoot fire from her eyes and burn him to a crisp.

"So you married me to make a fool of me, to humiliate me by keeping the truth from me and then springing it on me one day so that you could rub my nose in it and have a good laugh." As she spoke, the words fueled her anger and pain at being betrayed by him. Tears stung her eyes and she whirled away from him, not wanting him to see that she was nearly undone.

"Now, Dellie, don't be like that. After all, you're being a hypocrite."

She swiped at her eyes and cut him with a sharp glare. "What are you talking about? I'm not the one who just admitted to marrying someone just to—"

"Dellie, all you've done is try to teach everyone how to live their lives," he interrupted. "Every soul you come in contact with you try to mold into the person *you* think they should be."

"That's another lie," she said, giving him a shove that barely tested him.

"Oh? Who was it who made me do chores before I got a kiss?"

"You agreed to that. No one forced it on you."

"True, but leave it to you to think up such a trade."

"I was only trying to move you in the right direction."

"Yes, the direction you chose for me. When I told you I was managing this saloon—"

"Another lie!"

"—you didn't approve, and it wasn't a complete lie since I *am* managing it."

She started to tell him that her main objection to the saloon was the high price Taylor Terrapin would put on his head because of it, but he continued to fling accusations at her like stones.

"You won't let Sally marry who she wants without a fight from you."

"I tore up her contract."

"But only after lecturing her and ruining your friendship." He held up one hand to ward off her comment. "I admit, your friendship with her wasn't worth much, but you seemed to value it."

"I will not stand here and be lectured by you." She reached for her gloves. His hands settled on her shoulders.

"Dellie, don't leave mad."

"Let go of me."

"Look at it this way, we've both learned important things about each other—"

"You never meant to stay married to me," she charged, that one point sticking into her heart like a thorn. "You only meant to prove something."

"So did you! Hell, you used me to prove to the town that ordering a spouse is wrong. It backfired because you and I have gotten close, closer than you ever imagined."

She shook free of him, tears spilling onto her cheeks. "Yes, this marriage certainly has backfired. But don't worry, Reno. I've learned my lesson. I have seen the error of my ways." She fastened her gaze on him, extending him a cool look of disdain. "I know now that I should have sent you packing the minute you stepped off the train and saved myself this heartache."

"Dellie, don't—"

She knew it was futile to stay another moment, because she had no voice left, only sobs. Dodging his attempt to detain her, she opened the door and ran out of the room and down the stairs, hoping and praying he would not follow.

Reno lunged for her and tripped on the pile of bedclothes. Stubbing his toe, he cursed under his breath as pain shot up his foot to his ankle. He slammed the door behind her and ground his teeth together in impotent rage.

"Damn it all!" he bellowed, turning away to face the bed where he'd found heaven, only to lose it. "You are a sorry bastard, Gold."

*   *   *

Hurrying down the stairs, through the empty saloon, and out onto the boardwalk, Adele blinked away her tears. She sagged against a hitching post and dabbed at her wet face with a handkerchief. To steady herself she breathed deeply and staved off a fresh batch of tears.

She would not waste another tear on him, she thought, even as more blurred her vision. God's nightgown! If she wasn't the worst bawl-baby ever! Glancing around, she struggled to compose herself, not wanting anyone to witness her misery.

That's when she saw Terrapin stride from his saloon. He didn't look her way, but seemed focused on something down the street. Focused like a cat with a mouse in its sights. A grim smile rode his mouth. It sent a shiver of apprehension down Adele's spine and dried up her tears. Sunlight struck metal in his hand. Adele's heart shuddered when she saw that he held a gun.

Oh, no. Now what?

She shoved herself away from the hitching post and stepped into the street to see for herself what or who had earned Terrapin's wrath.

Her apprehension turned into stark terror when she recognized the woman walking toward her, blithely unaware of the danger stalking her.

"Mrs. McDonald!" Adele shouted. The woman waved, then froze and looked around, belatedly alert.

"I warned you, Doris," Terrapin yelled to her. "I told you I wouldn't tolerate your unfaithfulness, your ungratefulness. You asked for this. Just remember that when you get to hell."

The few people on the street scattered like buckshot

as Terrapin raised his gun. Mrs. McDonald whirled and started to run. Terrapin's gun kicked. Adele screamed, the sound reverberating in her head. Mrs. McDonald stumbled forward into the street, pushed by the impact of the bullet, then her body folded like an accordion.

Without a thought for her own safety, Adele ran to the injured woman and dropped to her knees, pulling Mrs. McDonald into her lap. Cradling her close, she tried vainly to protect her from the man who strode toward them, that chilling smile still on his face.

"Is she dead?" Terrapin asked.

Adele could feel a struggling pulse in Mrs. McDonald's neck, but she would sooner have died than tell him.

Looking around, fear shaking her insides, Adele searched for someone to help her. Nobody was on the street. "Someone get the doctor!" she screamed at the faces pressed against the windows of the barber shop and the General Store.

"Let go of her and I'll spare you," Terrapin said almost pleasantly.

"Stay away," she warned him, extending a hand to ward him off and wishing she had a gun in it. She could have blown Terrapin away without an ounce of remorse. "You stay away from us."

Terrapin made a *tsk* sound with his tongue. "You can't boss me like you do that husband of yours. No woman will ever be my boss. And no woman will ever betray me and live to brag about it. Just ask Dead-eye Doris there. Or maybe we should just call her Dead Doris now."

Mrs. McDonald moaned and moved fitfully. Beads

of perspiration broke out over Adele's forehead and dampened her palms. She held Mrs. McDonald more tightly, curving her body around the woman to shield her as Terrapin took careful aim again.

"Looks like she needs another ticket to send her to hell."

"No!" Adele bent over Mrs. McDonald, a cold tremble rising in her to make her teeth chatter. Through Terrapin's parted legs she saw Buck Wilhite come out of the Black Knight and walk confidently in their direction, his hand on the butt of his holstered gun. Her courage ebbing away, she grasped at her last ray of hope. "Reno!" she screamed. "Help, Reno, help!"

As if by magic, Reno materialized, gun in hand, not even breaking his stride as he fired on Wilhite, winging him in the shoulder. Grunting, Wilhite staggered and tried to raise his own gun. Reno fired again, and Wilhite jerked and fell onto his back.

"Thank you, thank you, thank you," Adele babbled, so relieved to see Reno that nothing else mattered, not the woman bleeding in her lap or the terror that shook her as Terrapin turned to face Reno.

Sunlight shimmered around Reno, while shadow draped Terrapin. Adele blinked, trying to clear her vision, trying to find a way to help Reno, who was always so willing to help her.

"I'm going to kill you, you son of a bitch," Reno said, and Adele hardly recognized his voice, it was so deathly deep, so full of rancor.

"I don't think so," Terrapin said, holstering his own gun. "But if you want to try, then let's face each other like men. Twenty paces, Gold."

Adele realized she was sobbing, but she couldn't stop. She felt for Mrs. McDonald's pulse again and found it thready and faint. Anchored by the woman's inert body and her own paralyzing fear, she could only watch as Reno holstered his gun and prepared for a contest that would leave one dead, one alive.

Wilhite, who Adele thought had been knocked unconscious by Reno's bullets, suddenly moved. Adele's blood froze in her veins. She opened her mouth to yell a warning to Reno, but managed only another sob.

Rising behind Reno like a specter, Wilhite leveled his gun at his back. A scream rattled from Adele, shrill and full of terror.

As Reno whirled to face the new menace, a small figure darted into the street from the direction of the Lucky Strike and disappeared behind Wilhite. When Buck groaned and wilted like a plucked flower without any report from a gun, Adele thought her eyes were playing tricks on her.

"What the hell?" Terrapin muttered, then cursed.

Little Nugget stood barefoot and clad in a pink nightgown, the neck of a shattered whiskey bottle clutched in one hand and a look of determination stamped on her face. The rest of the bottle lay in pieces around Wilhite, having made contact with the back of his head. This time he was out cold, thanks to Little Nugget's quick action.

Adele released a long sigh and her heart settled back into place, but then Terrapin reached for his gun. Fury and fear combined to give Adele a burst of strength.

Pushing Mrs. McDonald from her lap, Adele scrambled to her feet and lunged at Terrapin, throwing her body against his to ruin his aim. The bullet went foul, grazing Reno's gun hand, slicing through muscle, and sending his fingers into spasm. Dropping the Smith & Wesson, Reno cursed viciously and stared bleakly at his weapon lying in the dirt. Only a foot away, but it might as well have been a mile.

Adele tried to sink her nails into Terrapin's eyes, but he pushed her off. Screaming with fury, she threw herself at him again, trying to give Reno a chance to retrieve his gun. Terrapin backhanded her across the face and sent her sprawling in the dirt. Hot pain spread through her head and she choked on dust.

Through a red haze she saw Terrapin chuckle with fiendish delight as he aimed his gun at Reno.

"Good-bye, Gold," Terrapin said. "Time to shake hands with the Devil."

Chapter 23

"Taylor! What have you done?" Sally cried, running toward him, oblivious of the danger.

Terrapin frowned and waved her aside, but kept his eyes trained on Reno. "Get out of here, woman. Are you crazy? Can't you see I'm taking care of business?"

"But Taylor, you didn't shoot her, did you?" Sally asked, glancing fearfully at Mrs. McDonald.

Adele prayed Sally could appeal to any shred of decency Terrapin might still possess. She saw Reno signal Little Nugget to go back into the saloon and out of harm's way. Little Nugget hesitated, but then obeyed, running in a crouch to the Lucky Strike. Adele could see the hard glitter in Reno's eyes and his tight-lipped snarl.

"Taylor, answer me! You didn't shoot her, did you?" Sally demanded, grasping Terrapin's arm.

"It's what she deserved. I told you, she betrayed me. Now get out of the way."

"You're a coward," Adele said, anger making her voice shake. She glanced around, looking for allies, but saw only Yancy Stummer and a couple of his cronies crouched behind a water trough. The weasels.

Sally turned her face up to Terrapin's. "Taylor, please. This isn't right. Think of our future together. We have so much at stake. Don't throw it away. I know your pride is stinging over what she did, but it's over and done with. Don't be stupid."

Terrapin grabbed Sally by the hair and yanked. Crying out, she struggled, but only briefly. He wound his fingers more tightly into her hair and she sobbed.

"Taylor, let go! You're hurting me." Her voice quivered with uncertainty as she turned her eyes up to his face, a face contorted with rage. "Taylor . . . please?"

"You think I'm stupid, bitch?"

"Nn-o . . . d-darling." There was no mistaking the fear in her voice.

Adele knew the exact moment when Sally saw Taylor Terrapin for what he truly was, a monster with no conscience and no thought for anyone but himself. Staring at him, Sally's eyes rounded and her skin paled to ghostly white.

Searching for a way to tip the odds in Reno's favor, Adele's prayers were suddenly answered from an unlikely source. Rousing up from his stupor, Buck Wilhite let out a groan that startled Terrapin enough to make him flinch and loosen his hold on Sally so she could wrench free. She stumbled away from him even as he tried to recapture her, his hand grasping the air in front of her face.

"You disappoint me," Terrapin said, seeing that he'd lost her. "I thought you were a woman who knew her place and when to keep her mouth shut." He brought the gun around and aimed it at her, then slowly and with deliberate assurance. "I fear I can't allow any woman to call me stupid. How unfortunate for you, my dear."

The world ground to a halt. Even the horses and mules stood motionless as Sally Baldridge stared down the barrel of the gun. A whimper escaped through her white, trembling lips.

"No!" Adele screamed, feet flailing in the dirt as she tried to find purchase and stop Terrapin before he could pull the trigger.

That's when Reno lunged.

In a flurry of movement too fast for the eye to follow, Reno dropped to the ground and grabbed his .44 in both hands. He rolled, making himself a moving target. Terrapin fired over and over again, the bullets whizzing through the air, digging into the horse trough, the hitching rails, and the boardwalk. Women inside the buildings screamed. A baby wailed. One of the bullets knocked off Reno's hat. Another took a piece from the top of his shoulder.

Terrapin stood rooted to the spot, taking his shots, laughing as Reno tried to evade the bullets. Reno came to rest on his stomach and sighted his weapon with both hands. He fired. The bullet went wide, sailing over Sally's head. She jerked as if she'd been shot. Reno fired again. Terrapin grunted and took an involuntary step backward, the lump of lead burying itself in his shoulder and shattering bone, splitting muscle.

Reno rolled again as Terrapin roared with outrage and fired in a frenzy of blood lust. Each bullet was a fraction too late, finding dirt instead of Reno's flesh.

Click. Click. Click.

Adele heard the sound and knew that Terrapin's luck had run out, just like his ammunition. Reno knew it, too. He got to his feet, no longer having to dodge death.

The two men faced each other in an age-old battle of fate and final decisions. Terrapin dropped his empty gun. Adele released a sigh of relief. Sally, on her knees in a puddle of tears and shivers, sobbed in gratitude.

Then Terrapin reached across his body toward the other gun, which was strapped to his hip. He smiled with mad determination. Reno shook his head, silently advising the man not to go for the weapon. Terrapin was beyond sanity. He made a grab for the gun's grip. Reno fired, and Terrapin spun sideways, hit in the other shoulder. Still he did not stop. Drawing his Colt, he squeezed the trigger at the same moment as Reno fired again.

Adele flinched at each gun burst. For an instant of pure, heart-stopping terror, she couldn't tell who, if anyone, had been wounded. Then she saw the red blossom of death bloom on Terrapin's chest. He fell backward, kicked once, and stared sightlessly at the gray sky. Sally's hysterical sobs filled the eerie silence, and the smell of blood and gunpowder turned the air rancid.

Reno strode slowly to the sprawled body and looked down into Terrapin's face. Reno's haggard expression twisted Adele's heart and she went to him, tucking her arms around his waist and pressing her face into his shoulder. The smell of blood stung her nostrils, and she leaned back to take inventory. The left sleeve of his shirt was pink, and blood dripped off his fingertips.

"He's dead and you're alive," she whispered, touching his face. "And that's all that matters."

He swallowed and heaved a sigh, then seemed to shake himself into awareness. "Stummer!" he bellowed, motioning with his gun at the man cowering behind the horse trough. "You and your pals there, carry that woman to the doctor and make it quick!" He pointed to Mrs. McDonald, the back of whose dress was soaked in blood.

"Is she alive?" he asked Adele.

"Yes, I think so."

The men left their shelter reluctantly, giving Terrapin's body a wide berth as they approached the fallen woman. They reminded Adele of scurrying rats.

"Adele . . . I'm so sorry!" Sally wailed, still on her knees, her arms outstretched toward Adele. "Please forgive me! Please don't hate me!"

Adele could find no forgiveness at the moment, only profound gratitude that Reno was still standing. She clung to him, glad to feel his arm circle her waist.

"You're hurt," she said.

"It's nothing."

With another weary sigh, he let go of her and moved with heavy steps to Sally. She sat weeping, her face buried in a lacy handkerchief.

"Sally Ann?" He slipped his gun back into its holster, then touched the crown of her head. She looked up at him with red-rimmed, puffy eyes. "Get on up and let's go into the saloon. We could all use a drink."

Sally let him pull her to her feet and followed him and Adele to the Lucky Strike. People were venturing out of the buildings now, their eyes wide and wary. One grizzled man slapped Reno on the back and gave him a broad smile.

"Atta way, boy," the old-timer said. "I watched it all from inside the saloon. Glad it's you still on your feet and not that sneaky Terrapin."

Reno barely acknowledged him, moving with dogged determination to the shelter of his saloon.

Little Nugget sat huddled in a blanket on top of the bar. She eased off it and smiled wanly.

"Y'all okay? I saw it from in here. Taylor's dead." She raised herself on tiptoe and kissed Reno's cheek. "I won't forget what you did. I want to go see about Doris, but I'm as weak as a kitten."

Reno gestured toward the stairs. "You get on back to bed and I'll check on her in a bit."

"You going to be okay?" she asked, eyeing his bleeding shoulder and hand.

"Yeah. I just need a drink." He went around to the other side of the bar and set three glasses on the shiny surface.

Adele placed an arm gingerly around Little Nugget's tiny waist. "Let me help you up those stairs."

"I can make it. Will you look after Doris for me?"

"Of course." Adele stood at the bottom of the staircase and watched Little Nugget's slow ascent. The young woman turned and waved before shuffling back to her bedroom.

Sally fell into a chair. "Everybody in this town hates me now," she said, sniffing and dabbing at her eyes.

"*Now?*" Reno repeated with dry sarcasm.

"Reno," Adele scolded, but had to fight to keep from smiling. Sally sobbed and blew her nose.

"Aw, hell, Sally Ann, have a drink." Reno picked up the whiskey bottle and offered it to her. "You weren't the only one in Whistle Stop to kiss Terrapin's backside. The whole damn—"

A young man strode unsteadily into the saloon. His eyes were red-rimmed and he smelled of rum and sweat. "What's been going on? I want answers, by God!"

Reno regarded him curiously. "And who would you be?"

Adele swallowed a startled laugh, realizing that Reno hadn't met the town sheriff.

"Me? Why, I'm Sheriff Marcus Short." He slapped a hand to his chest where a tin star should have been pinned, but wasn't. Startled, he stared at his shirt, patted down his pockets, and looked as if he might cry. "Hell, I've lost another one."

"*You're* the sheriff?" Reno asked, incredulous. He glanced at Adele for confirmation, then shook his head in amazement. Draining his shot glass, he backhanded his mouth and gave a short, barking laugh. "You're just a kid."

Adele couldn't help but snicker when Terrapin's hand-picked sheriff turned beet red. He *was* a kid. Eighteen and good for nothing but drinking until he passed out in a whore's bed.

"Did you shoot Taylor Terrapin?" the boy sheriff demanded.

"Yes, son, I surely did," Reno replied affably. "And he shot me. I'm just a better marksman and a lucky bastard."

"I'll have to arrest you until this thing is sorted out."

Adele gaped at him. "You must be out of your mind!"

"Calm down, Dellie," Reno said, unconcerned, as he returned his attention to the sheriff. "He's not going to arrest anyone." He sauntered toward the red-faced boy, standing a foot taller and twice as broad. "I've been in this town awhile and I've opened up a business, but this is the first time I've seen you. Seems to me you're a day late and a dollar short, Sheriff Short."

"All I know is that a man is lying dead out there."

"He deserves to be dead," Sally spoke up, her tone lifeless.

"Mrs. Baldridge, isn't it?" the sheriff asked, removing his hat and clutching it to his chest as he approached her. His sticky blond hair swirled in a messy cowlick at the back of his head. "I'm sorry for your loss. I know you and Mr. Terrapin were—"

"He shot a woman in cold blood," Sally interrupted him, turning her dull, tear-washed eyes on him.

"Who did?" the sheriff asked, glaring accusingly at Reno.

"Not him. Taylor," Sally said. Then she raised her head higher and drew in a deep breath. "If it weren't for Reno Gold, we'd all be dead."

"If you want to arrest someone, arrest Buck Wilhite," Adele suggested.

"Wilhite? Where is he?" The sheriff spun around, nearly lost his balance, and had to grab onto a chair to keep from falling.

Adele sighed and marched to the door. "He's out here in the street. Are you blind?" But the street was empty except for Terrapin's body. "Well, I never!"

Adele turned back to the others. "He's gone."

Reno chuckled. "Like any no-good coyote, he knows when to make tracks." He lifted his glass to the sheriff. "You might learn from his example there, son. Terrapin is dead, which means your days as a lawman in this town are numbered."

Marcus Short's mouth worked, but no words came out. Mutely he stomped toward the double doors. By the time he had crossed the threshold, he'd recovered his voice. He turned back to them, his face pink, his nose red and veined.

"This body must be removed from the street," he announced.

Adele shook her head, pitying the uselessness of him. "Brilliant deduction," she allowed. "See to it." Resolutely she closed the doors, shutting him out.

"So that's the sheriff," Reno drawled. "Hell, he's barely out of knickers."

"I didn't know you hadn't met him."

"I've heard about him. He spends most of his time across the street at the Black Knight, where he gets his whores free because he's under Terrapin's thumb."

"*Was* under Terrapin's thumb," Adele amended. Her legs suddenly wobbled. She had enough steam left to stumble to a chair and sit beside Sally. She massaged her pounding temples and groaned. "Is it over? Is it really over? He's dead and we're all still breathing?"

"Was there ever a doubt about the outcome?" Reno asked, striding forward to plunk down two shot glasses full of whiskey before her and Sally. "Drink up before you pass out cold. You ladies are looking right peaked."

The whiskey sloshed through Adele with all the finesse of buckshot. She coughed and felt alive again.

"I never knew him, I suppose," Sally said suddenly. Her eyes were almost swollen shut. "He wasn't the man I thought he was."

Looking at Reno, Adele struggled with equal portions of pride and betrayal. She wondered if he loved her or could love her. She wanted to ask him if he thought they could forgive each other and start over, but he turned away and leaned on the bar. One of his shirtsleeves was stiff with blood. Adele winced, ashamed to be rehashing a lover's quarrel when he stood before her, bleeding.

She braced her hands on the edge of the table and pushed herself up. Her knees locked, much to her relief.

"Where are you going?" Sally asked.

"To see about Reno."

Reno frowned. "I'm okay. Why don't you go check on Mrs. McDonald?"

"Let me help clean the wound."

"I'll pour some of this whiskey on it. I'll be fine." He jerked away when she lifted a hand to touch him. "Go on now to the doctor's. I can take care of myself."

Stung by his sudden iciness toward her, Adele retreated, staring at his imposing back. She wanted to put her arms around him and lay her head on his blood-soaked shoulder and thank him for saving them. But at the same time she wanted him to beg her to forgive him for lying, for marrying her to teach her a lesson, for making her fall in love with him only to break her heart.

"Are you going now?" Sally asked. She stood and swayed for a moment before finding her balance.

"Yes," Adele said, hesitating, so as to give Reno a chance to change his mind and ask her to wait for him. He glanced over his shoulder at her, a frown creasing his brow. "Are you sure I can't do something for you?"

"I need to be alone, Dellie. I just killed a man." He turned away from her and ran a hand through his hair.

"You saved lives," she said.

"Yes, but I took one, too." He poured himself another drink. "Just leave me be for a spell."

Sally touched her arm and glanced pointedly to the doorway. Adele knew she was right. Reno wanted to be alone with his thoughts. But still she hesitated. Finally she laid a hand on his back, barely touching him, then went outside with Sally.

"I wish he'd let me help him," Adele said.

"You can help him later when he's got himself on a firm footing again." Sally winced, watching the sheriff and Hector, the Black Knight bartender, lift Terrapin's body and carry it in the direction of the undertaker's. Making a choking sound, she averted her gaze. Adele placed an arm around her shoulders and walked quickly with her in the opposite direction.

"He hates me," Sally said.

"Who?"

"Reno."

Adele sighed. "I doubt that."

"He's always hated me."

"No, he hasn't."

"You've been right about everything."

"Not about everything."

Sally wiped tears from her cheeks with her damp handkerchief. "I can't believe it. Taylor was going to shoot me! He would have killed me and not batted an eye in remorse or regret. He couldn't have loved me at all. Not at all." Her mouth twisted out of shape and she swallowed hard to keep from sobbing.

"Sally, you knew he was ruthless."

"But I never thought he'd hurt me. Never me. He told me I was a great lady. He worshiped me."

"Men say lots of things to get what they want." Adele wasn't proud of the bitter quality in her tone and was glad they'd reached the doctor's office, because she was beginning to see something about herself that she didn't like.

Sally hung back. "Maybe I shouldn't go in. After all, I was never . . . Well, I could have been more cordial to Mrs. McDonald."

Adele placed her hands on Sally's shoulders and turned her toward the door. "It's never too late to change, Sally, or to mend our ways." The words echoed back to her, shaming her. Sally went into the doctor's office and Adele followed, but her heart was suddenly heavy with hypocrisy.

Reno hadn't been truthful with her, but she hadn't been truthful with him either, she admitted to herself. She hadn't intended actually to marry him, but had been shamed and bullied into it. And she hadn't been forthright about her feelings for him. She hadn't told him that she'd fallen in love with him and didn't care if he were rich or poor, ambitious or lazy.

Was it too late now to correct those omissions?

She realized she was standing in the outer office. Sally had been conferring with Doc Martin and was now speaking to her.

". . . so we'll go in and sit with her while the doctor is down at the Lucky Strike, tending to Reno. How does that sound?"

"Will she pull through?" Adele asked.

"The doctor seems to think so," Sally said, taking her by the arm. "He wants one of us to sit with her until she comes to again."

"Okay." But Adele wished she could go back to the Lucky Strike and be with Reno. Once again they seemed to be at odds, with her wanting desperately for his company and him wanting to be shed of hers.

Doc Martin came out of an examination room, his black medical bag clutched in one hand. "I'll go see about Gold now. If Mrs. McDonald wakes up, just make her keep still."

Adele reached out to detain him. "Tell Reno that I—" She clamped her teeth shut. No. She needed to tell him *that* face to face. "Never mind, but Doctor, he didn't want to kill Terrapin. He had to, or he'd be the dead one right now. Make him understand that."

Doc Martin nodded, laying a hand on her shoulder and giving it a squeeze. "I imagine he knows that, but I'll mention it to him anyway."

"He seems troubled."

"Killing never goes down easy," Doc Martin said. "And it never should."

After he left, Adele sat with Sally at Mrs. McDonald's bedside, but her thoughts were on Reno and what he'd done, not only for her, but for the entire town. She decided that Whistle Stop should honor him.

When Terrapin was buried and the taint of blood was gone from the air, she'd open the restaurant doors and invite the whole town in to pay their respects to Reno Gold.

And afterward, when she was alone with him, she'd add her own special thank-you. She'd show him that she'd changed and that all was forgiven.

Chapter 24

The next day dawned gray and rainy. Taylor Terrapin was buried in a downpour. The funeral was not well attended. In fact, finding enough pallbearers was a problem. As soon as he was placed in the muddy ground, the sun came out. Most people thought that was more than coincidental.

"Sally was there," Adele told Mrs. McDonald at her bedside later that afternoon at Doc Martin's. "And I went to his funeral because Sally needed me."

"You and Sally are friends again?"

"Yes, but . . . Well, I don't think we'll ever be as close again."

"Give it time."

Adele nodded. "Perhaps." Her doubts outweighed her faith. "Reno was there, too."

"He was? Why did he go?"

"He said he thought he should, since he was the one who shot Terrapin." The memory of his drawn expression, his bleak eyes, tore at Adele's heart. She'd told him that she needed to see him that evening at the restaurant, and he had promised to come by at

345

eight. "He doesn't know about the celebration tonight. I just asked him to come by so that we could talk. I neglected to mention that most of the town will be there with me. I hope they keep their mouths shut and don't ruin the surprise. And I hope I'm doing the right thing. Reno seems so . . . depressed."

"He'll snap out of it," Mrs. McDonald said, her voice weak, but her eyes bright. Her color had almost returned to normal. The doctor said she had a strong constitution, otherwise she would surely have died from her injuries.

"You're one lucky lady," Adele told her. "Doc Martin told me that the bullet would have found your heart if not for your corset. One of the bone stays deflected it."

"Guess corsets are good for something after all," she said drolly. "How's Little Nugget? She didn't go to that rat's funeral, did she?"

"No. She's doing better, but her back is too tender for her to wear anything fitting or binding. A nightgown is about all she can manage for now. I wish you two were well enough to come to the surprise party tonight. Reno thinks so much of both of you."

"You give him our love tonight. Hey, was Buck at the funeral?"

"Nobody has seen Buck Wilhite since yesterday. Some folks are saying he's gone to Texas."

"Let Texas have him. He'll fit right in with the bandits and rattlesnakes and tumbleweeds."

"I saw Little Nugget before I came over here. Reno wasn't there. Little Nugget said he'd gone to the telegraph office and then to the bank." Adele plucked fretfully at the bedsheet covering Mrs. McDonald.

"What's wrong, hon?"

"Oh, it's just that . . . Little Nugget is talking about leaving Whistle Stop once she's well enough."

"That's probably for the best. She got a destination in mind?"

Adele stared at her in surprise. "I thought you'd be upset. I thought you'd want her to stay here with us."

"Well, sure, I'll miss her, but I'm thinking about what will be best for her, not for me. The whole town knows her for a whore, so what kind of future can she have here?"

Adele frowned. "That's what she said, but I told her you'd done well for yourself."

"With me it's different. I've had me a husband and I'm older. I'm not looking for a man to marry. Little Nugget is young and she's got a chance at landing herself a good husband, having herself a family."

"That's what she said, but I think she might meet a nice gentleman here."

"You didn't. Had to advertise for Mr. Reno. Any man who would take up with Little Nugget would have to be a saint, and Whistle Stop has a shortage of those. Your average man couldn't put up with the whole town snickering behind his back about what his wife used to do to make money." She shifted in the bed as if she was uncomfortable, but shook her head when Adele sat forward in concern. "I'm fine."

"I should leave."

"No." Mrs. McDonald clutched one of Adele's hands. "Stay awhile longer. Tell me about Mr. Reno. How bad was he hurt?"

"His arm is in a sling, but he told me at the funeral that he isn't in any pain. One of the bullets grazed his shoulder and another one skipped across the top of his hand. Flesh wounds, he called them. He said his muscles were stiff and sore but his wounds were healing fast."

"He's a tough one."

"Yes." But he had seemed vulnerable at the funeral, she thought, remembering the sadness in his eyes and voice when he'd spoken to her. "He's weary, as though he can barely put one foot in front of the other."

"Taking somebody's life, even if that somebody is a sorry soul like Terrapin, is a heavy burden to bear, I reckon."

"I hope tonight's surprise cheers him up."

"It should. Wish I could be there."

"We'll throw another party for you when you're up and about again."

Mrs. McDonald smiled and patted her hand. "I'll hold you to that. You've been so good to me, Mrs. Adele, I don't rightly know how to thank you."

"You don't have to, Mrs. McDonald. Your friendship is enough. You know, I've never had many friends and I treasure them as other people would gold."

"Is that why you held fast to Mrs. Baldridge, even when she was downright hateful?"

Adele nodded. "Sally was my first real girlfriend. I wanted her to be like a sister to me. I have a lot to learn about friendships, I guess."

"All you've got to know is that you can't ask more of people than they're willing to give. And friends, real friends, are hard to come by. If you have two, you're wealthy beyond measure."

"I'll remember that."

"Of course, the man you love should be your best friend. No one should be placed before him."

Adele lifted a brow. "You think I place people ahead of the man I love?"

"You might have, but I think you know better now."

"Yes, I've learned quite a few lessons over the past few days, Mrs. McDonald. I only hope I'm not too late to put my new knowledge to good use." She sighed. "I really must go and let you rest."

"Adele? Are you here?"

Startled, Adele turned toward the front of the building, recognizing Sally's voice. "Back here, Sally!"

Sally came into the room, her eyes wide. "Oh, good. I caught up with you. Hello, Mrs. McDonald. How are you feeling today?"

"Much better, Mrs. Baldridge."

"I'm glad to hear it." Sally smiled at her, then turned to Adele. "I was at the bank and I overheard Reno talking to the bank president. Reno said he was leaving, Adele. He said he had his bags packed and the saloon was closed. Did you know? He didn't say a thing about this at the funeral, did he?"

"No!" For a few moments, Adele thought she would burst into tears, then anger clamped down on that first instinct. "How dare he! He can't leave! I'm his wife!" She paced, her mind whirling, her emotions roiling. "He thinks he can hightail it out of town without discussing it with me first? Here I am planning a surprise party for him and he's busy cutting himself loose and making tracks. Oooh! He makes me so mad!" She rounded on Sally. "What else did he say?

Where's he going? Why is he leaving? Did he mention my name at all?"

"No. He said he was going to talk to you tonight and board the first train out in the morning." Sally wrung her hands in agitation. "I thought you two would patch things up. I know that's what you want."

"He's going to tell me tonight, is he? Blast his ornery hide." She stopped her pacing and tipped up her chin. "Come on, Sally. We have to prepare for the party tonight. I want you to help me look irresistible. If he's thinking of giving me the boot, I don't want to make it easy for him."

"Atta girl," Mrs. McDonald said, her voice suddenly stronger. "Put up a fight, hon."

"Don't worry," Adele assured her. "He's not the only tough customer in this town. I'm going to stick to him like a burr to a saddle blanket. Sally Ann, we have work to do."

"Yes, Adele," Sally said, sending Mrs. McDonald a wink before dutifully following Adele from the room.

The restaurant looked dark as Reno approached. Perfect for his mood, he thought, shoving one boot in front of the other. Ever since the shoot-out he'd felt as if he were walking through a heavy fog. Even seeing Adele at the funeral earlier that day hadn't helped. In fact, seeing her had made him feel worse, because he was reminded of what he was leaving behind, of what he'd lost.

He hitched his horse to the rail and reminded himself to ask Adele if she'd take care of the animal for him. If she didn't want to keep the horse, she could sell it. Removing the packed saddlebags and satchel, he set them under a bench on the depot platform.

Pausing, he surveyed the depot and thought of the day he'd stepped off the train and back into Adele's life. He wished he could stay with her, but he couldn't ask that of her. He'd betrayed her trust, after all, and a woman like Dellie could never get over that. No, too many lies had been told, too many chances had been missed. And in Dellie's right-or-wrong world, he was all wrong.

If he'd told her earlier about his wealth and why he had kept it from her, told her right after they'd become intimate, then things might have been different for them.

She probably thought that her world had spun out of control since he'd been in it. Yes, Terrapin was dead and Wilhite had disappeared like a ghost, but Mrs. McDonald and Little Nugget had both paid dearly. Reno blamed himself for their pain and predicament. After all, he'd placed them in danger by hiring them away from Terrapin. And he'd placed Dellie in danger, too. She must see that by now and would be secretly relieved when he told her he was leaving. She could piece her life back together without him in it.

But it would be hell for him, and he knew it. Squaring his shoulders and gathering in a deep breath, he told himself to face his heartache like a man. Striding to the door, he opened it and stepped inside the shadow-draped restaurant.

"Surprise!"

Reno jerked all over and his hand went automatically to his gun. Voices flooded the room and bodies popped up from behind the counter and from behind the tables. The kitchen door swung open and more people filed in, all laughing and slapping him on the back. Relaxing, his bandaged hand swinging away from the butt of his gun, he breathed a sigh of relief as he was blinded by face-splitting grins, deafened by shouts and laughter.

"What's going on here?" he asked, his sense of being in a foggy dream intensified.

"You're the town hero, so we're throwing you a party," Colleen said. "Let me take your hat and coat." She swept them away while other people crowded around him.

Someone pushed a glass of ginger ale into his hand. Chester, the feed store owner, guided him toward the counter and pushed him down onto one of the tall stools there. A chorus of "For he's a jolly good fellow" made Reno smile but shake his head in denial. Still, it was touching for these people to plan this, to show their gratitude. But wait. They hadn't planned it. No, this had a certain lady's touch.

Reno cast his gaze around the room, looking . . . searching . . . hoping . . . Ah, there! His heart thumped at the sight of her.

Adele stood across the room from him and the beauty of her smile clutched at him. Swathed in green satin, she was easily the most beautiful woman in the room. Hell, she was the most beautiful woman in the world to *him*! A slow smile claimed his mouth.

He wasn't even aware he'd stood up and moved until he was halfway across the room to her.

"You did this," he said, glancing around at the streamers and food and gaiety.

"Yes. You deserve it."

While the words were warm, he sensed an undercurrent of something he couldn't decipher. He chalked it up to her nerves and his moodiness.

"You're the real hero here." He reached for her hands and held them. The gold band on her finger mocked him. "You stood up to Terrapin before I came to town."

"But you rid the town of him."

He shrugged. "It's too bad blood had to be shed."

She stepped closer and lowered her voice. "You have nothing to be ashamed of or to regret, Reno. You defended yourself and us. Mrs. McDonald and Little Nugget wanted to be here, but they couldn't leave their sickbeds. Reno, if it weren't for you, we would have buried them this morning instead of Terrapin."

"I appreciate that, Dellie."

She raised herself on tiptoe and kissed his lips lightly. "And I mean it with all my heart, Reno."

A thrill surged through his body. He wanted to crush her to him and kiss her deeply, imprint himself on her, give her something to remember him by. But he wasn't alone with her, and the others were calling out his name, wanting to shake his hand. He let himself be pulled away, but throughout the next couple of hours, his gaze sought hers time and time again. Looking at her created an odd mixture of lust and sadness within him. How could he turn his back and walk away? He knew it would be the hardest test of all and one he could not fail. The sooner he was out of Dellie's way, the sooner she could put all the unhappiness behind her and go on with her life. He had hoped she would love him, but all he had earned was her gratitude. That would have to be enough.

At half past midnight Adele decided she'd have to do something drastic. Yes, she wanted the party to be successful, but it was *too* successful. Only a few people had left. The food was almost gone, but the revels continued. Adele had tried to suggest politely that the hour was growing late, but no one had taken the hint.

Someone had produced a case of whiskey, and Adele worried that Reno might drink too much and be incapacitated before she had a chance to talk with him. And she simply had to talk to him before the first train rolled in!

With her mind made up, she marched smartly to her quarters and fetched her aunt's rifle. Taking it outside, she stood on the depot platform, cocked the weapon and fired twice into the air. Shouts of laughter changed to shouts of alarm, and people stared at her through the windows. Some ran to see what new danger had developed.

Reno was the first one outside. He stopped a few feet from her and gave her a curious look. "What's going on?"

"Party's over," she said, arching a brow.

"Just like that?"

"Any complaints?"

"No, I—"

"What's wrong? Who you shooting at?" Ned, the blacksmith, asked, his eyes wild with panic.

"Nobody," Adele said, cradling the warm rifle in her arms. "I wanted to get everyone's attention. Do I have it?"

"You got mine," Ned assured her, then turned and cupped his hands around his mouth. "Hey y'all! Pipe down. Mrs. Adele has something to say!"

"Thank you, Ned." Adele cleared her throat. "The party's over, everyone. I appreciate you coming tonight, but it's morning now and time for us to toddle off to our beds." She shifted the weapon, just to make sure she had their attention. "Good night. Sleep tight."

"Better get along, folks," Reno said. "Take it from me, Dellie's good with that rifle. You don't want to rile her when she's armed." He grinned, making the others laugh off his warning. "I appreciate you sharing the evening with me, folks. I don't rightly deserve it, but that didn't stop me from having a few drinks and more than a few laughs. I thank you." He bowed from the waist.

Paul Green came forward to shake his hand. "Good night, Gold. Don't be a stranger."

"Night, Paul."

"You sure know how to shut down a good time," Ned grumbled at Adele, but he crushed his hat onto his head and shuffled off with his wife.

Others followed. Adele smiled pleasantly and waved, feeling a little guilty for forcing them to leave, but also impatient to see the last of them. She'd waited long enough to speak to Reno. As it was, her nerves were stretched to the breaking point. She'd thought he might announce to the others that he was planning to leave town, but evidently it was his little secret.

Not for long, she vowed silently. If he thought he would sneak out of town like a thief in the night and not tell a living soul, not even his wife. Well, she wouldn't let him go. Not that easily.

She saw Sally hustle Colleen and Helen upstairs when the last of the townspeople were gone. Suddenly the night was uncommonly quiet and the moon and stars provided the only illumination.

Reno walked to his horse, hitched at the railing, and ran a hand down the animal's sleek neck. "Thanks for everything, Adele. I was wondering if you'd see to my horse here. You see, I'm—" He clamped his teeth shut when he saw her raise the rifle and aim it at him. "Just what in the hell are you doing?"

"Just what in the hell are *you* doing?" she charged hotly. "If you think you're leaving, Reno Gold, think again."

Chapter 25

"**D**amn it all." He scowled at her. "How'd you find out? I was going to tell you as soon as we were alone, but as usual, someone beat me to it. That's been the way between us since the beginning—just when I work up the courage to tell you something, you've already heard it."

"And why do you need courage to tell me the truth?" she rejoined. "Do you perhaps feel guilty for tucking tail and running out of town without a backward glance?"

"I'm not running anywhere. I'm simply moving on."

"Need I remind you that we're married, Reno Gold?" She lowered the rifle and tapped her foot impatiently.

"I'm aware of that, Dellie. I figured I'd leave the divorce in your hands. I'll pay any fees, of course."

"How noble of you." She wished she was a man so that she could bust him one.

"What are you riled about?" He propped his hands on his hips and looked at her, clearly perplexed. "I

357

thought you'd be glad to see the last of me. After all we've been through, I figured—"

"Exactly," she interrupted him. "After all we've been through, the very least you could do is discuss this with me. But, no! You pack your bags." She shot a look at the saddlebags and satchel he'd tucked under the bench. "And don't think I didn't see your things hidden out of sight over there."

"Not hidden too well," he noted with a roll of his eyes. "For God's sake, Dellie—"

"And Little Nugget says she's leaving, too! I suppose you put that idea in her head. You think you can sweep in here, turn a person's life upside down, make a person care for you, and then just disappear like a puff of smoke? How dare you, Reno Gold!"

He swept his hat off his head in a gesture of irritation. "Hell's afire, Dellie. I can't figure you out to save my life. As for Little Nugget, she's a grown woman and knows what she wants. I haven't even talked to her about leaving."

Adele puffed out a breath. "Oh, that's just like you! Don't waste a thought on those you leave behind! You won't even miss her or me or anyone!"

He shook his head, having a devil of a time trying to win any points with her or even follow her circuitous train of thought. "That's not true." He hung his hat on the saddle horn and moved closer to her, watching her color rise and her breasts heave with her agitated breaths. She was so beautiful, so spirited, so furious, he just had to have her.

"I care," he told her, glancing at the rifle in her hands.

"I don't believe you."

"Then believe this." He closed the distance between them in two steps and with his good hand he wrenched the rifle from her and flung it aside. Wrapping his arm around her, he drowned out her startled cry with the pressure of his lips, the surge of his tongue, the power of his lust. She tasted sweet and spicy, hot and wild. Her struggles only made his blood run hotter.

She pushed at his shoulders; his injury stung him, but he was beyond caring about such inconsequential pain. He held her closer, stilling her movements against the solidness of his body and forcing her to experience his kiss fully. She made furious sounds for a few moments, and then a purr moved up her throat and echoed in his head. He stroked her tongue with his and covered one of her breasts with his hand— his wounded hand, he vaguely noted. But his wounds were nothing compared to the seduction of her body, the beading of her nipple beneath his palm and the layers of her clothing. He wanted to take that pearly flesh into his mouth, to lose himself in her again just one last time.

He lifted his mouth from hers and stared into her shining eyes. "Dellie, make love to me. Let's make love as if there's no tomorrow."

With a sudden frown she gave him a shove that jostled his wounded shoulder enough to make him curse softly and release her.

"Careful," he cautioned, "I took a bullet for you!" He was angling for a drop of sympathy, but she was bent on retaliation and offered not even a wince of remorse.

"The bullets took pieces of skin, that's all. Doc Martin said you'd be fully healed in a a couple of weeks," she informed him archly. "And how can you stand there and ask me to make love to you without regard for tomorrow?"

"I didn't say that. I asked you to—"

"I know what you said," she interrupted, whirling away from him. "And I'm telling you that I will *not* make love to you and then kiss you good-bye." She leaned over and retrieved the rifle, then took it inside.

Reno followed her, perplexed by her refusal. She wanted him as badly as he wanted her, damn it all! And he was making a hell of a sacrifice by leaving her. "I thought you'd be glad to see the last of me."

"Oh, did you?" She was holding the rifle again, both hands curled around it protectively. "And it never occurred to you to ask me what I wanted, what would make me happy, did it?"

"I was thinking of hanging around, maybe buying the old hotel and fixing it up," he admitted. "This town could use a good hotel with a great restaurant. I even imagined you managing it. You'd make a success of it, that's for sure." He shrugged. "But it would never work."

"Why is that?"

"Because I lied to you, and you'll never trust me again. You can't build a partnership of any kind without trust." He sat on one of the tall stools at the counter.

"All this thinking you've been doing, is that what's made you so distant and in such a dark mood?"

"You're the one in a strange mood, if you ask me." He eyed the rifle. "Asking folks to a party and then sending them home by firing off a round or two."

"I didn't think they'd spend the night! Besides, I needed to talk with you before the first train came in and you jumped on it."

"So you point that thing at me to make me listen to you? Asking nice would have accomplished the same thing."

"I got your attention." She hefted the rifle, curling a finger around the trigger. "Still have it."

"You don't need that, Dellie. A smile would do the trick."

"I've been smiling all night, but you're still determined to leave me. What's wrong, Reno? Why haven't you come around until now? You didn't say ten words to me at the funeral."

He ran a hand down his face. "Killing a man brings on sobering thoughts and summons inner demons," he allowed, staring at the floor and seeing the final minutes of Terrapin's life play out in his mind.

"You did what you had to do, Reno," Adele said, sitting next to him and leaning the rifle against the counter. "Terrapin was bound and determined to ruin you or kill you."

He nodded. "I know, Dellie, I know." His glance flickered to her. "He's not the first man I've shot. So far as I know, he's the first one I've killed, but there could have been others. I ran with a wild bunch a few years back. Gunfights were common, and I certainly couldn't turn my back and not get a knife stuck in it."

"What were you doing with people like that around you?"

"Prospecting and gambling." His smile turned rueful. "I've led a rambunctious life between Lawrence and Whistle Stop. When I came here, I admit it was a lark. I wanted to see you again and see how you'd changed, what had happened to drive you to placing an advertisement for a husband. A beautiful woman like you had to have a damn good reason, and I was dying of curiosity."

"I have changed, especially since you've been here," she admitted, her voice low. "Can you leave and not look back, Reno? Not ever think of me again?"

"Hell, no. I never said I could. But I figure I've put you through enough." He shook his head. "Aw, Dellie, I guess I've loved you since the first moment I laid eyes on you."

"Wh-what?" Adele stared at him in open-mouthed amazement. "Be serious."

"You mean I've finally told you something you didn't already know?" he teased, turning to face her, to take her hands in his. "Love at first sight is what fools and poets blabber on about, but I swear I've never felt like this for any other female. I was hoping you'd fall in love with me, too."

Emotion clogged her throat, and she had to swallow hard before she could speak. "Reno, I must tell you—"

"Yes, I know, you can't love a man you can't trust. I understand that. I should have been honest instead of bucking you at every turn, challenging you to like me in spite of my orneriness. I tested your patience, didn't I, sugar?"

"Many times," she agreed. "But Reno—"

"I can't stay here, Dellie. Not in the same town with you. It just wouldn't work. That's why I have to board the next train and get out of your life." He stood and looked out the window. After a few moments he slipped his arm out of the sling.

"Reno, you shouldn't," she advised.

He tossed the black square of cloth aside. "I don't need that damned thing." He rested a hand on his shoulder where the bullet had grazed him. The wound burned, but the discomfort was minimal compared to the ache around his heart. He never thought he'd end up a lovesick fool, but Dellie had reduced him to that sorry state.

"Back in Deadwood people thought I was the luckiest man alive. They thought I'd made up my last name and that I had a lucky charm given to me by one of my Gypsy ancestors. One fella even started a rumor that I wore a Cheyenne medicine bag that helped me find gold. I don't feel so lucky now."

Adele slipped off the stool and went to stand beside him at the window. Starlight painted his face and she admired his handsome profile.

"My legendary luck seems to have run out, Dellie."

"No, Reno," she protested, resting a hand on his arm.

"My big plans have fallen to dust. I wanted to open a print shop here." He flashed her a smile and her heart skipped a beat. "I've got ink in my blood."

And I have lust in mine, she thought, but tempered her needs for the moment. "The town could use a good hotel, and we've never had a newspaper. Why can't you stay?"

Hope lifted his heart, then set it down when he saw only curiosity in her eyes. "Whistle Stop no longer holds any appeal for me. But I have no hard feelings. I want us to part friends."

She snatched her hand from his arm and her anger bit hard again. "It's too late for that. I don't want to be your *friend*. Quitter! No wonder your luck soured," she told him. "You've lost faith in everything. Maybe the murder of Terrapin has taken more out of you than you're willing to admit. Maybe Terrapin won, after all. He beat you into submission."

His eyes were suddenly like a sky full of rain. "Why are you talking like that? You don't mean what you're saying. Why are you trying to hurt me?"

"Why do you think, you fool?" She wiped tears from her eyes. "I'm mad, I'm desolate! You come in here and tell me that you loved me at first sight and then you ask me for a divorce. What did you think I would do? Jump for joy?"

"I thought you might be relieved. I lied to you, Dellie. I strung you along and made you think—"

"I lied to you, too, Reno."

"What? When? Oh, are you talking about not intending to marry me at first?"

"I lied by not telling you something. Something you deserved to know."

He rubbed his wounded shoulder and frowned at her. "What's that?"

Adele stepped closer, careful to look him straight in the eyes as she rested her hands on his chest. His heart thumped against her palm. "I love you."

He spread one hand over hers, and she felt his heart leap and race. Then he narrowed his eyes with suspicion. "No, you don't. You said that out of pity."

"Pity? Is this pity?" Curling a hand behind his neck,

she pulled his mouth down to hers. His initial surprise dissolved into desire.

The slide of his hand down her spine held the stamp of possessiveness that renewed her faith that she could not only win him, but hold him. He opened his lips over hers and his tongue delved inside, courting hers into a dance of desire. Slanting his mouth over hers, he spiked her passion, took her breath away, and made her moan with pleasure.

No matter what he said, she knew he belonged to her, that no other woman would ever touch him as deeply, know him so completely. She smoothed the back of his hair and arched her body into his. Their nights together swam through her mind and heated her blood. If he'd asked her to make love to him right then, smack dab in the middle of the restaurant floor, she would have done it.

That realization sent her out of his arms. He groaned a complaint and reached for her, but she sidestepped, evading him. She needed his words of devotion more than his kisses of desire just now.

"Reno, do you really want a divorce?"

"No, but you—"

"Don't presume to think for me." She shook a cautionary finger at him. "You should know better than that by now."

"I should," he allowed with a crooked grin. "Kiss me again, Dellie, before I die from wanting you."

"Tell me you love me."

His eyes shone with it before his lips spoke of it. "I love you, Dellie."

"Oh, Reno . . ." She melted into his embrace again. His mouth touched hers, fanning a flame that raced from his body to hers and engulfed them both.

To Adele it was like walking into the sunlight after a long, cold winter. Sliding her hands under his jacket and up his back, she wanted to feel his flesh against hers, wanted him buried deeply within her.

"Dellie, Dellie, is this a dream?" he murmured, raining kisses upon her upturned face.

"No, Reno. How could you even *think* about leaving me?"

"You don't trust me."

"Oh, no. Only with my life." She mocked his look of surprise. "How many times must I place my life in your hands before you believe me? I was never so scared as when I faced Terrapin, but then you showed up and I was no longer afraid for myself, but only for you. If that isn't trust, if that isn't love, then what is?"

"But I've made you cry. I can't stand that. I only wanted to bring you smiles and laughter and love. It seems that all I've done is bring trouble to your doorstep."

"You *are* a lot of trouble, Reno Gold," she said, leaning back to beam at him. "But at times like this you're worth it—and you're certainly worth a few tears. Especially when they're tears of happiness." She caressed his face with trembling fingers. "And I am happy, Reno. I treated you badly. I shouldn't have lorded it over you, assumed you were a drifter with nothing to show for yourself. I'm ashamed of myself for thinking so badly of you."

He cupped her chin in his hand and studied her face. "I see the girl I used to know in your eyes. The girl with the big heart and patient soul and gentle spirit. Dellie, didn't you love me a little back in Kansas?"

She swept her lashes down. "Reno, I was so young back then I didn't know what love was. But I was smart enough to know that I shouldn't marry Win if I couldn't stop thinking about you and hoping you'd kiss me again."

"Are you saying this so I'll love you even more?"

"No." She looked up into his face, and her heart swelled with incredible, incurable devotion for him. "It's true. I might have married Win, if not for you."

"Speaking of marriage, will you stay married to me, Dellie?"

She nodded, happiness brimming over in her heart. "I'm glad I won't have to use that rifle on you to keep you here."

He grinned and kissed the tip of her nose. "I'll build us a house nearby. A big house for the family we'll have. I'll open that hotel and print shop."

"Those are big plans."

"Together we'll make Whistle Stop a good town, not just a place for trains to stop in, but a place to nurture families and dreams and love. A place worthy of you, Dellie."

His high opinion of her brought on a fresh crop of tears, which she blinked away, because she wanted to see his face clearly, to bask in his smile and the loving light in his eyes. He wasn't going anywhere, she assured herself. He was staying, staying with her. Putting down roots.

"I've got a lot of money, Dellie. You won't have to work here unless you want to."

His revelation dazzled her. Rich. He was rich! And

she was married to him. She had never pictured herself a lady of leisure, a woman of independent means.

"You're a good catch then?"

"A damn good catch."

"I suppose my mother would approve of this match."

"Your mother would be doing a jig of pure elation," he assured her. "Any woman who has had to work hard knows the value of a rich husband."

"You!" She pressed a gentle fist into his hard stomach. "Were you afraid I might love you for your money instead of for yourself? Is that why you kept the truth from me?"

"Damn straight. I spotted you for a gold digger right off," he teased.

"Watch out, Gold. I can still get to my rifle and remove a few of your toes."

"A woman with your beauty is a weapon unto herself." He smiled when she blushed.

"You're such a charmer." She slipped the coat off his shoulders and began unbuttoning his shirt as she walked him backward toward her quarters. "Being rich might be fun."

"Oh, it's tons of fun," he assured her. "Beats the hell out of being poor. But you're not staying married to me just for the money, are you?" he asked, teasing lights glinting in his blue eyes. He closed the door to her quarters behind him. Moonlight provided enough light for them to weave around her parlor furniture and into her bedroom. "You *do* want *me*, don't you, Dellie? For richer or for poorer?"

She stood on tiptoe and sandwiched his earlobe

gently between her teeth. "I want you and I want you *now*."

"Lordy, you're a bossy woman."

"I just know what I want, what I need." She peeled the shirt off him, *tsking* softly over his bandaged wound, kissing the other bandage on the back of his hand. He shivered with anticipation. She turned her gaze up to his, coquettishness swirling through her, curving her lips into a smile, placing a husky note in her voice "You see, I have a bad case of gold fever, and you're not leaving until I'm cured."

He growled low in his throat, and his hands slipped down her back to spread over the swell of her hips. "Sugar, there might not be a cure."

"You might be right." Her lips melted under his in a hungry kiss that left her panting for more. "This fever might be permanent, flaring up when we least expect it."

"That'll make life interesting," he murmured, kissing her shoulder while he unfastened the back of her dress.

Her lips rubbing his, she whispered, "That's a sure bet, gambling man."

"Get ready," he said, his tone devilishly sexy, his breath warm on her skin. "This gamblin' man is about to claim his winnings."

"Oh, you feel lucky, do you?"

He nodded and covered her breasts with his hands. "My Midas touch is back."

She flung back her head, her body responding to his touch, her lips parting on a sigh. "Reno, darling, it never left."

Epilogue

S ix months later the 10:42 stood on the tracks, waiting for passengers and another load of wood.

Adele hugged Little Nugget close, loath to let her board and head for a questionable future with a man she'd never met.

"Are you sure?" she asked the young woman.

"I'm sure," Little Nugget said with authority. "I'm going to be a married lady. My husband-to-be has lots of land and needs himself a wife. After a spell we'll have children. It's everything I've ever wanted."

"But you don't know him," Adele said, clutching Little Nugget's small shoulders. "You've never met him. What if he's a horrible man?"

"Hey, he's willing to marry me, sight unseen, so he can't be too bad."

"Let her go, Dellie," Reno said, stepping close and resting a hand on her shoulder. "Remember, you promised to let people live their own lives, to trust them to make their own decisions."

"I know." Adele sighed. Her hands slipped down Little Nugget's arms. "You'll write?"

"Yes'm."

"Write me, too," Doris McDonald said, taking her turn to hug Little Nugget. "If you don't, I'll hop on a train and hunt you down."

"Now that I know how to write, nobody can stop me," Little Nugget said with a proud smile. "I'll be sending so many letters you won't have time to read them all." Laughing, she drew in a deep breath as she gazed at the people who had come to see her off. Reno and Adele Gold, Doris, Colleen, and Helen. All dear to her. "I'll miss you. Every last one of you. But I have to take this chance at having the kind of life I've always dreamed of. And Kansas ain't so far away."

"You'll make him a fine wife," Reno said. "But remember you can always come back here."

"I'll remember." She shifted the doll she called Miss Tess from one arm to the other. "Guess I'd better go now. I'm so excited I can hardly stand it!"

"*All aboard!*"

The call for passengers brought tears of farewell to Adele's eyes. She embraced Little Nugget once more before opening her arms and releasing her for the last time.

Reno slipped an arm around her waist, his fingers moving over her slightly protruding stomach, where their first child grew. "I'm proud of you," he said. "I know how hard it is for you to let her go without giving her a stern lecture on the hazards of a mail-order marriage."

She looked up into his blue eyes. She hoped their child inherited those eyes. "How could I lecture her about that when I'm part of such a marriage?"

He arched a brow and grinned. "True enough. But our situation was different."

"Yes, the bride ordered the groom instead of the other way around."

"That's not what I meant." He pulled her closer, his gaze drifting down to her midsection, where a miracle flourished. "If she finds even half the happiness I've found with you, she'll be uncommonly blessed."

"Oh, Reno." Adele rested her head on his shoulder and counted herself unbelievably lucky. "I love you."

"I know." He kissed her temple as the locomotive strained forward, bells clanging and smoke rolling from its stack.

Little Nugget stuck her head out a window and waved happily.

"Be sure and write to tell me if y'all have a boy or a girl!" she called. "I'm betting it's a boy!"

"We'll miss you! Take care, Little Nugget!" Adele said, waving her soggy handkerchief.

"The name is Cassie," she called back, the train picking up speed and noise. "Cassie Mae Little! And in a few days it will be Mrs. Cassie Dalton!" She laughed, eyes shining with excitement and adventure.

"She's so young," Adele said, shaking her head.

"But she's a tough one," Mrs. McDonald said, wiping a tear from her eye. "And she knows how to make a man happy. Mr. A. J. Dalton of Kansas is getting himself a good, hard-working woman for a wife."

"What do you think?" Reno asked Adele.

"I think Mr. Dalton is a fortunate man."

"No, I mean, which do you think? A boy or a girl?"

She smiled. "I think it will be . . . a baby." She

looped her arms around his neck. "A beautiful, spoiled-rotten baby."

"That's a safe bet," he agreed. "Boy or girl, this child will be mightily loved."

"Another safe bet." Adele pressed her mouth to his, forgetting about everyone else, as was her custom when she looked into her husband's eyes or enjoyed his kiss. "And I bet we'll be the happiest couple in Whistle Stop."

Framing her face in his hands, he touched his smiling lips to hers. "Dellie, darlin', we already are."

Avon Romances—
the best in exceptional authors and unforgettable novels!